Pr...
CAN YOU K...

"Venturing beyond Saks and Barney's, the bestselling author of *Confessions of a Shopaholic* and *Shopaholic Ties the Knot* entertains readers with backstabbing office shenanigans, competition, scandal, love and sex. . . . Kinsella's down-to-earth protagonist is sure to have readers sympathizing and doubled over in laughter."
—*Publishers Weekly*

"Chick lit at its lightest and breeziest . . . filled with fabulous clothes, stalwart friends, and snotty enemies waiting to be taken down a peg." —*Orlando Sentinel*

"[Kinsella's] dialogue is sharp, even her minor characters are well drawn, and her parody of the marketing world is very funny." —*Washington Post Book World*

"[A] comedic frenzy of ill-fated events . . . punchy . . . fast-moving." —*Rocky Mountain News*

"Kinsella's witty take on mundane office and family life will really make you laugh out loud. . . . Move over, Bridget [Jones]!" —*Evening Chronicle* (U.K.)

"Hilarious." —*Sun* (U.K.)

"Kinsella's light touch keeps this very funny look at life and relationships flying along and builds Emma into a genuinely endearing character. Romantic, but refreshingly witty."
—*Sunday Mirror* (U.K.)

Also by Sophie Kinsella

CONFESSIONS OF A SHOPAHOLIC

SHOPAHOLIC TAKES MANHATTAN

SHOPAHOLIC TIES THE KNOT

CAN YOU KEEP A SECRET?

SHOPAHOLIC & SISTER

THE UNDOMESTIC GODDESS

SHOPAHOLIC & BABY

REMEMBER ME?

SOPHIE KINSELLA

Can You Keep a Secret?

A DIAL PRESS TRADE PAPERBACK

CAN YOU KEEP A SECRET?
A Dial Press Trade Paperback Book

PUBLISHING HISTORY
Dial Press hardcover edition published March 2004
Delta trade paperback edition / March 2005
Dial Press Trade Paperback edition / June 2005
Dial Press Trade Paperback reissue / March 2008

Published by
The Dial Press
A Division of Random House, Inc.
New York, New York

This is a work of fiction. Names, characters, places, and incidents either are the product of the author's imagination or are used fictitiously. Any resemblance to actual persons, living or dead, events, or locales is entirely coincidental.

Library of Congress Catalog Card Number: 2003055350

ISBN 978-0-385-33808-0

Printed in the United States of America
Published simultaneously in Canada

www.dialpress.com

BVG 20 19 18 17 16 15 14 13

To H, from whom I have no secrets. Well, not many.

One

OF COURSE I have secrets.

Of course I do. Everyone has a few secrets. It's completely normal.

I'm not talking about big, earth-shattering secrets. Not the-president-is-planning-to-bomb-Japan-and-only-Will-Smith-can-save-the-world type secrets. Just normal, everyday little secrets.

Like, for example, here are a few random secrets of mine, off the top of my head:

1. My Kate Spade bag is a fake.
2. I love sweet sherry, the least cool drink in the universe.
3. I have no idea what NATO stands for. Or even exactly what it is.
4. I weigh 128 pounds. Not 118, like my boyfriend, Connor, thinks. (Although, in my defense, I was

planning to go on a diet when I told him that. And, to be fair, it is only one number different.)

5. I've always thought Connor looks a bit like Ken. As in Barbie and Ken.

6. Sometimes, when we're right in the middle of passionate sex, I suddenly want to laugh.

7. I lost my virginity in the spare bedroom with Danny Nussbaum while Mum and Dad were downstairs watching *Ben-Hur*.

8. I've already drunk the wine that Dad told me to save for twenty years.

9. Sammy the goldfish at home isn't the same goldfish that Mum and Dad gave me to look after when they went to Egypt.

10. When my colleague Artemis really annoys me, I feed her plant orange juice. (Which is pretty much every day.)

11. I once had this weird lesbian dream about my flatmate Lissy.

12. My G-string is hurting me.

13. I've always had this deep-down conviction that I'm not like everybody else, and there's an amazingly exciting new life waiting for me just around the corner.

14. I have no idea what this guy in the gray suit is going on about.

15. Plus, I've already forgotten his name.

And I only met him ten minutes ago.

"We believe in multi-logistical formative alliances," he's saying in a nasal, droning voice, "both above and below the line."

"Absolutely!" I reply brightly, as though to say "Doesn't everybody?"

Multi-logistical. What does that mean, again?

Oh, God. What if they ask me?

Don't be stupid, Emma. They won't suddenly demand, What does "multi-logistical" mean? I'm a fellow marketing professional, aren't I? Obviously I know these things.

And anyway, if they mention it again, I'll change the subject. Or I'll say I'm post-logistical or something.

The important thing is to keep confident and businesslike. I can do this. This is my big chance, and I'm not going to screw it up.

I'm sitting in the offices of Glen Oil's headquarters in Glasgow, and as I glance at my reflection in the window, I look just like a top businesswoman. My shoulder-length hair is straightened, after half an hour with the hair dryer and a bottle of serum this morning. I'm wearing discreet gold swirl earrings like they tell you to in how-to-win-that-job articles. And I've got on my smart new Jigsaw suit. (At least, it's practically new. I got it from the Cancer Research shop and sewed on a button to replace the missing one, and you can hardly tell.)

I'm here representing the Panther Corporation, which is where I work. The meeting is to finalize a promotional arrangement between the new cranberry-flavored Panther Prime sports drink and Glen Oil, and I flew up this morning from London, especially.

When I arrived, the two Glen Oil marketing guys started on this long, show-offy "who's traveled the most?" conversation about air miles and the red-eye to Washington—and I think I bluffed pretty convincingly. But the truth is, this is the first time I've ever had to travel for work.

OK. The *real* truth is, this is the first business meeting I've attended on my own. I've been at the Panther Corporation for eleven months as a marketing assistant, which is the bottom level in our department. I started off just doing menial tasks like typing letters, getting the sandwiches, and collecting my boss Paul's dry cleaning. But after a couple of months, I was allowed to start checking copy. Then a few months ago, I got to write my very own promotional leaflet, for a tie-in with washing powder! God, I was excited. I bought a creative-writing book especially to help me, and I spent all weekend working on it. And I was really pleased with the result, even if it didn't have a misunderstood villain like the book suggested. And even if Paul did just glance at the copy and say "Fine" and kind of forget to tell anyone that I wrote it.

Since then I've done a fair bit of writing promotional literature, and I've even sat in on a few meetings with Paul. So I really think I'm moving up the ladder. In lots of ways I'm practically a marketing executive already!

Except for the tiny point that I still seem to do just as much typing as before. And getting sandwiches and collecting dry cleaning. I just do it *as well as* the other jobs. Especially so since our departmental secretary, Gloria, left a few weeks ago and still hasn't been replaced.

But it's all going to change; I know it is. This meeting is my big break. It's my first chance to show Paul what I'm really capable of. I had to beg him to let me go—after all, Glen Oil and Panther have done loads of deals together in the past; it's not like there'll be any surprises. But deep down I know I'm here only because I was in his office when he realized he'd double-booked with an awards lunch that most of the department were attending. So here I am, representing the company.

And my secret hope is that if I do well today, I'll get promoted. The job ad said "possibility of promotion after a year"—and it's nearly been a year. And on Monday I'm having my appraisal meeting. I looked up "Appraisals" in the staff induction book, and it said they are "an ideal opportunity to discuss possibilities for career advancement."

Career advancement! At the thought, I feel a familiar stab of longing. It would just show Dad I'm not a complete loser.

And Mum. And Kerry. If I could just go home and say, "By the way, I've been promoted to marketing executive."

Emma Corrigan, marketing executive.

Emma Corrigan, senior vice-president (marketing).

As long as everything goes well today. Paul said the deal was pretty much done and dusted, and all I had to do was raise one point about timing, and even I should be able to manage that. And so far, I reckon it's going really well!

OK, so I don't understand some of the terms they're using. But then I didn't understand most of my GCSE French Oral either, and I still got a B.

"Rebranding . . . analysis . . . cost-effective . . ."

The man in the gray suit is still droning on. As casually as possible, I extend my hand and inch his business card toward me so I can read it.

Doug Hamilton. That's right. I can remember this. Doug. Dug. Easy—I'll picture a shovel. Together with a *ham*. Which . . . which looks *ill* . . . and . . .

OK, forget this. I'll just write it down.

I write down "rebranding" and "Doug Hamilton" on my notepad and give an uncomfortable little wriggle. God, my knickers really are uncomfortable. I mean, G-strings are never that comfortable at the best of times, but these are particularly bad. Which could be because they're two sizes too small.

Which could possibly be because when Connor bought them for me, he told the lingerie assistant I weighed 118 pounds. Whereupon she told him I must be size 4. Size 4!

So it got to Christmas Eve, and we were exchanging presents, and I unwrapped this pair of gorgeous pale pink silk knickers. Size 4. And I basically had two options.

A: Confess the truth: "Actually, these are too small. I'm more of an eight, and by the way, I don't really weigh one hundred eighteen pounds."

B: Shoehorn myself into them.

Actually, it was fine. You could hardly see the red lines on my skin afterward. And all it meant was that I had to quickly cut the labels out of my clothes so Connor would never realize.

Since then, I've hardly ever worn this particular set of underwear, needless to say. But every so often I see them, looking all nice and expensive in the drawer, and think, Oh, come on, they can't be *that* tight, and somehow squeeze into them. Which is what I did this morning. I even decided I must have lost weight, because they didn't feel too bad.

I am such a deluded moron.

". . . unfortunately, since rebranding . . . major rethink . . . feel we need to be considering alternative synergies . . ."

Up to now I've just been sitting and nodding, thinking this business meeting is really easy. But now Doug Hamilton's voice starts to impinge on my consciousness. What's he saying?

". . . two products diverging . . . becoming incompatible . . ."

What was that about incompatible? What was that about a major rethink? I feel a jolt of alarm.

"We appreciate the functional and synergetic partnership that Panther and Glen Oil have enjoyed in the past," Doug Hamilton is saying, "but you'll agree that clearly we're going in different directions."

Different directions?

My stomach gives an anxious lurch.

He can't be—

Is he trying to pull out of the deal?

"Excuse me, Doug," I say in my most relaxed voice. "Obviously I was closely following what you were saying earlier." I give a friendly, we're-all-professionals-together smile. "But if you could just . . . um, recap the situation for all our benefits . . ."

In plain English, I beg silently.

Doug Hamilton and the other guy exchange glances.

"We're a little unhappy about your brand values," says Doug Hamilton.

"My brand values?" I echo in panic.

"The brand values of the *product*," he says, giving me an odd look. "As I've been explaining, we here at Glen Oil are going through a rebranding process at the moment, and we see our new image very much as a *caring* petrol, as our new daffodil logo demonstrates. And we feel Panther Prime, with its emphasis on sport and competition, is simply too aggressive."

"Aggressive?" I stare at him in bewilderment. "But . . . it's a fruit drink."

This makes no sense. Glen Oil is fume-making, world-ruining petrol. Panther Prime is an innocent cranberry-flavored drink. How can it be too aggressive?

"The values it espouses." He gestures to the marketing brochures on the table. "Drive. Elitism. Masculinity. The very slogan 'Don't Pause.' Frankly, it seems a little dated." He shrugs. "We just don't think a joint initiative will be possible."

No. No. This can't be happening. He can't be pulling out.

Everyone at the office will think it was my fault. They'll think I cocked it up and I'm completely crap.

My heart is thumping. My face is hot. I can't let this happen. But what do I say? I haven't prepared anything. Paul said the promotion was all set up, and all I had to do was tell them we wanted to bring it forward to June.

"We'll certainly discuss it again before we make a decision," Doug's saying. He gives me a brief smile. "And as I say, we would like to continue links with the Panther Corporation, so this has been a useful meeting, in any case. . . ."

He's pushing back his chair.

I can't let this slip away! I have to try to win them around.

"Wait!" I hear myself say. "Just . . . wait a moment! I have a few points to make."

There's a can of Panther Prime sitting on the desk, and I grab it for inspiration. Playing for time, I stand up, walk to the center of the room, and raise the can high into the air where we can all see it. "Panther Prime is . . . a sports drink."

I stop, and there's a polite silence. My face is prickling. "It, um, it is very . . ."

Oh, God. What am I doing?

Come *on,* Emma. *Think.* Think Panther Prime. . . . Think Panther Cola. . . . Think. . . . Think. . . .

Yes! Of course!

"Since the launch of Panther Cola in the late 1980s, Panther drinks have been a byword for energy, excitement, and excellence," I say fluently.

Thank God. This is the standard marketing blurb for Panther Cola. I've typed it out so many times, I could recite it in my sleep.

"Panther drinks are a marketing phenomenon," I continue. "The Panther character is one of the most widely recognized in the world, while the classic slogan 'Don't Pause' has made it into dictionaries. We are offering Glen Oil an exclusive opportunity to strengthen its association with this premium, world-famous brand."

My confidence growing, I start to stride around the room, gesturing with the can. "By buying a Panther health drink, the consumer is signaling that he will settle for nothing but the best." I hit the can sharply with my other hand. "He expects the best from his energy drink, he expects the best from his petrol, he expects the best from himself."

I'm flying! I'm fantastic! If Paul could see me now, he'd give me a promotion on the spot!

I come over to the desk and look Doug Hamilton right in the eye. "When the Panther consumer opens that can, he is making a choice that tells the world who he is. I'm asking Glen Oil to make the same choice."

As I finish speaking, I plant the can firmly in the middle of the desk, reach for the ring pull, and, with a cool smile, snap it back.

And a volcano erupts.

Fizzy cranberry-flavored drink explodes in a whoosh out

of the can, drenching the papers and blotters in lurid red liquid . . . and—oh, no, please no—spattering all over Doug Hamilton's shirt.

"Fuck!" I gasp. "I mean, I'm really sorry—"

"Jesus Christ," says Doug Hamilton irritably, standing up and getting a handkerchief out of his pocket. "Does this stuff stain?"

"Er . . ." I grab the can helplessly. "I don't know."

"I'll get a cloth," says the other guy, and leaps to his feet.

The door closes behind him and there's silence, apart from the sound of cranberry drink dripping slowly onto the floor.

I stare at Doug Hamilton, my face hot and blood throbbing through my ears.

"Please . . ." My voice is husky. "Don't tell my boss."

After all that, I screwed it up.

As I drag my heels across the concourse at Glasgow Airport, I feel completely dejected. Doug Hamilton was quite sweet in the end. He said he was sure the stain would come out, and promised he wouldn't tell Paul what happened. But he didn't change his mind about the deal.

My first big chance—and this is what happens. I feel like phoning the office and saying, "That's it. I'm never coming back again, and by the way, it was me who jammed the photocopier that time."

But I can't. This is my third career in four years. It *has* to work. For my own self-worth. For my own self-esteem. And also because I owe my dad four thousand quid.

I've arrived at the airport with an hour to go, and have headed straight for the bar. "So what can I get you?" says the Australian bartender, and I look up at him in a daze.

"Erm . . ." My mind is blank. "Er, white wine. No, actually, a vodka and tonic. Thanks."

As he moves away, I slump down again in my stool. An air

hostess with fair hair in a French plait comes and sits down two bar stools away. She smiles at me, and I smile weakly in return.

I don't know how other people manage their careers, I really don't. Like my oldest friend, Lissy. She's always known she wanted to be a lawyer—and now, ta-daah! She's a fraud barrister. But I left college with absolutely no clue. My first job was in an estate agency, and I only went into it because I've always quite liked looking around houses, plus I met this woman with amazing red lacquered nails at a career fair who told me she made so much money, she'd be able to retire when she was forty.

But the minute I started, I hated it. I hated all the other trainee estate agents. I hated saying things like "a lovely aspect." And I hated the way if someone said they could afford three hundred thousand we were supposed to give them details of houses costing at least four hundred thousand, and then kind of look down our noses, like, "You only have three hundred thousand pounds? God, you complete loser."

So after six months I announced I was changing careers and was going to be a photographer instead. It was *such* a fantastic moment, like in a film or something. My dad lent me the money for a photography course and camera, and I was going to launch this amazing new creative career, and it was going to be the start of my new life. . . .

Except it didn't quite happen like that.

For a start, do you have any idea how much a photographer's assistant gets paid?

Nothing. It's nothing.

Which, you know, I wouldn't have minded if anyone had actually *offered* me a photographer's assistant's job.

I heave a sigh and gaze at my doleful expression in the mirror behind the bar. As well as everything else, my hair's gone all frizzy. So much for "Salon Serum—For That 24-Hour Professional Salon Look."

At least I wasn't the only one who didn't get anywhere.

Out of the eight people in my course, one became instantly successful and now takes photos for *Vogue,* one became a wedding photographer, one had an affair with the tutor, one went traveling, one had a baby, one works at Snappy Snaps, and one is now at Morgan Stanley.

Meanwhile, I got more and more into debt, so I started temping and applying for jobs that actually paid money. And eventually, eleven months ago, I started as a marketing assistant at the Panther Corporation.

The barman places a vodka and tonic in front of me and gives me a quizzical look. "Cheer up!" he says. "It can't be that bad!"

"Thanks," I say gratefully, and take a sip. That feels a bit better.

I ought to call Paul and give him a report. But I just can't face it. Anyway, he's probably still out at his awards lunch. He won't want me disturbing him on his mobile. It can wait until Monday.

I'm just taking a second sip of vodka when my mobile starts to ring. I feel a beat of nerves. If it's the office, I'll just pretend I didn't hear.

But it's not; it's our home number flashing on the little screen.

I press "answer." "Hi," I say.

"Hiya!" comes Lissy's voice. "Only me! So how did it go?"

Lissy is not only my oldest friend but my flatmate, too. She has tufty dark hair and an IQ of about 600 and is the sweetest person I know.

"It was a disaster," I say miserably.

"It can't have been that bad!"

"Lissy, I drenched the marketing director of Glen Oil in cranberry drink!"

Along the bar, I can see the air hostess hiding a smile, and I feel myself flush. Great. Now the whole world knows.

"Oh, dear." I can almost *feel* Lissy trying to think of something positive to say. "Well, at least you got their attention!" she says at last. "At least they won't forget you in a hurry."

"I suppose," I say morosely. "So, did I have any messages?"

"Oh! Erm, no. I mean, your dad did phone, but, um, you know, it wasn't . . ." She trails off evasively.

"Lissy. What did he want?"

There's a pause.

"Apparently your cousin's won some industry award," she says apologetically. "They're going to be celebrating it on Saturday, as well as your mum's birthday."

"Oh. Great."

I slump deeper in my chair. That's all I need. My cousin Kerry triumphantly clutching some silver best-office-furniture-salesperson-in-the-whole-world-no-make-that-universe trophy.

"And Connor rang, too, to see how you got on," adds Lissy quickly. "He was really sweet. He said he didn't want to ring your mobile during your meeting, in case it disturbed you."

"Really?"

For the first time today, I feel a lift in spirits.

Connor. My boyfriend. My lovely, thoughtful boyfriend.

"He's such a sweetheart!" Lissy is saying. "He said he's tied up in a big meeting all afternoon, but he's canceled his squash game especially, so do you want to go out to supper tonight?"

"Oh," I say, pleased. "Oh, well, that'll be nice. Thanks, Lissy."

I click off and take another sip of vodka, feeling much more cheerful.

My boyfriend.

It's just like Julie Andrews said. When the dog bites, when the bee stings . . . I simply remember I have a boyfriend—and suddenly things don't seem quite so completely shit.

Or however she put it.

And not just any boyfriend. A tall, handsome, clever boyfriend whom *Marketing Week* called "one of the brightest sparks in marketing research today."

I sit nursing my vodka, allowing thoughts of Connor to comfort me. The way his blond hair shines in the sunshine, and the way he's always smiling. And the way he upgraded all the software on my computer the other day without my even asking, and the way he . . . he . . .

My mind's gone blank. This is ridiculous. I mean, there's so much that is wonderful about Connor. From his . . . his long legs. Yes. And his broad shoulders. To the time he looked after me when I had the flu. I mean, how many boyfriends do that? Exactly.

I'm so lucky. I really am.

I put my phone away, run my fingers through my hair, and glance at the clock behind the bar. Forty minutes before the flight. Not long to go now. Nerves are starting to creep over me like little insects, and I take a deep gulp of vodka, draining my glass.

It'll be fine, I tell myself for the zillionth time. It'll be absolutely fine.

I'm not frightened. I'm just . . . I'm just . . .

OK. I'm frightened.

16. I'm scared of flying.

I've never told anyone I'm scared of flying. It just sounds so lame. And I mean, it's not like I'm phobic or anything. It's not like I can't *get on* a plane. It's just . . . all things being equal, I would prefer to be on the ground.

On the way up here this morning, I was so excited about the meeting, it was almost a distraction from my fear. But even so, I kept feeling bursts of panic. I kept having to close my eyes and take deep breaths. And ever since I landed, it's been ticking away at the back of my mind: I have to fly back again. I have to get on a plane again.

I never used to be scared. But over the last few years, I've gradually got more and more nervous. I know it's completely irrational. I know thousands of people fly every day and it's practically safer than lying in bed. You have less chance of being in a plane crash than . . . than finding a man in London, or something.

But still. I just don't like it.

Maybe I'll have another quick vodka.

By the time my flight is called, I've drunk two more vodkas and am feeling a lot more positive. I mean, Lissy's right. At least I made an impression, didn't I? At least they'll remember who I am.

As I stride toward the gate, clutching my briefcase, I almost start to feel like a confident businesswoman again. A couple of people smile at me as they pass, and I smile broadly back, feeling a warm glow of friendliness. You see. The world's not so bad after all. It's all just a question of being positive. Anything can happen in life, can't it? You never know what's around the next corner.

I reach the entrance to the plane, and there at the door, taking boarding passes, is the air hostess with the French plait who was sitting at the bar earlier.

"Hi again!" I say, smiling. "This is a coincidence!"

The air hostess stares at me. "Hi. Erm . . ."

"What?" Why does she look embarrassed?

"Sorry. It's just . . . Did you know that . . ." She gestures awkwardly to my front.

"What is it?" I say pleasantly. I look down, and freeze, aghast.

Somehow my silky shirt has been unbuttoning itself while I've been walking along. Three buttons have come undone and it's gaping at the front.

My bra shows. My pink lacy bra. The one that went a bit blobby in the wash.

That's why those people were smiling at me. Not because the world is a nice place but because I'm Pink-Blobby-Bra Woman.

"Thanks," I mutter, and do up the buttons with fumbling fingers, my face hot with humiliation.

"It hasn't been your day, has it?" says the air hostess sympathetically, holding out a hand for my boarding pass. "Sorry. I couldn't help overhearing earlier."

"That's all right." I raise a half smile. "No, it hasn't been the best day of my life." There's a short silence as she studies my boarding pass.

"Tell you what," she says in a low voice. "Would you like an onboard upgrade?"

"A what?"

"Come on. You deserve a break."

"Really? But . . . can you just upgrade people like that?"

"If there are spare seats, we can. We use our discretion. And this flight is so short." She gives me a conspiratorial smile. "Just don't tell anyone, OK?"

She leads me into the front section of the plane and gestures to a big, wide seat. I've never been upgraded before in my life! I can't quite believe she's really letting me do this.

"Is this first class?" I whisper, taking in the hushed luxury atmosphere. A man in a smart suit is tapping at a laptop to my right, and two elderly women in the corner are plugging themselves into headsets.

"Business class. There's no first class on this flight." She lifts her voice to a normal volume. "Is everything OK for you?"

"It's perfect! Thanks very much."

"No problem." She smiles again and walks away, and I push my briefcase under the seat in front.

Wow. This really is lovely. Comfortable seats, and footrests, and everything. This is going to be a completely pleasurable experience from start to finish. I reach for my seat belt and buckle it up nonchalantly, trying to ignore the flutters of apprehension in my stomach.

"Would you like some champagne?" It's my friend the air hostess, beaming down at me.

"That would be great," I say. "Thanks!"

Champagne!

"And for you, sir? Some champagne?"

There's a man in the seat next to mine who hasn't even looked up yet. He's wearing jeans and an old sweatshirt and is staring out of the window. As he turns to answer, I catch a glimpse of dark eyes, stubble, a deep frown etched on his forehead.

"Just a brandy. Thanks."

His voice is dry and has an American accent. I'm about to ask him politely where he's from, but he immediately turns back and stares out the window again.

Which is fine, because to be honest I'm not much in the mood for talking either.

Two

OK. THE TRUTH IS, I don't like this.

I know it's business class; I know it's all a lovely luxury. But my stomach is still a tight knot of fear.

It's about ten minutes into the flight, and they've switched off the seat belt signs. While we were taking off, I counted very slowly with my eyes closed, and that kind of worked. But I ran out of steam at three hundred and fifty, so now I'm just sitting, sipping champagne, attempting to read an article called "30 Things to Do Before You're 30" in *Cosmo*. I'm trying really hard to look like a relaxed business-class top marketing executive. But every tiny sound makes me start; every vibration makes me catch my breath.

With an outward veneer of calm, I reach for the laminated safety instructions and run my eyes over them for the fifth time. *Safety exits. Brace position. If life jackets are required, please assist the elderly and children first.* Oh, God—

Why am I even *looking* at this? How will it help me to gaze at pictures of little stick people jumping into the ocean while their plane explodes behind them? I stuff the safety instructions quickly back in their pocket and take a gulp of champagne.

To distract myself, I look around the cabin. The two elderly women I noticed earlier are both laughing at something. The guy with the laptop is still typing. Behind him is a little blond boy of maybe two, sitting with a beautiful dark girl. As I watch, the boy drops a plastic wheel on the floor. It rolls away, and immediately he starts to wail. The two elderly ladies pause in their laughter, and I'm aware of the man next to me looking up.

"Is everything OK? Can I help?" An air hostess is rushing up to the toddler's seat.

"Don't worry." The dark girl waves her arm. "He'll calm down."

"Are you his mum?" The air hostess smiles at her.

"Nanny." She reaches in her bag and produces a lolly, which she starts to unwrap. "He'll keep quiet now."

"Excuse me," I say. "He dropped his toy." Everyone turns to look at me and I flush. "That might be why he's crying," I explain.

The dark girl looks at me without expression. "It's just a piece of plastic. He'll get over it." She jams the lolly in the boy's mouth and he starts to suck it, but tears are rolling down his cheeks.

Poor little thing. Isn't she even going to *try* to get the toy?

Suddenly my eye is caught by a patch of bright color on the floor. It's the wheel. It's rolled under a row of empty seats, right over to the window.

"Oh!" I say. "Look—there it is!"

To my slight disbelief, the nanny shrugs. "He's not bothered," she says.

"He *is* bothered!" I retort. "Don't worry," I add to the child, "*I'll* help you."

Telling myself it can make absolutely no difference to the

safety of the plane if I stand up, I unbuckle my seat belt. Somehow I force myself to my feet. Then, with everyone's eyes on me, I bend coolly down to retrieve the wheel.

OK. Now I can't reach the bloody thing.

Well, I'm not giving up, after I've made this big deal about it. Without looking at anyone, I lie right down on the plane floor.

Oh, God. It's more wobbly than I expected.

What if the floor suddenly collapsed and I fell through the sky?

No. Stop it. Nothing's going to collapse. I shuffle forward, stretch as far as possible . . . and at last my fingers close around the plastic wheel. As nonchalantly as I can, I get to my feet, banging my elbow on a seat tray, and hand the plastic wheel to the little boy.

"Here," I say in my best Superman, all-in-a-day's-work voice. "I think this is yours."

He clasps it tightly to his chest, and I glow with pride.

A moment later, he hurls the wheel on the floor, and it rolls away, to almost exactly the same place.

The nanny gives a stifled giggle, and I can see one of the elderly ladies smiling.

"Right," I say after a pause. "Right. Well . . . enjoy your flight."

I get back into my seat, trying to look unfazed, as though this is what I planned all along.

"Nice try," says the American guy next to me, and I turn, suspicious. But he doesn't look as if he's laughing at me.

"Oh." I hesitate. "Thanks."

I buckle up my seat belt and reach for my magazine again. That's it. I'm not moving from this seat again.

"Excuse me, madam." An air hostess with red curls has appeared by my side. "Are you traveling on business?"

"Yes." I smooth down my hair. "Yes, I am."

She hands me a leaflet titled "Executive Facilities," on

which there's a photo of businesspeople talking animatedly in front of a clipboard with a wavy graph on it.

"This is some information about our new business–class lounge at Gatwick. We provide full conference call facilities and meeting rooms, should you require them. Would you be interested?"

I am a top businesswoman. I am a top high-flying business executive.

"Quite possibly," I say, looking casually at the leaflet. "Yes, I may well use one of these rooms to . . . brief my team. I have a large team, and obviously they need a lot of briefing. On business matters." I clear my throat. "Mostly . . . multi-logistical."

"I see." The hostess looks a little nonplussed.

"Actually, while you're here," I add, "I was just wondering. Is that sound normal?"

"What sound?" The air hostess cocks her head.

"That sound. That kind of whining, coming from the wing?"

"I can't hear anything." She looks at me sympathetically. "Are you a nervous flyer?"

"No!" I say at once, and give a little laugh. "No, I'm not *nervous*! I just . . . was wondering. Just out of interest."

"I'll see if I can find out for you," she says kindly. "Here you are, sir. Some information about our executive facilities at Gatwick."

The American man takes his leaflet wordlessly and slips it into the seat pocket in front of him without even looking at it. The hostess moves on, staggering a little as the plane gives a bump.

Why is the plane bumping?

Oh, God. An avalanche of fear hits me with no warning. This is madness. Madness! Sitting in this big, heavy box with no way of escape, thousands and thousands of feet above the ground . . .

I can't do this on my own. I have an overpowering need to talk to someone. Someone reassuring. Someone safe.

Connor.

Instinctively I fish out my mobile phone, but immediately the air hostess swoops down on me.

"I'm afraid you can't use that on board the plane," she says with a bright smile. "Could you please ensure that it's switched off?"

"Oh. Er, sorry."

Of course I can't use my mobile. They've only said it about fifty-five zillion times. I am such a durr-brain.

Shall I use the seat phone?

No. It doesn't matter. I don't need to bother Connor. It's ridiculous. This is just a tiny flight from Glasgow. I'm fine. I put my mobile away in my bag and look at my watch.

Only five minutes have passed since I last looked. Fifty-five to go.

OK, don't think about that. Just take each minute as it comes. I lean back and try to concentrate on the old episode of *Fawlty Towers* that is showing on the screen.

Maybe I'll start counting again. Three hundred and forty-nine. Three hundred and fifty. Three hundred and—

Fuck. My head jerks up. What was that bump? Did we just get *hit*?

OK, don't panic. It was just a bump. I'm sure everything's fine. We probably just flew into a pigeon or something. Where was I?

Three hundred and fifty-one. Three hundred and fifty-two. Three hundred and fifty—

And then I hear the screams like a wave over my head, almost before I realize what's happening.

Oh, God. Oh God, oh God, oh God, oh . . . OH . . . NO. NO. NO.

We're falling. Oh, God, we're falling.

The plane's plummeting through the air like a stone. A

man across from me has just shot up through the air and banged his head on the ceiling. He's bleeding. I'm clutching on to the arms of my seat, but I can feel myself being wrenched upward; it's like someone's tugging me, like gravity's suddenly switched the other way. Bags are flying around, drinks are spilling, one of the cabin crew has fallen over, she's gripping a seat . . .

Oh, God. Oh, God. OK, the plane is leveling off now. It's . . . it's better.

I look at the American man, and he's grasping on to his seat as tightly as I am.

I feel sick. I think I might be sick.

"Ladies and gentlemen," comes a voice over the intercom, and everyone looks up. "This is your captain speaking."

My heart is juddering in my chest. I can't listen. I can't think.

"We're currently hitting some clear-air turbulence, and things may be unsteady for a while. I have switched on the seat belt signs and would ask that you all return to your seats as quickly as—"

There's another huge lurch, and his voice is drowned by screams and cries all around the plane.

It's like a bad dream. A bad roller-coaster dream.

The cabin crew are all strapping themselves into their seats. One of the hostesses is mopping blood on her face. A minute ago they were happily doling out honey-roasted peanuts.

I always knew something like this was going to happen to me. I just knew. All those people who said flying was perfectly safe—they were lying.

"We have to keep calm!" one of the elderly women is saying. "Everyone, keep calm!"

Keep *calm*? I can't breathe, let alone keep calm. What are we going to do? Are we all supposed to just *sit* here while the plane bucks like an out-of-control horse?

I can hear someone behind me reciting "Hail Mary, full of

grace . . ." and a fresh, choking panic sweeps through me. People are praying. This is real.

We're going to die.

We're going to die.

"I'm sorry?" The American man in the next seat looks at me, his face tense and white.

Did I just say that aloud?

"We're going to die." I stare into his face. This could be the last person I ever see alive. I take in the lines etched around his dark eyes; his strong jaw, shaded with stubble.

The plane suddenly drops again, and I give an involuntary shriek.

"I don't think we're going to die," he says. "They said it was just turbulence—"

"Of course they did!" I can hear the hysteria in my voice. "They wouldn't exactly say, 'OK, folks, that's it—you're all goners'!"

The plane gives another terrifying swoop, and I find myself clutching the man's hand in panic. "We're not going to make it. I know we're not. This is it. I'm twenty-five years old, for God's sake. I'm not ready. I haven't achieved anything. I've never had children. I've never saved a life. The one time I tried to do the Heimlich maneuver, the guy thought I was coming on to him. . . ." I feel myself clutching the magazine in my lap, still open at the "30 Things to Do Before You're 30" article. "I haven't ever climbed a mountain, I haven't got a tattoo, I don't even *know* if I've got a G spot. . . ."

"I'm sorry?" says the man, sounding taken aback, but I barely hear him.

"My career's a complete joke. I'm not a top businesswoman at all." I gesture half tearfully to my suit. "I haven't got a team! I'm just a crappy assistant, and I just had my first-ever big meeting and it was a complete disaster. Half the time I haven't got a clue what people are talking about. I don't know what multilogistical means, I'm never going to get promoted, and I owe my dad four thousand quid, and I've never really been in love. . . ."

The plane levels off again, and I draw myself up short with a jolt. "I'm sorry," I say, and exhale sharply. "You don't want to hear all this."

"That's quite all right," says the man.

God. I'm completely losing it.

And anyway, what I just said wasn't true. Because I am in love with Connor. It must be the altitude or something, confusing my mind.

Flustered, I push the hair off my face and try to get hold of myself. OK, let's try counting once more. Three hundred and fifty . . . six. Three hundred and—

Oh, God. Oh, God. No. Please. The plane's lurching again. We're plummeting.

"I've never done anything to make my parents proud of me." The words come spilling out of my mouth before I can stop them. "Never."

"I'm sure that's not true," says the man kindly.

"It's true. Maybe they used to be proud of me. But then my cousin Kerry came to live with us, and suddenly it was like my parents couldn't see me anymore. All they could see was her. She was fourteen when she arrived, and I was ten, and I thought it was going to be great, you know. Like having an older sister. But it didn't work out like that. . . ."

I can't stop talking. I just can't stop.

Every time the plane bumps or jolts, another torrent of words comes rushing out of my mouth. Like a waterfall.

". . . she was a swimming champion, and an everything champion, and I was just . . . nothing in comparison. . . ."

". . . photography course and I honestly thought it was going to change my life. . . ."

". . . eight stone three. But I was planning to go on a diet. . . ."

"I applied for every single job in the world. I was so desperate, I even applied to . . ."

". . . awful girl called Artemis. This new desk arrived the other day, and she just took it, even though I've got this really grotty little desk. . . ."

". . . sometimes I water her stupid spider plant with orange juice, just to serve her right. . . ."

". . . sweet girl Katie, who works in Personnel. We have this secret code where she comes in and says, 'Can I go through some numbers with you, Emma?' and we go and get a coffee and have a gossip. . . ."

". . . coffee at work is the most disgusting stuff you've ever drunk, absolute poison. So we usually nip out to Starbucks. . . ."

". . . put 'Maths GCSE grade A' on my CV, when I really only got a C. I know it was dishonest. I know I shouldn't have done it, but I *so* wanted to get the job. . . ."

What's happened to me? Normally there's a kind of filter that stops me from blurting out everything I'm thinking, but the filter's stopped working. Everything's piling out in a big, random stream, and I can't stop it.

"Sometimes I think I believe in God, because how else did we all get here? But then I think, Yes, but what about war. . . ."

". . . wear G-strings because they don't give you VPL. But they're *so* uncomfortable. . . ."

". . . size four, and I didn't know what to do, so I just said, 'Wow, those are absolutely fantastic. . . .' "

". . . roasted peppers, my complete favorite food . . ."

". . . joined a book group, but I just couldn't get through

Great Expectations. So I just skimmed the back and pretended I'd read it. . . ."

". . . I gave him all his goldfish food. I honestly don't know what happened. . . ."

". . . just have to *hear* that Carpenters song 'Close to You' and I start crying. . . ."

". . . perfect date would start off with champagne just *appearing* at the table, as if by magic. . . ."

I'm unaware of anything around us. The world has narrowed to me and this stranger, and my mouth, spewing out all my innermost thoughts and secrets.

". . . name was Danny Nussbaum. Mum and Dad were downstairs watching *Ben-Hur,* and I remember thinking, If this is what the world gets so excited about, then the world's mad. . . ."

". . . lie on my side, because that way your cleavage looks bigger. . . ."

". . . works in Market Research. I remember thinking the very first time I saw him, Wow, he's good-looking. He's very tall and blond, because he's half-Swedish, and he has these amazing blue eyes. So he asked me out. . . ."

". . . always have a glass of sweet sherry before a date, to calm my nerves. . . ."

"He's wonderful. Connor's completely wonderful. He's sweet, and he's good, and he's successful, and everyone calls us the perfect couple. . . ."

". . . I'd never tell anyone this in a million years. But sometimes I think he's almost *too* good-looking. A bit like one of those dolls? Like Ken. Like a blond Ken."

And now I'm on the subject of Connor, I'm saying things I've never said to anyone. Things I never even realized were in my head.

". . . gave him this lovely leather watch for Christmas, but he wears this orange digital thing, because it can tell him the temperature in Poland or something stupid. . . ."

". . . took me to all these jazz concerts and I pretended to enjoy them to be polite, so now he thinks I love jazz. . . ."

". . . every single Woody Allen film off by heart and says each line before it comes, and it drives me crackers. . . ."

". . . determined to find my G spot, so we spent the whole weekend doing it in different positions, and by the end I was just knackered. All I wanted was a pizza and *Friends*. . . ."

". . . he kept saying, What was it like, what was it like? So I just made some stuff up, I said it was absolutely amazing, and it felt as though my whole body were opening up like a flower, and he said what sort of flower, so I said a begonia. . . ."

". . . can't expect the initial passion to last. But how do you tell if the passion's faded in a good, long-term-commitment way or in a crap, we-don't-fancy-each-other-anymore way. . . ."

". . . knight in shining armor is not a realistic option. But there's a part of me that wants a huge, amazing romance. I want passion. I want to be swept off my feet. I want an earthquake, or a . . . I don't know, a huge whirlwind . . . something *exciting*. Sometimes I feel as if there's this whole new, thrilling life waiting for me out there, and if I can just—"

"Excuse me, miss?"

"What?" I look up dazedly. "What is it?" The air hostess with the French plait is smiling down at me.

"We've landed."

"We've *landed*?"

How can we have landed? I look around—and glimpse the airport terminal through the window. The plane's still. We're on the ground.

I feel like Dorothy. A second ago I was swirling around in Oz, clicking my heels together, and now that I've woken up, all is flat and quiet and normal again.

"We aren't bumping anymore," I say stupidly.

"We stopped bumping quite a while ago," says the American man.

"We're . . . we're not going to die."

"We're not going to die," he agrees.

I look at him as though for the first time—and suddenly it hits me. I've been blabbering nonstop this whole time to a complete stranger. God alone knows what I've been saying.

I want to get off this plane right now. "I'm sorry," I say awkwardly. "You should have stopped me."

"That would have been a little difficult." There's a tiny smile at his lips. "You were on a bit of a roll."

"I'm so embarrassed!" I try to smile, but I can't even look this guy in the eye. I mean, I told him about my knickers. I told him about my *G spot*. My whole face is hot with mortification.

"Don't worry about it. We were all stressed-out. That was some flight." He hesitates. "Will you be OK getting back home?"

"Yes!" My voice is shrill. "I'll be fine, thanks!" I scrabble hurriedly under the seat for my briefcase. I have to get out of here. Now.

"You're sure you're OK?"

"Fine! Thanks very much." I undo my seat belt and get to my feet, stumbling a little. "I hope you have a nice visit."

"Thanks." He smiles up at me, and I nod back, then walk away as quickly as I can.

As I step onto the solid ground of the terminal, the relief hits me again. I'm alive. I'm safe. Slowly, trying to keep control of myself, I make my way along the carpeted corridors toward Arrivals. I feel sweaty, my hair's all over the place, and my head is starting to throb.

The airport seems so bright and calm after the intense atmosphere of the plane. The ground seems so firm. I sit quietly on a plastic chair for a while, trying to get myself together, but as I stand up at last, I still feel dazed. I walk through Customs in a blur, hardly able to believe I'm here.

"Emma!" I hear someone calling as I come out of Arrivals, but I don't look up. There are loads of Emmas in this world.

"Emma! Over here!"

I raise my head in disbelief. Is that . . .

No. It can't be, it can't—

It's Connor.

He looks heartbreakingly handsome. His skin has that Scandinavian tan, and his eyes are bluer than ever, and he's running toward me. This makes no sense. What's he doing here? As we reach each other, he grabs me and pulls me tight to his chest.

"Thank God," he says huskily. "Thank God. Are you OK?"

"Connor, what—what are you doing here?"

"I thought I'd surprise you. When I got here, they told me the plane had hit turbulence." He closes his eyes briefly. "Emma, I watched your plane land. They sent an ambulance straight out to it. Then you didn't appear. I thought . . ." He swallows hard. "I don't know exactly what I thought."

"I'm fine. I was just trying to get myself together. Oh, God, Connor, it was terrifying." My voice is suddenly all shaky, which is ridiculous, because I'm perfectly safe now. "At one point I honestly thought I was going to die."

"When you didn't come through the barrier . . ." Connor breaks off and looks at me silently for a few seconds. "I think I realized for the first time quite how deeply I feel about you."

"Really?" I falter.

"Emma, I think we should . . ."

Get married? My heart jumps in fear. Oh, my God. He's going to ask me to marry him, right here in the airport. What am I going to say? I'm not ready to get married. But if I say no, he'll stalk off in a huff. Shit. OK. What I'll say is, Gosh, Connor, I need a little time to . . .

". . . move in together," he finishes.

Well, of course. Obviously he wasn't going to ask me to *marry* him.

"What do you think?" He strokes my hair gently.

"Erm . . ." I rub my face, playing for time, unable to think straight. Move in with Connor. It kind of makes sense.

All at once, some of the things I said on the plane slide into my head. Something about my never having been properly in love. Something about Connor's not understanding me properly.

But then . . . that was just drivel, wasn't it? I mean, I thought I was about to die. I wasn't exactly at my most lucid.

"Connor, what about your big meeting?" I say, suddenly recalling.

"I canceled it."

"You canceled it?" I stare at him. "For me?"

I feel really wobbly now. My legs are barely holding me up. I don't know if it's the aftermath of the plane journey, or love.

Oh, God, just look at him. He's tall and he's handsome, and he canceled a big meeting, and now he wants to rescue me.

It's love. It has to be love.

"I'd love to move in with you, Connor," I whisper, and, to my utter astonishment, burst into tears.

Three

I WAKE UP the next morning with sunlight warming my eyelids and the delicious smell of coffee in the air.

"Morning!" comes Connor's voice from far above.

"Morning," I mumble without opening my eyes.

"D'you want some coffee?"

"Yes, please."

I turn over and bury my throbbing head in the pillow, trying to sink into sleep again for a couple of minutes, which normally I would find very easy. But today something's niggling at me. What have I forgotten?

As I half listen to Connor clattering around in the kitchen, and the tinny background sound of the telly, my mind gropes blearily around for clues. It's Saturday morning. I'm in Connor's bed. We went out for supper—oh, God, that awful awful plane ride . . . He came to the airport, and he said . . .

We're moving in together!

I sit up just as Connor comes in with two mugs and a coffee pot. He's dressed in a white waffle robe, his skin is glowing with health, and his blond hair is dappled in the morning sunlight. He looks completely gorgeous—and I'm not being biased here. Connor could easily be in a catalog. Or a film. He'd be one of those characters called Good-Looking Guy. I feel a prickle of pride and reach over to give him a kiss.

"Hi," he says, laughing. "Careful." He hands me my coffee. "How are you feeling?"

"All right." I push my hair back off my face. "A bit groggy."

"I'm not surprised." Connor raises his eyebrows. "Quite a day yesterday."

"Absolutely." I nod and take a sip of coffee. "So. We're . . . going to live together!"

"If you're still on for it?"

"Of course! Of course I am!" I smile brightly.

I feel as though I've turned into a grown-up overnight. I'm moving in with my boyfriend! Finally my life is going the way it should!

"I'll have to give Andrew notice. . . ." Connor gestures toward the wall, on the other side of which is his flatmate's room.

"And I'll have to tell Lissy and Jemima."

"And we'll have to find the right place. And you'll have to promise to keep it tidy." He gives me a teasing grin.

"I like that!" I feign outrage. "You're the one with fifty million CDs!"

"That's different!"

"How is it different, may I ask?" I plant my hand on my hip, like someone in a sitcom, and Connor laughs.

There's a pause, as though we've both run out of steam, and we both take a sip of coffee.

"So, anyway," says Connor after a while, "I should get going." Connor is attending a course on computers this weekend. "I'm sorry I'll miss your parents," he adds.

And he really is. I mean, as if he weren't already the perfect boyfriend, he actually *enjoys* visiting my parents.

"That's OK," I say benevolently. "It doesn't matter."

"Oh, and I forgot to tell you!" Connor reaches into his briefcase and pulls out an envelope. "Guess what I've got tickets for."

"Ooh!" I say excitedly. "Um . . ." I'm about to say "Paris!"

"The jazz festival!" Connor beams. "The Dennisson Quartet! It's their last concert of the year. Remember we heard them at Ronnie Scott's?"

For a moment I can't quite speak.

"Wow!" I manage at last. "The . . . Dennisson Quartet! I do remember!"

They played clarinets. On and on and on, for about two hours, without even taking a breath—

"I knew you'd be thrilled!" Connor touches my arm affectionately.

"Oh, I am!"

The thing is, I probably will get to like jazz one day. In fact, I'm positive I will.

I watch with fondness as he gets dressed, flosses his teeth, and picks up his briefcase.

"You wore my present," he says, glancing at my discarded underwear on the floor, obviously pleased.

"I . . . often wear them!" I say, crossing my fingers behind my back. "They're so beautiful."

"Have a lovely day with your family." Connor comes over to the bed to kiss me, and then hesitates. "Emma?"

"Yes?"

He sits down on the bed and gazes seriously at me with his bright blue eyes. "There's something I wanted to say." He bites his lip. "You know we always speak frankly to each other about our relationship."

"Er, yes," I say, feeling a little apprehensive.

"This is just an idea. You may not like it. I mean . . . it's completely up to you. . . ."

I have never seen Connor look so squirmy. Oh, my God. Is he going to start getting kinky? Does he want me to dress up in outfits and stuff?

I wouldn't mind being a nurse, actually. Or Catwoman from *Batman*! That would be cool. I could get some shiny boots. . . .

"I was thinking that . . . perhaps . . . we could . . ." He stops awkwardly.

"Yes?" I put a supportive hand on his arm.

"We could . . ." He stops again.

"Yes?"

There's another silence. I almost can't breathe for anticipation.

"We could start calling each other 'darling,' " he says in an embarrassed rush.

"What?" I say stupidly.

"It's just that . . ." Connor's whole face is suffused with blood. "We're going to be living together. It's quite a commitment. And I noticed recently, we never seem to use any . . . terms of endearment."

I stare at him, feeling caught out. "Don't we?"

"No."

"Oh." I take a sip of coffee. Now that I think about it, he's right. We don't. Why don't we?

"So how do you feel about it? Only if you wanted to—"

"Absolutely! I mean, you're right! Of course we should." I clear my throat. "Darling!"

"Thanks, darling," he says lovingly, and I smile back, trying to ignore the tiny protests inside my head.

This doesn't feel right.

I don't feel like a darling.

Darling is a married person with pearls and a four-wheel drive.

"Emma?" Connor looks perturbed. "Is something wrong?"

"I'm not sure!" I give a self-conscious laugh. "I just don't know if I feel like a 'darling'! But . . . you know. It may grow on me."

"Really? Well, we can use something else. What about 'dear'?"

Dear? Is he serious?

"No," I say quickly. "I think 'darling' is better."

"Or 'sweetheart' . . . 'honey' . . . 'angel' . . ."

"Maybe. Look, can we just leave it?"

Connor's face falls, and immediately I feel bad. Come on. I can call my boyfriend "darling." This is what growing up's all about.

"Connor, I'm sorry," I say. "I don't know what's wrong with me. Maybe I'm still a bit tense after that flight." I take his hand. "Darling."

"That's all right, darling." He gives me a kiss, his sunny expression restored. "See you later."

You see. Easy.

Oh, God.

It takes me about half an hour to get from Connor's place in Maida Vale to Islington, which is where I live, and as I open the door, I find Lissy on the sofa. She's surrounded by papers and has a frown of concentration on her face.

She works so hard, Lissy. When she's preparing a case, she spends days at home, reading technical documents and wandering around and scrawling notes to herself. And one thing I've learned is *never* to throw anything away when she's in this phase. Ever since the awful time I chucked out an empty packet of Rice Krispies that had a bit of scribble on the back— and it turned out the scribble was her entire opening speech.

"What are you working on?" I say sympathetically. "Is it that fraud case?"

Most of Lissy's cases are to do with fraud and offshore companies and stuff. It's pretty dry, to be honest. She says she enjoys it—but even she looks a bit jaded sometimes. Which I think is a bit sad, because when we were at school, she preferred the creative side of things. I think she'd have loved to go into the arts.

Her parents would never have let her be an artist, though. She once told her dad she'd like to be a painter—and he gave her this whole tirade about how she wouldn't make any money and she'd starve, and he wouldn't bail her out, if that's what she thought. Poor old Lissy was really freaked out. I mean, she was only seven.

"Er, no, it's not a case. It's this article," says Lissy. She lifts up a glossy magazine, looking a bit sheepish. "It says since the days of Cleopatra, the proportions of beauty have been the same, and there's a way to work out how beautiful you are, scientifically. You do all these measurements. . . ."

"Oh, right!" I say with interest. "So, what are you?"

"I'm just working it out." She frowns at the page again. "That makes fifty-three . . . subtract twenty . . . makes . . . Oh, my God!" She stares at the page in dismay. "I only got thirty-three!"

"Out of what?"

"A hundred! Thirty-three out of a hundred!"

"Oh, Lissy. That's crap!"

"I know," says Lissy seriously. "I'm ugly. I knew it. You know, all my life I've kind of secretly *known,* but—"

"No!" I say, trying not to laugh. "I meant the magazine's crap! You can't measure beauty with some stupid index! Just *look* at you!" Lissy is tall and slim, has the biggest gray eyes in the world, has gorgeous clear, pale skin, and is frankly stunning, even if her last haircut was a bit severe. "I mean, who are you going to believe? The mirror or a stupid, mindless magazine article?"

"A stupid, mindless magazine article," says Lissy as though it's perfectly obvious.

I know she's half joking. But ever since her boyfriend Simon chucked her, two months ago, Lissy's had really low self-esteem. In fact, I've been quite worried about her.

What's so weird is, when she's in the courtroom, Lissy has more confidence than anyone I know. In fact, her nickname is the Rottweiler. The last time I watched her in court, some fraudster was trying to spin a story about how he didn't know what he was doing, it was all the fault of his computer software . . . and Lissy completely annihilated him. Then one of the opposing barristers got some technical point wrong—and she annihilated him, too.

But then last week she went on a blind date, and the guy made an excuse and left after half an hour—and she came home totally convinced it was because of her thighs. Apparently he glanced at them as he left.

"Is that the golden proportion of beauty?" says our other flatmate, Jemima, tapping into the room in her kitten heels. She's wearing pale pink jeans and a tight white top, and as usual she looks perfectly tanned and groomed. In theory, Jemima has a job, working in a Bond Street gallery. But all she ever seems to do is have bits of her waxed and plucked and massaged and go on dates with city bankers, whose salary she always checks out before she says yes.

I do get on with Jemima. Kind of. It's just that she tends to begin all her sentences "*If* you want a rock on your finger," and "*If* you want an SW3 address," and "*If* you want to be known as a seriously good dinner party hostess."

I mean, I wouldn't *mind* being known as a seriously good dinner party hostess. You know. It's just not exactly highest on my list of priorities right now.

Plus, Jemima's idea of being a seriously good dinner party hostess is inviting lots of rich friends over, decorating the whole flat with twiggy things, getting caterers to cook loads of yummy food and telling everyone she made it herself, then sending her flatmates (me and Lissy) out to the cinema for the night and looking affronted when they dare creep back in at midnight and make themselves a hot chocolate.

"I did that quiz," she says now, picking up her pink Louis Vuitton bag. Her dad bought it for her as a present when she broke up with a guy after three dates. Like she was heart-broken.

Mind you, he had a yacht, so she probably *was* heartbroken.

"What did you get?" says Lissy.

"Eighty-nine." She spritzes herself with perfume, tosses her long, blond hair back, and smiles at herself in the mirror. "So, Emma, is it true you're moving in with Connor?"

"How did you know that?" I say in shock.

"Word on the street. Andrew called Rupes this morning about cricket, and he told him."

"Are you moving in with Connor?" says Lissy incredu-lously. "Why didn't you tell me?"

"I was about to. Isn't it great?"

"Bad move, Emma." Jemima shakes her head. "Very bad tactics."

"Tactics?" says Lissy, rolling her eyes. "*Tactics?* Jemima, they're having a relationship, not playing chess!"

"A relationship *is* a game of chess!" retorts Jemima, brush-ing mascara onto her lashes. "Mummy says you always have to look ahead. You have to plan strategically. If you make the wrong move, you've had it."

"That's rubbish!" says Lissy. "A relationship is about like minds! It's about soul mates finding each other."

"Soul mates!" says Jemima dismissively, and looks at me. "Just remember, Emma, *if* you want a rock on your finger, don't move in with Connor."

Her eyes give a swift, Pavlovian glance to the photograph

on the mantelpiece of her meeting Prince William at a charity polo match.

"Still holding out for royalty?" says Lissy. "How much younger is he than you again, Jemima?"

"Don't be stupid!" she snaps, color tinging her cheeks. "You're so immature sometimes, Lissy."

"Anyway, I don't *want* a rock on my finger," I return.

Jemima raises her arched eyebrows as though to say, "You poor, ignorant fool," and picks up her bag.

"Oh," she adds, her eyes narrowing. "Has either of you borrowed my Joseph jumper?"

There's a tiny beat of silence.

"No," I say innocently.

"I don't even know which one it is," says Lissy, flipping a page.

I can't look at Lissy. I'm sure I saw her wearing it the other night.

Jemima's blue eyes are running over us like radar scanners. "Because I have very slender arms," she says warningly, "and I really don't want the sleeves stretched. And don't think I won't notice, because I will. Ciao."

The minute she's gone, Lissy and I look at each other.

"Shit," says Lissy. "I think I left it at work. Oh, well, I'll pick it up on Monday." She shrugs and goes back to reading the magazine.

OK. So the truth is, we do both occasionally borrow Jemima's clothes. Without asking. But in our defense, she has so many, she hardly ever notices. Plus, according to Lissy, it's a basic human right that flatmates should be able to borrow one another's clothes. She says it's practically part of the un-written British constitution.

"And anyway," adds Lissy, "she owes it to me for writing her that letter to the council about all her parking tickets. You know, she never even said thank you!" She looks up from an article on Nicole Kidman. "So, what are you doing later on? D'you want to see a film?"

"I can't," I say reluctantly. "I've got my mum's birthday lunch."

"Oh, yes, of course." Lissy is the only person in the world who has any idea how I feel about visiting home. She pulls a sympathetic face. "Good luck. I hope it's OK."

Four

BUT AS I SIT on the train down, I resolve that this time will be better. I was watching a Cindy Blaine show the other day, all about reuniting long-lost daughters with their mothers, and it was so moving I had tears running down my face. At the end, Cindy gave this little homily about how our families are far too easy to take for granted and that they gave us life and we should cherish them. And I felt really chastened.

So these are my resolutions for today:

I will not:
Let my family stress me out.
Feel jealous of Kerry, or let Nev wind me up.
Look at my watch, wondering how soon I can leave.
I will:
Stay serene and loving and remember that we are all
    sacred links in the eternal circle of life.

(I got that from Cindy Blaine, too.)

Mum and Dad used to live in Twickenham, which is where I grew up. But now, since Dad's retirement, they've moved farther out of London to Stanning St. John, which is a village in Hampshire. Dad used to work for a textile company, and he took early retirement when he didn't get on the board.

He made lots of jokes about it at his retirement do, and everyone kind of winced. Especially the guy who *did* get on. I almost think Dad was hoping they'd suddenly offer it to him. But they didn't. So he and Mum decided to "get out of the rat race"—even though Twickenham isn't exactly inner city—and bought a big golden brick house with a half-acre garden, which Dad calls "land."

I arrive at the house just after twelve, to find Mum in the kitchen with my cousin Kerry. She and her husband, Nev, have moved out, too, to a village about five minutes' drive from Stanning St. John, so they see one another all the time.

I feel a familiar pang as I see them, standing side by side by the stove. They look more like mother and daughter than aunt and niece. It's not that their faces are similiar. Kerry's is all pointy nose and jutting chin, whereas Mum has the same dimples as me. But they've become similar in other ways. They've both got the same feather-cut blond hair—although Kerry's is highlighted more strongly than Mum's. They're both wearing brightly colored tops that show a lot of tanned cleavage and probably came from the same shop. And they're both laughing. On the counter, I notice a bottle of white wine already half gone.

"Happy birthday!" I say, hugging Mum with a thrill of anticipation. I have got Mum the *best* birthday present. I can't wait to give it to her!

"Hi*ya*!" says Kerry, turning around in her apron. Her blue eyes are heavily made-up, and around her neck she's wearing a diamond cross, which I haven't seen before. Every time I see Kerry, she has a new piece of jewelry. "Great to see you, Emma! We don't see enough of you. Do we, Auntie Rachel?"

"We certainly don't," says Mum, giving me a hug.

"Shall I take your coat?" says Kerry as I put the bottle of champagne I've brought into the fridge. "And what about a drink?"

This is how Kerry always talks to me. As though I'm a visitor.

But never mind. I'm not going to stress about it. Sacred links in the eternal circle of life. "It's OK!" I say, trying to sound pleasant. "I'll get it." I open the cupboard where glasses are always kept, to find myself looking at tins of tomatoes.

"They're over here now," says Kerry, on the other side of the kitchen. "We moved everything around! It makes much more sense now."

"Oh, right. Thanks." I take the glass she gives me and sip my wine. "Well done on your award, by the way."

"You've got quite an array now!" pipes up Mum. "Haven't you, Kerry love?"

"Five." Kerry smirks. "Seven, including the regional ones."

"That's fantastic!" I force a smile. "Really great. So . . . can I do anything to help?"

"I don't *think* so . . ." says Kerry, looking critically around the kitchen. "Everything's pretty much done. So I said to Elaine," she adds to Mum, " 'Where did you get those shoes?' And she said M & S! I couldn't believe it!"

"Who's Elaine?" I say, trying to join in.

"At the golf club," says Kerry.

Mum never used to play golf. But then when she moved to Hampshire, she and Kerry took it up together. And now all I hear about is golf matches, golf club dinners, and endless parties with chums from the golf club.

I did once go along, to see what it was all about. But first of all, they have all these stupid rules about what you can wear, which I didn't know, and some old guy nearly had a heart attack because I was in jeans. (Mum said she thought Kerry had told me what to wear. But she hadn't.) So they had to find me a skirt and a spare pair of those clumpy shoes with spikes. And then when we got onto the course, I couldn't hit the ball. Not that I couldn't hit the ball *well:* I literally could not make contact with the ball. So in the end they all exchanged pitying glances and said I'd better wait in the club-house.

"Sorry, Emma. Can I just get past you?" Kerry reaches over my shoulder for a serving dish.

"Sorry," I say, and move aside. "So, is there really nothing I can do, Mum?"

"You could feed Sammy," she says, giving me a pot of goldfish food. She frowns anxiously. "You know, I'm a bit worried about Sammy."

"Oh!" I say, feeling a spasm of alarm. "Er, why?"

"He just doesn't seem *himself*." She peers at him in his bowl. "What do you think? Does he look right to you?"

"Er . . ." I follow her gaze and pull a thoughtful face as though I'm studying Sammy's features.

Oh, God. I never thought she would notice. I tried as hard as I could to get a fish that looked just like Sammy. I mean, he's orange, he's got two fins, he swims around . . . what's the difference?

"He's probably just a bit depressed," I say at last. "He'll get over it."

Please don't let her take him to the vet or anything, I silently pray. I didn't even check if I got the right sex. Do goldfishes even *have* sexes?

"Anything else I can do?" I start sprinkling fish food lavishly over the water in an attempt to block her view of him.

"We've pretty much got it covered," replies Kerry kindly.

"Why don't you go and say hello to Dad?" A cloud of steam rises as Mum sieves some peas. "Lunch won't be for another ten minutes or so."

I find Dad and Nev in the sitting room, in front of the cricket. Dad's graying beard is as neatly trimmed as ever, and he's drinking beer from a silver tankard. The room has recently been redecorated with stripy wallpaper, but on the wall there's still a display of Kerry's swimming cups. Mum polishes them all regularly, every week.

Plus my two riding rosettes. I think she kind of dusts those, too.

"Hi, Dad," I say, giving him a kiss.

"Emma!" He puts a hand to his head in mock surprise. "You made it! No detours! No visits to historic cities!"

"Not today!" I give a little laugh. "Safe and sound."

There was one time, just after Mum and Dad had moved to this house, when I took the wrong train on the way down and ended up in Salisbury, and Dad always teases me about it.

"Hi, Nev." I peck him on the cheek, trying not to choke on the amount of aftershave he's wearing. He's in chinos and a tight white roll-neck that shows off his thick, muscular chest and glares off his reddened skin. Around his wrist is a heavy gold bracelet, and on his ring finger is a wedding ring with a diamond set in it. Nev runs his family's company, which supplies water coolers all around the country, and he met Kerry at some convention for young entrepreneurs. Apparently they struck up conversation admiring each other's Rolex watches.

"Hi, Emma," he says. "D'you see the new motor?"

"What?" I suddenly recall a glossy new car on the drive when I arrived. "Oh, yes! Very smart."

"Mercedes Five Series. Forty-two grand list price."

"Gosh."

"Didn't pay that, though." He taps the side of his nose. "Have a guess."

"Erm, forty?"

"Guess again."

"Thirty-nine?"

"Got him down to thirty-seven-two-fifty," says Nev triumphantly. "And free CD changer. Tax deductible," he adds.

"Right. Wow."

I don't really know what else to say, so I perch on the side of the sofa and eat a peanut.

"That's what you're aiming for, Emma!" says Dad. "Executive level! Think you'll ever make it?"

"I . . . don't know! Er, Dad, that reminds me. I've got a check for you." I awkwardly reach into my bag and get out a check for three hundred pounds.

"Well done," says Dad. "That can go on the tally." His green eyes twinkle as he puts it in his pocket. "It's called learning the value of money. It's called learning to stand on your own two feet!"

"Valuable lesson," says Nev, nodding. He takes a slug of beer and grins at Dad. "Just remind me, Emma—what career is it this week?"

When I first met Nev, it was just after I'd left the estate agency to become a photographer. Two and a half years ago. And he makes the same joke every time I see him. Every single, bloody—

OK, calm down. Happy thoughts. Cherish your family. Cherish Nev.

"It's still marketing!" I say brightly. "Has been for almost a year now!"

"Ah. Marketing. Good, good!"

There's silence for a few minutes, apart from the cricket commentary. Suddenly Dad and Nev simultaneously groan as something or other happens on the cricket pitch. A moment later they groan again.

"Right," I say. "Well, I'll just . . ."

As I get up from the sofa, they don't even turn their heads.

I go out to the hall and pick up the small carton I brought down with me. Then I go through the side gate, knock on the annex door, and push it cautiously.

"Grandpa?"

Grandpa is Mum's dad, and he's lived with us ever since he had his heart operation, ten years ago. At the old house in Twickenham, he just had a bedroom, but this house is bigger, so he has his own annex of two rooms and a tiny little kitchen, tacked onto the side of the house. He's sitting in his favorite leather armchair, with the radio playing classical music and his eyes tight shut. On the floor in front of him are about six cardboard packing cases crammed with stuff. I glimpse sheaves of papers, books dotted with age, an old wireless, an old-fashioned alarm clock, a set of plastic flowerpots, a slide projector, an Ordinance Survey map dating from 1977.

"Hi, Grandpa!" I say.

"Emma!" As he opens his eyes, his face lights up. "Darling girl! Come here!" I bend over to give him a kiss, and he squeezes my hand tight. His skin is dry and cool, and his hair is even whiter than it was last time I saw him.

"I've got some more Panther Bars for you," I say, nodding to my box. Grandpa is completely addicted to Panther energy bars, and so are all his friends at the bowling club, so I use my discount allowance to buy him a boxful every time I come home. (Apparently Panther employees used to get all the products for free. But then some guys from Design were found to be selling Panther Cola cheap over the Internet, so they clamped down.)

"Thank you, my love!" Grandpa beams. "You're a good girl, Emma."

"Where should I put them?"

We both look helplessly around the cluttered room.

"What about over there, by the fireplace?" says Grandpa at last. I pick my way across the room, dump the box on the floor, then retrace my steps, picking between a bundle of newspapers tied together with string, a pile of postcards and letters, and a heap of stuff that looks like total rubbish.

"Pineapple and papaya?" Grandpa's reading the label on the box. He looks up in dismay. "What happened to apple and black currant?"

"They're pushing the tropical flavors," I explain, sitting down on one of the packing cases. "There's a whole ad campaign around it. 'Transport Yourself.' These guys are playing volleyball, and they take a bite of a Panther Bar, and suddenly they're on this exotic beach. . . ."

I trail off as Grandpa shakes his head.

"Papaya! Would you put papaya on your porridge?" He looks so disgusted I want to laugh.

"Er, well, but these are oat health bars—"

"Exactly. Oats. Porridge!"

"I'll get you some apple and black currant ones. I promise—"

"Apple and oats, yes. Pineapple and oats . . ." Grandpa pauses. "Barf."

I nearly choke in surprise. *"Barf?"*

"It's the new slang," says Grandpa. "I read it in the paper. It means 'to be sick.' I'm surprised you haven't heard of it, Emma."

"Well, I have. But—"

"And another thing," adds Grandpa before I can continue. "I read a very worrying newspaper article the other day, about safety in London." He gives me a beady look. "You don't travel on public transport in the evenings, do you?"

"Erm, hardly ever," I say, crossing my fingers behind my back. "Just now and then, when I absolutely have to. . . ."

"Darling girl, you mustn't!" says Grandpa, looking agitated. "Teenagers in hoods with flick-knives roam the Underground, it said. Drunken louts breaking bottles, gouging one another's eyes out . . ."

"It's not *that* bad—"

"Emma, it's not worth the risk! For the sake of a taxi fare or two!"

I'm pretty sure that if I asked Grandpa what he thought the average taxi fare was in London, he'd say five shillings.

"Honestly, Grandpa, I'm really careful." I adopt a reassuring tone. "And I do take taxis."

Sometimes. About once a year.

"Anyway. What's all this stuff?" I ask to change the subject, and Grandpa gives a gusty sigh.

"Your mother cleared out the attic last week. I'm just sorting out what to throw away and what to keep."

"That seems like a good idea." I look at the pile of rubbish on the floor. "Is this the stuff you're throwing out?"

"No! I'm keeping all that!" He puts a protective hand over it.

"So, where's the stuff to throw?"

There's silence. Grandpa avoids my gaze.

"Grandpa! You have to throw *some* of this away!" I exclaim, trying not to laugh. "You don't need all these old newspaper cuttings! And what's this?" I reach past the newspaper cuttings and fish out an old yo-yo. "This is rubbish, surely."

"Jim's yo-yo!" Grandpa's reaches for the yo-yo, his eyes softening. "Good old Jim."

"Who was Jim?" I've never even heard of a Jim before. "Was he a good friend of yours?"

"We met at the fairground. Spent the afternoon together. I was nine." Grandpa is turning the yo-yo over and over in his fingers.

"Did you become friends?"

"Never saw him again." He shakes his head. "I've never forgotten it."

The trouble with Grandpa is, he never forgets anything.

"Well . . . what about some of these cards?" I pull out a bundle of old Christmas cards.

"I never throw away cards." Grandpa gives me a long look. "When you get to my age; when the people you've known and loved all your life start to pass away . . . you want to hang on to any memento. However small."

"I can understand that," I say more quietly. Maybe this is all souvenirs of Granny. She died when I was seven, and Grandpa still visits her grave every two weeks.

I reach for the nearest card and open it, and my expression changes. "Grandpa! This is from Smith's Electrical Maintenance, 1965!"

"Frank Smith was a very good man," starts Grandpa.

"Grandpa." I try to sound firm. "You can't possibly need to keep this. Nor do you need one from . . ." I open the next card. "Southwestern Gas Supplies. And you don't need twenty old copies of *Punch*." I deposit them on the pile. "And what are these?" I reach into the box again and pull out an envelope of photos. "Are these actually of anything you really want to—"

I stop. I'm looking at a photograph of me and Dad and Mum sitting on a bench in a park. Mum's wearing a flowery dress, and Dad's wearing a stupid sun hat, and I'm on his knee, aged about nine, eating an ice cream. We all look so happy together.

Wordlessly, I turn to another photo. I've got Dad's hat on, and we're all laughing helplessly at something. Just us three.

Just us. Before Kerry came into our lives.

I still remember the day she arrived as though it were yesterday. I remember red suitcases in the hall and a new voice in the kitchen and an unfamiliar smell of perfume in the air. I

Can You Keep a Secret?

walked in and there she was, a stranger, all the way from Hong Kong, drinking a cup of tea. She was wearing a school uniform, but she still looked like a grown-up to me. She already had an enormous bust, and gold studs in her ears, and streaks in her hair. And at suppertime, Mum and Dad let her have a glass of wine. Mum kept telling me I had to be very kind to her, because her mother had died and her father, Mum's brother, was too busy traveling to look after her. She was going to live with us for the moment, and then maybe her daddy would get a new job and move back to Britain. But in the meantime we all had to be very kind to Kerry. That was why she got my room.

I leaf through the rest of the pictures, trying to swallow the lump in my throat. There's the park we used to go to, with swings and slides. I loved that place so much. But it was too boring for Kerry, and I desperately wanted to be like her, so I said it was boring, too, and we never went again.

"Knock, knock!"

I look up with a start, and Kerry's standing at the door, holding her glass of wine.

"Lunch is ready!"

"Thanks," I say. "We're just coming."

"Now, Gramps!" Kerry wags her finger reprovingly at Grandpa and gestures at the packing cases. "Haven't you got anywhere with this yet?"

"It's difficult," I hear myself saying defensively. "There are loads of memories in here. You can't just throw them out."

"If you say so." Kerry rolls her eyes. "If it were me, the whole lot'd go in the bin."

I cannot cherish her. I cannot do it. I want to throw my treacle tart at her.

We've been sitting around the table now for forty minutes, and the only voice we've heard is Kerry's.

"It's all about image," she's saying now. "It's all about the right clothes, the right look, the right walk. When I walk along the street, the message I give the world is 'I am a successful woman.'"

"Show us!" says Mum admiringly.

"Well." Kerry gives a false-modest smile. "Like this." She pushes her chair back and wipes her mouth with her napkin.

"You should watch this, Emma!" says Mum. "Pick up a few tips!"

As we all watch, Kerry starts striding around the room. Her chin is raised, her boobs are sticking out, her eyes are fixed on the middle distance, and her bottom is jerking from side to side.

She looks like a cross between an ostrich and one of the androids in *Attack of the Clones*.

"I should be in heels, of course," she says without stopping.

"When Kerry goes into a conference hall, I tell you, heads turn," says Nev proudly, and takes a sip of wine. "People stop what they're doing and stare at her!"

I bet they do.

Oh, God. I want to giggle. I mustn't. I mustn't.

"Do you want to have a go, Emma?" says Kerry. "Copy me?"

"Er, I don't think so," I say. "I think I probably . . . picked up the basics."

I can't control the snort of laughter that erupts, so I turn it into a cough.

"Kerry's trying to help you, Emma!" says Mum. "You should be grateful!" She beams at Kerry, who simpers back. "You are good to Emma, Kerry."

I just take a swig of wine.

Yeah, right. Kerry really wants to help me.

That's why when I was completely desperate for a job after

the photography disaster and asked her for work experience at her office furniture company, she said no. I wrote her this really long, careful letter, saying I realized it put her in an awkward situation, but I'd really appreciate any chance, even a couple of days of running errands, to gain experience.

And she sent back a standard rejection letter saying she'd "keep my details on file."

I was so totally mortified, I never told anyone. Especially not Mum and Dad.

"You should listen to some of Kerry's business tips, Emma," Dad is saying sharply. "Maybe if you paid more attention, you'd do a bit better in life."

"It's only a walk!" quips Nev with a chortle. "It's not a miracle cure!"

"Nev!" Mum frowns in half reproof.

"Emma knows I'm joking, don't you, Emma?" says Nev easily, and fills up his glass with more wine.

"Of course!" I force a merry smile.

Just wait till I get promoted.

Just wait. Just wait.

A sudden image of the cranberry drink spraying over Doug Hamilton pops into my head, and I feel a twinge of unease. Not one of my best moments. And when I got home yesterday night, I found a message from Paul on my mobile, asking how the meeting went and saying we'd speak on Monday.

But I have to think positive. He wouldn't not promote me just because of one mistake, would he? I mean, if it was anyone's fault, it was the design department's! They should make better cans. Or the drink should be less fizzy. . . .

"Emma! Earth to Emma!" Kerry is waving a comical hand in front of my face. "Wake up, dopey! We're doing presents!"

"Oh, right." I come to. "OK. I'll just go and get mine."

As Mum opens a camera from Dad and a purse from

Grandpa, I start to feel excited. I *so* hope Mum likes my present.

"It doesn't look much," I say as I hand her the pink envelope. "But you'll see when you open it. . . ."

"What can it be?" Mum says, looking intrigued. She rips open the envelope and takes out the flowered card, and her whole face lights up. "Oh, Emma!"

"What is it?" says Dad.

"It's a day at a spa!" exclaims Mum. "A whole day of pampering!"

"What a good idea!" says Grandpa, and pats my hand. "You always have good ideas for presents, Emma!"

"Thank you, love! How thoughtful!" Mum leans over to kiss me, and I feel a surge of pleasure. I had the idea a few months ago. It's a really nice daylong package, with free treatments and everything.

"You get champagne lunch," I say eagerly. "And you can keep the slippers!"

"Wonderful!" says Mum. "I'll look forward to it! Emma, that's a lovely present!"

"Oh, dear!" says Kerry with a little laugh. She looks at the large creamy envelope in her own hands. "My present's slightly upstaged, I'm afraid. Never mind. I'll change it."

I look up, alert. There's something about Kerry's voice. I know something's up. I just know it.

"What do you mean?" says Mum.

"It doesn't matter," says Kerry. "I'll just . . . find something else. Not to worry." She starts to put the envelope away in her bag.

"Kerry, love!" says Mum. "Stop that! Don't be silly! What is it?"

"Well," says Kerry. "It's just that Emma and I seem to have had the same idea." She hands Mum the envelope with another little laugh. "Can you believe it?"

My whole body stiffens.

There's complete silence as Mum opens the envelope.

"Oh, my goodness!" she says, taking out a gold-embossed brochure. "What's this? Le Spa Meridien?" Something falls into her hands, and she lifts it. "Tickets to *Paris*? Kerry!"

She's ruined my present.

"For both of you," adds Kerry a little smugly. "Uncle Brian, too."

"Kerry!" says Dad in delight. "You marvel!"

"It *is* supposed to be rather good," says Kerry with a complacent smile. "Five-star accommodation . . . The chef has three Michelin stars."

"I don't believe this!" says Mum. She's leafing excitedly through the brochure. "Look at the swimming pool! Look at the gardens!"

My flowery card is lying, forgotten, amid the wrapping paper.

Suddenly I feel close to tears. She knew. She *knew*.

"Kerry, you knew," I suddenly blurt out, unable to stop myself. "I told you I was giving Mum a spa treat. I *told* you! We had that conversation about it, months ago. In the garden!"

"Did we?" says Kerry casually. "I don't remember."

"You do! Of course you remember!"

"Emma!" says Mum sharply. "It was a simple mistake. Wasn't it, Kerry?"

"Of course it was!" says Kerry, opening her eyes in wide innocence. "Emma, if I've spoiled things for you, I can only apologize—"

"There's no need to apologize, Kerry love!" says Mum. "These things happen. And they're *both* lovely presents. *Both* of them." She looks at my card again. "Now, you two girls are best friends! I don't like to see you quarreling! Especially on my birthday!"

Mum smiles at me, and I try to smile back. But inside, I feel about ten years old again. Kerry always manages to wrong-foot me. She always has, ever since she arrived. Whatever she did, everyone took her side. She was the one whose mother had died. We all had to be nice to her. I could never, ever win.

Trying to pull myself together, I reach for my wineglass and take a huge swig. Then I find myself surreptitiously glancing at my watch. I can leave at four if I make an excuse about trains running late. That's only another hour and a half to get through. And maybe we'll watch telly or something. . . .

"A penny for your thoughts, Emma," says Grandpa, patting my hand, and I look up guiltily.

"Er, nothing," I say. "I wasn't really thinking about . . . anything."

Five

ANYWAY. It doesn't matter, because I'm going to get a promotion. Then Nev will stop making cracks about my career, and I'll be able to pay back Dad. . . . Everyone will be really impressed.

I still have to explain to Paul why the Glasgow meeting went wrong. I'm not looking forward to that. But even so, I can't help feeling optimistic as I wake up on Monday morning. It's my yearly appraisal today. And if you ignore that one teeny incident—if you look at the bigger picture—I've been doing really well recently. I *know* I have.

The thing about Paul is, he doesn't heap you with praise. But I bet he's noticed all the extra jobs I've been doing. He's probably been writing it all down in a little book or something. He'll bring it out and flick through the pages and say, "You know, effort doesn't go uncredited in this company, Emma."

As I get dressed, I can feel a growing fizz of anticipation. I even wonder whether to put on a smart suit again—just to *show* Paul what a great executive I'd make. But no. He might think I'm being pretentious. I'll just wear my usual work outfit. Jeans and a nice top, this one from French Connection.

Well . . . not exactly French Connection. To be honest, I bought it at Oxfam. But the *label* says French Connection. And while I'm still paying off Dad, I don't have much choice about where I shop. I mean, a new top from French Connection costs about fifty quid, whereas this one cost £7.50! And it's practically new!

As I skip up the tube steps at Blackfriars, the air is fresh and the sky is a bright morning blue. Office workers are hurrying along the street, holding cups of tea and coffee, clutching bags and cases, jostling one another at the traffic lights. A guy in a raincoat and heavy shoes strides past and almost squashes my foot, but I'm too distracted to react. I'm imagining if I do get promoted. Mum will say, "How was your week?" and I'll say, "Well, actually—"

No, what I'll do is wait until I go home and then just nonchalantly hand over my new business card—

"Emma!"

I look around to see Katie, my friend from Personnel, climbing the tube steps behind me, panting slightly. Her curly red hair is all tousled, she's holding one shoe in her hand, and her green eyes are even wider than usual, giving her an air of surprise.

I heard a group of girls talking about Katie in the loos at work once. Their theory was that she always looks surprised because she plucks her eyebrows so high. But the truth is, quite a lot of the time Katie *is* surprised by life. It's like she's unprepared. Like she was never given the instruction manual.

"What on earth happened?" I say as she reaches the top of the steps.

"My stupid shoe!" she exclaims. "I only had it mended the other day, and the heel's just come off!" She flaps it at me. "I paid six quid for that heel! God, this day is such a disaster.

The milkman forgot to bring me any milk, and I had a *terrible* weekend."

"I thought you were spending it with Charlie!" I say in surprise. "What happened?"

Charlie is Katie's latest man. They've been seeing each other for a few weeks, and this weekend she was supposed to be visiting his country cottage, which he's doing up at the weekends.

"It was awful! As soon as we arrived, he said he was going off to play golf."

"Oh, right." I try to find a positive angle. "Well . . . at least he's comfortable with you. He can just act normal."

"Maybe." She looks doubtful. "So then he said, how did I feel about helping out a bit while he was gone? So I said of course—and then he gave me this paintbrush and three pots of paint and said I should get the sitting room done if I worked fast."

"What?"

"And then he came back at six o'clock . . . and said my brushwork was careless!" Her voice rises in woe. "It wasn't careless! I only smudged one bit, and that's because the stupid ladder wasn't long enough."

I stare at her in disbelief. "Katie, you're not telling me you actually painted the room."

"Well . . . yes. You know, to help out. But now I'm starting to think . . . Is he just using me?"

I'm almost speechless.

"Katie, of course he's using you!" I manage at last. "He wants a free painter-decorator! You have to chuck him! Immediately! Now!"

Katie is silent for a few seconds, and I eye her with apprehension. Her face is still, but I can tell lots of things are going on beneath the surface.

"Oh, God, you're right!" she suddenly bursts out. "You're right! He's been using me! It's my own fault. I should have realized when he asked me if I had any experience in plumbing or roofing—"

"When did he ask you that?" I say incredulously.

"On our first date! I thought he was just, you know, making conversation. . . ."

"Katie, it's not your fault." I squeeze her arm. "You weren't to know!"

"But what is it about me?" Katie stops still in the street. "Why do I only attract complete shits?"

"You don't!"

"I do! Look at the men I've been out with." She starts counting off on her fingers. "Daniel borrowed all that money off me and disappeared to Mexico, Eric chucked me as soon as I found him a job, David was two-timing me. . . . Do you see a pattern emerging?"

"I, um, possibly . . ."

"I just think I should give up." Her face falls. "I'm never going to find anyone nice."

"No!" I say at once. "Don't give up! Katie, I just know your life is going to turn around. You're going to find some lovely, kind, wonderful man—"

"But where?"

"I . . . don't know!" I cross my fingers behind my back. "But I know it'll happen. I've got a really strong feeling about it."

"Really?" She blinks. "You do?"

"Absolutely!" I think for a moment. "Look, here's an idea. Why don't you try . . . going to have lunch at a different place today. Somewhere completely different. And maybe you'll meet someone there!"

"You think?" She gazes at me. "OK. I'll try it."

We start walking along the pavement again. "The *only* good thing about the weekend," she adds as we reach the corner, "is I finished making my new top! What do you think?"

She proudly takes off her jacket and does a twirl, and I stare at her for a few seconds, not quite sure what to say.

It's not that I don't *like* crochet—

OK. It is that I don't like crochet.

Especially pink scoop-neck open-weave crochet tops. You can actually see glimpses of her bra through it.

"It's . . . amazing!" I manage at last. "Absolutely fantastic!"

"Isn't it great?" She gives me a pleased smile. "And it was so quick to do! I'm going to make the matching skirt next!"

"That's great!" I say faintly. "You're so clever."

"Oh, it's nothing! I just enjoy it."

She smiles modestly and puts her jacket back on. "So anyway, how about you?" she adds as we start to cross the road. "Did you have a nice weekend? I bet you did. I bet Connor was completely wonderful and romantic. I bet he took you out for dinner or something."

"Actually, he asked me to move in with him," I say, feeling a bit awkward.

"Really?" Katie gazes at me wistfully. "God, Emma, you two make the perfect couple. You give me faith that it can happen. It all seems so easy for you."

I can't help feeling a little flicker of pleasure inside. Me and Connor. The perfect couple. Role models for other people.

"It's not *that* easy!" I try to sound modest. "I mean, we argue, like anyone else!"

"Do you?" Katie looks surprised. "I've never seen you argue."

"Of course we do!"

I rack my brain for a moment, trying to remember the last time Connor and I had a fight. I mean, obviously we do *have* arguments. Loads of them. All couples do. It's only healthy.

Come on, this is silly. We must have—

Yes! There was that time by the river when I thought those big white birds were geese and Connor thought they were swans. Exactly.

———

The Panther building is a big steel and glass office block on Farringdon Road. As we walk up the pale stone steps, each with a granite panther jumping across it, my stomach starts jumping a little with nerves. What shall I say to Paul about the meeting at Glen Oil?

Well, obviously I'll be completely frank and honest. Without actually telling him the truth—

"Hey, look!" Katie's voice interrupts me, and I follow her gaze. Through the glass front of the building, I can see a commotion in the foyer. This isn't normal. What's going on?

God, has there been a fire or something?

As Katie and I push our way through the heavy revolving glass doors, we look at each other, baffled. The whole place is in turmoil. People are scurrying about, someone's polishing the brass banister, someone else is polishing the fake plants, and Cyril, the senior office manager, is shooing people into lifts.

"Could you please go to your offices! We don't want you hanging around the reception area. You should all be at your desks by now." Cyril sounds completely stressed-out. "There's nothing to see down here! Please go to your desks!"

"What's happening?" I say to Dave the security guard, who's lounging against the wall with a cup of tea as usual. He takes a sip, swills it around his mouth, and gives us a grin. "Jack Harper's visiting."

"What?" We both gawk at him.

"Today?"

"Are you *serious*?"

In the world of the Panther Corporation, this is like saying the Pope's visiting. Or Father Christmas. Jack Harper is the joint founder of the Panther Corporation. He *invented* Panther Cola. I know this because I've typed out blurbs about him approximately a million times. *"It was 1987 when young, dynamic business partners Jack Harper and Pete Laidler bought up the ailing Zoot soft drinks company, repackaged Zootacola as Panther Cola, invented the slogan 'Don't Pause,' and thus made marketing history."*

No wonder Cyril's in a tizz.

"In about five minutes." Dave consults his watch. "Give or take."

"But . . . but how come?" says Katie. "I mean, just out of the blue like this . . ."

Dave's eyes twinkle. He's obviously been telling people the news all morning and is thoroughly enjoying himself. "He wants to have a look around the U.K. operation, apparently."

"I thought he wasn't interested in the business anymore!" says Jane from Accounts, who's come up behind us and is listening, agog. "I thought ever since Pete Laidler died, he was all grief-stricken and reclusive. He was going to take a career break, wasn't he? On his ranch, or whatever it is."

"That was a year ago," points out Katie. "Maybe he's feeling better."

"Maybe he wants to sell us off, more like," says Jane darkly.

"My theory," says Dave, and we bend our heads to listen, "is he wants to see if the plants are shiny enough." He nods his head toward Cyril, and we all giggle.

"Be careful," Cyril is snapping. "Don't damage the stems." He glances up. "What are you all still doing there?"

"Just going!" says Katie, and we head toward the stairs, which I always use because it means I don't have to bother with the gym. Plus, luckily Marketing is on the first floor. We've just reached the landing when Jane squeaks, "Look! Oh, my God! It's him!"

A limousine has purred up in the street, right in front of the glass doors. Like clockwork, a lift at the other end of the foyer suddenly opens, and out strides Graham Hillingdon, the chief executive, plus the managing director and about six others, all looking immaculate in dark suits.

"That's enough!" Cyril is hissing at the poor cleaners in the foyer. "Go! Leave it!"

The three of us stand, goggling like children, as the passenger door of the limousine opens. A moment later, out gets a man with sleek blond hair in a navy blue overcoat. He's wearing dark glasses and black leather gloves and is holding a titanium briefcase. His trousers are pressed to razor-sharp pleats at the front, and his hair is so perfect, it looks like each follicle has been individually trimmed.

He looks like a million dollars.

Graham Hillingdon and the others are all outside by now, lined up on the steps. They all shake his hand in turn, then usher him inside, where Cyril is waiting. The blond man scans the foyer over his dark glasses, then flicks some dust off his coat.

"Welcome to the Panther Corporation U.K.," Cyril says fulsomely. "I hope your journey was pleasant?"

"Not too bad, thanks," says the man, in an American accent.

"As you can see, this is very much a *normal* working day. . . ."

"Hey, look," murmurs Katie. "Kenny's stuck outside the doors."

Kenny Davey, one of the designers, is hovering uncertainly on the steps outside in his jeans and baseball boots, not knowing whether to come in or not. He puts a hand to the door, then retreats a little, then comes up to the door again and peers uncertainly inside.

"Come in, Kenny!" says Cyril, opening the door with a rather savage smile. "One of our designers, Kenny Davey. You should have been here ten minutes ago, Kenny! Still, never mind!" He pushes a bewildered Kenny toward the lifts, then glances up and shoos us away in irritation.

"Come on," says Katie, "we'd better go." And, trying not to giggle, the three of us hurry up the stairs.

The atmosphere in the marketing department is a bit like my bedroom used to be before we had parties in the sixth form. People are brushing their hair, spraying perfume, shuffling papers around, and gossiping excitedly. As I walk past the office of Neil Gregg, who is in charge of media strategy, I see him carefully lining up his *Marketing Week* awards on his desk, while Fiona, his assistant, is polishing all the framed photographs of him shaking hands with famous people.

I'm just hanging up my coat on the rack when the head of our department, Paul, pulls me aside.

"What the fuck happened at Glen Oil? I had a very strange e-mail from Doug Hamilton this morning. You poured a drink over him?"

I don't believe it. Doug Hamilton *told* Paul? But he promised he wouldn't! "It wasn't like that," I say quickly. "I was just trying to demonstrate the many fine qualities of Panther Prime and I . . . I kind of spilled it."

Paul raises his eyebrows, and not in a friendly way. "All right. Well, I've smoothed it over with them. I guess it was a lot to ask of you."

My heart plummets. Please don't say one stupid can has ruined my chances. "It wasn't!" I say quickly. "What I mean is, if you just give me another opportunity to prove myself, I'll do better. I promise."

"We'll see." He looks at his watch. "You'd better get on. Your desk is a fucking mess."

"OK. Um, what time will my appraisal be?"

"Emma, in case you hadn't heard, Jack Harper's visiting us today," says Paul in his most sarcastic voice. "But of course, if you think your appraisal's more important than the guy who *founded* the company—"

"No! I didn't mean . . . I just . . ."

"Go and tidy your desk," says Paul in a bored voice. "And if you spill fucking Panther Prime over Harper, you're fired."

As I scurry to my desk, Cyril comes into the room looking hassled. His round face is a little sweaty, and his striped shirt is edging out of his double-breasted suit.

"Attention!" he says, clapping his hands. "Attention, everyone! This is an informal visit, nothing more. Mr. Harper will come in, perhaps talk to one or two of you, observe what you do. . . . So I want you all just to act normal, but obviously, at your highest standards. . . . What are these papers?" he suddenly snaps, looking at a neat pile of proofs in the corner next to Fergus Grady's desk.

"That's the, um, artwork for the new Panther Gum campaign," says Fergus, who is very shy and creative. "I haven't quite got room on my desk. . . ."

"Well, they can't stay here!" Cyril picks them up and shoves them at him. "Get rid of them! Now, if he asks any of you a question, just be pleasant and natural. When he arrives, I want you all at work. Just doing typical tasks that you would naturally be doing in the course of a normal day." He looks around distractedly. "Some of you could be on the phone; some could be typing at your computers. . . . A couple of you could be creatively brainstorming. . . . Remember, this department is the very hub of the company. The Panther Corporation is renowned for its marketing brilliance!"

He stops, and we all stare dumbly at him.

"Get on!" He claps his hands again. "Don't just stand there! You!" He points to me. "Come on! Move!"

Oh, God. My desk is completely covered with stuff. I open a drawer and sweep a whole load of papers inside, then, in slight panic, begin to tidy the pens in my stationery pot. At the next desk, Artemis Harrison is redoing her lipstick.

"It'll be really inspirational to meet him," she says, admiring herself in her hand mirror. "You know, a lot of people think he single-handedly changed the face of marketing practice." Her eyes fall on me. "Is that a new top, Emma? Where's it from?"

"Er, French Connection," I say after a pause.

"I was in French Connection at the weekend." Her eyes are narrowing. "I didn't see that design."

"Well . . . they'd probably sold out!" I turn away and pretend to be reorganizing my top drawer.

"What do we call him?" Caroline, a product manager, is saying. "Mr. Harper or Jack?"

"Five minutes alone with him," Nick, one of the marketing executives, is saying feverishly into his phone. "That's all I need. Five minutes to pitch him the Web site idea. I mean, Jesus, if he went for it—"

God, the air of excitement is infectious! With a spurt of adrenaline, I find myself reaching for my comb and checking my lip gloss. I mean, you never know. Maybe he'll somehow spot my potential. Maybe he'll pull me out of the crowd!

"OK, folks," says Paul, striding into the department. "He's on this floor. He's going into Admin. first. . . ."

"On with your everyday tasks!" exclaims Cyril. "Now!"

Fuck. What's my everyday task?

I pick up my phone and press my voice mail code. I can be listening to my messages.

I look around the department—and see that everyone else has done the same thing.

We can't *all* be on the phone. This is so stupid! OK, I'll just switch on my computer and wait for it to warm up.

As I watch the screen changing color, Artemis starts talking in a loud voice.

"I think the whole essence of the concept is *vitality,*" she says, her eye constantly flicking toward the door. "D'you see what I mean?"

"Er, yes," says Nick. "I mean, in a modern marketing environment, I think we need to be looking at a, um, fusion of strategy and forward-thinking vision."

God, my computer's slow today. Jack Harper will arrive and I'll still be sitting here like a waxwork.

I know what I'll do. I'll be the person getting a coffee. I mean, what could be more natural than that?

"I think I'll get a coffee!" I say, and get up from my seat.

"Could you get me one?" says Artemis, looking up briefly. "So anyway, on my M.B.A. course . . ."

The coffee machine is near the entrance to the department, in its own little alcove. As I'm waiting for the noxious liquid to fill my cup, I glance up and see Graham Hillingdon walking out of the admin. department, followed by a couple of others. Shit! He's coming!

OK. Keep cool. Just wait for the second cup to fill, nice and natural. . . .

And there he is! With his blond hair and his expensive-looking suit and his dark glasses. But to my slight surprise, he steps back, out of the way.

In fact, no one's even looking at him. Everyone's attention is focused on some other guy. A guy wearing jeans and a black turtleneck, who's walking out now . . .

As I stare in fascination, he turns.

Oh, my God. As I see his face, I feel an almighty thud, as though a bowling ball's landed hard in my chest.

It's him.

The same dark eyes. The same laugh lines. The stubble's gone, but it's definitely him.

It's the man from the plane.

What's *he* doing here?

And . . . and why is everyone's attention on him? He's speaking now, and everyone is lapping up every word he says.

He turns again, and I instinctively duck back out of sight, trying to keep calm. What's he doing here? He can't—

That can't be—

That can't possibly be—

With wobbly legs, I walk back to my desk, trying not to drop the coffee on the floor.

"Hey," I say to Artemis, my voice pitched slightly too high. "Erm, do you know what Jack Harper looks like?"

"No," she says, and takes her coffee. "Thanks."

"Dark hair," says someone.

"Dark?" I swallow. "Not blond?"

"He's coming this way!" hisses someone. "He's coming!"

I sink into my chair and sip my coffee, wincing automatically at the disgusting taste.

". . . our head of Marketing and Promotion, Paul Fletcher," I can hear Graham saying.

"Good to meet you, Paul," comes the same dry American voice.

It's him. It's definitely him.

OK, keep calm. Maybe he won't remember me. It was one short flight. He probably takes a lot of flights.

"Everyone." Paul is leading him into the center of the office. "I'm delighted to introduce our founding father, the man who has influenced and inspired a generation of marketeers . . . Jack Harper!"

A round of applause breaks out, and Jack Harper shakes his head, smiling. "Please," he says. "No fuss. Just do what you would normally do."

He starts to walk around the office, pausing now and then to talk to people. Paul is leading the way, making all the introductions, and following them silently everywhere is the blond man.

"Here he comes!" Artemis suddenly murmurs, and everyone at our end of the office stiffens.

My heart starts to thump, and I shrink into my chair, trying to hide behind my computer.

Maybe he won't recognize me. Maybe he won't remember. Maybe he won't—

Fuck. He's looking at me. I see the flash of surprise in his eyes, and he raises his eyebrows.

He recognizes me.

Please don't come over, I silently pray. Please don't come over.

"And who's this?" he says to Paul.

"This is Emma Corrigan, one of our junior marketing assistants."

He's walking toward me. Artemis has stopped talking. Everyone's staring. I'm hot with embarrassment.

"Hello," he says pleasantly.

"Hello," I manage, "Mr. Harper."

OK, so he recognizes me. But that doesn't necessarily mean he remembers anything I said. A few random comments thrown out by a person in the next-door seat. Who's going to remember that? Maybe he wasn't even *listening*—

"And what do you do?"

"I, um, assist the marketing department, and I help with setting up promotional initiatives," I mumble.

"Emma was in Glasgow only last week on business," puts in Paul, giving me a completely phony smile. "We believe in giving our junior staff responsibility as early as possible."

"Very wise," says Jack Harper, nodding. His gaze runs over my desk and alights with sudden interest on my polystyrene cup. He looks up and meets my eye. "How's the coffee?" he asks pleasantly. "Tasty?"

Like a tape recording in my head, I suddenly hear my own stupid voice, prattling on.

The coffee at work is the most disgusting stuff you've ever drunk, absolute poison. . . .

"It's great!" I say. "Really . . . delicious!"

"I'm very glad to hear it." There's a spark of amusement in his eyes, and I feel myself redden.

He remembers. Fuck. He remembers.

"And this is Artemis Harrison," says Paul. "One of our brightest young marketing executives."

"Artemis," says Jack Harper thoughtfully. He takes a few steps toward her workstation. "That's a nice big desk you've got there, Artemis." He smiles at her. "Is that new?"

. . . This new desk arrived the other day, and she just took it . . .

He remembers everything, doesn't he? Everything.

Oh, God. What the fuck else did I say?

While Artemis makes some show-offy reply, I'm sitting

perfectly still with my pleasant, good-employee expression. But inside, my mind is frantically spooling back, trying to remember, trying to piece together what I said. I mean, I told this man everything about myself. *Everything.* I told him what sort of knickers I wear, and what flavor ice cream I like, and how I lost my virginity, and—

Suddenly my blood runs cold.

I'm remembering something I should not have told him.

Something I should not have told anyone.

. . . I know I shouldn't have done it, but I so wanted to get the job . . .

I told him about faking the A grade on my CV.

Well, that's it. I'm dead.

He'll fire me. I'll get a record for being dishonest and no one will ever employ me again, and I'll end up on a *Britain's Worst Jobs* documentary, cleaning up cow poo, saying brightly, "It's not too bad, really. . . ."

OK. Don't panic. There must be something I can do. I'll apologize. Yes. I'll say it was an error of judgment that I now deeply regret, and I never meant to mislead the company, and—

No. I'll say, "Actually, I *did* get an A grade, ha-ha—silly me—I forgot!" And then I'll forge a GCSE certificate with one of those calligraphy kits. I mean, he's American. He'll never know—

No. He's bound to find out.

OK, maybe I'm overreacting here. Let's just get things in proportion. Jack Harper is a huge, important guy. Look at him! He's got limos and flunkies, and a great big company that makes millions every year. He doesn't care if one of his employees got a poxy A grade or not! I mean, honestly!

I laugh out loud in my nerves, and Artemis gives me an odd look.

"I'd just like to say that I'm very glad to meet you all," says Jack Harper, looking around the silent office. "And also introduce my assistant, Sven James." He gestures to the guy with blond hair. "I'll be staying here for a few days, so I hope I'll get to know a few of you better. As you know, Pete Laidler, who founded the Panther Corporation with me, was British. For that reason, among many others, this country has always been immensely important to me."

A sympathetic murmur goes around the office. He lifts a hand, nods, and walks away, followed by Sven and all the executives. There's silence until he's gone, then an excited babble breaks out.

I feel my whole body sag in relief. Thank God. Thank *God*.

Honestly, I'm ridiculous. Fancy thinking even for a moment that Jack Harper would remember what I said. Let alone care about it! Fancy thinking he would actually take time out of his busy, important schedule for something as insignificant as whether I faked my CV or not! As I reach for my mouse and click on a new document, I'm actually smiling.

"Emma." I look up to see Paul standing over my desk. "Jack Harper would like to see you," he says curtly.

"What?" My smile fades away. "Me?"

"The meeting room in five minutes."

"Did he say . . . why?"

"No."

Paul strides off, and I gaze unseeingly at my computer screen, feeling sick.

I was right the first time. I'm going to lose my job.

I'm going to lose my job because of one stupid comment on one stupid plane ride.

Why did I have to get upgraded? *Why* did I have to open my stupid mouth?

"Why does Jack Harper want to see you?" says Artemis, sounding put out.

"I don't know," I say.

"Is he seeing anyone else?"

"I don't know!" I say distractedly.

To stop her from asking any more questions, I start typing drivel into my computer, my mind whirring around and around.

I can't lose this job. I can't ruin yet another career.

I mean, obviously, if he'd *told* me he was my employer, I would never have mentioned my CV. Or . . . any of it.

And anyway, it's not like I faked my *degree,* is it? It's not like I've got a criminal record or something. I'm a good employee. I try really hard and I don't skive off that often, *and* I put in all that overtime with the sportswear promotion, *and* I organized the Christmas raffle. . . .

I'm typing harder and harder, and my face is growing red with agitation.

"Emma." Paul is looking meaningfully at his watch.

"Right." I take a deep breath and stand up.

I'm not going to let him fire me. I'm just not going to let it happen.

I stride across the office and down the corridor to the meeting room, knock on the door, and push it open.

Jack Harper is sitting on a chair at the conference table, scribbling something in a notebook. As I come in, he looks up, and there's a grave expression on his face that makes my stomach turn over.

But I have to defend myself. I *have* to keep this job.

"Hi," he says. "Can you close the door?" He waits until I've done so, then looks up. "Emma, we need to talk about something."

"I'm aware that we do," I say, trying to keep my voice steady. "But I'd like to say my part first, if I may."

For a moment Jack Harper looks taken aback—then he raises his eyebrows. "Sure. Go ahead."

I walk into the room and look him straight in the eye.

"Mr. Harper, I know what you want to see me about. I know it was wrong. It was an error of judgment that I deeply regret. I'm extremely sorry, and it will never happen again.

But in my defense . . ." I can hear my voice rising in emotion. "In my defense, I had no idea who you were on that plane ride. And I don't believe I should be penalized for what was an honest, genuine mistake!"

There's a pause.

"You think I'm penalizing you?" says Jack Harper at last, with a frown.

"Yes! You must realize I would never have mentioned my CV if I'd known who you were! It was like a . . . honey trap! You know, if this were a court, the judge would throw it out! They wouldn't even let you—"

"Your CV?" Jack Harper's brow suddenly clears. "Ah! The A grade on your résumé." He gives me a penetrating look. "The falsified A grade, I should say."

Hearing it out loud like that silences me. I can feel my face growing hotter and hotter.

"You know, a lot of people would call that fraud," says Jack Harper, leaning back in his chair.

"I know they would. I know it was wrong. I shouldn't have . . . But it doesn't affect the way I do my job! It doesn't *mean* anything—"

"You think?" He shakes his head thoughtfully. "I don't know. Going from a C grade to an A grade . . . that's quite a jump. What if we need you to do some math?"

"I can do math," I say desperately. "Ask me a math question. Go on—ask me anything."

"OK." His mouth is twitching. "Eight nines."

I stare at him, my heart racing, my mind blank. Eight nines. I've got no idea. Fuck. OK, once nine is nine. Two nines are—

No. I've got it. Eight tens are 80. So eight *nines* must be—

"Seventy-two!" I cry, and flinch as he gives a tiny half smile. "It's seventy-two," I add more calmly.

"Very good." He gestures politely to a chair. "Now. Have you finished what you wanted to say, or is there more?"

"I . . ." I rub my face confusedly. "You're . . . not going to fire me?"

"No," says Jack Harper patiently. "I'm not going to fire you. Now can we talk?"

As I sit down, a horrible suspicion starts growing in my mind. "Was . . ." I clear my throat. "Was my CV what you wanted to see me about?"

"No," he says mildly. "That wasn't what I wanted to see you about."

I want to die.

"Right." I smooth back my hair, trying to compose myself, trying to look businesslike. "Right. Well. So, er, what did you . . . what . . ."

"I have a small favor to ask you."

"Right!" I feel a tweak of anticipation. "Anything! I mean . . . what is it?"

"For various reasons," says Jack Harper, "I would prefer it that nobody knows I was in Scotland last week." He meets my eyes. "So I would like it very much if we could keep the fact that we met that day between ourselves."

"Right!" I say after a pause. "Of course! Absolutely. I can do that."

"You haven't told anyone?"

"No. No one! Not even my . . . I mean, no one. I haven't told anyone."

"Good. Thank you very much. I appreciate it." He smiles and gets up from his chair. "Nice to meet you again, Emma. I'm sure I'll see you again."

"That's it?"

"That's it. Unless you had anything else you wanted to discuss—"

"No!" I get to my feet hurriedly, banging my ankle on the table leg.

I mean, what did I think? That he was going to ask me to head up his exciting new international project?

Jack Harper opens the door and holds it politely for me. And I'm halfway out when I stop. "Wait."

"What is it?"

"What shall I say you wanted to talk to me about?" I say awkwardly. "Everyone's going to ask me."

"Why not say we were discussing logistics?" He raises his eyebrows and closes the door.

Six

HE WAS A STRANGER. He was supposed to be a *stranger*. As I travel home that evening, I'm still reeling with the injustice of it all. The whole point about strangers is, they disappear into the ether and you never see them again. They don't turn up at the office. They don't ask you what eight nines are. They don't turn out to be your mega-boss employer.

Well, all I can say is, that's taught me. My parents always said never talk to strangers, and they were right. I'm never telling a stranger anything again. *Ever.*

I've arranged to go to Connor's flat this evening, and as I arrive, I feel my body expand in relief. Away from the office. Away from all the endless Jack Harper talk. And Connor's already cooking. I mean, how perfect is that? The kitchen is full of a wonderful garlicky-herby smell, and there's a glass of wine already waiting for me on the table.

"Hi!" I say, and give him a kiss.

"Hi, darling!" he says, looking up from the stove.

Shit. I totally forgot to say "darling." OK, how am I going to remember this?

I know. I'll write it on my hand.

"Have a look at those! I downloaded them from the Internet." Connor gestures to a folder on the table. I open it and find myself looking at a grainy black and white picture of a room with a sofa and a potted plant.

"Flat details!" I say, taken aback. I check the postcode. It's in Maida Vale. In fact, just around the corner from here. I don't remember agreeing on Maida Vale. But then, it doesn't really matter.

"Wow!" I say. "That's quick! I haven't even given notice yet."

"Well, we need to start looking," says Connor. "Look—that one's got a balcony. And there's one with a working fireplace!"

"Gosh!"

I sit down on a nearby chair and peer at the blurry photograph, trying to imagine me and Connor living in it together. Sitting on that sofa. Just the two of us, every single evening.

I wonder what we'll talk about.

Well! We'll talk about . . . whatever we always talk about.

Maybe we'll play Monopoly. Just if we get bored or anything.

I turn to another sheet and feel a sudden pang of excitement.

This flat has wooden floors and shutters! I've *always* wanted wooden floors and shutters. And look at that cool kitchen, with all-granite work tops. . . .

Oh, this is going to be so great.

I take a happy slug of wine and am just sinking comfortably back as Connor says, "So! Isn't it exciting about Jack Harper coming over!"

Oh, God. Please. Not *more* talk about bloody Jack Harper.

"Did you get to meet him?" he adds, coming over with a bowl of peanuts. "I heard he went into Marketing. . . ."

"Um . . . yes, I met him."

"He came into Research this afternoon, but I was at a meeting." Connor looks at me, agog. "So, what's he like?"

"He's . . . I don't know. Dark hair . . . American. . . . So, how did the meeting go?"

Connor totally ignores my attempt to change the subject. "Isn't it exciting, though?" His face is glowing. "Jack Harper!"

"I suppose so." I shrug. "Anyway—"

"Emma! Aren't you excited?" says Connor in astonishment. "We're talking about the founder of the company! We're talking about the man who came up with the concept of Panther Cola! Who took an unknown brand, repackaged it, and sold it to the world! He turned a failing company into a huge, successful corporation. And now we're all getting to meet him! Don't you find that thrilling?"

"Yes," I say at last. "It's . . . thrilling!"

"This could be the opportunity of a lifetime for all of us! To learn from the genius himself! You know, he's never written a book. He's never shared his thoughts with anyone except Pete Laidler. . . ." He reaches into the fridge for a can of Panther Cola and cracks it open. Connor has to be the most loyal employee in the world. I once bought a Pepsi when we were out on a picnic, and he nearly had a heart attack.

"You know what I would love above anything?" he says, taking a gulp. "A one-to-one with him." His eyes shine. "A one-to-one with Jack Harper! Wouldn't that be the most fantastic career boost?"

A one-to-one with Jack Harper.

Yup, that really boosted my career.

"I suppose," I say reluctantly.

"Of course it would be! Just having the chance to listen to him! To hear what he has to say! I mean, the guy's been shut away for a year. What ideas must he have been generating all this time? He must have so many insights and theories, not just about marketing but about business . . . about the way people work . . . about life itself—"

Connor's enthusiastic voice is like salt on sore skin. So, let's just see quite how spectacularly I have played this wrong, shall we? I'm sitting on a plane next to the great Jack Harper, creative genius and source of all wisdom on business and marketing, not to mention the deepest mysteries of life itself.

And what do I do? Do I ask him insightful questions? Do I engage him in intelligent conversation? Do I learn anything from him at all?

No. I blabber on about fascinating subjects such as what kind of underwear I prefer.

Great career move, Emma. One of the best.

The next day, Connor is off to a meeting first thing, but before he goes, he digs out an old magazine article about Jack Harper.

"Read this," he says through a mouthful of toast. "It's good background information."

I don't *want* any background information! I feel like saying, but Connor's already out the door.

I'm tempted to leave it behind and not even bother looking at it, but it's quite a long journey from Maida Vale to work, and I haven't got any magazines with me. So I take the article and grudgingly start reading it on the tube. I suppose it is quite an interesting story. How Jack Harper and Pete Laidler were friends ever since they met at some small marketing agency, and they decided to go into business, and Jack was the creative one and Pete was the extroverted playboy one, and they became multimillionaires together, and they were so close they were practically like brothers. There's some quote from a business mogul saying how annoying it was having meetings with them because they were so in tune with each other and expected everyone else to follow their thoughts.

And then Pete crashed his Mercedes and died the next day. And Jack was so devastated he shut himself away from the world and said he was giving it all up.

And of course now that I read all this, I'm starting to feel a bit stupid. I should have recognized Jack Harper. I mean, I certainly recognize Pete Laidler. For one thing, he looks—looked—just like Robert Redford. And for another, he was all over the papers when he died. I can remember it vividly now, even though I had nothing to do with the Panther Corporation then.

I emerge from the underground into a bright morning, and head toward the juice bar where I usually pop in before work. I've got into the habit of picking up a mango smoothie every morning, because it's healthy.

And also because there is a very cute New Zealand guy who works behind the counter, called Aidan. He has cropped brown hair, the whitest of white teeth, and the most amazing body. (In fact, I actually had a miniature crush on him before I started going out with Connor.) When he isn't working in the smoothie bar, he's doing a course on sports science, and he's always telling me stuff about essential minerals and what your carb ratio should be.

"Hiya," he says as I come in. "How's the kickboxing going?"

"Oh!" I say, coloring slightly. "It's great, thanks!"

"Did you try that new maneuver I told you about?"

"Erm, yes! It really helped!"

"I thought it would," he says, looking pleased, and goes off to make my mango smoothie.

The truth is, I don't really do kickboxing. I did try it once, at our local leisure center, and to be honest, I was shocked! I had no idea it would be so *violent*. But Aidan was so enthused about it and kept saying how it would transform my life, I couldn't bring myself to admit I'd given up after only one session. So I kind of . . . fibbed. I mean, he'll never know. It's not like I ever see him outside the smoothie bar.

"That's one mango smoothie," says Aidan.

"And . . . a chocolate brownie," I say. "For . . . my colleague." Aidan picks up the brownie and pops it in a bag.

"You know, that colleague of yours needs to think about her refined sugar levels," he says with a concerned frown. "She's averaging three brownies a week."

"I know," I say earnestly. "I'll . . . tell her. Thanks, Aidan."

"No problem!" says Aidan. "And remember: one-two-swivel!"

"One-two-swivel," I repeat. "I'll . . . remember!"

As I arrive at the office, everything's quiet apart from a couple of people murmuring on the phone. It's as though, after the hubbub of yesterday, everyone's a bit exhausted. In fact, as I hang my jacket up, Nick gives an enormous yawn—then sees me watching him and scowls.

"Emma." Paul appears out of his office and snaps his fingers at me. "Appraisal."

My stomach gives an almighty lurch, and I nearly choke on my last bite of chocolate brownie. Oh, God. This is it. I'm not ready.

Yes, I am. Come on. Exude confidence. I am a woman on her way somewhere.

Suddenly I remember Kerry and her I-am-a-successful-woman walk. I know Kerry's an obnoxious cow, but she does have her own company and make zillions of pounds a year. She must be doing something right. Maybe I should give it a go. Cautiously I stick out my bust, lift my head, and start striding across the office with a fixed, alert expression on my face.

"Is something wrong, Emma?" says Paul as I reach his door.

"Er, no."

"Well, you look very odd. Now. Sit down." He shuts the door, sits down at his desk, and opens a form marked "Staff Appraisal Review." "I'm sorry I couldn't see you yesterday. But what with Jack Harper's arrival, everything got buggered up."

"That's OK."

I try to smile, but my mouth is suddenly dry. I can't believe how nervous I feel. This is worse than a school report. I watch Paul as he leafs through his notes. It occurs to me that objectively he's quite good-looking, despite his receding hairline. He's tall and slim and has an infectious laugh. If you met him at a party, you'd probably enjoy chatting with him.

But I've never met him at a party. I've only ever seen him here. My scary boss.

"OK. So . . . Emma Corrigan." He looks at the form and starts ticking boxes. "Generally, you're doing fine. You're not generally late. . . . You understand the tasks given to you. . . . You're fairly efficient. . . . You work OK with your colleagues . . . blah, blah . . . blah . . . Any problems?" he says, looking up.

"Er, no."

"Do you feel racially harassed?"

"Er, no."

"Good." He ticks another box and starts writing in a panel at the bottom of the sheet. "Well, I think that's it. Well done. Can you send Nick in to see me?"

What? Has he forgotten? "Um, what about my promotion?" I say, trying not to sound too anxious.

"Promotion?" He pauses in his writing. "What promotion?"

"To marketing executive."

"What the fuck are you talking about?"

"It said in the ad for my job. . . ." I pull the crumpled ad out of my jeans pocket, where it's been since yesterday.

" 'Possible promotion after a year.' It says it right there." I push it across the desk, and he looks at it with a frown.

"Emma, that was only for exceptional candidates. You're not ready for a promotion. You'll have to prove yourself first." He hands the ad back.

"But . . . I'm doing everything as well as I can! If you just give me a chance—"

"You had the chance at Glen Oil." Paul raises his eyebrows at me, and I feel a twinge of humiliation. "Emma, bottom line is, I don't think you're ready for a higher position. In a year we'll see."

A *year*?

"OK? Now, hop to it."

My mind is whirling. I have to accept this in a calm, dignified way. I have to say something like "I respect your decision, Paul," shake his hand, and leave the room. This is what I have to do.

The only trouble is, I can't seem to get up out of my chair.

After a few moments Paul looks at me, puzzled. "That's it, Emma."

I can't move. Once I leave this room, it's over.

"Emma?"

"I've done everything I can!" The words spill out before I can stop them. "I've been writing copy for leaflets, I've been making contacts, I sorted out that whole mess with the ice-skating promotion. . . . Plus, I've been doing all the typing and stuff. . . . I mean, it's more like two jobs I've been doing!"

"I see." Paul looks grave. "Well, if you're finding it too much—"

"No! It's not that. . . ." I crumple the ad in frustration. "I just want to be doing more interesting things! I've had loads of ideas. . . . Like, it was me who came up with the idea of giving away Panther Gum with health club towels. Remember?"

Paul puts down his pen and sighs. "Emma, I'm not saying you haven't done well—"

"Please promote me! It's the only thing I want in the whole world, and I'll work so hard—I promise. I'll come in at weekends, and I'll . . . I'll wear smart suits. . . ."

"What?" Paul is staring at me as though I've turned into a goldfish.

OK, I have to calm down here. Take a deep breath. Nice and steady. "I feel I deserve a promotion."

There are my cards. Right on the table.

"And I feel you're not yet up to it," replies Paul without hesitation.

The trouble is, I've never been any good at cards. "Right." I bite my lip. "So, when—"

"Emma, moving up to marketing executive is a big step. If you want to get ahead, you have to create your own chances. You have to carve out your own opportunities. Now, seriously. Could you please fuck off out of my office and get Nick for me?"

As I leave, I can see him raising his eyes to heaven and scribbling something else on my form.

I walk, dejected, back to my desk, and Artemis looks up with a beady expression.

"Oh, Emma," she says, "your cousin Kerry just called for you."

"Really?" I say in surprise. Kerry never phones me at work. In fact she never phones me at all. "Did she leave a message?"

"Yes, she did. She wanted to know, have you heard about your promotion yet?"

This is now official. I hate Kerry. "Right," I say, trying to sound as though this is some boring, everyday inquiry. "Thanks."

"Are you being promoted, Emma? I didn't know that!" Her voice is high and piercing, and I see several people raise their heads in interest. "So, are you going to become a marketing executive?"

"No," I mutter, my face hot with humiliation. "I'm not."

"Oh!" Artemis pulls a puzzled face. "So, why did she—"

"Shut up, Artemis," says Caroline. I give her a grateful look and slump into my chair.

Another whole year. Another whole year of being the crappy marketing assistant, and everyone thinking I'm useless. Another year of being in debt to Dad, and Kerry and Nev laughing at me, and feeling like a complete failure. I switch on my computer and summon up the copy for a new Panther Lite brochure. But suddenly all my energy's gone.

"I think I'll get a coffee," I say. "Does anyone want one?"

"You can't get a coffee," says Artemis, giving me an odd look. "Haven't you seen?"

"What?"

"They've taken the coffee machine away," says Nick. "While you were in with Paul."

"Taken it away? But . . . why?"

"Dunno," he says, walking off toward Paul's office. "They just came and carted it away."

"We're getting a new machine!" says Caroline, walking past with a bundle of proofs. "That's what they were saying downstairs. A really nice one, with proper coffee. Ordered by Jack Harper, apparently."

Jack Harper ordered a new coffee machine?

"Emma!" Artemis is snapping. "Did you hear that? I want you to find the leaflet we did for the Tesco promotion two years ago. Sorry, Mummy?" she says into the phone. "Just telling my assistant something."

Her assistant. God, it pisses me off when she says that.

But to be honest, I'm feeling a bit too dazed to get annoyed.

It's nothing to do with me, I tell myself firmly as I root around at the bottom of the filing cabinet. He was probably planning to order new coffee anyway. He was probably—

I stand up with a pile of files in my arms and nearly drop them all on the floor.

There he is.

Standing right in front of me, wearing jeans and a slate-gray jumper.

"Hello again." His dark eyes crinkle in a smile. "How are you doing?"

"Er . . . good, thanks." I swallow hard. "I just heard about the coffee machine. Um, thanks."

"No problem."

"Now, everyone!" Paul comes striding up behind him. "Mr. Harper is going to be sitting in on the department this morning."

"Please." Jack Harper smiles. "Call me Jack."

"Right you are. *Jack* is going to be sitting in this morning. He's going to observe what you do, find out how we operate as a team. Just behave normally; don't do anything special. . . ." Paul's eyes alight on me and he gives me an ingratiating smile. "Hi there, Emma! How are you doing? Everything OK?"

"Er, yes, thanks, Paul," I mutter. "Everything's great."

"Good! A happy staff, that's what we like. And while I've got your attention"—he coughs, a little self-conscious—"let me just remind you that our corporate family day is coming up, a week on Saturday. A chance for us all to let our hair down, enjoy meeting each other's families, and have some fun!"

A couple of people exchange looks. Until this moment, Paul has always referred to this as the corporate fuckwit day and said he'd rather have his balls torn off than bring any member of his family to it.

"Anyway, back to work, everyone! Jack, let me get you a chair."

"Just ignore me," says Jack Harper as he sits down. "Behave normally."

Behave normally. Right. Of course.

So that would be sit down, take my shoes off, check my e-mails, put some hand cream on, eat a few Smarties, read my horoscope on iVillage, read Connor's horoscope, send an e-mail to Connor, wait a few minutes to see if he replies, take a swig of mineral water, and then finally get around to finding the Tesco leaflet for Artemis.

I don't think so.

As I sit back down at my desk, my mind is working quickly. Create your own chances. Carve out your own opportunities. That's what Paul said.

And what is this if not an opportunity?

Jack Harper himself is sitting here, watching me work. The great Jack Harper. Boss of the entire corporation. Surely I can impress him *somehow*?

OK, perhaps I haven't gotten off to the most brilliant start with him.

But maybe this is my chance to redeem myself! If I can just somehow show that I'm really bright and motivated . . .

As I sit, leafing through the file of promotional literature, I'm aware that I'm holding my head slightly higher than usual, as though I'm in a posture class. And as I glance around the office, everyone else seems to be in a posture class, too. Before Jack Harper arrived, Artemis was on the phone to her mum, but now she's put on her horn-rimmed glasses and is typing briskly, occasionally pausing to smile at what she's written in a what-an-intelligent-person-I-am way. Nick was reading the sports section of the *Telegraph,* but now he stands up and comes over to Fergus's desk.

"Did you have any more thoughts on the artwork for the

Panther Gum promotion?" he says, in a loud, too casual voice. "Because I really think it needs to rock. We need to get to these kids, yeah?"

"Er, yeah," says Fergus, looking bewildered.

"So this is the giveaway." Nick picks up a small, multi-colored plastic toy. "Yeah. Well, you know, maybe we can *use* this in some way. Take the concept . . . turn it inside out, and play with it. Have some fun."

Oh, God. He's totally showing off. This is so embarrassing.

"You've got it upside down," comes Jack Harper's dry voice. Everyone stiffens, and Nick turns around, clearly joyful at having attracted Jack Harper's attention.

"Absolutely! I see what you mean." He nods a few times. "So, what, like, the concept needs to be turned upside down? *Reversed,* if you like—"

"Not the concept," says Jack. "The toy."

Nick looks blankly at the toy in his fingers.

"It sits the other way up. You pull the rip cord and it spins." Jack gives Nick an appraising look. "You knew that, right?"

A faint color creeps up Nick's face, clashing with his pale red hair. "Er, sure," he says. "Of course I did! So, anyway. We'll . . . we'll brainstorm, OK?"

There's an excruciating silence as he puts the toy back on Fergus's desk and stiffly walks back to his own.

I want to laugh. But I'm too petrified. What if Jack Harper picks on me next?

"Emma?" says Artemis in a falsely sweet voice. "Have you found that leaflet I was asking you for? Not that there's *any* hurry—"

"Er, yes, I have!" I say. I push back my chair, stand up, and walk over to her desk.

I'm trying to look as natural as possible. But God, this is

like being on telly or something. My legs aren't working properly and my smile is pasted onto my face and I have a horrible conviction I might suddenly shout "Pants!" or something.

"Here you are, Artemis!" I say, and carefully lay the leaflet on her desk.

"Bless you!" says Artemis. Her eyes meet mine, and I realize she's completely acting, too. She puts her hand on mine and gives me a twinkly smile. "I don't know what we'd do without you, Emma!"

"That's quite all right!" I say, matching her tone. "Anytime!"

Shit, I think as I walk back to my desk. I should have said something cleverer. I should have said something like "Teamwork is what keeps this operation together."

OK, never mind. I can still be impressive.

Trying to act as normal as possible, I open a document and start to type as quickly and efficiently as I can, my back ramrod straight. I've never known the office this quiet. Everyone's tapping away; no one's chatting. It's like being in an exam. My foot's itching, but I don't dare scratch it.

How on earth do people do those fly-on-the-wall documentaries? I feel completely exhausted, and it's only been about five minutes.

"It's very quiet in here," says Jack Harper after a while. "Is it normally this quiet?"

"Er . . ." We all look around uncertainly at one another.

"Please, don't mind me. Talk away like you normally would. You must have office discussions." He gets up from his seat, spreads his arms, and begins to walk around. "When I worked in an office, we talked about everything under the sun. Politics, books . . . For instance, what have you all been reading recently?"

"Actually, I've been reading the new biography of Mao Tse-tung," says Artemis at once. "Fascinating stuff."

"I'm in the middle of a history of fourteenth-century Europe," says Nick.

"I'm just rereading Proust," says Caroline with a modest shrug. "In the original French."

"Ah." Jack Harper nods, his face unreadable. "And . . . Emma, is it? What are you reading?"

"Um, actually . . ." I swallow, playing for time.

I cannot say *Horoscopes for Lovers*. Even though it is actually very good. Quick. What's a serious book?

"You were reading *Great Expectations,* weren't you, Emma?" says Artemis. "For your book club."

"Yes!" I say in relief. "Yes, that's right—"

And then I stop abruptly as I meet Jack Harper's gaze.

Fuck.

Inside my head, my own voice from the plane is babbling away innocently.

. . . just skimmed the back and pretended I'd read it. . . .

"*Great Expectations,*" says Jack Harper thoughtfully. "What did you think of it, Emma?"

I don't *believe* he asked me that.

For a few moments I can't speak.

"Well!" I clear my throat at last. "I thought it . . . it was really . . . extremely . . ."

"It's a wonderful book," says Artemis earnestly. "Once you fully understand the symbolism . . ."

Shut *up*, you stupid show-off. Oh, God. What am I going to say?

"I thought it really . . . resonated," I say at last.

"What resonated?" says Nick puzzledly.

"The, um . . ." I clear my throat. "The resonances."

"The resonances . . . resonated?" says Artemis.

"Yes," I say defiantly. "They did. Anyway, I've got to get on with my work." I turn away with a roll of my eyes and start typing feverishly.

OK. So the book discussion didn't go that well. But that

was just sheer bad luck. Think positive. I can still do this. I can still impress him—

"I just don't know what's wrong with it!" Artemis is saying in a girly voice. "I water it every day. . . ."

She pokes her spider plant. "Do you know anything about plants, Jack?"

"I don't, I'm afraid," says Jack, and looks over at me, his face deadpan. "What do you think could be wrong with it, Emma?"

. . . sometimes, when I'm pissed off with Artemis . . .

"I . . . I have no idea," I say at last, and carry on typing, my face flaming.

Never mind. It doesn't matter. So I watered one little plant with orange juice. It's still alive, isn't it?

"Has anyone seen my World Cup mug?" says Paul, walking into the office with a frown. "I can't seem to find it anywhere."

. . . I broke my boss's mug last week and hid the pieces in my handbag . . .

Shit.

Never mind. So I broke one tiny mug, too. Just keep typing—

"Hey, Jack," says Nick in a matey, lads-together voice, "just in case you don't think we have any fun, look up there!" He nods toward the picture of a photocopied, G-stringed bottom that has been up on the notice board since Christmas. "We still don't know who it is . . ."

. . . I had a few too many drinks at the last Christmas party . . .

Now I want to die. Someone, please kill me—

"Hi, Emma!" comes Katie's voice, and I look up to see her hurrying into the office, her face pink with excitement. When she sees Jack Harper, she stops dead. "Oh!"

"It's all right. I'm simply a fly on the wall." He waves an easy hand at her. "Go ahead. Say whatever you were going to say."

"Hi, Katie!" I manage. "What is it?"

As soon as I say her name, Jack Harper raises his head, looking animated.

What did I tell him about Katie? What? My mind spools furiously back. What did I say? What did I—

Suddenly I remember.

. . . we have this secret code where she comes in and says, "Can I go through some numbers with you, Emma?" and it really means "Shall we nip out to Starbucks . . ."

I told him our skiving code.

I focus desperately on Katie's eager face, trying somehow to convey the message to her.

Do not say it. Do *not* say you want to go over some numbers with me.

But she's completely oblivious.

"I just, erm . . ." She clears her throat in a businesslike way and glances self-consciously at Jack Harper, who has strolled over toward my desk. "Could I possibly go over some numbers with you, Emma?"

Fuck.

I can feel my face flooding with color. My whole body is prickling.

"You know," I say in a bright, artificial voice, "I'm not sure that'll be possible today."

Katie looks instantly crestfallen. "But I have to . . . I really *need* you to go over some numbers with me." She nods in consternation.

There's obviously something on her mind. But what am I supposed to do?

"I'm quite tied up here with my work, Katie!" I force a smile, simultaneously trying to telegraph "Shut *up*!"

"It won't take long! Just quickly."

"I really don't think so."

Katie is practically hopping from foot to foot. "But, Emma, they're very . . . *important* numbers. I really need to . . . to tell you about them . . ."

"Emma." At Jack Harper's voice I jump as though I've been stung. He leans toward me confidentially. "Maybe you should go over the numbers."

For a few moments I can't quite speak.

"Right," I manage after a long pause. "OK. I'll do that."

Seven

I WALK ALONG the street with Katie, half numb with fear and half wanting to burst into hysterical laughter. Everyone else is in the office, trying as hard as they can to impress Jack Harper. And here I am, strolling off nonchalantly under his nose for a cappuccino.

"I'm sorry I interrupted you!" says Katie as we push our way through the doors of Starbucks. "With Jack Harper there and everything! I had no idea he'd be just *sitting* there! But you know, I was really subtle." She adds reassuringly, "He'll never know what we're up to."

"I'm sure you're right!" I manage. "He'll never guess in a million years!"

"Are you OK, Emma?" Katie looks at me curiously.

"I'm fine!" I say with a kind of shrill hilarity. "I'm absolutely fine! So . . . why the emergency summit?"

We edge our way past two mothers with pushchairs and reach the counter.

"I *had* to tell you. Two cappuccinos, please." Katie beams at me excitedly. "You won't believe it!"

"What is it?"

"I've got a date! I met a new guy!"

"No!" I say, staring at her. "Really? That was quick!"

"Yes! It happened yesterday, just like you said! I deliberately walked farther than usual in my lunch hour, and I found this really nice place where they were serving lunch. And there was this nice man in the line next to me—and he struck up conversation with me. Then we shared a table and chatted some more . . . and I was just leaving, when he said did I fancy having a drink sometime?" She takes the cappuccinos from the counter. "So we're going out this evening!"

"That's fantastic!" I say in delight. "So, come on, what's he like?"

"He's lovely! He's got these lovely sparkly eyes, and he's really charming and polite, and he's got a great sense of humor. . . ."

"He sounds great!"

"I know! I have a really good feeling about him! He just seems different. And I know this sounds really stupid, Emma. . . ." She hesitates. "But I feel like you somehow *brought* him to me."

"Me?"

"You gave me the confidence to speak to him."

"But all I said was—"

"You said you knew I'd meet someone. You had faith in me. And I did!" Suddenly her eyes begin to shine. "I'm sorry," she whispers, and dabs her eyes with a napkin. "I'm just a bit overcome."

"Oh, Katie."

"I just really think my life is going to turn around! I think everything's going to get better. And it's all down to you, Emma!"

"Really, Katie," I say awkwardly. "It was nothing—"

"It wasn't nothing!" She gulps. "And I wanted to do something for you in return." She rummages in her bag and pulls out a large piece of orange crochet. "So I made you this last night." She looks at me expectantly. "It's a head scarf!"

For a few moments, I can't move. A crochet head scarf.

"Katie!" I manage at last, turning it over in my fingers. "Really, you . . . you shouldn't have!"

"I wanted to! To say thank you." She looks at me earnestly. "Especially after you lost that crochet belt I made for you for Christmas—"

"Oh!" I say, feeling a pang of guilt. "Er, yes. That was . . . such a shame." I swallow. "It was a lovely belt. I was really upset to lose it . . ."

"Oh, what the hell!" Her eyes well up again. "I'll make you a new belt, too!"

"No!" I say in alarm. "No, Katie, don't do that!"

"But I want to!" She leans forward and gives me a hug. "That's what friends are for!"

It's another twenty minutes before we finish our second cappuccinos and head back for the office. As we approach the Panther building, I glance at my watch and see to my dismay that we've been gone thirty-five minutes in all.

"Isn't it amazing we're getting new coffee machines?" says Katie as we hurry up the steps.

"Er, yes. It's great."

My stomach tightens as I think of facing Jack Harper again. I haven't felt so nervous since I took my grade one clarinet exam, and when the examiner asked me what my name was, I burst into tears.

"Well, see you later," says Katie as we reach the first floor. "And thanks, Emma."

"No problem!" I say. "See you later."

As I head along the corridor toward the marketing department, I'm aware that my legs aren't moving quite as quickly as usual. In fact, as the door is nearing, they're getting slower and slower . . . and slower . . .

I can't go in there.

Yes, I can. It'll be fine. I'll just sit down very quietly and get on with my work.

Maybe he won't even notice me.

Come on. The longer I leave it, the worse it'll be. I take a deep breath, close my eyes, walk into the marketing department, and open them.

There's a hubbub around Artemis's desk, and no sign of Jack Harper.

"I mean, maybe he's going to rethink the whole company," someone's saying.

"I've heard this rumor he's got a secret project . . ."

"He can't completely centralize the marketing function," Artemis is saying, trying to raise her voice above everyone else's.

"Where's Jack Harper?" I say, trying to sound casual.

"He's gone," says Nick, and I feel a whoosh of relief. Gone! He's gone!

"Is he coming back?"

"Don't think so," he replies. "Emma, have you done those letters for me yet? Because I gave them to you several days ago—"

"I'll do them now," I say, and beam at Nick. As I sit down at my desk, I feel as light as a helium balloon. I cheerfully kick off my shoes, reach for my Evian bottle—and stop.

There's a folded piece of paper resting on my keyboard, with "Emma" written on it in a handwriting I don't recognize.

Puzzled, I look around the office. No one's looking at me, waiting for me to find it. In fact, no one seems to have noticed. My desk is half hidden behind the photocopier. And besides, they're all too busy talking about Jack Harper.

Slowly I unfold it. There's a message inside.

Hope your meeting was productive. I always find numbers give me a real buzz.

Jack Harper

It could have been worse. It could have read, "Clear your
desk."

But even so, for the rest of the day, I'm completely on
edge. Every time anyone walks into the department, I feel a
little spasm of panic. And when someone starts talking loudly
outside our door about "Jack says he may pop back into
Marketing," I seriously consider hiding out in the loos until
he's gone.

On the dot of five-thirty, I stop typing mid-sentence, close
my computer down, and grab my coat. I'm not waiting around
for him to reappear. I all but run down the stairs, and only begin to relax when I'm safely on the other side of the big glass
doors.

The tubes are miraculously quick for once, and I arrive
home within twenty minutes. As I push open the front door
of our flat, I can hear a strange noise coming from Lissy's
room. A kind of thumping, bumping sound. She's probably
moving her furniture around. Which would make sense.

Lissy had a big victory in court yesterday—and every time
she finishes a case, it's the same thing. She gathers all her bits
of paper together and puts them in a file box. She tidies her
room and puts all her clothes away. And then she invites me
in to admire, and says, "*This* is how I'm going to live from
now on."

Sure.

"Lissy," I call as I go into the kitchen. "You will not believe what happened today." I grab a bottle of Evian from the
fridge and hold it against my hot forehead. Then I wander
out into the hall again, to see Lissy's door opening.

"Lissy!" I begin. "What on earth were you—"

And then out of the door comes not Lissy but a man.

A man! A tall, thin guy in trendy black trousers and steel spectacles. He's got jutting cheekbones and a pretty good physique, I can't help noticing, and as he sees me, he inclines his head politely.

"Oh," I say, taken aback. "Er, hi."

"Emma!" says Lissy, following him out. She's wearing a T-shirt over some gray leggings I've never seen before, is drinking a glass of water, and looks startled to see me. "You're home early."

"I know. I was in a hurry."

"This is Jean-Paul," says Lissy, clearly flustered. "Jean-Paul, my flatmate Emma."

"Hello, Jean-Paul," I say, as though this were all perfectly normal.

"Good to meet you, Emma," says Jean-Paul in a French accent.

God, French accents are sexy.

"Jean-Paul and I were just, um, going over some case notes," says Lissy.

"Oh, right," I say. "Lovely!"

Case notes. That would really make a whole load of thumping noises.

Lissy is such a dark horse!

"I must be going . . ." says Jean-Paul, looking at Lissy.

"I'll just see you out."

She disappears through the front door, and I can hear the two of them murmuring on the landing.

I walk into the sitting room and slump down on the sofa. My whole body aches from tension. This is seriously bad for my health. How am I going to survive a whole week of Jack Harper?

"So!" I demand as Lissy returns. "What's going on?"

"What do you mean?"

"You and Jean-Paul! How long have you two been . . ."

"We're not . . ." starts Lissy, turning red. "It's not . . . We were going over case notes. That's all."

"Sure you were."

"We were! That's all it was!"

"OK." I raise my eyebrows. "If you say so."

Lissy sometimes gets like this, all shy and abashed. I'll just have to get her pissed one night, and she'll admit it.

"So, how was your day?" she asks, sitting down on the floor and reaching for a magazine.

I don't even know where to start.

"My day," I say at last. "My day was a bit of a nightmare."

"Really?" says Lissy, looking up in surprise.

"No, take that back. It was a *complete* nightmare."

"What happened? Tell me!"

"OK." I take a deep breath and smooth my hair back, wondering where on earth to start. "OK, remember I had that awful flight back from Scotland last week?"

"Yes!" Lissy's face lights up. "And Connor came to meet you and it was all really romantic. . . ."

"Yes. Well." I clear my throat. "Before that. On the flight. There was this . . . this man sitting next to me. And the plane got really turbulent." I bite my lip. "And the thing is, I honestly thought we were all going to die and this was the last person I would ever see, and . . . I . . ."

"Oh, my God!" Lissy claps her hand over her mouth. "You didn't have sex with him."

"Worse. I told him all my secrets!"

I'm expecting Lissy to gasp, or say something sympathetic like "Oh, no!" but her face is blank.

"What secrets?"

"My secrets. You know."

Lissy looks as if I've suddenly told her I've got an artificial leg.

"You have *secrets*?"

"Of course I have secrets!" I say. "Everyone has a few secrets."

"I don't!" she says at once, looking offended. "I don't have
any secrets."

"Yes, you do!"

"Like what?"

"Like . . . like . . . OK." I start counting off on my fingers.
"You never told your dad it was you who lost the garage key
that time."

"That was ages ago!"

". . . You never told Simon you were hoping he might
propose to you."

"I wasn't!" says Lissy, coloring. "Well, OK, maybe I was . . ."

". . . You think that sad guy next door fancies you."

"That's not a *secret!*" she says, rolling her eyes.

"Oh, right. Shall I tell him, then?" I lean back toward the
open window. "Hey, Mike," I call. "Guess what? Lissy thinks
you—"

"Stop!" says Lissy frantically.

"You see? You have got secrets. Everyone has secrets. The
Pope probably has a few secrets—"

"OK," says Lissy. "OK. You've made your point. But I
don't understand what the problem is. So you told some guy
on a plane your secrets—"

"And now he's turned up at work."

"What?" Lissy goggles at me. "Are you serious? Who is
he?"

"He's . . ." I'm about to say Jack Harper's name when I remember the promise I made. "He's just this . . . this guy
who's come in to observe."

"Is he senior?"

"He's . . . yes. You could say he's pretty senior."

"Blimey." Lissy frowns, thinking for a few moments.
"Well . . . does it really matter? If he knows a few things
about you . . ."

"Lissy, it wasn't just a *few* things." I feel myself flush. "It was *everything*. I told him I faked a grade on my CV . . ."

"You faked a grade on your *CV*?" echoes Lissy in shock. "Are you serious?"

". . . I told him about feeding Artemis's spider plant orange juice. I told him I find G-strings uncomfortable . . ."

I trail off to see Lissy's aghast expression.

"Emma," she says at last. "Have you ever *heard* the phrase 'too much information'?"

"I didn't *mean* to say any of it!" I know I sound defensive. "It just kind of came out! I'd had three vodkas and champagne, and I thought we were about to die. Honestly, Lissy, you would have been the same. Everyone was screaming, people were praying, the plane was bouncing around . . ."

"So you blab all your secrets to your boss!"

"But he *wasn't* my boss on the plane!" I cry in frustration. "He was just some stranger! I was never supposed to see him again!"

There's silence as Lissy takes this all in.

"You know, this is like what happened to my cousin," she says at last. "She went to a party, and there, right in front of her, was the doctor who'd delivered her baby two months before."

"Ooh." I pull a face.

"Exactly! She said she was so embarrassed, she had to leave. I mean, he'd seen everything! She said somehow it didn't matter when she was in a hospital room, but when she saw him standing there, holding a glass of wine and chatting about house prices, it was a different matter—"

"Well, this is the same! He knows all my most intimate, personal details! But the difference is, I can't just leave! I have to sit there and pretend to be a good employee! And he *knows* I'm not—"

"So, what are you going to do?"

"I don't know! I suppose all I can do is try to avoid him!"

"How long is he over for?"

"The rest of the week," I say in despair. "The whole week."

I pick up the zapper and turn on the television, and for a few moments we both silently watch a load of dancing models in Gap jeans.

The ad finishes, and I raise my head. Lissy has a curious look on her face.

"What?" I say. "What is it?"

"Emma . . ." She clears her throat awkwardly. "You don't have any secrets from *me,* do you?"

"From *you*?" I say, slightly thrown. "Er . . ."

A series of images flashes rapidly through my mind. That weird dream I once had about Lissy and me being lesbians. Those times I've bought supermarket carrots and sworn to her they were organic. The time when we were fifteen and she went to France and I got off with Gary Appleton, whom she had a complete crush on, and never told her.

"Er, no! Of course not!" I say, and quickly take a sip of water. "Why? Have you got any from me?"

Two dots of pink appear on Lissy's cheeks. "No! Of course I haven't!" she says in a stilted voice. "I was just . . . wondering." She reaches for the TV guide and starts to flip through it, avoiding my gaze. "You know. Just out of interest."

"Yes, well." I shrug, trying to look nonchalant. "So was I."

Wow. Lissy's got a secret. I wonder what it—

Of course. Like she was really going over case notes with that guy. Does she think I'm a complete idiot?

Eight

I ARRIVE AT WORK the next morning with exactly one aim: Avoid Jack Harper.

It should be easy enough. The Panther Corporation is a huge company in a huge building. He'll be busy in other departments today. He'll probably be tied up in loads of meetings. He'll probably spend all day on the eleventh floor or something.

Even so, as I approach the big glass doors, my pace slows down, and I find myself peering inside to see if he's about.

"All right, Emma?" says Dave the security guard, coming to open the door for me. "You look lost."

"No! I'm great! Thanks!" I give a relaxed little laugh, my eyes darting about the foyer.

I can't see him anywhere. This is going to be fine. He probably isn't in yet. He probably isn't even coming in today! I throw my hair back, walk briskly across the marble floor, and start to head up the stairs.

"Jack!" I suddenly hear as I'm nearing the first floor. "Have you got a minute?"

"Sure."

It's his voice. Where on earth—

Bewildered, I look around and suddenly spot him on the landing above, talking to Graham Hillingdon.

Shit. If he looked down now, he'd see me.

Why does he have to stand right *there*? Doesn't he have some big, important office he can go to?

Anyway. I'll just . . . take a different route. Very slowly I tiptoe back down the stairs, trying not to click my heels on the marble.

As soon as I'm out of his view, I feel myself relax, and walk more quickly back down to the foyer. I'll go by lift instead. No problem. I step confidently across the floor, and I'm right in the middle of the huge expanse of marble when I freeze.

"That's right." It's his voice again. And it seems to be getting nearer. Or am I just paranoid?

". . . think I'll take a good look at . . ."

My head is swiveling around bewilderedly. Where is he now? Which direction is he going in?

". . . really think that . . ."

Shit. He's coming down the stairs. There's nowhere to hide!

Without thinking twice, I fly to the glass doors, push them open, and hurry out of the building. I scuttle down the steps, run about a hundred yards down the road, and stop, panting.

This is not going well.

OK, I can't stay out here on the street all day. Come on, think. There must be a way around this. There must be—

Yes! I have a totally brilliant idea. This will definitely work.

Three minutes and a trip to the newsstand later, I once

more approach the doors of the Panther building, totally engrossed in an article in *The Times*. I can't see anything around me. And no one can see my face. This is the perfect disguise!

I push the door open with my shoulder and walk across the foyer and up the stairs, all without looking up. As I stride along the corridor toward the marketing department, I feel all cocooned and safe, buried in my *Times*. I should do this more often. No one can get me in here. It's a really reassuring feeling, almost as though I'm invisible, or—

"Ow! Sorry!"

I've crashed into someone. Shit. I lower my paper, to see Paul staring at me, rubbing his head.

"Emma, what the fuck are you doing?"

"I was just . . . reading *The Times*. I'm really sorry. . . ."

"All right. Anyway, where the hell have you been? I want you to do tea and coffee at the departmental meeting. Ten o'clock."

"What tea and coffee?" I say, puzzled. They don't usually have any refreshments at the departmental meeting. In fact, usually about six people turn up, if that.

"We're having tea and coffee today. And biscuits. All right?"

I automatically start to reply, "Yes, of course."

Then I stop. Now that I think about it, this isn't all right.

"Paul, when are you going to replace Gloria? I mean, this is the kind of thing she used to do."

There's silence.

"We're in the process of recruitment," Paul says at last.

He's not quite meeting my eye.

All of a sudden I remember a conversation I overheard in the lifts a few weeks ago. Two women from Personnel were talking about staff budgets and the word "trimming" came up.

Like trimming a tree? Or like trimming split ends?

"You are *going* to get a new departmental secretary, aren't you?" I try to sound lighthearted—but inside I can feel twinges of alarm. If they don't replace Gloria, guess who'll end up as the general dogsbody.

"Of course!" Paul pauses. "Probably."

"Probably?"

"Emma, I really don't have time for this!" says Paul impatiently. "Jack Harper's coming to the meeting. I've got a lot to do—"

"What?" I feel a new consternation, sweeping all thoughts of trimming from my head.

"Jack Harper's coming to the meeting. So hurry up."

"Do I have to go?" I say before I can stop myself.

"What?"

"I was just wondering if I . . . have to go, or whether . . ." I trail off.

"Emma, if you can serve tea and coffee by telepathy," says Paul sarcastically, "then you're more than welcome to stay at your desk. If not, would you most kindly get your arse in gear and up to the conference room. You know, for someone who wants to advance their career . . ." He shakes his head and stalks off.

How can this day have gone so wrong already and I haven't even sat down yet?

I dump my bag and jacket at my desk, hurry back down the corridors to the lifts, and press the Up button. A moment later the doors open.

No. No.

This is a bad dream.

Jack Harper is standing alone in the lift, in old jeans and a brown cashmere sweater, with a mobile phone in his hand.

Before I can stop myself, I take a startled step backward. Jack Harper puts his mobile away, tilts his head to one side, and gives me a quizzical look. He looks disheveled and there are shadows under his eyes.

"Are you getting into the elevator?"

"Um . . ."

I'm stuffed. I can't say, "No, I just pressed the button for fun, ha-ha!"

"Yes," I say at last, and walk into the lift with stiff legs. "Yes, I am."

The doors close, and we begin to travel upward in silence. I've got a knot of tension in my stomach.

"Erm, Mr. Harper," I begin, and he looks up. "I just wanted to apologize for my . . . for the, um, shirking episode the other day. It won't happen again."

"You have drinkable coffee now," says Jack Harper. "So you shouldn't need to go to Starbucks, at any rate . . ."

"I know. I'm really sorry." My face is hot. "And may I assure you, that was the very last time I ever do such a thing." I clear my throat. "I am fully committed to the Panther Corporation, and I look forward to serving this company as best I can, giving one hundred percent, every day, now and in the future."

I almost want to add "Amen."

"Really." Jack nods, looking serious. "That's great." He thinks for a moment. "Emma, can you keep a secret?"

"Er, yes!" I say apprehensively. "What is it?"

Jack leans close and whispers, "I used to play hooky, too."

"What?" I say in astonishment.

"In my first job. I had a friend I used to hang out with. We had a code, too. One of us would ask the other to bring him the Leopold file."

"What was the Leopold file?"

"It didn't exist." He grins. "It was just an excuse to get away from our desks."

"Oh. Oh, right!"

Suddenly I feel a bit better. Jack Harper used to *skive*? I would have thought he was too busy being brilliant.

The lift stops at floor three and the doors open, but no one gets in.

"So, your colleagues seemed a very agreeable lot," says Jack as we start traveling up again. "A very friendly, industrious team. Are they like that all the time?"

"Absolutely!" I say at once. "We enjoy cooperating with one another, in an integrated, team-based, um, operational . . ." I'm trying to think of another long word when I make the mistake of catching his eye.

He *knows* this is bullshit, doesn't he?

Oh, God. What's the point?

"OK." I lean against the lift wall. "In real life, we don't behave anything like that. Paul usually shouts at me six times a day, and Nick and Artemis hate each other, and we don't usually sit around discussing literature. We were all faking it."

"You amaze me." His mouth twitches. "The atmosphere in the admin. department also seemed very false. My suspicions were aroused when two employees spontaneously started singing the Panther Corporation song. I didn't even know there *was* a Panther Corporation song."

"Neither did I," I say in surprise. "Is it any good?"

"What do you think?" He grimaces in mock horror and I give a little giggle.

It's bizarre, but the atmosphere between us isn't remotely awkward anymore. In fact, it almost feels like we're old friends or something.

"How about this corporate family day?" he says. "Looking forward to it?"

"Like having teeth pulled out."

"I got that vibe." He nods, looking amused. "And what . . ." He hesitates. "What do people think about me?" He casually rumples his hair. "You don't have to answer if you don't want to—"

"No, everyone likes you!" I think for a few moments. "Although . . . some people think your friend is creepy."

"Who, Sven?" Jack stares at me for a minute, then throws back his head and laughs. "I can assure you, Sven is one of my oldest, closest friends, and he's not in the least bit creepy. In fact—"

He breaks off as the lift doors ping. We both snap back into impassive expressions and move slightly away from each other. The doors open, and I freeze.

Connor is standing on the other side.

When he sees Jack Harper, his face lights up as though he can't believe his luck.

"Hi there!" I say, trying to sound natural.

"Hi," he says, his eyes shining with excitement.

"Plenty of room," says Jack easily.

There's an infinitesimal pause—then he moves a couple of steps closer to me.

Somewhere in my body a tiny pulse starts beating. Which must be because of the weirdness of the situation.

"Which floor would you like?" says Jack.

"Nine, please."

Jack reaches past to press the button. I catch the faint smell of his musky aftershave, familiar from the plane. I don't move. I don't dare look up.

"Mr. Harper, may I quickly introduce myself?" Connor eagerly holds out his hand. "Connor Martin from Research. You're coming to visit our department later on today."

"It's a pleasure to meet you, Connor," says Jack. "Research is vital for a company like ours."

"You're so right!" says Connor, thrilled. "In fact, I'm looking forward to discussing with you the latest research findings on Panther Sportswear. We've come up with some very fascinating results involving customer preferences on fabric thickness. You'll be amazed!"

"I'm . . . sure I will," says Jack. "I look forward to it."

Connor gives me an excited grin. "You've already met Emma Corrigan from our marketing department?" he says.

"Yes, we've met." Jack's tone gives nothing away.

We travel for a few seconds in an awkward silence.

"How are we doing for time?" says Connor. He glances at his watch, and in horror I see Jack glance at it, too.

Oh, God.

. . . I gave him a really nice watch, but he insists on wearing this orange digital thing . . .

"Wait a minute!" says Jack, dawn breaking over his face. He peers at Connor as though seeing him for the first time. "Wait a minute. You're Ken."

Oh, no.

Oh no, oh no, oh no, oh no, oh no, oh—

"It's Connor." Connor looks puzzled. "Connor Martin—"

"I'm sorry!" Jack hits his head with his fist. "Connor. Of course. And you two"—he gestures to me—"are an item?"

Connor looks uncomfortable. "I can assure you, sir, that at work, our relationship is strictly professional. However. In a private context, Emma and I are . . . yes, having a personal relationship."

"That's wonderful!" says Jack encouragingly.

Connor looks as thrilled as a head prefect receiving a good-conduct badge. "In fact," he adds proudly, "Emma and I have just decided to move in together."

"Is that so?" Jack shoots me a look of genuine surprise. "That's . . . great news. When did you make that decision?"

"Just a couple of days ago," says Connor. "At the airport."

"At the airport," echoes Jack Harper after a short silence. "Very interesting."

I can't look at him. I'm staring desperately at the floor. Why can't this bloody lift go quicker?

"Well . . . I'm sure you'll be very happy together," Jack Harper says to Connor. "You seem very compatible."

"Oh, we are!" says Connor at once. "We both love jazz, for a start."

"Is that so?" says Jack. "You know, I can't think of anything nicer in the world than a shared love of jazz."

He's teasing me. This is unbearable.

"Really?" says Connor eagerly.

"Absolutely." Jack nods. "I'd say jazz, and . . . Woody Allen films."

"We love Woody Allen films!" says Connor in amazed delight. "Don't we, Emma!"

"Yes," I say, my voice hoarse. "Yes, we do."

"Now, Connor, tell me," says Jack in confidential tones. "Did you ever find Emma's . . ."

If he says "G spot," I will die. I will die. I will *die*.

". . . presence here distracting? Because I can imagine I would!" Jack gives Connor a friendly smile, but Connor doesn't smile back.

"As I said, sir," he begins a little stiffly, "Emma and I operate on a strictly professional basis while at work. We would never dream of abusing the company's time for our own . . . ends." He flushes. "I mean . . . by ends, I don't mean . . . I meant . . ."

"I'm glad to hear it," says Jack.

God, why does Connor have to be such a . . . *goody-goody*?

The lift pings, and I feel relief drain over me. Thank God, at last I can escape—

"Looks like we're all going to the same place," says Jack Harper. "Connor, why don't you lead the way?"

I can't cope with this. I just can't cope. As I pour out cups of tea and coffee for members of the marketing department, I'm outwardly calm, smiling at everyone and even chatting. But inside I'm all unsettled and confused. I don't want to admit it to myself, but seeing Connor through Jack Harper's eyes has thrown me.

I love Connor. I didn't mean any of what I said on the plane. I love him. I run my eyes over his face, trying to reassure myself. There's no doubt about it. Connor is good-looking by any standards. He glows with good health. His hair is shiny and his eyes are blue, and he's got a gorgeous dimple when he smiles.

Jack Harper never seems to shave. His hair is all over the place. *And* there's a hole in his jeans. But even so. It's like he's some kind of magnet. I'm sitting here, my attention firmly on the tea trolley—and yet, somehow I can't keep my eyes off him.

It's because of the plane, I keep telling myself. It's just because we were in a traumatic situation together, and . . . and that's why. No other reason.

"We need more lateral thinking, people," Paul is saying. "The Panther Bar is simply not performing as it should. Connor, you have the latest research statistics?"

Connor stands up, and I feel a little flip of apprehension on his behalf. I can tell he's really nervous from the way he keeps fiddling with his cuffs.

"That's right, Paul." He picks up a clipboard and clears his throat. "In our latest survey, one thousand teenagers were questioned on aspects of the Panther Bar. Unfortunately, the results were inconclusive."

He presses his remote control. A graph appears on the screen behind him, and we all regard it obediently.

"Seventy-four percent of ten-to-fourteen-year-olds felt the texture could be more chewy," says Connor earnestly. "However, sixty-seven percent of fifteen-to-eighteen-year-olds felt the texture could be more crunchy, while twenty-two percent felt it could be *less* crunchy."

I glance over Artemis's shoulder and see she's written "Chewy/crunchy??" on her notepad.

Connor presses the remote control again, and another graph appears.

"Forty-six percent of ten-to-fourteen-year-olds felt the flavor was too tangy. However, thirty-three percent of fifteen-to-eighteen-year-olds felt it was not tangy enough, while . . ."

Oh, God. I know it's Connor. And I love him and everything. But can't he make this sound a bit more . . . *interesting*? And anyway, what's the point of all these stupid percentages that don't really mean anything? Those teenagers couldn't give a shit. They probably all lied on their forms.

I glance over to see how Jack Harper is taking it, and he raises his eyebrows at me. Immediately I flush, feeling disloyal.

"Ninety percent of female teenagers would prefer the calorie content to be reduced," Connor concludes. "But the same proportion would also like to see a thicker chocolate coating." He gives a helpless shrug.

"They don't know what the hell they want," says someone.

"We polled a broad cross-section of teenagers," says Connor, "including Caucasians, Afro-Caribbeans, Asians, and, er"—he peers at the paper—"Jedi knights. At least, that's what they put."

"Teenagers!" says Artemis, rolling her eyes.

"Briefly remind us of our target market, Connor," says Paul with a frown.

"Our target market"—Connor consults another clipboard—"is aged ten to eighteen, in full- or part-time education. He/she drinks Panther Cola four times a week, eats burgers three times a week, visits the cinema twice a week, reads magazines and comics but not books, is most likely to agree with the lifestyle statement 'It's more important to be cool than rich.' . . ." He looks up. "Shall I go on?"

"Does he/she eat toast for breakfast?" says somebody thoughtfully. "Or cereal?"

"I . . . I'm not sure," says Connor, riffling through his pages. "We could do some more research . . ."

"I think we get the picture," says Paul. "Does anyone have any thoughts on this?"

All this time, I've been plucking up the courage to speak, and now I take a deep breath. "You know, my grandpa really likes Panther Bars!" I say. Everyone swivels in their chairs to look at me, and I feel my face grow hot.

"What relevance does that have?" says Paul with a frown.

"It's just that . . ." I swallow. "He really doesn't like the new papaya and pineapple flavor . . ."

"With all due respect, Emma," says Connor in an almost patronizing tone, "your grandfather is hardly in our target demographic!"

"Unless he started very young," quips Artemis.

I flush, feeling stupid, and pretend to be reorganizing the tea bags.

To be honest, I feel a bit hurt. Why did Connor have to say that? I know he wants to be all professional and proper when we're at work. But that's not the same as being mean, is it? I'd always stick up for him.

"My own view," Artemis is saying, "is that if the Panther Bar isn't performing, we should axe it. It's quite obviously a problem child—"

I look up in dismay. They can't axe the Panther Bar! What will Grandpa take to his bowling tournaments?

"Surely a fully cost-based, customer-oriented rebranding—" begins somebody.

"I disagree." Artemis leans forward. "If we're going to maximize our concept innovation in a functional and logistical way, then surely we need to focus on our strategic competencies—"

"Excuse me," says Jack Harper, lifting a hand. It's the first time he's spoken, and everyone turns to look. There's a sudden prickle of anticipation in the air, and Artemis glows smugly. "Yes, Mr. Harper?" she says.

"I have no idea what you're talking about," he says.

The whole room reverberates in shock, and I cough with laughter without quite meaning to.

"As you know, I've been out of the business arena for a while," Jack adds. "Could you please translate what you just said into standard English?"

"Oh," says Artemis, looking discomfited. "Well, I was simply saying that from a strategic point of view, notwithstanding our corporate vision . . ." She trails off at his expression.

"Try again. Without using the word 'strategic.' "

"Oh," says Artemis again, and rubs her nose. "Well, I was just saying that . . . we should . . . concentrate on . . . on what we do well."

"Ah! Now I understand. Please, carry on."

As Artemis starts talking again, Jack shoots me the briefest of glances. And I can't help giving a tiny grin back.

After the meeting, people trickle out of the room, still talking, and I go around the table, picking up coffee cups.

"It was very good to meet you, Mr. Harper," I can hear Connor saying eagerly. "If you'd like a transcript of my presentation . . ."

"You know, I don't think that will be necessary," Jack says in that dry voice. "I think I more or less got the gist."

Oh, God. Doesn't Connor *realize* he's trying too hard?

I balance all the cups in precarious piles on the trolley, then start collecting the biscuit wrappers.

"Now, I'm due in the design studio right about now," Jack's saying, "but I don't quite remember where it is . . ."

"Emma!" says Paul sharply. "Can you please show Jack to the design studio? You can clear up the rest of the coffee later."

I freeze, clutching an orange cream wrapper.

Please, no more.

"Of course," I manage at last. "It would be a . . . pleasure. This way."

Awkwardly, I usher Jack Harper out of the meeting room and we begin to walk down the corridor, side by side. My face is tingling slightly as people try not to gawk at us. I'm aware of everyone else turning into self-conscious robots as soon as they see him. People in adjacent offices are nudging one another excitedly, and I hear at least one person hissing, "He's coming!"

Is it like this everywhere he goes?

Mind you, he doesn't even seem to notice.

"So," says Jack Harper. "You're moving in with Ken."

"It's *Connor,*" I say. "And yes. Yes, we are."

"Looking forward to it?"

"Yes. Yes, I am."

We've reached the lifts and I press the button. I can feel his eyes on me. I can *feel* them. "What?" I say defensively, turning to look at him.

"Did I say anything?" As I see the amusement in his eyes, I feel stung. What does he know about it?

"I know what you're thinking," I say, lifting my chin defiantly. "But you're quite wrong."

"I'm wrong?"

"Look. I know I might have made certain . . . comments to you on the plane," I begin, clenching my fists tightly at my sides. "But what you have to know is that that conversation took place under duress, in extreme circumstances . . . and I said a lot of things that I didn't really mean!"

"I see," says Jack thoughtfully. "So . . . you *don't* like double chocolate chip Häagen-Dazs ice cream."

For an instant, I'm thrown.

"Some things, obviously, I *did* mean—"

The lift doors ping, and both our heads jerk up.

"Jack!" says Cyril, standing on the other side of the lift doors. "I wondered where you were!"

"I've been having a nice chat with Emma here," says Jack. "She offered to show me the way."

"Ah." Cyril's dismissive eyes run over me. "Well, they're waiting for you in the studio."

"So, um, I'll just go, then."

"See you later," says Jack. "Good talking to you, Emma."

Nine

As I leave the office in the evening, I feel all agitated, like one of those snow globes you see resting peacefully on shop counters. I was perfectly happy being an ordinary, dull little Swiss village. But now Jack Harper's come and shaken me up, and there are snowflakes all over the place, whirling around until I don't know what I think anymore.

And bits of glitter, too. Tiny bits of shiny, secret excitement.

Every time I catch his eye or hear his voice, it's like a little dart to my chest.

Which is ridiculous. Ridiculous.

Connor is my boyfriend. Connor is my future. He loves me and I love him and I'm moving in with him. And we're going to have all-wooden floors and shutters and granite work tops. So there.

So there.

I arrive home to find Lissy on her knees in the sitting

room. She's still in her smart suit and white shirt from court and is helping Jemima into the tightest black suede dress I've ever seen.

"Wow!" I say as I put down my bag. "That's amazing!"

"There!" pants Lissy, and sits back on her heels. "That's the zip done. Can you breathe?"

Jemima doesn't move a muscle. Lissy and I glance at each other.

"Jemima!" says Lissy in alarm. "Can you breathe?"

"Kind of," says Jemima at last. "I'll be fine." Very slowly, with a totally rigid body, she totters over to where her Louis Vuitton bag is resting on a chair. Her skin is golden brown with Saint-Tropez tan, her hair is smooth blond, and her makeup has the kind of perfection you only get with time and very expensive brushes. All to get a rock on her finger.

"Did you *go* to work today?" inquires Lissy.

"Of course I did." Jemima gives her a scathing look. "Till three."

"How on earth do you get away with it?"

"I sold a seventy-thousand-pound painting yesterday, thank you very much." Jemima speaks in short snatches, gasping for breath in between. "This dress is my commission."

"Jemima, what happens if you need to go to the loo?" I ask.

"Or go back to his place?" says Lissy with a giggle.

"It's only our second date! I'm not going to go back to his place!" Jemima says in horror. "Mummy says that's not the way to . . ." She struggles for breath. ". . . to get a rock on your finger."

Jemima's mother is her total role model. She's taller than Jemima, thinner than Jemima, and has a 10.5-carat rock on her finger, which in Jemima's world makes her God. Living with Jemima, I've gotten to know Mummy's opinions on pretty much all subjects, including tattoos (vulgar), gays ("as long as they *dress* well"), and whether one should wear a backless gown when entertaining minor royalty at a charity ball (no).

"But what if you get carried away with desire for each other?" Lissy is needling Jemima.

"What if he gropes you in the taxi?" I join in.

"He's not *like* that," says Jemima. "He happens to be the First Assistant Under-Secretary to the Secretary of the Treasury, *actually*."

I meet Lissy's eyes and can't help giggling.

"Emma, don't laugh," says Lissy, deadpan. "There's nothing wrong with being a secretary. He can always move up, get himself a few qualifications. . . ."

"Oh ha-ha, very funny," says Jemima crossly. "You know, he'll be knighted one day. I don't think you'll be laughing then."

"Oh, I expect I will," says Lissy. "Even more so." She suddenly focuses on Jemima, who is still standing by the chair, trying to reach her bag. "Oh, my God! You can't even pick up your bag, can you?"

"I can!" says Jemima, making one last, desperate effort to bend her body. "Of course I can! There!" She manages to scoop up the strap on the end of one of her acrylic fingernails and triumphantly swings it onto her shoulder. "You see?"

"What if he suggests dancing?" says Lissy slyly. "What will you do then?"

A look of total panic crosses Jemima's face, then disappears. "He won't," she says scornfully. "Englishmen never suggest dancing."

"Fair point. Have a good time."

As Jemima vanishes out of the door, I sit down and flick on the telly. A Cindy Blaine show is just starting, with the tag line "I'm Going to Propose to the Father of My Twins!" and I settle back comfortably on the sofa.

"Look, Liss," I say. "It's your favorite show."

Lissy always tries to be appalled when I watch Cindy Blaine. She says it's all so demeaning for everyone involved and *she's* going to go and do some work. (She usually reaches the door, and watches the rest from there.)

But Lissy isn't listening. She has a preoccupied look on her face. "Conditional!" she says suddenly. "Of course! How could I have been so *stupid*?"

She scrabbles around under the sofa, pulls out several old newspaper crosswords, and starts searching through them.

Honestly. As if being a top lawyer didn't use up enough brainpower, Lissy spends her whole time doing crosswords and games of chess by correspondence, and special brainy puzzles that she gets from her geeky society of extra-clever people. (It's not *called* that, of course. It's called something like "Mindset—For People Who Like to Think." Then at the bottom it casually mentions that you need an IQ of 600 in order to join.)

And if she can't solve a clue, she doesn't just throw it out, saying "stupid puzzle," like I would. She saves it. Then about three months later, when we're watching *EastEnders* or something, she'll suddenly come up with the answer. And she's ecstatic! Just because she gets the last word in the box, or whatever.

Lissy's my oldest friend, and I really love her. But sometimes I really do *not* understand her.

"What's that?" I say as she writes in the answer. "Some crossword from 1993?"

"Ha-ha," she says absently. "So, what are you doing this evening?"

"Watching Cindy, of course," I say, gesturing to the screen. "There's no finer entertainment."

"Oh, right. So you won't be interested in this . . ." She fishes in her bag and slowly pulls out a large, rusty key ring, to which a brand-new Yale is attached.

"What's that?" Suddenly I realize. "No!"

"Yes! I'm in!"

"Oh, my God! Lissy!"

"I know!" Lissy beams at me. "Isn't it fab?"

The key that Lissy is holding is the coolest key in the world. It opens the door to a private members' club in Clerkenwell, which is completely happening and impossible to get into . . . except someone at Lissy's chambers is on the founding committee.

"Lissy, you're a star!"

I take the key from her and look at it in fascination, but there's nothing on it. No name, no address, no logo, no nothing. It looks a bit like the key to my dad's garden shed, I find myself thinking. But obviously way, way cooler, I add hastily. "Apparently Madonna's a member!" I look up. "And Jude Law! And that gorgeous new actor from *EastEnders*. Except everyone says he's gay, really—"

"Emma," interrupts Lissy. "You do know celebrities aren't guaranteed."

"I know!" I say, a little offended.

Honestly. Who does Lissy think I am? I'm a cool and sophisticated Londoner. "*Actually,* I was just thinking how it probably spoils the atmosphere if the place is stuffed full of celebrities," I say. "I mean, can you think of anything worse than sitting at a table, trying to have a nice, normal conversation, while all around you are movie stars and supermodels and . . . and pop stars . . ."

There's a pause while we both consider this.

"So," says Lissy casually, "we might as well go and get ready."

"Why not," I say with equal nonchalance.

Not that it will take long. I mean, I'm only going to throw on a pair of jeans. And maybe quickly wash my hair, which I was going to do anyway.

And maybe do a quick face mask.

An hour later Lissy appears at the door of my room, dressed in jeans, a tight black corset top, and her Bertie heels, which I happen to know always give her a blister.

"What do you think?" she says in the same casual voice. "I mean, I haven't really made much effort—"

"Neither have I," I say, blowing on my second coat of nail polish. "I mean, it's just a relaxed evening out. I'm hardly even bothering with makeup." I look up and study Lissy's face. "Are those false eyelashes?"

"No! I mean . . . yes. But you weren't supposed to notice. They're called natural look." She goes over to the mirror and bats her eyelids. "Are they really obvious?"

"No!" I say reassuringly, and reach for my blusher brush. When I look up again, Lissy is staring at my shoulder.

"What's that?"

"What?" I say innocently, and touch the little diamanté heart on my shoulder blade. "Oh, *this*. Yes, it just sticks on. I thought I'd wear it for fun." I reach for my halter neck top, tie it on, and slide my feet into my pointy suede boots. I got them in a Sue Ryder shop a year ago, and they're a bit scuffed up, but in the dark you can hardly tell.

"Do you think we look too much?" says Lissy as I go and stand next to her in front of the mirror. "What if they're all in jeans?"

"We're in jeans!"

"But what if they're in big, thick jumpers and we look really stupid?"

Lissy is always completely paranoid about what everyone else will be wearing. When it was her first chambers Christmas party and she didn't know whether "black tie" meant long dresses or just sparkly tops, she made me come and stand outside the door with about six different outfits in carrier bags so she could quickly change. (Of course, the original dress she'd put on was fine. I *told* her it would be.)

"They won't be wearing big, thick jumpers!" I say. "Come on—let's go."

"We can't!" Lissy looks at her watch. "It's too early."

"Yes, we can. We can be just having a quick drink on our way to *another* celebrity party."

"Oh, yes." Lissy brightens. "Cool. Let's go!"

It takes us about fifteen minutes to get from Islington to Clerkenwell. Lissy leads me down an empty road near Smithfield Market, full of warehouses and empty office buildings. Then we turn a corner, and then another corner, until we're standing in a small alley.

"Right," says Lissy, standing under a street lamp and consulting a tiny scrap of paper. "It's all hidden away somewhere."

"Isn't there a sign?"

"No. The whole point is, no one except members knows where it is. You have to knock on the right door and ask for Alexander."

"Who's Alexander?"

"Dunno." Lissy shrugs. "It's their secret code."

Secret code! This gets cooler and cooler. As Lissy squints at an intercom set in the wall, I look idly around. This street is completely nondescript. In fact, it's pretty shabby. Just rows of identical doors and blanked-out windows and barely any sign of life. But just think. Hidden behind this grim facade is the whole of London celebrity society!

"Hi, is Alexander there?" says Lissy nervously. There's a moment's silence, then, as if by magic, the door clicks open.

This is like Aladdin or something. Looking apprehensively at each other, we make our way down a lit corridor pulsing with music. We come to a flat stainless-steel door, and Lissy reaches for her key. As it opens, I quickly tug at my top and casually rearrange my hair.

"OK," Lissy mutters. "Don't look. Don't stare."

"All right," I mutter back, and follow Lissy into the club. As she shows her membership card to a girl at a desk, I stare studiously at her back, and as we walk through into a large, dim room, I keep my eyes fixed on the beige carpet. I'm not going to gawk at the celebrities. I'm not going to stare. I'm not going to—

"Look out!"

Oops. I was so busy gazing at the floor, I blundered right into Lissy.

"Sorry," I whisper. "Where shall we sit down?"

I don't dare look around the room for a free seat, in case I see Madonna and she thinks I'm ogling her. "Here," says Lissy, gesturing to a wooden table with an odd little jerk of her head.

Somehow we manage to sit down, stow our bags, and pick up the lists of cocktails, all the time rigidly staring at each other.

"Have you seen anyone?" I murmur.

"No. Have you?"

"No." I scan the cocktail menu, keeping my eyes down.

God, this is a strain. My eyes are starting to ache. I want to *see* the place. "Lissy," I hiss. "I'm going to have a look around."

"Really?" Lissy peers at me anxiously, as though I'm Steve McQueen announcing he's going over the wire. "Well . . . OK. But be careful. Be *discreet*."

"I will. I'll be fine!"

OK. Here we go. A quick, non-gawking sweep. I lean back in my chair, take a deep breath, then allow my eyes to skim swiftly around the room, taking in as much detail as quickly as I can. Low lighting . . . lots of purple sofas and chairs . . . a pair of guys in T-shirts . . . three girls in jeans and jumpers—God, Lissy's going to freak—a couple whispering to each other and giggling . . . a guy with a beard, reading *Private Eye* . . . and that's it.

That can't be it.

This can't be right. Where's Robbie Williams? Where's Jude Law? Where are all the supermodels?

"Who did you see?" hisses Lissy, still staring at the cocktail menu.

"I'm not sure," I whisper uncertainly. "Maybe that guy with the beard is some famous actor?"

Casually, Lissy turns in her seat and gives him a look. "I don't think so," she says at last, turning back.

"Well, how about the guy in the gray T-shirt?" I say, gesturing hopefully. "Is he in a boy band or something?"

"Mmm . . . no. I don't think so."

There's silence as we look at each other.

"Is *anyone* famous here?" I say at last.

"Celebrities aren't guaranteed!" says Lissy defensively.

"I know! But you'd think—"

"Hi!" A voice interrupts us and we both look around, to see two of the girls in jeans approaching our table. One of them is smiling at me nervously. "I hope you don't mind, but my friends and I were just wondering—aren't you that new one in *Hollyoaks*?"

Oh, for God's sake.

I can't help feeling a bit disappointed. Not to see a *single* famous person.

But never mind. We didn't come here to see tacky celebrities taking coke and showing off, I tell myself. We just came to have a nice, quiet drink together.

We order strawberry daiquiris and some luxury mixed nuts (£4.50 for a small bowl—don't even *ask* how much the drinks cost). And I have to admit, I feel a bit more relaxed, now that I know there's no one famous to impress.

"How's your work going?" I ask as I sip my drink.

"Oh, it's fine," says Lissy with a shrug. "I saw the Jersey Fraudster today."

The Jersey Fraudster is this client of Lissy's who keeps being charged with fraud and appealing and—because Lissy's so brilliant—getting let out. One minute he's wearing handcuffs; the next he's dressed in handmade suits and taking her to lunch at the Ritz.

"He tried to buy me a diamond brooch," says Lissy, rolling her eyes. "He had this Asprey's catalog and he kept saying 'That one's rather jolly.' And I was like, 'Humphrey, you're in prison! Concentrate!' " She shakes her head, takes a sip of her drink, and looks up. "So . . . what about your man?"

I know at once she means Jack, but I don't want to admit that's where my mind has leapt to, so I attempt a blank look and say, "Who, Connor?"

"No, you dope! Your stranger on the plane. The one who knows everything about you."

"Oh, *him.*" I feel a flush coming to my cheeks and look down at my embossed paper coaster.

"Yes, him! Have you managed to avoid him?"

"No," I admit. "He won't bloody leave me alone."

Lissy gives me a close look. "Emma, do you fancy this guy?"

"No, of course I don't *fancy* him," I say hotly. "He just . . . disconcerts me, that's all! It's a completely natural reaction. You'd be the same. Anyway, it's fine. I only have to get through until Friday. Then he'll be gone."

"And then you'll be moving in with Connor. Lucky you!" Lissy takes a sip of her daiquiri and leans forward. "You know, I reckon he's going to ask you to marry him!"

"Really?" I say, feeling as though I've swallowed a chunk of ice. "I mean . . . yes. Connor's just . . . great." I start to shred my paper coaster into little bits.

"Emma?" I lift my head to see Lissy peering at me questioningly. "Is something wrong?"

"I suppose the only *tiny* little thing would be . . . that it's not that romantic anymore."

"You can't expect it to be romantic forever! Things change. It's natural to become a bit more steady."

"Oh, I know that! We're two mature, sensible people in a loving, steady relationship. Which . . . you know, is just what I want. Except . . ." I clear my throat awkwardly. "We don't have sex *that* often anymore."

"That's a common problem in long-term relationships," says Lissy knowledgeably. "You need to spice it up."

"With what?"

"Have you tried handcuffs?"

"No! Have you?" I stare at Lissy, riveted.

"A long time ago," she says with a dismissive shrug. "They weren't all that." She leans forward. "Emma . . ."

"Yes?" I hold my breath. Is she going to give me advice on bondage gear?

"You've got something stuck between your teeth."

"Ooh!" I say in horror, and pull out my compact, but it's too dim in here to see my reflection. "I'll just pop to the loo." I stand up and grab my bag. "Can you order me another drink?"

The ladies' room is all limestone and glass basins and chrome taps, which you operate by waving your arms about. I fix my teeth, then redo my lipstick and get out my hairbrush. And I'm just starting to brush my hair when I hear a moan from a cubicle.

I ignore it and carry on brushing. But then there's another one. Then another, much longer one. I pause and look at the cubicle door, feeling uncertain. Should I do anything? Maybe some girl is ill in there.

Or maybe she's taken a drug overdose, I think in sudden horror. It's a celebrity on heroin. I knew it. There's another moan, and a muffled knocking sound against the door. I feel a faint queasiness. Has she passed out?

"Er, hello?" I say softly.

There's no answer. Now what do I do?

A cry of pain breaks the silence and I clap a hand over my mouth. She must be in agony. She must have cracked her head on the floor.

"It's OK!" I say quickly, getting down onto my knees and craning to see underneath the door. I'll try to make eye contact with her and establish a bond, then I'll go into the next cubicle and somehow climb over the partition—

Hang on.

I'm looking at three feet. Two in pink suede kitten heels . . . and one in a heavy black brogue. As I watch, the other brogue appears on the floor.

And now the knocking sound has started again. Except it's more of a . . . rocking. And the moaning is more like—

I don't believe this.

I scramble to my feet, feeling a wash of embarrassment. What, they're just having blatant sex and not bothering about anyone else? Connor and I would never do that. Not in a million years. I mean, the very *thought* of Connor and me getting it together in some public place, where someone could easily come across us . . .

I catch sight of my own flushed reflection.

Actually . . . that's an idea.

I hurry out of the ladies', down the corridor, and back through the dim bar to our table, where Lissy looks up in excitement.

"Emma! Where *were* you! You'll never—"

"I have it," I interrupt, sliding into my chair. "I have the answer. It came to me in the loo. I'm going to seduce Connor in public. Like, at work or somewhere. That'll put the fizz back in our sex life. What do you think?"

"Emma, you just missed Ewan McGregor! He just came in here! He was in this amazing dark suit and he looked totally gorgeous! And he was *alone*!"

For a full five minutes I cannot speak.

I missed him. I missed a genuine A-list celebrity. By trying to help someone who didn't need help at all! That's it—I'm never helping anyone again.

But at last the feeling returns to my face. At last Lissy persuades me that if Ewan came here once, he will again—and she promises we'll return as many times as it takes to see him.

"And I think your idea is fantastic!" she adds encouragingly. "It'll definitely work!"

This finally cheers me up enough to have another cocktail. In fact, the more I think about my plan, the more pleased I feel with myself. I'll shag Connor at work tomorrow, and it will be the best sex we've ever had . . . and the sparkle will come back . . . and we'll be madly in love again. Easy. And that will show Jack Harper.

No. This is nothing to do with Jack Harper. I don't know why that slipped out.

There's only one tiny hitch to my scheme. Which is that it's not quite as easy to shag your boyfriend at work as you'd think. I hadn't quite appreciated before how . . . *open* everything is in our office. And how many glass partitions there are. And how many people there are, walking around all the time.

By eleven o'clock the next morning, I still haven't managed to put a game plan together. I think I'd kind of pictured doing it behind a potted plant somewhere. But now that I actually look at them, potted plants are tiny. And all frondy. There's no way Connor and I would be able to hide behind one, let alone risk any . . . movement.

We can't do it in the loos. The girls' loos always have people in there, gossiping and putting on their makeup, and the men's loos . . . yuck. No way.

We can't do it in Connor's office, because the walls are

completely made of glass and there aren't any blinds or any-thing.

Oh, this is ridiculous. People having affairs must have sex at the office all the time. Is there some special secret shagging room I don't know about?

I can't e-mail Connor and ask for suggestions, because it's crucial that I surprise him. The shock element will be a huge turn-on and make it really sizzling hot and romantic. Plus, there's a tiny risk that if I warn him, he'll go all corporate on me and insist we take an hour's unpaid leave for it, or some-thing.

I'm just wondering whether we could creep out onto the fire escape, when Nick comes out of Paul's office, talking about margins.

My head jerks up, and I feel a nervous twinge. There's something I've been trying to pluck up courage to say to him since that big meeting yesterday.

"Hey, Nick," I say as he walks by my desk. "Panther Bars are your product, aren't they?"

"If you can call them a product."

"Are they going to axe them?"

"More than likely."

"Well, listen," I say quickly. "Can I have a tiny bit of the marketing budget to put a coupon ad in a magazine?"

Nick swivels to face me. "Do what?"

"Put in an ad! It won't be very expensive. I promise. No one will even notice."

"Where?"

"*Bowling Weekly,*" I say, flushing slightly. "My grandpa gets it."

"*Bowling* What?"

"Please! Look, you don't have to do anything. I'll sort it all out. It'll be less than a thousand quid. It's a drop in the ocean, compared to all the other ads you've run. . . ." I'm *willing* him to say yes. "Please . . . please . . ."

"Oh, all right!" he says impatiently.

"Thanks!" I beam at him, then, as he walks off, reach for the phone and dial Grandpa's number.

"Hi, Grandpa!" I say as his answering machine beeps. "I'm putting a money-off coupon ad for Panther Bars in *Bowling Weekly*. So tell all your friends! You can stock up cheaply! I'll see you soon, OK?"

"Emma?" Grandpa's voice suddenly booms into my ear. "I'm here! Just screening."

"Screening?" I echo. Grandpa screens?

"It's my new hobby. Have you not heard of it? You listen to your friends leaving messages and laugh at them. Most amusing."

"So you'll buy *Bowling Weekly*?"

"I certainly will. And I'll spread the word at the club. Now, Emma, I was meaning to ring you. I saw a very alarming piece on the news yesterday about muggings in central London."

Not this again. "Grandpa—"

"Promise me you don't take London transport, Emma!"

"I, er, promise," I say, crossing my fingers. "Grandpa, I have to go, really. But I'll call again soon. Love you."

"Love you, too, darling girl."

As I put the phone down I feel a tiny glow of satisfaction.

"I'll just have to go and fish it out of the archives," Caroline is saying to Fergus across the office.

Hang on.

The archive room. Of course. Of course! No one goes to the archive room unless they absolutely have to. It's way down in the basement, and it's all dark with no windows, and loads of old books and magazines.

It's perfect!

"I'll go," I say, trying to sound nonchalant. "If you like. What do you have to find?"

"Would you?" says Caroline gratefully. "Thanks, Emma!

It's an old ad in some defunct magazine. This is the reference." She hands me a piece of paper, and as she walks away I pick up my phone and dial Connor's number.

"Hey, Connor," I say in a low, husky voice when he picks up. "Meet me in the archive room. I've got something I want to show you."

"What?"

"Just . . . be there," I say, feeling like Kim Cattrall.

I hurry down the corridor as quickly as I can, but as I pass Admin., I'm accosted by Wendy Smith, who wants to know if I'd like to play on the netball team. So I don't actually get to the basement for a few minutes, and when I open the door, Connor is standing there, looking at his watch.

That's rather annoying. I'd planned to be waiting for him. I was going to be sitting on a pile of books that I would have quickly constructed, one leg crossed over the other and my skirt hitched up seductively.

Oh, well.

"Hi," I say, and push back my hair with a languorous gesture.

"Hi," says Connor with a frown. "Emma, what is this? I'm really busy this morning."

"I just wanted to see you. A lot of you." I push the door shut and trail my finger down his chest, like an aftershave commercial. "We never make love spontaneously anymore."

"What?" Connor seems stunned.

"Come on." I start unbuttoning his pink shirt with what I hope is a sultry expression on my face. "Let's do it. Right here, right now."

To be honest, I'm not feeling that turned-on myself. But I'll just have to do what I can. They say if you smile even when you don't feel like it, you send happy thoughts to your brain and cheer yourself up. So if I *behave* as though I'm full of desire, then surely . . .

"Are you *crazy*?" says Connor, pushing my fingers out of

the way and hastily rebuttoning his shirt. "Emma, we're in the office!"

Of course, it would help if Connor joined in . . .

"We're young. We're supposed to be in love—" I trail a hand even farther down, and Connor's eyes widen.

"Stop!" he hisses. "Stop right now! Emma, are you drunk or something?"

"I just want to have sex! Is that too much to ask?"

"Is it too much to ask to suggest we do it in bed like normal people?"

"But we don't *do* it in bed! I mean, hardly ever!"

There's a sharp silence.

"Emma," says Connor at last. "This isn't the time or the place—"

"It is! It could be! This is how we get the spark back! Lissy said—"

"You discussed our sex life with Lissy?" Connor looks appalled.

"Obviously I didn't mention *us*," I say, hastily backtracking. "We were just talking about . . . about couples in general . . . Come on, Connor!" I shimmy close to him and pull one of his hands inside my bra. "Don't you find this exciting? Just the thought that someone could be walking down the corridor right now, reaching toward the door . . ." I come to a halt as I hear a sound.

I think someone *is* walking down the corridor right now.

Oh, shit.

"I can hear footsteps!" Connor pulls sharply away from me, but his hand stays exactly where it is, inside my bra. He stares at it in shock. "I'm stuck! My bloody watch! It's snagged on your jumper!" He yanks at it. "Fuck! I can't move my arm!"

"Pull it!"

"I am pulling it!" He looks frantically around. "Where are some scissors?"

"You're not cutting my jumper!" I say in horror.

"Do you have any other suggestions?" He yanks sharply again, and I give a muffled shriek. "Ow! Stop it! You'll ruin it!"

"Oh, I'll ruin it. And that's our major concern, is it?"

"I've always hated that stupid watch! If you'd just worn the one I gave you—" I break off. There are definitely footsteps approaching. They're nearly outside the door.

"Fuck!" Connor is desperate. "Fucking . . . fucking . . ." He gives an almighty wrench, and his watch comes free just as the door opens.

Jack Harper is standing in the doorway, holding a big bundle of old magazines. Behind him I can see Anthea Adams, who is Graham Hillingdon's personal assistant and never, ever cracks a smile.

"Hello," says Jack.

"Er, hi!" I say, forcing a natural tone. "I was . . . We were just having . . . I was *researching* . . ." I seize on the word in relief. "Researching something."

"So was I," puts in Connor.

"I see." Jack's voice is blank and unreadable. His gaze passes from Connor to me—and back again.

Suddenly a flash of color catches my eye. A strand of pink wool. Looped around Connor's watch.

Pink wool from my jumper.

Oh . . . fuck.

"Well, I'll leave you to it," says Jack, putting the magazines down on a table. He pauses as though to say something more—then opens the door and leaves.

I just catch a glimpse of Anthea's dismissive gaze as the door closes. We both stand frozen.

I wish . . . I don't know what I wish.

"You've wrecked my jumper!" I say at last, suddenly feeling irritated beyond belief with Connor.

"You nearly wrecked both our careers!" Connor's voice is

high-pitched with outrage. "Do you *realize* what would have happened if—"

"Oh, shut up," I snap, and stalk out of the room. Any desire I had for sex has vanished. I feel completely livid with myself. And Connor. And everybody.

Ten

It's the following day. And Jack Harper is leaving. Thank God.

I really couldn't cope with any more of . . . of *him*. If I can just keep my head down and avoid him until five o'clock and then run out the door, then everything will be fine. Life will be back to normal and I will stop feeling like my radar's been skewed by some invisible magnetic force.

I don't know why I'm in such a jumpy, irritable mood. Because although I nearly died of embarrassment yesterday, my brilliant plan worked. As soon as we got back to our desks, Connor started sending me apologetic e-mails. And then last night we had sex. Twice. With scented candles.

I think Connor must have read somewhere that girls like scented candles during sex. Maybe in *Cosmo,* which I know he sometimes flicks through to get hints. Because he always looks really pleased with himself when he lights them.

I mean, scented candles are lovely; don't get me wrong. But it's not like they actually *do* anything, is it?

Anyway. So we had sex.

And tonight we're going to look at a flat together. It doesn't have a wooden floor or shutters—but it has a Jacuzzi in the bathroom, which is pretty cool. So my life is coming together nicely. I don't know why I'm feeling so pissed off. I don't know what's—

I don't want to move in with Connor, says a tiny voice in my brain before I can stop it.

No. That can't be right. That cannot possibly be right. Connor is perfect. Everyone knows that.

But I don't want to—

Shut up. We're the perfect couple. We have sex with scented candles. And we go for walks by the river. And we read the papers on Sundays with cups of coffee, in pajamas. That's what perfect couples do.

I feel the prick of panic and swallow hard. Connor is the one good thing in my life. If I didn't have Connor . . . what would I have?

The phone rings on my desk, interrupting my thoughts, and I pick it up.

"Hello, Emma?" comes a familiar dry voice. "This is Jack Harper."

My heart gives a leap of fright and I nearly spill my coffee. I should never have answered my phone.

In fact, I should never have come in to work today. "Oh," I say. "Er, hi!"

"Would you mind coming up to my office for a moment?"

"What . . . me?"

"Yes, you."

I clear my throat. "Should I . . . bring anything?"

"No, just yourself."

I put my phone down, feeling nervous. Why does Jack Harper want to see me?

Is this going to be about what happened yesterday?

I take a deep breath, stand up, and make my way up to the eleventh floor. There's a desk outside his suite, but no secretary, so I go straight up to the door and knock.

"Come in."

I cautiously push the door open. The room is huge and bright and paneled in pale wood, with a view over the Thames all the way along to Tower Bridge. I never realized you could see so much from up here. Jack is sitting at a circular table, with six people gathered around on chairs. Six people I've never seen before, I suddenly realize, all with trendy haircuts and a kind of casual smartness. One guy has bleached, cropped hair and a nylon mesh shirt under his jacket. It looks like he was talking before I came in.

They all slowly turn toward me. I can feel the tension in the atmosphere.

"Hello," I say, trying to keep as composed as possible. But my face is hot, and I know I look flustered.

"Hi." Jack's face crinkles in a smile. "Emma . . . relax. There's nothing to worry about. I just wanted to ask you something."

"Oh, right." I'm totally confused. What on earth could he have to ask me?

Jack reaches for a piece of paper and holds it up so I can see it clearly. "What do you think this is a picture of?" he says.

Oh, fucketty fuck.

This is your worst nightmare. This is like when I went for that interview at Laines Bank and they showed me a squiggle and I said I thought it looked like a squiggle.

Everyone is focused on me. I so want to get it right. If only I knew what right was.

I stare at the picture, trying to stay calm. It's a graphic of two round objects. Kind of irregular in shape. I have absolutely no idea what they're supposed to be. None at all. They look like . . . They look like . . .

Suddenly I see it. "It's nuts! Two walnuts!"

Jack explodes with laughter, and a couple of people give muffled giggles, which they stifle.

"Well, I think that proves my point," says Jack.

"Aren't they walnuts?" I look around the table.

"They're supposed to be ovaries," says a man with rimless spectacles, in a tight voice.

"Ovaries?" I stare at the page. "Oh, right! Well, yes. Now that you say it, I can definitely see a . . . an ovary-like . . ."

"Walnuts." Jack wipes his eyes.

"I've explained, the ovaries are simply *part* of a range of symbolic representations of womanhood," says the bleached-blond guy defensively. "Ovaries to represent fertility, an eye for wisdom, this tree to signify the earth mother . . ."

"The point is, the images can be used across the entire range of products," says a woman with black hair, leaning forward. "The health drink, clothing, a fragrance . . ."

"The target market responds well to abstract images," adds rimless-spectacle guy. "The research has shown—"

"Emma." Jack looks at me again. "Would *you* buy a drink with ovaries on it?"

"Er . . ." I clear my throat, aware of a couple of hostile faces pointing my way. "Well . . . probably not."

A few people exchange glances.

"This is so irrelevant," someone is muttering.

"Jack, three creative teams have been at work at this," the blond woman says earnestly. "We can't start from scratch. We simply cannot."

Jack takes a sip of water, wipes his mouth, and looks at her. "You know I came up with the slogan 'Don't Pause' in two minutes on a bar napkin?"

"Yes, we know," mutters the guy in rimless spectacles.

"We are not selling a drink with ovaries on it." Jack exhales sharply and runs a hand through his hair. Then he pushes his chair back. "OK, let's take a break. Emma, would you be kind enough to assist me in carrying some of these folders down to Sven's office?"

God, I wonder what all that was about. But I don't quite dare ask. Jack marches me down the corridor in silence, and into a lift. He presses the ninth-floor button. After we've descended for about two seconds, he presses the emergency button, and we grind to a halt. Then, finally, he looks at me.

"Are you and I the only sane people in this building?"

"Um . . ."

"What happened to instincts?" His face is incredulous. "No one knows a good idea from a terrible one anymore. Ovaries." He shakes his head. "Fucking *ovaries!*"

I can't help it. He looks so outraged, and the way he says *"ovaries!"* seems the funniest thing in the world, and before I know it, I've started laughing. For an instant Jack looks astounded, and then his face kind of crumples, and suddenly he's laughing, too. His nose screws right up when he laughs, just like a baby's, and somehow this makes this moment seem about a million times funnier.

Oh, God. I really am laughing now. I'm giving tiny little snorts, and my ribs hurt, and every time I look at him, I gurgle again. My nose is running, and I haven't got a tissue. . . . I'll have to blow my nose on the picture of the ovaries . . .

"Emma . . . why are you with that guy?"

"What?" I look up, still laughing, until suddenly I realize that Jack's stopped. He's looking at me with an unreadable expression on his face.

"Why are you with that guy?" he repeats.

I push my hair back off my face. "What do you mean?"

"Connor Martin. He's not going to make you happy. He's not going to fulfill you."

For a moment I'm wrong-footed. "Who says?"

"I've gotten to know Connor. I've sat in meetings with him. I've seen how his mind works. He's a nice guy—but you need more than a nice guy." Jack gives me a long, shrewd look. "My guess is, you don't really want to move in with him. But you're afraid of ducking out."

I feel a swell of indignation. How dare he read my mind and get it so . . . so *wrong*. Of course I want to move in with Connor.

"Actually, you're quite mistaken," I say in cutting tones. "I'm looking forward to moving in with him. In fact . . . in fact, I was just sitting at my desk, thinking how I can't wait!"

Jack's shaking his head. "You need someone with a spark. Who . . . excites you."

"I told you, I didn't *mean* what I said on the plane. Connor *does* excite me!" I give him a defiant look. "You know when you found us in the archive room? You want to guess what we were doing?"

"I'm pretty sure I know what you were doing," says Jack. "I assumed it was a desperate attempt to spice up your love life."

"That was not a desperate attempt to spice up my love life!" I almost spit at him. "That was simply a . . . a spontaneous act of passion."

"Sorry. My mistake."

"Anyway, why do you care?" I fold my arms. "What does it matter to you whether I'm happy or not?"

There's a sharp silence, and suddenly I realize I'm breathing rather quickly. I meet his dark eyes and quickly look away again.

"I've asked myself that same question," says Jack. "Maybe it's because we experienced that extraordinary plane ride together. Maybe it's because you're the only person in this whole company who hasn't put on some kind of phony act for me."

I would have put on an act! I feel like retorting. If I'd had a choice!

"Maybe it's because you make me laugh," he adds.

I feel a rush of surprise. I make him laugh? In a good way?

"I guess what I'm saying is . . . I feel as if you're a friend," Jack continues. "And I care what happens to my friends."

"Oh," I say, and rub my nose.

I'm about to say politely that he feels like a friend, too, when he adds, "Plus, anyone who recites Woody Allen films line for line *has* to be a loser."

I feel a surge of outrage on Connor's behalf. "You don't know anything about it!" I exclaim. "You know, I wish I'd never sat next to you on that stupid plane. You go around saying all these things to . . . to wind me up, behaving as though you know me better than anyone else—"

"Maybe I do," he says quick as lightning.

"What?"

"Maybe I do know you better than anyone else."

I feel a breathless mixture of outrage and exhilaration. It's as though we're playing tennis. Or dancing.

"You do not know me better than anyone else!" I retort in the most scathing tones I can muster.

"I know you won't end with Connor Martin."

"You don't know that."

"Yes, I do."

"No, you don't."

"I do." He's starting to laugh.

"No, you don't! If you want to know, I'll probably end up marrying Connor!"

"Marry Connor?" says Jack, as though this were the funniest joke he's ever heard.

"Yes! Why not? He's tall, and he's handsome, and he's kind, and he's very . . . He's . . ." I'm floundering slightly. "And

anyway, this is my personal life! You're my boss, and you only
met me last week, and frankly this is none of your business!"

Jack's laughter vanishes, and he looks as though I've slapped
him. For a few moments he says nothing. Then he takes a step
back and releases the lift button. "You're right," he says. The
teasing edge has vanished from his voice. "Your personal life
is none of my business. I overstepped the mark . . . and I
apologize."

I feel a spasm of dismay. "I . . . I didn't mean—"

"No. You're right." He stares at the floor for a few moments, then looks up. "So, I leave for the States tomorrow. It's
been a very pleasant stay, and I'd like to thank you for all your
help. Will I see you at the drinks party tonight?"

"I . . . I don't know," I say.

The atmosphere has disintegrated.

This is awful. I'm standing, clenching the folders more and
more tightly. Jack's face is impassive. I want to say something,
I want to put it back to the way it was before, all easy and joking. But I can't find the words.

We reach the ninth floor, and the doors open.

"I think I can manage these from here," Jack says. "I really
only asked you along for the company."

Awkwardly, I transfer the folders to his arms.

"Well, Emma," he says in the same formal voice, "in case I
don't see you later on . . . it was nice knowing you." He meets
my eyes, and a glimmer of his old, warm expression returns.
"I really mean that."

"You, too."

I don't want him to go. I feel like suggesting a quick drink.
I feel like clinging on to his hand and saying, "Don't leave." I
don't want this to be the end.

God, what's *wrong* with me?

"Have a good journey," I manage as he shakes my hand.
Then he turns on his heel and walks off down the corridor.

I open my mouth to call after him—but what would I

say? By tomorrow morning he'll be on a plane back to his life. And I'll be left here in mine.

I feel leaden for the rest of the day. Everyone else is talking about going out for a drink tonight, but I leave work half an hour early. I go straight home to an empty flat—Lissy's doing a case in Birmingham and Jemima's probably having a French manicure or something. I make myself some hot chocolate, and am sitting on the sofa, lost in my own thoughts, when Connor lets himself into the flat.

I look up as he walks into the room, and immediately I know something's different. Not with him. He hasn't changed a bit.

But I have. I've changed.

"Hi," he says, and kisses me lightly on the head. "Shall we go?"

"Go?"

"To look at the flat on Edith Road! Oh, and my mother's given us a housewarming present. It was delivered to work."

He hands me a cardboard box, and I pull out a glass teapot.

"You can keep the tea leaves separate from the water. Mum says it really does make a better cup of tea—"

"Connor . . ." I hear myself saying. "I can't do this."

"It's quite easy. You just have to lift the—"

"No." I shut my eyes, trying to gather some courage. At last I open them again. "I can't do *this*. I can't move in with you."

"What?" Connor's face kind of freezes. "Has something happened?"

"Yes. No." I swallow. "I've been having doubts for a while. About us. And recently they've . . . they've been confirmed. If we carry on, I'll be a hypocrite. It's not fair to either of us."

"*What?* Emma, are you saying you want to . . . to . . ."

"I want to break up," I say, my eyes fixed on the carpet.

"You're joking."

"I'm not joking!" I say in sudden anguish. This is harder than I was expecting. Connor looks so totally crushed. Although what was I expecting? That he'd say, "Hmm, yes, good idea"?

"But . . . this is ridiculous! It's ridiculous!" Connor's pacing around the room like an agitated lion. Suddenly he looks at me.

"It's that plane journey."

"What?" Every cell in my body jumps. "What do you mean?"

"You've been different ever since that plane ride down from Scotland!"

"No, I haven't!"

"You have! You've been edgy; you've been tense. . . ." Connor squats down in front of me and takes my hands. "Emma, I think maybe you're still suffering some kind of trauma. You could have counseling. . . ."

"Connor, I don't need counseling!" I jerk my hands away. "But maybe you're right. Maybe that plane ride did . . ." I swallow. ". . . affect me. Maybe it brought my life into perspective and made me realize a few things. And one of the things I've realized is, we aren't right for each other."

Slowly Connor sinks down onto the carpet, bewildered. "But things have been great! We've been having lots of sex—"

"I know."

"Is there someone else?"

"No!" I say sharply. "Of course there's no one else!" My thoughts swirl in uncertain circles. Why can't he stop quizzing me?

"This isn't you talking!" says Connor suddenly. "It's just the mood you're in. I'll run you a nice, hot bath, light some scented candles . . ."

"Connor, please!" I exclaim. "No more scented candles!

You have to listen to me. And you have to believe me." I look straight into his eyes. "I want to break up."

"I *don't* believe you!" he says, shaking his head. "I *know* you, Emma! You're not that kind of person! You wouldn't just throw away something like that! You wouldn't—"

He stops in shock as, with no warning, I hurl the glass teapot to the floor.

Stunned, we both watch it bounce on the floorboards.

"It was supposed to break," I explain after a pause. "And that was going to signify that yes, I would throw something away, if I knew it wasn't right for me."

"I think it *has* broken," says Connor, picking it up and examining it. "At least, there's a hairline crack."

"There you go."

"We could still use it—"

"No. We couldn't."

"We could get some Sellotape—"

"But it would never work properly. It just . . . wouldn't work."

"I see," says Connor after a pause.

And I think, finally, he does.

"Well . . . I'll be off, then," he says at last. "I'll phone the flat people and tell them that we're . . . ." He stops and takes a deep breath. "You'll want your keys back, too."

"Thanks," I say in a voice that doesn't sound like mine. "Can we keep it quiet from everyone at work?" I add. "Just for the moment."

"Of course," he says gruffly. "I won't say anything."

He's halfway out the door when suddenly he turns back, reaching in his pocket. "Emma . . . here are the tickets for the jazz festival. You have them."

"What?" I stare at them in horror. "No! Connor, you have them! They're yours!"

"*You* have them. I know how much you've been looking

forward to hearing the Dennisson Quartet." He pushes the brightly colored tickets roughly into my hand, together with the keys of the flat, and closes my fingers over them.

"I . . . I . . ." I swallow. "Connor . . . I just . . . I don't know what to say . . ."

"We'll always have jazz," says Connor in a choked-up voice, and closes the door behind him.

Eleven

SO NOW I HAVE NO PROMOTION *and* no boyfriend. And everyone thinks I'm mad.

"You're mad," Jemima says approximately every ten minutes. It's Saturday morning, and we're in our usual routine of dressing gowns and coffee and nursing hangovers. Or, in my case, breakups. "You do realize you had him?" She frowns at her toenail, which she's painting baby pink. "I would have predicted a rock on your finger within six months."

"I thought you said I'd ruined all my chances by agreeing to move in with him," I say sulkily.

"Well, in Connor's case I think you would have been safe." She shakes her head. "You're crazy."

"Do you think I'm crazy?" I say, turning to Lissy, who's sitting in the rocking chair with her arm around her knees, eating a piece of raisin toast. "Be honest."

"Er, no!" says Lissy unconvincingly. "Of course not!"

"You do!"

"It's just . . . you just seemed like such a great couple."

"I know we did. I know we looked great on the outside." I pause, trying to explain. "But the truth is, I never felt I was being myself. It was always a bit like we were . . . acting. You know. It didn't seem *real,* somehow—"

"That's *it*?" interrupts Jemima, as though I'm talking gibberish. "That's the reason you broke up!"

"It's a pretty good reason, don't you think?" says Lissy loyally.

"Of course not! Emma, if you'd just stuck it out and acted being the perfect couple for long enough . . . you would have *become* the perfect couple."

"But . . . but we wouldn't have been happy!"

"You would have been the perfect couple," says Jemima, as though explaining something to a stupid child. "*Obviously* you would have been happy." She cautiously stands up, her toes splayed by bits of pink foam, and starts making her way toward the door. "And anyway. Everyone pretends in a relationship."

"No, they don't! Or at least, they shouldn't . . ."

"Of course they should! Mummy says all this being honest with each other is totally overrated! She's been married to Daddy for thirty years, and he still has no idea she isn't a natural blonde."

As Jemima disappears out of the room, I exchange glances with Lissy. "Do you think she's right?" I say.

"No," says Lissy uncertainly. "Of course not! Relationships should be built on . . . on trust . . . and truth . . ." She pauses and looks at me anxiously. "Emma, you never told me you felt that way about Connor."

"I . . . didn't tell anyone." This isn't quite true, I immediately realize. But I'm hardly going to let on to my best friend that I told more to a complete stranger than to her, am I?

"Well, I really wish you'd confided in me more," says Lissy earnestly. "Emma, let's make a new resolution. We'll tell each other *everything* from now on. We shouldn't have secrets from each other, anyway! We're best friends!"

"It's a deal!" I say with a warm burst of emotion. Impulsively I lean forward and give her a hug.

Lissy's so right. We shouldn't keep things from each other. I mean, we've been friends for over twenty years!

"So, if we're telling each other everything . . ." Lissy takes a bite of raisin toast and gives me a sidelong look. "Did your chucking Connor have anything to do with that man? The man from the plane?"

I feel a pang, which I ignore by taking a sip of coffee. "No," I say without looking up. "Nothing."

We both watch the television screen for a few moments, where Kylie Minogue is being interviewed.

"Oh, OK!" I say, suddenly remembering. "So, if we're asking each other questions . . . what were you *really* doing with that guy Jean-Paul in your room?"

Lissy takes a breath.

"And don't tell me you were looking at case notes," I add. "Because that wouldn't make all that thumping, bumping noise."

"Oh!" says Lissy, looking cornered. "OK. Well . . . we were . . ." She takes a gulp of coffee and avoids my gaze. "We were, um, having sex."

"What?" I stare at her, disconcerted.

"Yes. We were having sex. That's why I didn't want to tell you. I was embarrassed."

"You and Jean-Paul were having sex?"

"Yes!" She clears her throat. "We were having . . . passionate . . . raunchy . . . animalistic sex."

There's something wrong here. Something about her tone just doesn't ring true. When Lissy talks about sex, that's not how she sounds. And she'd never use the word "animalistic." Or "raunchy," for that matter.

She's lying!

"I don't believe you!" I give her a long look. "You weren't having sex!"

The pink dots on Lissy's cheeks immediately deepen in color. "Yes, we were!"

"No, you weren't. Lissy, what were you *really* doing?"

"We were having sex, OK?" says Lissy, now agitated. "He's my new boyfriend, and . . . that's what we were doing! Now, just leave me alone!" She gets up, scattering raisin toast crumbs, and heads out of the room, tripping slightly on the rug.

Why is she lying? What on earth was she doing in there? What's more embarrassing than sex, for God's sake? I'm so intrigued, I almost feel cheered up.

To be honest, it's not the greatest weekend of my life. It's made even less great when the post arrives and I get a postcard from Mum and Dad from Le Spa Meridien, telling me what a fantastic time they're having. And even *less* great when I read my horoscope in the *Mail,* and it tells me, "You may just have made a rash mistake. Examine your motives carefully."

I lie in bed on Saturday night, unable to sleep. Then, at about three in the morning, I find myself replaying that final meeting with Jack over and over in my mind. I even start composing light, friendly postcards to send him in America. *Hope you had a good trip back . . . It was great to meet you . . .*

But who am I kidding? I'm not going to send him any card. He's probably forgotten who I am already. It was an interesting experience meeting him—and now it's over.

By the time I wake up on Monday morning, I feel a lot better. My new life starts today. I'm going to forget all about love and romance and concentrate on my career. As I get ready for work, I reach for my smartest trousers and a neck scarf that isn't very nice but shouts "career woman." I'll show Paul who's ready for a promotion.

Maybe I'll even look for a new job. Yes!

As I come out of the tube station, I fantasize applying for a job as marketing executive at Coca-Cola. And I'll get it. And Paul will suddenly realize what a terrible mistake he made, not promoting me. And he'll ask me to stay, but I'll say, "It's too late. You had your chance." And then he'll beg, "Emma, is there anything I can do to change your mind?" And then *I'll* say—

By the time I reach the building, Paul is groveling on the floor as I sit nonchalantly on his desk, holding one knee (I also seem to be wearing a new suit and Prada shoes) and saying, "You know, Paul, all you had to do was treat me with a little respect—"

Shit. My eyes suddenly focus and I stop in my tracks, hand on the glass doors. There's a blond head in the foyer.

Connor. I can't go in there. I can't do it. I can't—

Then the head moves, and it's not Connor at all; it's Andrea from Accounts. I push the door open, feeling like a complete flake. God, I'm a mess. I have to get a grip on myself, because I will run into Connor before too long, and I'm just going to have to handle it.

At least no one at work knows yet, I think as I walk up the stairs. That would make things a million times harder. To have people coming up to me and saying—

"Emma, I'm so sorry to hear about you and Connor!"

"What?" I stop still in shock and see a girl called Nancy coming toward me.

"It was such a bolt from the blue! Of all the couples to split up, I would never have said you two. But it just shows, you never can tell . . ."

"How . . . how do you know?"

"Oh, everyone knows!" says Nancy. "You know there was

a little drinks do on Friday night? Well, Connor came to it, and he got quite drunk. And he told everyone. In fact, he made a little speech!"

"He . . . he did what?"

"It was quite touching, really. It was all about how the Panther Corporation felt like his family and how he knew we would all support him through this difficult time. And you, of course," she adds as an afterthought. "Although since you were the one who broke it off, Connor's really the wounded party." She leans forward confidentially. "I have to say, a lot of the girls were saying you must have a screw loose!"

I cannot believe this. Connor gave a speech about our breakup. After promising to keep it quiet. And now everyone's on *his* side.

"Right," I say at last. "Well, I'd better get on—"

"It just seems such a shame!" Nancy's inquisitive eyes run over me. "You two seemed so perfect!"

"I know we did." I force a smile. "Anyway. See you later."

I head for the new coffee machine, trying to get my head around this, when a tremulous voice interrupts me. "Emma?"

I look up in apprehension. It's Katie, peering at me as though I've suddenly grown three heads.

"Oh, hi!" I say, trying to sound breezy.

"Is it true?" she whispers. "Is it true? Because I won't believe it's true until I hear you say it with your own lips."

"Yes," I say reluctantly. "It's true. Connor and I have broken up."

"Oh, God." Katie's breathing becomes quicker and quicker. "Oh, my God. It's true. Oh my God, oh my God, I really can't cope with this . . ."

Shit. She's hyperventilating. I grab an empty sugar bag and shove it over her mouth.

"Katie, calm down!" I say helplessly. "Breathe in . . . and out . . ."

"I've been having panic attacks all weekend," she manages between breaths. "I woke up last night in a cold sweat and I just thought to myself, If this is true, the world doesn't make sense anymore. It simply makes no sense."

"Katie, we broke up! That's all! People break up all the time."

"But you and Connor weren't just people! You were *the* couple." She removes the bag from her face. "I mean, if you can't make it, why should any of the rest of us bother even trying?"

"Katie, we weren't *the* couple!" I say, trying to keep my temper. "We were *a* couple. And it went wrong, and . . . and these things happen!"

"But—"

"And to be honest, I'd rather not talk about it."

"Oh," she says. "Oh, God, of course. Sorry, Emma. I didn't . . . I just . . . You know, it was such a shock."

"Come on—you haven't told me how your date with Philip went yet," I say firmly. "Cheer me up with some good news."

The kettle switches off, and I reach for the coffee grounds. Katie's breathing has gradually calmed.

"Actually . . . it went really well," she says. "We're going to see each other again!"

"Well, there you go!"

"He's so charming. And gentle. And we have the same sense of humor, and we like the same things . . ." A bashful smile spreads across Katie's face. "Actually, he's lovely!"

"He sounds wonderful! You see?" I squeeze her arm. "You and Philip will probably be a far better couple than Connor and I ever were. Do you want a coffee?"

"No, thanks, I've got to go. We've got a meeting with Jack Harper about personnel. See you."

"OK, see you," I say absently.

About five seconds later, my brain clicks into gear. "Wait a second." I hurry down the corridor and grab her shoulder. "Did you just say . . . Jack Harper?"

"Yes."

"But . . . but he's gone. He left on Friday."

"No, he didn't. He changed his mind."

"So . . ." I swallow. "So . . . he's here?"

"Of course he's here!" says Katie with a laugh. "He's upstairs!"

Suddenly my legs won't work properly. "Why . . ." I clear my throat, which has gone a little grainy. "Why did he change his mind?"

"Who knows?" Katie shrugs. "He's the boss. He can do what he likes, can't he? Mind you, I've always thought he seems very down-to-earth." She reaches into her pocket for a packet of gum and offers it to me. "He was really nice to Connor after he gave his little speech . . ."

I feel a fresh jolt. "Jack Harper heard Connor's speech? About our breaking up?"

"Yes! He was standing right next to him." Katie unwraps her gum. "And afterward he said something really nice like he could just imagine how Connor was feeling. Wasn't that sweet?"

I need to sit down. I need to think. I need to . . .

"Emma, are you OK?" says Katie in dismay. "God, I'm so insensitive—"

"No. It's fine," I say in a daze. "I'm fine. I'll see you later."

This is not the way it was supposed to happen. Jack Harper was supposed to be back in America. He was supposed to have no idea that I went straight home from our conversation and chucked Connor.

I feel humiliated. He'll think I chucked Connor because of what he said to me in the lift, won't he? He'll think it was all because of him. Which it so *wasn't*.

At least . . . not completely . . .

Maybe that's why—

No. It's ridiculous to think that his staying has anything to do with me. Ridiculous.

As I near my desk, Artemis looks up from a copy of *Marketing Week.* "Oh, Emma. I was sorry to hear about you and Connor."

"Thanks," I say. "But I don't really want to talk about it, if that's OK—"

"Fine," says Artemis. "Whatever. I was just being polite." She looks at a Post-it on her desk. "There's a message for you from Jack Harper, by the way."

"What?" I start.

"Could you please take the . . ." She squints at the paper. ". . . the Leopold file to his office. He said you'd know what it was. But if you can't find it, it doesn't matter."

The Leopold file.

It was just an excuse to get away from our desks . . .

It's a secret code. He wants to see me.

Oh, my God. Oh, my God.

I have never been more thrilled and petrified. Both at once.

I sit down and stare at my blank screen for a minute. Then, with trembling fingers, I take out a blank file. I wait until Artemis has turned away, then write "Leopold" on the side of it, trying to disguise my handwriting.

Suddenly I stop. Am I being really, really stupid here? Is there a real Leopold file?

Hastily I go into the company database and do a quick search for "Leopold." But nothing comes up.

OK. I was right the first time.

I'm about to push my chair back when I suddenly have a paranoid thought. What if someone stops me and asks what the Leopold file is? Or what if I drop it on the floor and everyone sees it's empty?

Quickly, I open a new document, invent a fancy letter-head, and type a letter from a Mr. Ernest P. Leopold to the Panther Corporation. I send it over to print, stroll over to the printer, and whisk it out before anyone else can see what it is. Not that anyone else is remotely interested.

"Right," I say casually, tucking it into the cardboard folder. "Well, I'll just take that file up, then . . ."

Artemis doesn't even raise her head.

As I walk through the corridors, I'm pulsing with nerves. I feel as though everyone in the building must know what I'm doing.

Why does Jack Harper want to see me? Because if it's just to tell me he was right all along about Connor, then he can just . . . he can just bloody well . . . Suddenly I have a flash-back to that awful atmosphere in the lift. What if it's really awkward?

I don't have to go, I remind myself. He did give me an out. I could easily phone his secretary and say, "Sorry, I couldn't find the Leopold file," and that would be the end.

For an instant I hesitate, my fingers tightly clutching the cardboard. And then I carry on walking.

The door of Jack's office is being guarded not by one of the secretaries but by Sven. As he hears me coming, he looks up and his pale eyes give a flicker, like a lizard's. He doesn't smile.

Oh, God. I know Jack has said he's his oldest friend, but I can't help it. I do find this guy creepy. "Hi," I say. "Er, Mr. Harper asked me to bring up the Leopold file."

Sven looks at me, and for an instant it's like a little silent communication is passing between us. He knows, doesn't he? He probably uses the Leopold file code himself. He picks up his phone and after a moment says, "Jack, Emma Corrigan is here with the Leopold file." Then he puts down the phone and says, "Go straight in."

I walk in, feeling all prickly with self-consciousness. Jack's sitting behind a big wooden desk, wearing the black turtleneck he wore on the first day. As he looks up, his eyes are warm, and I feel myself relax just a bit.

"Hello," he says.

"Hello," I reply. "So, um, here's the Leopold file." I hand him the cardboard folder.

"The Leopold file." He laughs. "Very good." Then he opens it and looks at the sheet of paper in surprise. "What's this?"

"It's a . . . it's a letter from Mr. Leopold of Leopold and Company."

"You composed a letter from Mr. Leopold?" He seems astonished. Suddenly I feel really stupid.

"Just in case I dropped the file on the floor and someone saw," I mumble. "I thought I'd just quickly make something up. It's not important . . ." I try to take it back, but Jack moves it out of my reach.

" 'From the office of Ernest P. Leopold,' " he reads aloud. "I see he wishes to order six thousand cases of Panther Cola. Quite a customer, this Leopold."

"It's for a corporate event," I explain. "He normally uses Pepsi, but recently one of his employees tasted Panther Cola, and it was so good . . ."

"He simply had to switch," finishes Jack. " 'May I add that I am delighted with all aspects of your company, and have taken to wearing a Panther jogging suit, which is quite the most comfortable sportswear I have ever known.' " He's silent for a moment, then looks up with a smile. To my surprise, his eyes are shining. "You know, Pete would have adored this."

"Pete Laidler?" I say hesitantly.

"Yup. It was Pete who came up with the whole Leopold file maneuver. This was the kind of stuff he did all the time." He taps the letter. "Can I keep it?"

"Of course," I say, touched. He folds it up and puts it in his pocket, and for a few moments there's silence.

"So," says Jack at last. He raises his head and gives me a long, searching look. "You broke up with Connor."

Wow. So we're straight to the point.

"So," I reply defiantly. "You decided to stay."

"Yes, well . . ." He stretches out his fingers and studies them briefly. "I thought I might take a closer look at some of the European subsidiaries." He looks up. "How about you?"

He wants me to say I chucked Connor because of him, doesn't he? Well, I'm not going to. No way.

"Same reason." I nod. "European subsidiaries."

There's a flash of amusement in Jack's eyes. "I see. And are you . . . OK?"

"I'm fine. Actually, I'm enjoying the freedom of being single again." I gesture widely with my arms. "You know, the liberation, the flexibility . . ."

"That's great. Well, then, maybe this isn't a good time to . . ." He stops.

"To what?" I say a little too quickly.

"I know you must be hurting right now," he says carefully. "But I was wondering." He pauses for what seems like forever. My throat gradually tightens, but I don't dare swallow. "Would you like to have dinner sometime?"

He's asked me out. He's asked me out.

I almost can't move my mouth.

"Yes," I say at last. "Yes, that would be lovely."

"Great!" He pauses. "The only thing is, my life is kind of complicated right now. And what with our office situation . . . It might be an idea to keep this to ourselves."

"Oh, I completely agree," I say quickly. "We should be discreet."

"So, shall we say . . . how about <u>tomorrow</u> night? Would that suit you?"

"Tomorrow night would be perfect."

"I'll come and pick you up. If you e-mail me your address. Eight o'clock?"

"Eight it is!"

As I leave Jack's office, Sven glances up questioningly, but I don't say anything. I head back to the marketing department, trying as hard as I can to keep my face dispassionate and calm. But excitement is bubbling away inside, and a huge smile keeps breaking through.

Oh, my God. Oh, my God. I'm going out to dinner with Jack Harper. I just . . . I can't believe—

Oh, who am I kidding? I knew this was going to happen. As soon as I heard he hadn't gone to America. I knew.

Twelve

I HAVE NEVER SEEN JEMIMA look so appalled.

"He knows all your *secrets*?" She's looking at me as though I've just told her I'm going out with a mass murderer. "What on earth do you mean?"

"I sat next to him on a plane, and I told him everything about myself."

I frown at my reflection in my mirror and tweak out another eyebrow hair. It's seven o'clock, I've had my bath, and now I'm sitting in my robe, putting on my makeup.

"And now he's asked her out," says Lissy, reaching for my new mascara and studying it. "Isn't it romantic?"

"You are joking, aren't you?" says Jemima. "Tell me this is a joke." She's standing at the door of my room, wearing a new, dark green dress. Tonight she's got a date with the guy who bought the seventy-thousand-pound painting. Apparently he loves green.

"Of course I'm not joking! What's the problem?"

"You're going out with a man who knows everything about you."

"Yes."

"And you're asking me what's the *problem*?" she says incredulously. "Are you *crazy*?"

"Of course I'm not crazy!"

"I *knew* you fancied him," says Lissy for about the millionth time. "I knew it. Right from the moment you started talking about him." She looks at my reflection. "I'd leave that right eyebrow alone now."

"Really?" I peer at my face.

"Emma, you don't tell men all about yourself! You have to keep something back! Mummy always says you should never let a man see your feelings or the contents of your handbag."

"Well, too late. He's seen it all."

"Then it's never going to work," says Jemima. "He'll never respect you."

"Yes, he will!"

"Emma," says Jemima in a pitying voice. "Don't you understand? You've already lost."

"I haven't *lost*!"

Sometimes I think Jemima sees men as alien robots who must be conquered by any means possible.

"You're not being very helpful, Jemima," puts in Lissy. "Come on. You've been on loads of dates with rich businessmen. You must have some good advice!"

"All right." Jemima sighs and puts her bag down. "It's a hopeless cause, but I'll do my best." She starts ticking off on her fingers. "The first thing is to look as well groomed as possible."

"Why do you think I'm plucking my eyebrows?" I say with a grimace.

"Fine. OK, the next thing is, you can show an interest in his hobbies. What does he like?"

"Er . . . dunno. Cars, I think. He has all these vintage cars on his ranch, apparently."

"Well, then!" Jemima brightens. "That's good. Pretend you like cars. Suggest visiting a car show. . . . You could flick through a car magazine on the way there . . ."

"I can't," I say, taking a sip from my pre-date relaxer glass of Harveys Bristol Cream. "I told him on the plane that I hate vintage cars."

"You did *what*?" Jemima looks like she wants to hit me. "You told the man you're dating that you hate his favorite hobby?"

"I didn't know I would be going on a date with him then, did I?" I say defensively, reaching for my foundation. "And anyway, it's the truth! I hate vintage cars! The people in them always look so pleased with themselves . . ."

"What's the *truth* got to do with anything?" Jemima's voice rises in agitation. "Emma, I'm sorry; I can't help you. This is a disaster. You're completely vulnerable. It's like going into battle in a nightie."

"Jemima, this is not a battle!" I retort. "And it's not a chess game! It's dinner with a nice man!"

"You're so cynical, Jemima!" chimes in Lissy. "*I* think it's really romantic! They're going to have the perfect date, because there won't be any of that awkwardness. He knows what Emma likes. He knows what she's interested in. They're already compatible!"

"Well, I wash my hands of it," says Jemima, still shaking her head. "What are you going to wear?" Her eyes suddenly narrow. "Where's your outfit?"

"My black dress. And my strappy sandals." I gesture to the back of the door, where my black dress is hanging up.

Jemima's eyes narrow even further. She would have made a really good SS officer, I often think.

"You're not going to borrow anything of mine."

"No!" I say in indignant tones. "Honestly, Jemima, I do have my own clothes, you know."

"Fine. Well. Have a good time."

Lissy and I wait until her footsteps have tapped down the corridor and the front door has slammed.

"Right!" I say, but Lissy lifts a hand.

"Wait."

We both sit still for about five minutes. Suddenly there's the sound of the front door being opened very quietly.

"She's trying to catch us out," whispers Lissy. "Hi!" she says, raising her voice. "Is anyone there?"

"Oh, hi," says Jemima, appearing at the door of the room. "I forgot my lip gloss." Her eyes do a quick sweep of the room.

"I don't think you'll find it in here," says Lissy innocently.

"No. Well." Her eyes travel around the room again. "OK. Have a nice evening."

Again her footsteps tap down the corridor, and again the front door slams.

"Right!" says Lissy. "Let's go."

We unpeel the Sellotape from Jemima's door, and Lissy makes a little mark where it was. "Wait!" she says as I'm about to push the door open. "There's another one at the bottom."

"You should have been a spy," I say, watching her carefully peel it off.

"OK," she says, her forehead furrowed with concentration. "There have to be some more booby traps."

"There's Sellotape on the wardrobe, too," I say. "And . . . look!" I point up. A glass of water is balanced on top of the wardrobe, ready to drench us if we open the door.

"That cow!" says Lissy as I reach up for it. "You know, I had to spend all evening fielding calls for her the other night, and she wasn't even grateful."

She waits until I've put the water down safely, then reaches for the door. "Ready?"

"Ready."

Lissy takes a deep breath, then opens the wardrobe door. Immediately a loud, piercing siren begins to wail. *"Wee-oo wee-oo wee-oo . . ."*

"Shit!" she says, banging the door shut. "Shit! How did she do that?"

"It's still going! Make it stop! Make it stop!"

"I don't know how to! You probably need a special code!"

We're both jabbing at the wardrobe, patting it, searching for an off switch.

"I can't see a button or a switch or anything. . . ."

Abruptly the noise stops, and we both stare at each other, panting.

"Actually," says Lissy after a long pause. "Actually, I think that might have been a car alarm outside."

"Oh," I say. "Oh, right. Yes, maybe it was."

Looking a bit sheepish, Lissy reaches for the door again—and this time it's silent. "OK," she says. "Here goes."

"Wow," we breathe as one as she swings the door open.

Jemima's wardrobe is like a treasure chest. New, shiny, gorgeous clothes, all neatly folded and hung on padded hangers. All the shoes in shoe boxes with Polaroids on the front. All the belts are hanging neatly from hooks. All the bags are neatly lined up on a shelf. It's been a while since I borrowed anything from Jemima, but every single item seems to have changed since then.

"She must spend about an hour a day keeping this tidy," I say, thinking of the jumble that is my own wardrobe.

"She does," says Lissy. "I've seen her."

Mind you, Lissy is even worse. She has all these good intentions—but when she's working hard on a case, her wardrobe basically ends up being a chair in her room, on which all her garments get heaped.

"So!" says Lissy with a grin, and reaches for a white sparkly dress. "What look would Madam like this evening?"

I don't wear the white sparkly dress. But I do try it on. In fact, we both try on quite a lot of stuff, and then have to put it all back, very carefully. At one point another car alarm goes off outside, and we both jump in terror, then immediately pretend we weren't fazed.

In the end, I go for this amazing new red top with slashed shoulders, over my own black DKNY chiffon trousers (twenty-five pounds from the Notting Hill Housing Trust shop), and Jemima's silver high heels from Prada. And then, although I wasn't intending to, at the last minute, I grab a little black Gucci bag.

"You look amazing!" says Lissy as I do a little twirl. "Completely fab!"

"Do I look too smart?"

"Of course not! Come on—you're going out to dinner with a multimillionaire!"

"Don't *say* that!" I exclaim, feeling a clutch of nerves. I look at my watch. It's almost eight o'clock.

Oh, God. In the fun of getting ready, I'd almost forgotten what it was all for.

Keep calm, I tell myself. It's just dinner. That's all it is. Nothing out of the—

"Fuck!" Lissy's looking out the window in the sitting room. "Fuck! There's a great big car outside!"

"What? Where?" I hurry to join her. As I follow her gaze, I almost can't breathe.

An enormous, posh car is waiting outside our house. I mean *enormous*. It's all silver and shiny and looks incredibly conspicuous in our tiny little street. In fact, I can see some curious neighbors looking out of the house opposite.

What am I doing? This is a world I know nothing about. When we were sitting in the plane, Jack and I were just two people on an equal level. But now, look at the world he lives in—and look at the world I live in.

"Lissy," I say in a tiny voice. "I don't want to go."

"Yes, you do!" says Lissy—but I can see she's just as freaked out as I am.

The buzzer goes, and we both jump.

I feel like I might throw up.

OK. OK. Here I go. "Hi," I say into the intercom. "I'll . . . I'll be right down." I replace the phone and look at Lissy.

"Well," I say. "This is it!"

"Emma." Lissy grabs my hands. "Before you go. Don't take any notice of what Jemima said. Just have a lovely time." She hugs me tightly. "Call me if you get a chance!"

"I will!"

I take one last look at myself in the mirror, then make my way down the stairs.

I open the front door, and Jack's standing there, wearing a jacket and tie. His hair is brushed. He looks tidy. For an instant, I feel even more nervous.

Then he smiles—and all my fears fly away like butterflies. Jemima's wrong. This isn't me against him. This is me *with* him.

"Hi," he says. "You look very nice."

"Thanks."

I reach for the door handle, but a man in a peaked cap rushes forward to open it for me.

"Silly me!" I say with a nervous laugh.

I can't quite believe I'm getting into this car. Me. Emma Corrigan. I feel like a princess. I feel like a movie star.

I sit down on the plushy seat, trying not to think how different this is from any car I've ever been in, ever.

"Are you OK?" says Jack.

"Yes! I'm fine!" My voice is a squeak.

"Emma," says Jack. "We're going to have fun. I promise. Did you have your pre-date sweet sherry?"

How did he know—

Oh, yes. I told him on the plane. "Yes, I did, actually," I admit.

"Would you like some more?" He opens the bar, and I see a bottle of Harveys Bristol Cream sitting on a silver platter.

"Did you get that especially for me?" I say in disbelief.

"No, it's my favorite tipple." His expression is so deadpan, I can't help laughing.

"I'll join you," he says as he hands me a glass. "I've never tasted this before." He pours himself a deep measure, takes a sip, and splutters. "Are you serious?"

"It's yummy! It tastes like Christmas!"

"It tastes like . . ." He shakes his head. "I don't even want to tell you what it tastes like. I'll stick to whisky, if you don't mind."

"You're missing out." I take another sip and grin happily at him.

I'm completely relaxed already.

This is going to be the perfect date.

Thirteen

WE ARRIVE at a restaurant in Mayfair that I've never been to before. It's so completely posh, whyever would I?

"It's kind of a small place," Jack murmurs as we walk through a pillared courtyard. "Not many people know about it. But the food is fabulous."

"Mr. Harper. Miss Corrigan," says a man in a Nehru suit, appearing out of nowhere. "Please come this way."

They know my name? Wow.

We glide past more pillars into a softly lit room decorated with huge abstract paintings, candles burning in alcoves, and only a few linen-covered tables. Three other couples are already seated. All the women have diamonds flashing on their hands and ears.

"This is so not my world," I mutter nervously to Jack.

At once he stops. He turns to me, his face serious, while the waiter hovers. "Emma." His voice is low, but distinct. "You are here, having dinner. This is as much your world as any other. OK?" He meets my eyes as though issuing a command, and I feel a ripple of pleasure.

"OK."

There's a couple to our right, and as we walk past, a middle-aged woman with platinum hair and a gold lamé jacket suddenly catches my eye.

"Well, hello!" she says. "Rachel!"

"What?" I halt, bewildered. Is she looking at me?

She gets up from her seat, makes her way over, and plants a kiss on my cheek before I can react. "How are you, darling? We haven't seen you for ages!"

"Not your world, huh?" says Jack in my ear.

You can smell the alcohol on her breath from five yards away. And as I glance over at her dinner partner, he looks just as bad.

"I think you've made a mistake," I say politely. "I'm not Rachel."

"Oh!" The woman frowns for a moment. Then she glances at Jack, and her face snaps in understanding. "Oh! Oh, I see. Of course you're not." She gives me a little wink.

"No!" I say in horror. "You don't understand. I'm *really* not Rachel. I'm Emma!"

"Emma! Of course!" She nods conspiratorially. "Well, have a wonderful dinner! And call me sometime!"

As she stumbles back to her chair, Jack gives me an inquiring look. "Is there something you want to tell me?"

"Yes," I say, trying to keep a straight face. "That woman is extremely drunk."

"Aha." Jack nods. "So, shall we sit down? Or do you have any more long-lost friends you'd like to greet?"

"No . . . I think that's probably it."

"If you're sure," says Jack. "Take your time. You're sure that elderly gentleman over there isn't your grandfather?"

I feel a laugh rising and quell it. This is a posh restaurant. I have to behave with decorum.

We're shown to a table in the corner, by the fire. A waiter helps me into my chair and fluffs my napkin over my knee, while another pours out some water and yet another offers me a bread roll. Exactly the same is happening on Jack's side of the table. We have six people dancing attendance on us! I want to catch Jack's eye and laugh, but he looks unconcerned, like this is perfectly normal.

Perhaps it *is* normal for him, it suddenly strikes me. Oh, God. Perhaps he has a butler who makes him tea and irons his newspaper every day.

But what if he does? I mustn't let any of this faze me.

"Actually, my grandpa never comes to London if he can help it," I say, and give Jack a teasing look. "He thinks it's too full of Americans these days."

"He's absolutely right," replies Jack without a flicker. "Would this be the grandpa who likes Panther bars? Who taught you to ride a bike?"

"That's the one," I say, watching as a waiter adjusts the flowers in our vase. "Do you have a grandpa? Any grandparents?"

"All dead, I'm afraid."

There's a pause. I'm waiting for Jack to add something else. Some detail or other. But . . . he doesn't.

Well, maybe he doesn't like talking about his grandparents.

"So!" I say as the waiting staff melt away. "What shall we have to drink?" I've already eyed up the drink that that woman in gold has. It's all pink and has shaved slices of watermelon decorating the glass, and looks absolutely delicious.

"Already taken care of," says Jack with a smile as one of the waiters brings over a bottle of champagne, pops it open, and starts pouring. "I remember your telling me on the plane, your perfect date would start off with a bottle of champagne appearing at your table as if by magic."

"Oh," I say, quelling a tiny feeling of disappointment. "Er, yes! So I did."

"Cheers," says Jack, and lightly clinks my glass.

"Cheers." I take a sip, and it's delicious champagne. It really is.

I wonder what the watermelon drink tastes like.

Stop it. Champagne is perfect. "The first time I ever had champagne was when I was six years old—" I begin.

"At your aunt Sue's," says Jack. "You took all your clothes off and threw them in the pond."

"Oh, right," I say, halted mid-track. "Yes, I've told you, haven't I?"

So I won't bore him with that anecdote again. I sip my champagne and quickly try to think of something else to say. Something that he doesn't already know.

Is there anything?

"I've chosen a very special meal, which I think you'll like," Jack says, taking a sip of his champagne. "All preordered, just for you."

"Gosh!" I say, taken aback. "How . . . wonderful!"

A meal specially preordered for me! That's incredible.

Except . . . choosing your food is half the fun of eating out, isn't it? It's almost my favorite bit.

Anyway. It doesn't matter. It'll be perfect. It *is* perfect. "Um, so . . . what do you like doing in your spare time?" I ask.

Jack considers for a moment. "I hang out. I watch baseball. I fix my cars . . ."

"You have a collection of vintage cars!" I exclaim. "That's right. I really, um . . ."

"You hate vintage cars." He looks amused. "I remember."

Damn. I was hoping he might have forgotten. "I don't hate the cars themselves!" I say quickly. "I hate the people who . . . who . . ."

Shit. That didn't quite come out right. I take a quick gulp of champagne, but it goes down the wrong way and I start coughing. Oh, God. I'm really spluttering. My eyes are tearing.

And now the other six people in the room have all turned to stare.

"Are you OK?" says Jack in alarm. "Have some water. You like Evian, right?"

"Er, yes. Thanks."

Oh, bloody hell. I hate to admit that Jemima could be right about anything. But it would have been a lot easier if I could just have said, "Oh, I adore vintage cars!"

Anyway. Never mind.

As I'm gulping my water, a plate of roasted peppers somehow materializes in front of me. "I love roasted peppers!" I exclaim in delight.

"I remembered." Jack looks rather proud of himself. "You said on the plane that your favorite food was roasted peppers."

"Did I?" I say in surprise.

I don't remember that. I mean, I *like* roasted peppers, but I wouldn't have said—

"So I called the restaurant and had them make it specially for you. Peppers disagree with me," Jack adds as a plate of scallops appears in front of him, "otherwise, I would join you."

I gape at his plate. Oh, my God. Those scallops look amazing. I *adore* scallops.

"Bon appétit!" says Jack cheerfully.

"Er, yes! *Bon appétit."*

I take a bite of roasted pepper. It's delicious. And it was very thoughtful of him to remember.

But . . . I can't help eyeing his scallops. They're making my mouth water.

"Would you like a bite?" says Jack, following my gaze.

"No!" I say, jumping. "No, thanks! These peppers are absolutely . . . perfect!" I beam at him and take another huge bite.

Suddenly Jack claps a hand on his pocket. "My cell," he says. "Emma . . . would you mind if I took this? It could be something important."

———

When he's gone, I just can't help it. I reach over and spear one of his scallops. I close my eyes as I chew it, letting the flavor flood through my mouth. That is just divine. That is the best food I've ever tasted in my life. I'm just wondering whether I could get away with eating a second one if I shifted the others around his plate a bit, when I smell a whiff of gin. The woman in the golden jacket is right by my ear.

"Tell me quickly!" she says. "What's going on?"

"We're . . . having dinner."

"I can see that!" she says impatiently. "But what about Jeremy? Does he have any idea?"

"Look. I'm not who you think I am—"

"I can see that! I would never have thought you had this in you!" The woman squeezes my arm. "Well, good for you! Have some fun—that's what I say! You took your wedding band off," she adds, glancing at my left hand. "Smart girl . . . oops! He's coming! I'd better go!"

She moves away as Jack sits back down in his place, and I lean forward, already half giggling. Jack is going to love this.

"Guess what!" I say. "I have a husband called Jeremy! My friend over there just came over and told me. So, what do you reckon? Has Jeremy been having a dalliance, too?"

There's silence, and Jack looks up, a strained expression on his face. "I'm sorry?" he says.

He didn't hear a word I said.

I can't say the whole thing again. I'll just feel stupid. In fact . . . I already feel stupid. "It . . . doesn't matter."

There's another silence, and I cast around for something to say. "So, um, I have a confession to make," I say, gesturing to his plate. "I pinched one of your scallops."

I wait for him to pretend to be shocked, or angry. Or *anything*.

"That's OK," he says, and begins to fork the rest of them into his mouth.

I don't understand. What's happened?

———

By the time we've finished our tarragon chicken with rocket salad and chips, my entire body is tense with misery. This date is a disaster. A complete disaster. I've made every effort possible to chat, and joke, and be funny. But Jack's taken two more calls, and the rest of the time he's been all broody and distracted, and to be honest, I might as well not be here.

I feel like crying with disappointment. We were getting on so well. What went wrong?

"I'll . . . just go and freshen up," I say as our main-course plates are removed, and Jack simply nods.

The ladies' is more like a palace than a loo, with spotlit mirrors, dressing tables, plushy chairs, and a woman in uniform to give you a towel. For a moment I feel a bit shy, phoning Lissy in front of her—but she must have seen it all before, mustn't she?

"Hi," I say as Lissy picks up. "It's me."

"Emma! How's it going?"

"It's awful."

"What do you mean?" she says in horror. "How can it be awful? What's happened?"

"That's the worst thing!" I slump into a chair. "It all started off brilliantly. We were laughing and joking, and the restaurant's amazing, and he'd ordered this special menu just for me, all full of my favorite things . . ."

I swallow hard. Now that I put it like that, it does all sound pretty perfect.

"It sounds wonderful!" says Lissy in astonishment. "So, how come—"

"So then he had this call on his mobile." I grab a tissue from a tortoiseshell box and blow my nose. "And ever since, he's barely said a word to me! He keeps disappearing off to take calls, and I'm left on my own, and when he comes back, the conversation's all strained and stilted, and he's obviously only half paying attention."

"Maybe he's worried about something, but he doesn't want to burden you with it," says Lissy after a pause.

"That's true," I say slowly. "He does look pretty hassled."

"Maybe something awful has happened, but he doesn't want to ruin the mood. Just try talking to him."

"OK," I say, feeling more cheerful. "OK, I'll try that. Thanks, Lissy."

I walk back to the table, feeling slightly more positive. A waiter materializes to help me with my chair, and as I sit down I give Jack the warmest, most sympathetic look I can muster. "Jack, is everything OK?"

He frowns. "Why do you say that?"

"Well . . . you keep disappearing off. I just wondered if there was anything . . . you wanted to talk about."

"It's fine," he says curtly. "Thanks." His tone is very much "subject closed," but I'm not going to give up that easily.

"Have you had some bad news?"

"No."

"Is it . . . a business thing?" I persist. "Or . . . or is it some kind of personal . . ."

Jack looks up, a flash of anger in his face. "I said it's nothing. Quit it."

That puts me in my place, doesn't it?

"Would you both care for dessert?" A waiter's voice interrupts me, and I smile as best I can.

"Actually, I don't think so." I've had enough of this evening. I want to go home.

"Very well. Any coffee?"

"She does want dessert," says Jack over my head.

What? *What* did he just say? The waiter looks at me in hesitation.

"No, I don't!"

"Come on, Emma," says Jack, and suddenly his warm,

teasing tone is back. "You don't have to pretend with me. You told me on the plane, this is what you always say. You say you don't want a dessert, when really you do."

"Well, this time I really don't!"

"It's specially created for you." Jack leans forward. "Häagen-Dazs, meringue, Baileys sauce on the side . . ."

I feel completely patronized. How does he know what I want? Maybe I just want fruit. Maybe I want nothing. "I'm not hungry." I push my chair back.

"Emma, I know you. You want it, really—"

"You *don't* know me!" I cry angrily before I can stop myself. "Jack, you may know a whole load of random facts about me. But that doesn't mean you know me!"

"What?"

"If you knew me, you would have realized that when I go out to dinner with someone, I like them to listen to what I'm saying. I like them to treat me with a bit of respect, and not tell them to 'quit it' when all they're doing is trying to make conversation . . ."

Jack looks totally astonished.

"Emma, are you OK?"

"No. I'm not OK! You've practically ignored me all evening."

"That's not fair."

"You have! You've been on autopilot. Ever since your mobile phone started going . . ."

"Look." Jack sighs, thrusting his fingers through his hair. "A few things are going on in my life at the moment. They're very important—"

"Fine. Well, let them go on without me."

Tears are stinging my eyes as I stand up and reach for my bag. I so wanted this to be a perfect evening. I had such high hopes.

"That's right! You tell him!" the woman in gold supportively calls from across the room. "You know, this girl's got a lovely husband of her own!" she exclaims to Jack. "She doesn't need you!"

"Thank you for dinner," I say, gazing fixedly at the table-cloth as one of the waiters magically appears at my side with my coat.

"Emma," says Jack, getting to his feet in disbelief. "You're not seriously going."

"I am."

"Give it another chance. Please. Stay and have some coffee. I promise I'll talk—"

"I don't want any coffee," I say as the waiter helps me on with my coat.

"Mint tea, then. Chocolates! I ordered you a box of Godiva truffles specially . . ." His tone is entreating, and just for an instant I waver. I love Godiva truffles.

No, I've made up my mind. "I don't care. I'm going. Thank you very much," I add to the waiter. "How did you know I wanted my coat?"

"We make it our business to know," says the waiter discreetly.

"You see?" I say to Jack. "*They* know me."

There's an instant of silence.

"Fine," says Jack at last in resignation. "Fine. Daniel will take you home. He should be waiting outside in the car—"

"I'm not going home in your car! I'll make my own way, thanks."

"Emma, don't be stupid—"

"Good-bye. And thanks very much," I add to the waiter. "You were all very attentive and nice to me."

I hurry out of the restaurant to discover it's started to rain. And I don't have an umbrella.

Well, I don't care. I stride along the streets, skidding slightly on the wet pavement, feeling raindrops mingling with tears on my face. I have no idea where I am. I don't even know where the nearest tube is or where . . .

Hang on. There's a bus stop. The Islington bus runs from here.

Well, fine. I'll take the bus home. And then I'll have a nice cup of hot chocolate. And maybe some ice cream in front of the telly.

It's one of those bus shelters with a roof and little seats, and I sit down, thanking God my hair won't get any wetter.

What happened? Did I do something wrong? Did I break some rule I wasn't even aware of? One minute everything's great. The next, it's a disaster. It doesn't make any sense. My mind is running back and forth, trying to work it out, trying to pinpoint the exact moment when things started going wrong, when a big silver car purrs up at the pavement.

I don't believe it.

"Please," says Jack, getting out. "Let me take you home."

"No," I say without turning my head.

"You can't stand here in the rain."

"Yes, I can! Some of us live in the real world, you know."

What does he think? That I'll meekly say "Thank you!" and get in? That just because he's got a fancy car he can behave how he likes?

I turn away and pretend to be studying a poster all about AIDS. The next moment Jack has arrived in the bus shelter. He sits down in the little seat next to mine, and for a while we're both silent.

"I know I was terrible company this evening," he says eventually. "And I'm sorry. And I'm also sorry I can't tell you anything about it. But my life is . . . complicated. And some bits of it are very delicate. Do you understand?"

No, I want to say. No, I don't understand, when I've told you every single, little thing about me.

"I suppose," I say at last.

The rain is beating down even harder, thundering on the roof of the shelter and creeping into my—Jemima's—silver sandals. God, I hope it won't stain them.

"I'm sorry the evening was a disappointment to you," says Jack, lifting his voice above the noise.

"It wasn't," I say, suddenly feeling bad. "I just . . . I had such high hopes! I wanted to get to know you a bit . . . and I wanted to have fun . . . and for us to laugh . . . and I wanted one of those pink cocktails, not champagne . . ."

Shit. *Shit.* That slipped out before I could stop it.

"But . . . you like champagne!" says Jack, looking stunned. "You told me. Your perfect date would start off with champagne."

I can't quite meet his eye. "Yes, well. I didn't know about the pink cocktails then, did I?"

Jack throws back his head and laughs. "Fair point. Very fair point. And I didn't even give you a choice, did I?" He shakes his head ruefully. "You were probably sitting there thinking, 'Damn this guy. Can't he tell I want a pink cocktail?' "

"No!" I say at once, but my cheeks are turning crimson, and Jack is looking at me with such a comical expression, I want to hug him.

"Oh, Emma. I'm sorry." He shakes his head. "I wanted to get to know you, too. And I wanted to have fun, too. It sounds like we both wanted the same things. And it's my fault we didn't get them."

"It's not *your* fault—" I mumble.

"This is not the way I planned for things to go." He looks at me seriously. "Will you give me another chance? Tomorrow night?"

A big red double-decker bus rumbles up to the bus stop, and we both look up.

"I've got to go," I say, standing up. "This is my bus."

"Emma, don't be silly. Come in the car."

I feel a flicker of temptation. The car will be all warm and cozy and comfortable.

But something deeper inside me resists it. I want to show

Jack that I was serious. That I didn't come running out here expecting him to follow me.

"I'm going on the bus."

The automatic doors open, and I step onto the bus. I show my travel card to the driver and he nods.

"You're seriously considering riding on this thing?" says Jack, stepping on behind me. He peers dubiously at the usual motley collection of night bus riders. A man with bulbous eyes looks up at us and hunches his plastic hood over his head. "Is this *safe*?"

"You sound like my grandpa! Of course it's safe. It goes to the end of my road."

"Hurry up!" says the driver impatiently to Jack. "If you haven't got the money, get off."

"I have American Express . . ." says Jack, feeling in his pocket.

"You can't pay a bus fare with American Express!" I say. "Don't you know anything? And anyway"—I stare at my travel card for a few seconds—"I think maybe we should call it an evening. I'm pretty tired."

I'm not really tired. But somehow I want to be alone. I want to clear my head and start again.

"I see," says Jack in a more serious voice. "I guess I'd better get off," he says to the driver. Then he looks at me. "You haven't answered me. Can we try again? Tomorrow night. And this time we'll do whatever you want. You call the shots."

"OK." I try to sound noncommittal, but as I meet his eye, I find myself smiling, too. "Tomorrow."

"Eight o'clock again?"

"Eight o'clock. And leave the car behind," I add firmly. "We'll do things my way."

"Great! I look forward to it. Good night, Emma."

"Good night."

As he turns to get off, I climb the stairs to the top deck of the bus. I head for the front seat, the place I always used to sit when I was a child, and look out at the dark, rainy London night. If I gaze for long enough, the streetlights become blurred like a kaleidoscope. Like a fairyland.

That date was nothing like I expected it to be.

Not that I knew what to expect. But I did have the odd imaginary scenario in my head, ranging from dreadful (he doesn't turn up; it turns out he's a Nazi) to fantastic (we end up making love on a speedboat on the Thames and he asks me to marry him. Actually I think that one might have been a dream).

The real thing was somehow better and worse, all at once. I wasn't expecting to storm out. I wasn't expecting to cry. I wasn't expecting Jack to have made such an effort.

Swooshing around my mind are images of the woman in gold, the pink cocktail, Jack's expression as I said I was leaving, the waiter bringing me my coat, Jack's car arriving at the bus stop. Everything's jumbled up. I can't quite straighten my thoughts. All I can do is sit there, aware of familiar, comforting sounds around me. The old-fashioned grind and roar of the bus engine. The noise of the doors swishing open and shut. The sharp ring of the request bell. People thumping up the stairs and thumping back down again.

I can feel the bus swaying as we turn corners, but I'm barely even aware of where we're going. Until after a while, I start to take in familiar sights outside, and I realize we're nearly at my street. I gather myself, reach for my bag, and totter along to the top of the stairs.

Suddenly the bus makes a sharp swing left, and I grab for a seat handle, trying to steady myself. Why are we turning left? I look out of the window, thinking I'll be really pissed off if I end up having to walk, and blink in astonishment.

We're in my tiny little road.

And now we've stopped outside my house.

I hurry down the stairs, nearly breaking my ankle.

"Forty-one Elmwood Road," the driver says with a flourish.

No. This can't be happening.

I look around the bus in bewilderment, and a couple of drunk teenagers leer at me.

"What's going on?" I look at the driver. "Did he *pay* you?"

"Five hundred quid," says the driver, and winks at me. "Whoever he is, love, I'd hold on to him."

Five hundred quid? "Thanks," I manage. "I mean . . . thanks for the ride."

Feeling as though I'm in a dream, I get off the bus and head for the front door. But Lissy has already got there and is opening it. She looks totally mystified.

"What on earth's a *bus* doing here?"

"It's my bus," I say. "It took me home."

I wave to the driver, who waves back, and the bus rumbles off into the night.

Fourteen

OK. DON'T TELL ANYONE. Do *not* tell anyone that you were on a date with Jack Harper last night.

As I arrive at work the next day, I feel almost convinced I'm going to blurt it out by mistake. Or someone's going to guess. I mean, surely it must be obvious from my face. From my clothes. From the way I'm walking. I feel as though everything I do screams, "Hey, guess what I did last night!"

"Hiya," says Caroline as I make myself a cup of coffee. "How are you?"

"I'm fine, thanks!" I say, giving a guilty jump. "I just had a quiet evening in last night. With my flatmate. We watched three videos, *Pretty Woman, Notting Hill,* and *Four Weddings.* Just the two of us. No one else."

"Right!" says Caroline, looking a bit bemused. "Er, lovely!"

I'm losing it. Everyone knows this is how criminals get caught. They add too many details and trip themselves up.

Right, no more babbling.

"Hi," says Artemis as I sit down at my desk.

"Hi," I say, forcing myself to keep it at that. I won't even mention which kind of pizza Lissy and I ordered, even though I've got a whole story ready about how the pizza company thought we said green pepper instead of pepperoni, ha-ha, what a mix-up.

I'm supposed to be working on a money-off flyer for Panther Prime this morning. But instead, I find myself taking out a piece of paper and starting a list of possible date venues where I can take Jack tonight.

1. Pub. No. Far too boring.
2. Movie. No. Too much sitting, not talking to each other.
3. Ice-skating. Jack and I will glide around to music in seamless harmony . . . No. I can't skate. I'll end up twisting my ankle.
4.

I've run out of ideas already. How crap is this?

Suddenly I have a thought. I read this article on marketing innovation last month that said if your mind was blank, you should write buzzwords like SUCCESS and CUSTOMER and DE-SIRES on a piece of paper and wait for them to stimulate your brain.

I think for a bit, then write down, JACK, DATE, ROMANCE, KISS. I gaze at the words, trying to focus. But it's hard to concentrate when my brain is half tuning in to the idle conversation going on around me.

". . . really working on some secret project, or is that just a rumor?"

". . . company in a new direction, apparently, but no one knows exactly what he's . . ."

". . . *is* this Sven guy anyway? I mean, what function does he have?"

"He's Jack's bodyguard, isn't he?" says someone.

That's it. That's exactly what Sven looks like. A body-guard. Or a hit man. Maybe he's in charge of "dealing" with Jack's competitors.

"He's with Jack, isn't he?" says Amy, who works in Finance but fancies Nick, so she's always finding excuses to come into our office. "He must be Jack's lover."

"What?" I say, sitting up suddenly and snapping the point of my pencil. Luckily everyone's too busy gossiping to notice.

Jack gay? Jack gay?

That's why he didn't kiss me good night. He only wants me to be a friend. He'll introduce me to Sven and I'll have to pretend to be all cool with it, like I knew all along—

"Is Jack Harper gay?" Caroline is saying in astonishment.

"I just assumed he was," says Amy with a shrug. "There's no woman on the scene—"

"But he doesn't look groomed enough!"

"I don't think he looks gay!" I chip in, trying to sound lighthearted and just kind of vaguely interested.

"He's not gay," chimes in Artemis authoritatively. "I read an old profile of him in *Newsweek,* and he was dating the female president of Origin Software. And it said before that he went out with some supermodel."

A huge surge of relief floods through me.

Obviously I knew he wasn't gay.

"So, is Jack seeing anyone at the moment?"

"Who knows?"

"He's pretty sexy, don't you think?" says Caroline with a wicked grin. "I wouldn't mind."

"Yeah, right," says Nick. "You probably wouldn't mind his limo, either."

"Apparently, he hasn't had a relationship since Pete Laidler died," says Artemis crisply. "So I doubt you've got much of a chance."

"Bad luck, Caroline," says Nick with a laugh.

Just for an instant, I find myself imagining what would

happen if I stood up and said, "Actually I had dinner with Jack Harper last night." They'd all be utterly dumbfounded. There'd be gasps, and questions . . .

Oh, who am I kidding? They wouldn't believe me, would they? They'd say I was suffering from delusions.

"Hi, Connor," comes Caroline's voice, interrupting my thoughts.

Connor? I look up and there he is, with no warning, approaching my desk.

What's he doing here?

Has he found out about me and Jack?

I push my hair back, feeling nervous. I've spotted him a couple of times around the building, but this is our first moment face-to-face since we broke up.

"Hi," he says.

"Hi," I reply awkwardly, and there's silence.

Suddenly I notice my unfinished list of date ideas lying on my desk, with KISS clearly visible. Shit. Trying to stay casual, I reach for it, ball it up, and drop it in the bin.

Around us, all the gossip about Sven and Jack has petered out. I know everyone in the office is listening to us, even if they're pretending to be doing something else. It's like we're the in-house soap opera or something.

And I know which character I am. I'm the heartless bitch who chucked her lovely, decent man for no good reason.

The thing is, I do feel guilty. Every time I see Connor, or even think about him, I get a horrible tight feeling in my chest. But does he *have* to have such an expression of injured dignity on his face? A kind of you've-mortally-wounded-me-but-I'm-such-a-good-person-I-forgive-you kind of look.

I can feel my guilt ebbing away and annoyance starting to rise.

"I only came up," says Connor at last, "because I'd put us down to do a stint on the Pimm's stall together at the corporate family day. Obviously when I did so, I thought we'd be—"

He breaks off, looking more martyred than ever. "Anyway. But I don't mind going through with it. If you don't."

I'm not going to be the one to say I can't bear to stand next to him for half an hour. "I don't mind!" I say.

"Fine."

"Fine."

There's another awkward pause.

"I found your blue shirt, by the way," I say. "I'll bring it in."

"Thanks. I think I've got some stuff of yours, too . . ."

"Hey," says Nick, coming over toward us with a wicked, eyes-gleaming, let's-stir-shit expression. "I saw you with someone last night."

I feel a spasm of terror. Fuck! Fuck, fuck. OK . . . OK . . . It's OK. He's not looking at me. He's looking at Connor.

Who the hell was Connor with?

"That was just a friend," says Connor stiffly.

"Are you sure?" says Nick. "You looked pretty friendly to me—"

"Shut up, Nick," says Connor, looking pained. "It's far too early to be thinking of . . . moving on. Isn't it, Emma?"

"Er, yes." I swallow several times. "Absolutely. Definitely."

Oh, God.

Anyway. I'm not going to worry about Connor. I have an important date to think about. And thank goodness, by the end of the day I have at last come up with the perfect venue. It only takes me about half an hour to persuade Lissy that when they said, "The key shall in no circumstances be transferred to any nonmember" in the rules, they didn't really mean it.

At last she reaches into her bag and hands it to me, an anxious expression on her face. "Don't lose it!"

"I won't! Thanks, Liss." I give her a hug.

"You remember the password, don't you?"

"Yes. 'Alexander.' "

"Where are you going?" says Jemima, coming into my room in a black trouser suit and enormous creamy pearls. She gives me a critical look. "Nice top. Where's it from?"

"Oxfam. I mean Whistles."

I've decided tonight I'm not even going to *try* to borrow anything from Jemima. I'm going to wear my nice gray velvet top and black satin skirt, and if Jack doesn't like it, he can lump it.

"I was meaning to ask," Jemima says, narrowing her eyes. "You two didn't go into my room last night, did you?"

"No," says Lissy innocently. "Why—did it look like we had?"

Jemima was out until three last night, and by the time she got back, everything was back in place. Sellotape and everything. We couldn't have been more careful.

"No," admits Jemima. "Nothing was out of place. But I just got a *feeling*. As though someone had been in there."

"Did you leave the window open?" says Lissy. "Because I read this article recently, about how monkeys are being sent into houses to steal things."

"Monkeys?"

"Apparently. The thieves train them."

Jemima looks from Lissy to me, perplexed, and I force myself to keep a straight face.

"Anyway," I say to change the subject. "You might like to know that you were wrong about Jack. I'm going out with him again tonight! It wasn't a disastrous date at all!"

There's no need to add that we had a big row and I stormed out and he had to follow me to the bus stop. Because the point is, we're having a second date.

"I wasn't wrong," says Jemima. "You just wait. I predict doom." She glances at herself in the mirror and adjusts her necklace.

"Nice pearls," says Lissy. "First date?"

Jemima always follows Mummy's rule: on first dates you wear "prestige jewelry"—that is, real gems, not something cute from Accessorize. You also drop it into the conversation that you collect Tahitian pearls, diamonds, or whatever, and that you're allergic to base metal.

The rule was started years ago, apparently, after Jemima's mother had a date with an oil billionaire and wore a simple silver chain. The following day a box arrived from Cartier—containing another simple silver chain and a note from the oil billionaire about how he'd had to restrain himself from buying anything more ostentatious.

And then, two weeks later, he died. Apparently she's never really got over it.

"Well, ciao. See you later." Jemima tweaks her pearls one last time, smooths her hair down, and leaves the room. I pull a face at her skinny back and start putting on my mascara.

Honestly. Doom. She's just *trying* to spoil things.

"What's the time?" I say, frowning as I blob a bit on my eyelid.

"Ten to eight," says Lissy. "How are you going to get there?"

"Cab."

Suddenly the buzzer goes, and we both look up.

"He's early," says Lissy. "That's a bit weird."

"He can't be early!" We both hurry into the sitting room, and Lissy gets to the window first.

"Oh, shit," she says, looking down to the street below. "It's Connor."

"*Connor?*" I stare at her in horror. "Connor's here?"

"He's holding a box of stuff. Shall I buzz him up?"

"No! Pretend we're not in!"

"Too late," says Lissy, and pulls a face. "Sorry. He's seen me."

The buzzer sounds again, and we exchange helpless looks.

"OK," I say at last. "I'm going down."

Shit, shit, shit . . .

I pelt downstairs and open the door. And there, standing on the doorstep, is Connor, wearing the same martyred expression he had at the office.

"Hi," he says. "Here are the things I was telling you about. I thought you might need them."

"Er, thanks," I say, grabbing the box, which seems to contain one bottle of L'Oréal shampoo and some jumper I've never seen in my life. "I haven't quite sorted out your stuff yet, so I'll bring it to the office, shall I?"

I dump the box on the stairs, and quickly turn back before Connor thinks I'm inviting him in.

"So, um, thanks," I say. "It was really good of you to stop by."

"No problem," says Connor. He gives a heavy sigh. "Emma . . . I was thinking perhaps we could use this as an opportunity to talk. Maybe we could have a drink, or supper, even . . ."

"Gosh," I say. "I'd love that. I really would. But to be honest, now isn't a *brilliant* time . . ."

"Are you going out?" His face falls.

"Um, yes. With Lissy." I glance at my watch. It's six minutes to eight. "So anyway, I'll see you soon. You know, around the office . . ."

"Why are you so flustered?"

"I'm not flustered!" I say, and lean casually against the door frame.

"What's wrong?" His eyes narrow, and he looks past me into the hall. "Is something going on?"

"Connor." I put a reassuring hand on his arm. "Nothing's going on. You're imagining things."

At that moment, Lissy appears behind me at the door. "Um, Emma, there's a very urgent phone call for you," she says

in a really stilted voice. "You'd better come straightaway . . .
Oh, hello, Connor!"

The trouble is, Lissy is the worst liar in the world.

"You're trying to get rid of me!" says Connor, looking
from Lissy to me in shock.

"No, we're not!" says Lissy, flushing bright red.

"Hang on," says Connor suddenly, staring at my outfit.
"Hang on a minute. I don't . . . Are you going on a . . . date?"

My mind works quickly. If I deny it, we'll probably get
into some huge argument. But if I admit the truth . . . maybe
he'll stalk off in a huff! "You're right," I say. "I've got a date."

There's a shocked silence.

"I don't believe this," says Connor, shaking his head, and,
to my dismay, descends heavily down onto the garden wall. I
glance at my watch. Three minutes to eight. Shit!

"Connor—"

"You told me there wasn't anyone else! You promised,
Emma!"

"There wasn't! But . . . there is now. And he'll be here
soon . . . Connor, you really don't want to get into this." I
grab his arm and try to lift him, but he weighs about 160
pounds. "Connor, please. Don't make this more painful for
everyone."

"I suppose you're right." At last Connor gets to his feet.
"I'll go."

He walks to the gate, his back hunched in defeat, and I feel
a sudden pang of guilt mixed with a desperate desire for him
to hurry. Then, to my horror, he turns back. "So, who is it?"

"It's . . . it's someone you don't know," I say, crossing my
fingers behind my back. "Look, we'll have lunch soon and
have a good talk. Or something. I promise."

"OK," says Connor, looking more wounded than ever.
"Fine. I get the message."

I watch, unable to breathe, as he shuts the gate behind him

and walks slowly along the street. Keep walking, keep walking . . . Don't stop . . .

As Connor finally rounds the corner, Jack's silver car appears at the other end of the street.

"Bloody hell," murmurs Lissy. "If Jack had been a *minute* early . . ."

"Don't!" I collapse onto the stone wall. "Lissy, I can't cope with this."

I feel all shaky. I think I need a drink. Abruptly I realize I've only got mascara on one set of eyelashes.

The silver car pulls up in front of the house, and out gets the same uniformed driver as before. He opens the passenger door, and Jack steps out. The formal jacket and tie have gone—he's wearing a casual blue shirt over jeans.

"Hi!" he says, looking taken aback to see me. "Am I late?"

"No! I was just, um, sitting here. You know. Taking in the view." I gesture across the road, where I notice for the first time that a man with a huge belly is changing a tire on his Fiat. "Anyway!" I say, hastily standing up. "Actually . . . I'm not quite ready. Do you want to come up for a minute?"

"Sure. That would be nice."

"And send your car away!" I add. "You weren't supposed to have it!"

"You weren't supposed to be sitting outside your house and catch me," counters Jack. "OK, Daniel, that's it for the night." He nods to the driver. "I'm in this lady's hands from now on."

"This is Lissy, my flatmate," I say as the driver gets back into the car. "Lissy, Jack."

"Hi," says Lissy, looking a bit self-conscious as they shake hands.

As we make our way up the stairs to our flat, I'm suddenly aware of how narrow they are and how the cream paint on the walls is all scuffed and the carpet smells of cabbage. Jack probably lives in some enormous, grand mansion. He probably has a marble staircase or something.

But so what? It's probably awful. All cold and clattery.

"Emma, if you want to get ready, I'll fix Jack a drink," says Lissy, with a smile that says, "he's nice!"

"Thanks," I say, shooting back an "isn't he?" look. I hurry into my room and hurriedly start applying mascara to my other eye.

A few moments later there's a little knock at my door.

"Hi!" I say, expecting Lissy. But in comes Jack, holding out a glass of sweet sherry.

"Oh, thanks!" I say gratefully. "I could do with a drink."

"I won't come in—"

"No, it's fine. Sit down!"

I gesture to the bed, but it's covered with clothes. And my dressing table stool is piled high with magazines. Damn, I should have tidied up a bit.

"I'll stand," says Jack. He takes a sip of what looks like a whisky and looks around my room in fascination. "So this is your room. Your world."

"Yes." I flush slightly, unscrewing my lip gloss. "It's a bit messy—"

"It's very nice. Very homey." I can see him taking in the shoes piled in the corner, the fish mobile hanging from my light, the mirror with necklaces strung over the side, and a new skirt hanging on the wardrobe door.

"Cancer Research?" he says puzzledly, looking at the label. "What does that—"

"It's a shop," I say, a little defiant. "A secondhand shop."

"Ah." He nods in tactful comprehension. "Nice bedspread," he adds, smiling.

"It's ironic," I say in haste. "It's an ironic statement."

God, how embarrassing. I should have changed it.

Now Jack's staring incredulously at my open dressing table

drawer crammed with makeup. "How many lipsticks do you have?"

"Er, a few . . ." I say, closing it.

Maybe it wasn't such a great idea to let Jack come in here. Now he's picking up my Perfectil vitamins and examining them. I mean, what's so interesting about *vitamins*?

"Did you grow up in the city?" I say to distract him. "Or in the country?"

"Kind of between." Jack looks up from the Perfectil pack. "So these are beauty vitamins? You don't take them for the health benefits?"

"Well." I clear my throat, feeling a bit shallow. "Obviously I take them for both health *and* beauty reasons. . . ." I reach for my earring box. "So . . . which do you prefer? Town or country?"

Jack doesn't seem to hear. He's looking at Katie's crochet belt. "What's this? A snake?"

"It's a belt," I say, screwing up my face as I put in an earring. "I know. It's hideous. I can't stand crochet."

Where's my other earring? Where?

Oh, OK, here it is. Now what's Jack doing?

I turn to see him looking in fascination at my exercise chart, which I put up in January after I'd spent the entire Christmas eating chocolates.

" 'Monday, seven A.M.' " he reads aloud. " 'Brisk jog around block. Forty sit-ups. Lunch time: yoga class. Evening: Pilates tape. Sixty sit-ups.' " He takes a sip of whisky. "Very impressive. You do all this?"

"Well," I say after a pause, "I don't exactly manage every *single* . . . I mean, it was quite an ambitious . . . you know, er, anyway!" I quickly spritz myself with perfume. "Let's go!"

I have to get him out of here quickly before he does something like spot a Tampax and ask me what it is. I mean, honestly! Why on earth is he so *interested* in everything?

Fifteen

As we head out into the balmy evening, I feel light and happy with anticipation. This evening already has a completely different atmosphere from yesterday night. No scary cars; no posh restaurants. It feels more casual. More fun.

I hail a cab, and as we whizz along Upper Street, I feel quite proud of myself. It just shows, I'm a true Londoner. I can take my guests to little places off the beaten track. I can find spots that aren't just the obvious venues to go. I mean, not that Jack's restaurant wasn't amazing. But how much cooler will this be? A secret club! And I mean—who knows—Ewan might come back this evening!

We stop at some traffic lights. Outside, plastered across a building, is a huge billboard advertising Panther Cola.

"It must be weird being you," I say without thinking. Jack looks at me, and I realize that came out wrong. "I just mean . . . it's all around you. Everywhere you look, the Panther logo. Like a symbol of your success."

"Well, sure," he says, giving me a wry look. "And of course my failures."

Failures? "You've never failed at anything!" I say, affronted. "You're a successful, creative marketing genius. Everyone knows that."

Jack laughs. "You think I've had nothing but success? You want to hear about some of the great Panther failures? Like . . ." He considers for a moment. "The Panther tan tattoo."

"The what?"

"We developed this back in the eighties. A transparent sticky plastic shape. You stuck it on your skin, sunbathed, and . . . zowee. When you peeled it off at the end of a day in the sun, you had a shape on your back. A pair of lips, a flower, whatever. Let me tell you, this was going to be the latest craze." He pauses. "Before skin cancer came in, of course."

"What happened?"

"We lost half a million dollars," says Jack simply. "A lot, back then."

"Blimey."

I'm utterly taken aback. I've never thought of Jack as failing at anything.

"Then there was the Panther pogo stick . . . and the Panther pool cue. What a disaster." Jack shakes his head reminiscently. "Pete's fault. He started playing pool every night. Fine. But he couldn't leave it at that." He puts on a British accent. " 'Jack, believe me. Every red-blooded male, deep down, wants his own pool cue.' " Jack gives me a rueful look. "Like hell they do."

I laugh at his comical expression. Then all of a sudden the light fades from his eyes, and he looks out of the window, frowning. It's like he's trying to control himself.

"You still miss Pete?" I say hesitantly.

"Yeah."

"It must be really hard," I say, feeling inadequate.

"It's hard." He nods. "And it's tiring. Doing it all alone.

Pete and I . . . we spoke a kind of shorthand. We bounced off each other. Gave each other energy. We worked hard . . . but it wasn't all meetings and formality." Jack pauses. "You know, we took a vacation together every summer. People didn't understand it. But that's where we got the most work done all year."

"He must have been . . . an amazing person." I bite my lip.

Jack's silent, and I feel a dart of nerves. Maybe I shouldn't have asked about Pete. Maybe I've gone too far.

"He had a glow about him," he says suddenly. "He had this phenomenal . . . energy. Pete was the kind of guy who'd walk into a meeting, take the room over, and make a bunch of promises he couldn't fulfill. Then somehow . . . he'd fulfill them." Jack turns to look at me. He's smiling, but his eyes are shiny. " 'Don't Pause.' That was Pete."

"That'll be eight-fifty," comes the cabbie's voice from the front, and I give a startled jump. We're in Clerkenwell. I'd almost forgotten what we were doing.

As we get out into the fresh air, the intense mood of the taxi ride disappears. I insist on paying the fare and lead Jack down the alley.

"Very interesting!" says Jack, looking around. "So, where are we going?"

"Just wait," I say enigmatically. I head for the door, press the buzzer, and take Lissy's key out of my pocket with a little frisson of excitement.

He is going to be so impressed. He is going to be *so* impressed!

"Hello?" comes a voice.

"Hello," I say casually. "I'd like to speak to Alexander, please."

"Who?" says the voice.

"Alexander," I repeat, and give a little knowing smile. Obviously they have to double-check.

"Ees no Alexander here."

"You don't understand. Al-ex-an-der," I enunciate clearly.

"Ees no Alexander."

Maybe this is the wrong door, it suddenly occurs to me. I mean, I remember it as being this one—but maybe it was this other one, with the frosted glass. Yes. This one looks quite familiar, actually.

"Tiny hitch." I smile at Jack and press the new bell.

There's silence. I wait a few minutes, then try again, and again. There's no reply.

OK. So . . . it's not this one, either.

Fuck.

I am a moron. Why didn't I check the address? I was just so sure I'd remember where it was.

"Is there a problem?" says Jack.

"No!" I say at once. "I'm just not *entirely* sure . . ."

I look up and down the street, trying not to panic. Which one was it? Am I going to have to ring every doorbell in the street? I take a few steps along the pavement to trigger my memory. And suddenly, through an arch, I spy another alley almost identical to this one.

I feel cold with horror. Am I in the right *alley,* even? I dart forward and peer into the other alley. It looks exactly the same: rows of nondescript doors and blanked-out windows.

What am I going to do? I can't try every single doorbell in every bloody alley in the vicinity. It never once occurred to me that this might happen. Not once. I never even thought to—

OK, I'm being stupid. I'll call Lissy! She'll tell me.

I pull out my mobile and dial home, but immediately it clicks onto voice mail.

"Hi, Lissy, it's me," I say, trying to sound light and casual. "A small problem has arisen, which is that I can't remember exactly which door the club is behind. Or actually . . . which alley it's in, either. So if you get this, could you give me a call? Thanks!"

I switch off, then turn to Jack with the brightest, most I'm-in-control expression I can muster.

"Just a slight glitch," I say, and give a relaxed little laugh. "There's this secret club along here somewhere, but I can't quite remember where."

"Never mind," says Jack. "These things happen."

I feel a sinking sensation at his polite voice. He's just being kind. These things never happen to him. Of course they don't.

I jab the number for home again, but it's still engaged. Quickly I dial Lissy's mobile number, but it's switched off.

Oh, fuck. Fuck. We can't stand here in the street all night.

"Emma," says Jack, "would you like me to make a reservation at—"

"No!" I jump as though stung. Jack's not going to reserve anything. I've said I'll organize this evening, and I will. "No, thanks. It's OK." I make a snap decision. "Change of plan. We'll go to Antonio's instead."

"I could call the car—" begins Jack.

"We don't need the car!" I stride toward the main road, and, thank God, a taxi's coming toward us with its light on. I flag it down, open the door for Jack, and say to the driver, "Hi, Antonio's on Sanderstead Road in Clapham, please."

Hurrah. I have been grown-up and decisive and saved the situation.

"What's Antonio's?" says Jack as the taxi begins to speed away.

"It's a bit out of the way, in south London. But it's really nice. Lissy and I used to go there when we lived in Wandsworth. It's got huge pine tables and gorgeous food and sofas and stuff. And they never chivvy you."

"It sounds perfect," says Jack.

———

OK, it should *not* take this long to get from Clerkenwell to Clapham. We should have gotten there ages ago. I mean, it's only down the road! After we've sat in one solid congested patch of traffic for five minutes, I lean forward and say to the driver yet again, "Is there a problem?"

"Traffic, love." He gives an easy shrug. "What can you do?"

You can find a clever traffic-avoiding back route like taxi drivers are supposed to! I want to yell furiously. But instead I say politely, "So . . . how long do you think it'll be before we get there?"

"Who knows?"

I lean back on my seat, feeling my stomach churning with frustration. We should have gone somewhere in Clerkenwell. Or Covent Garden. I am such a moron . . .

"I'm sorry," I mumble. "This hasn't been one of my greatest successes . . ."

"Don't worry about it."

"I had it all planned out—"

"Emma, really. Don't worry. Everything's fine."

Just then the taxi swings sharply around a corner, and I'm thrown up against Jack. Without my intending to, my brain immediately catalogs that his shirt is crisp, that his body feels hard and muscular, that he's got the faintest five o'clock shadow, that the skin of his neck is completely different from Connor's, that I have the strongest urge to reach up and touch him . . .

"Sorry!" I laugh. "These taxis . . ." I pull away and start to fumble with my seat belt, aware that my cheeks are flaming.

I really am taking the prize for least cool date in the universe.

"Since we're on the subject," says Jack, as though nothing just happened. "What have been your greatest successes?"

"My what?"

"Just off the top of your head. Since I told you about my failures . . ." He gives me a wry look.

"Well . . . OK."

I think for a moment. My successes in life. It's not exactly a long list. "I suppose the first would be getting my job. Second would be . . ." I come to a halt.

"Or something you're proud of," puts in Jack. "Anything."

"Getting Lissy out of her room after her boyfriend chucked her," I reply promptly. "She was a total wreck. She didn't wash her hair and she didn't eat, and she had this big case she had to prepare for, but she just kept crying and saying she didn't care anymore . . ."

"So, what did you do?" Jack sits up, looking intrigued.

"I tricked her. I pretended to set the kitchen on fire. The smoke alarms were going off, and I was shrieking. She came rushing out . . . and there was a tea party waiting for her. With a big cake." I can't help smiling at the memory. "So she cried some more. But at least she was out . . ."

"You two must be close," says Jack.

"We've just been best friends forever." I shrug. "You know . . ."

"I do." Jack nods.

Suddenly I realize what I've said. Oh, God. I hope I haven't upset him.

"There's a third!" I exclaim, trying to lighten the atmosphere. "I have three successes to my name."

"Three?" Jack responds with mock amazement. "Are you superhuman?"

"I got a joke published in a magazine when I was ten!"

"You had a joke published?" He sounds genuinely impressed. "Tell it to me."

" 'A ghost walks into a bar. And the barman says . . .' "

" 'We don't serve spirits.' " Jack gives me a quizzical look. "That's a very old joke."

"They didn't say it had to be original," I retort. "I still got five quid for it."

I glance out of the window. We're still only in Battersea. How can we be going so *slowly*?

"You know, that's a perfect exercise in marketing," Jack is saying. "Take an old product . . . repackage it . . . sell it. People have written books about how to do this. You obviously have the natural instinct."

"Well, you know . . . maybe I'll make millions one day, like you," I say lightly.

"Is that what you want?" asks Jack. "To make millions?"

"Absolutely!" I'm uncertain whether he's teasing or not. "Billions, preferably."

"I'm serious. What does Emma Corrigan want out of life? Money? Fame? Security?"

"Happiness, I suppose. Doing what I want to be doing. Feeling I've made my mark on the world."

A promotion, I add silently. And thinner thighs would be nice.

I look out of the window again and feel a lift in spirits. At last. We're in Clapham! Nearly there . . . As we halt at a red light, I can barely keep still on my seat for frustration. Precious time is ticking away and the driver's just sitting there like it doesn't matter . . .

Green! It's green! Go now!

OK, calm down, Emma. Here's the street. We're finally here. "So this is it!" I say, trying to sound relaxed as we get out of the taxi. "Sorry it took a while . . ."

"No problem," says Jack. "This place looks great."

As I hand the fare to the taxi driver, I have to admit, I'm pretty pleased we came. Antonio's looks absolutely amazing! There are fairy lights decorating the familiar green facade, and helium balloons tied to the canopy, and music and laughter spilling out of the open door. I can even hear people singing inside.

"It's not normally quite *this* buzzing!" I say with a laugh, and head for the door. I can already see Antonio standing just inside. His thick, graying hair is as bushy as ever, and he's as plump as one of his own ravioli bundles.

"Hi!" I say as I push the door open. "Antonio!"

"Emma!" says Antonio. His cheeks are rosy; he's holding a glass of wine and is beaming even more widely than usual. *"Bellissima!"*

He kisses me on each cheek, and I feel a flood of warm relief. I was right to come here. I know the management. They'll make sure we have a wonderful time.

"This is Jack."

"Jack! Wonderful to meet you!" Antonio kisses Jack on each cheek, too.

"So, could we have a table for two?"

"Ah . . ." He pulls a face of regret. "Sweetheart, we're closed!"

"What? But . . . but you're not closed. People are here!" I look around at all the merry faces.

"It's a private party!" He raises his glass to someone across the room and shouts something in Italian. "My nephew's wedding. You ever meet him? Guido. He served here a few summers ago . . ."

"I . . . I'm not sure."

"He met a lovely girl at the law school. You know, he's qualified now! You ever need legal advice . . ."

"Thanks. Well . . . congratulations."

"I hope the party goes well," says Jack, and squeezes my arm. "Never mind, Emma. You couldn't have known."

"Darling, I'm sorry!" says Antonio, seeing my face. "Another night, I'll give you the best table we have. You call in advance—you let me know . . ."

"I'll do that." I manage a smile. "Thanks, Antonio."

I can't even look at Jack. I dragged him all the way down to bloody Clapham for this.

I have to redeem this situation. Quickly. "We'll go to the pub!" I say as soon as we're outside on the pavement. "I mean, what's wrong with just sitting down with a nice drink?"

"Sounds good," says Jack, and follows me as I hurry down the street to a sign reading "The Nag's Head" and push the door open. I've never been in this pub before, but surely it's bound to be fairly—

OK. Maybe not.

This has to be the grimmest pub I've ever seen in my life. Threadbare carpet, no music, and with no signs of life except a single man with a paunch.

I cannot have a date with Jack in here. I just can't. "Right!" I say, swinging the door shut again. "Let's think again." I quickly look up and down the street, but apart from Antonio's everything is shut except for a couple of grotty take-away places and a minicab firm. "Well . . . let's just grab a taxi and head back to town!" I say with a kind of shrill brightness. "It won't take too long."

I stride to the edge of the pavement and stick out my hand.

During the next three minutes, not a single car passes by. Not just no taxis. No vehicles at all.

"Kind of quiet," observes Jack at last.

"Well, this is really kind of a residential area. Antonio's is a bit of a one-off."

Outwardly, I'm still quite calm. But inside I'm starting to panic. What are we going to do? Should we try to walk to Clapham High Street? But it's bloody miles away.

I glance at my watch and am shocked to see that it's nine-fifteen. We've spent over an hour faffing about and we haven't even had a drink. And it's all my fault.

I can't even organize one simple evening without its going catastrophically wrong.

Suddenly I want to burst into tears. I want to sink down on the pavement and bury my head in my hands and sob.

"How about pizza?" says Jack, and I feel a pinprick of hope.

"Why? Do you know a pizza place around—"

"I see pizza for sale." He nods at one of the grotty take-away places. "And I see a bench." He gestures to the other side of the road, where there's a tiny railed garden with paving and trees and a wooden bench. "You get the pizza. I'll save the bench."

I have never felt so mortified in my entire life. Ever.

Jack Harper takes me to the grandest, poshest restaurant in the world, and I take him to a park bench in Clapham.

"Here's your pizza," I say, carrying the hot boxes over to where he's sitting. "I got margherita, ham and mushroom, and pepperoni."

I can't quite believe this is going to be our supper. I mean, they aren't even *nice* pizzas. They aren't even gourmet, roasted-artichoke type of pizzas. They're just cheap slabs of dough pastry with melted, congealed cheese and a few dodgy toppings.

"Perfect," says Jack. He takes a large bite, then reaches into his inside pocket. "Now, this was supposed to be your going-home present, but since we're here . . ."

I gape as he produces a small stainless steel cocktail shaker and two matching cups. He unscrews the top of the shaker and, to my astonishment, pours a pink, transparent liquid into each cup.

Is that . . .

"I don't believe it!" I gaze at him, wide-eyed.

"Well, come on. I couldn't let you wonder all your life what it tasted like, could I?" He hands me a cup and raises his toward me. "Your good health."

"Cheers." I take a sip of the cocktail . . . and—oh, my God—it's yummy. Sharp and sweet, with a kick of vodka.

"Good?"

"Delicious!" I say, and take another sip.

He's being so nice to me. He's pretending he's having a good time. But what does he think inside? He must despise me. He must think I'm a complete and utter dizzy cow.

"Emma . . . are you OK?"

"Not really," I say in a thick voice. "Jack . . . I'm so sorry. I really am. I honestly had it all planned. We were going to go to this really cool club where celebrities go, and it was going to be really good fun . . ."

"Emma." Jack puts his drink down and looks at me. "I wanted to spend this evening with you. And that's what we're doing."

"Yes. But—"

"That's what we're doing," he repeats firmly.

He leans toward me, and my throat tightens in excitement. This is it. He's going to kiss me. He's going to—

Suddenly I stiffen in a rictus of horror.

Jack stops moving, puzzled. "Emma? Are you OK?"

"It's just . . . a spider," I manage through clenched teeth, and jerk my head at my leg.

A big black spider is slowly crawling up my ankle. I feel almost sick, just looking at it.

With one brisk swipe, Jack brushes the spider off onto the grass, and I subside back on the bench, trying to regain my composure.

"Planes *and* spiders, huh?" says Jack.

"Yeah, kind of. I suppose you're not afraid of anything," I add, trying to laugh it off.

"Real men don't get afraid," he says lightly.

He seems to have forgotten all about kissing me. Misery sinks over me like a cold cloud. Why do I have to be scared of bloody spiders? As soon as I get home tonight, I'm booking myself on a hypnosis course. Spiders, flying, and screechy nails on blackboards. I'm going to zap them all.

In the distance I can hear a group of people leaving Antonio's, shouting to one another in Italian.

"So, how did you get that scar?" I say, to make conversation. I gesture to his wrist, where a faint line snakes underneath his cuff.

"It's a long, boring story. You don't want to hear it."

Yes, I do! an inner voice protests. Jack's not exactly the best at talking about himself.

"You have tomato sauce on your chin," he says, and reaches up with a napkin. His fingers brush gently against my face, and I feel a huge bound of hope. Maybe I didn't ruin things. He's bending toward me again. This is it. This is really it. This is—

"Jack."

We both leap in shock, and I spill my cocktail on the ground. I turn around, and there's Sven, standing at the gate of the tiny garden.

What the bloody fuck is Sven doing here?

"Great timing," murmurs Jack. "Hi, Sven."

"But . . . but what's he doing here?" I stare at Jack. "How did he know where we were?"

"He called while you were getting the pizza." Jack sighs and rubs his face. "I didn't know he'd get here this quickly. Emma . . . something's come up. I need to have a quick word with him. I promise it won't take long. OK?"

"OK," I reply, trying to sound cheerful. After all, what else *can* I say? I reach for the cocktail shaker, pour the remains of the pink cocktail into my cup, and take a deep swig.

Jack and Sven are standing by the gate, having an animated conversation in low voices. I take a sip of cocktail and casually shift along the bench so I can hear better.

". . . what to do from here . . ."

". . . plan B . . . back up to Glasgow . . ."

". . . urgent . . ."

I look up and find myself meeting Sven's eye. Quickly I look away again, pretending to be studying the ground. Their voices get even lower, and I can't hear a word. Then suddenly Jack breaks off and comes toward me.

"Emma . . . I'm really sorry about this. But I'm going to have to go."

"Go?"

"I'm going to have to go away for a few days. I'm sorry." He sits down beside me on the bench. "But . . . it's pretty important."

"Oh. Oh, right."

"Sven's ordered a car to take you home."

Great, I think savagely. Thanks a lot, Sven. "That was really . . . thoughtful of him," I say, and trace a pattern in the dirt with my shoe.

"Emma, I really have to go," says Jack. "But I'll see you when I get back, OK? At the company family day. And we'll . . . take it from there."

"OK." I try to smile. "That would be great."

"I had a good time tonight."

"So did I." My eyes are lowered. "I know it wasn't exactly clockwork . . . but I had a really good time."

"We'll have a good time again." He gently lifts my chin until I'm looking straight at him. "I promise, Emma."

He leans forward, and this time there's no hesitation. His mouth lands on mine, sweet and firm. He's kissing me. Jack Harper is kissing me on a park bench.

His mouth is opening mine; his stubble is rough against my face. His arm creeps around me and pulls me toward him, and my breath catches in my throat. I find myself reaching under his jacket, feeling the ridges of muscle beneath his shirt. Oh, God, I want this. I want more.

Suddenly he pulls away, and I feel like I've been wrenched out of a dream.

"Emma, I have to go."

My mouth is prickly wet. I can still feel his skin on mine. My entire body is throbbing. This can't be the end. It can't.

"Don't go," I hear myself saying thickly. "Half an hour."

What am I suggesting? That we do it under a *bush*?

Frankly, yes. Anywhere would do.

"I don't want to go." His dark eyes are almost opaque. "But I have to."

"So . . . I'll . . . I'll see you." I can barely talk properly.

"I can't wait."

"Neither can I."

"Jack." We both look up to see Sven at the gate.

"OK," calls Jack. We both stand up, and I discreetly look away from Jack's rather strange posture.

I could ride along in the car and—

No. *No*. Rewind. I did not think that.

As we reach the road, there are two silver cars waiting by the pavement. Sven is standing by one, and the other is obviously for me. Bloody hell. I feel like I've suddenly become part of the royal family or something.

As the driver opens the door for me, Jack touches my hand briefly. I want to grab him for a final snog, but somehow I manage to control myself.

" 'Bye," he murmurs.

" 'Bye," I murmur back.

Then I get into the car, the door closes with an expensive clunk, and we purr away.

Sixteen

WE'LL TAKE IT FROM THERE. That could mean . . .

Or it could mean . . .

Oh, God. Every time I think about it, I feel an excited little fizz. I can't concentrate at work. I can't think about anything else.

The corporate family day is a company event, I keep reminding myself. *Not* a date. It'll be a work occasion, and there probably won't be any chance at all for Jack and me to do more than say hello in a formal, boss-employee manner. Possibly shake hands. Nothing more.

We'll take it from there.

Oh, God. Oh, God . . .

On Saturday morning I get up extra early, exfoliate all over, shave under my arms, rub in my most expensive body cream, and paint my toenails.

Just because it's always a good thing to be well groomed. No other reason.

I choose my Gossard lacy bra and matching knickers, and my most flattering bias-cut summer dress.

Then, with a slight blush, I pop some condoms into my bag. Simply because it's always good to be prepared. This is a lesson I learned when I was eleven years old at Brownies, and it's always stayed with me. OK, maybe Brown Owl was talking about spare hankies and sewing kits rather than condoms . . . but the principle is the same, surely?

The family day is happening at Panther House, which is the Panther Corporation's country house in Hertfordshire. They use it for training and conferences and creative brainstorming days, none of which I ever get invited to. So I've never been here before, and as I get out of the taxi, I have to admit I'm pretty impressed. It's a really nice big old mansion, with lots of windows and pillars at the front. Probably dating from the . . . older period.

I follow the sounds of music and walk around the house to find the event in full swing on the vast lawn. Brightly colored bunting is festooning the back of the house, tents are dotting the grass, a band is playing on a little bandstand, and children are shrieking on a bouncy castle.

"Emma!" I look up to see Cyril advancing toward me, dressed as a joker with a red and yellow pointy hat. "Where's your costume?"

"Costume!" I try to look surprised. "Gosh! Um, I didn't realize we had to have one."

This is not entirely true. Yesterday evening at about five o'clock, Cyril sent around an urgent e-mail to everyone in the company, reading: A REMINDER: AT THE CFD, COSTUMES ARE COMPULSORY FOR ALL PANTHER EMPLOYEES.

But honestly. How are you supposed to produce a costume with five minutes' warning? And no way was I going to come here today in some hideous nylon outfit from the party shop.

Plus, let's face it, what can they do about it now? "Sorry," I say vaguely, looking around for Jack. "Still, never mind—"

"You people! It was on the memo; it was in the news-letter. . . ." He takes hold of my shoulder as I try to walk away. "Well, you'll have to take one of the spare ones."

"What?" I look at him blankly. "What spare ones?"

"I had a feeling this might happen," says Cyril with a slight note of triumph, "so I made advance provisions."

A cold feeling starts to creep over me. He can't mean—

He can't possibly mean—

"We've got plenty to choose from . . ." he's saying.

No. No way. I have to escape. Now.

I give a desperate wriggle, but his hand is like a clamp on my shoulder. He pushes me into a tent, where two middle-aged ladies are standing beside a rack of . . . Oh, my God. The most revolting, lurid man-made–fiber costumes I've ever seen. Worse than the party shop. Where did he *get* these from?

"No," I say in panic. "Really. I'd rather stay as I am . . ."

"Everybody has to wear a costume!" says Cyril firmly. "It was in the memo!"

"But . . . but this *is* a costume!" I quickly gesture to my dress. "I forgot to say. It's, um . . . a twenties summer garden-party costume, very authentic . . ."

"Emma, this is a fun day," snaps Cyril. "And part of that fun derives from seeing our fellow employees and family in amusing outfits. Which reminds me, where is your family?"

"Oh." I pull the regretful face I've been practicing all week. "They . . . Actually, they couldn't make it."

Which could be because I didn't tell them anything about it.

"You did tell them about it?" He eyes me suspiciously. "You sent them the leaflet?"

"Yes!" I cross my fingers behind my back. "Of course I told them! They would have loved to be here!"

"Well. You'll have to mingle with other families and colleagues. Here we are. Snow White." He shoves a horrendous nylon dress with puffy sleeves toward me.

"I don't want to be Snow White—" I begin, then break off as I see Moira from Accounts miserably being pushed into a big, shaggy gorilla costume. "OK." I grab the dress. "I'll be Snow White."

I almost want to cry. My beautiful, flattering dress is lying in a calico bag, ready for collection at the end of the day. And I am wearing an outfit that makes me look like a six-year-old. A six-year-old with zero taste and color blindness.

As I emerge disconsolately from the tent, the band is briskly playing the "Oom-Pah-Pah" song from *Oliver!* and someone is making an incomprehensible, crackly announcement over the loudspeaker. I look around, squinting against the sun, trying to work out who everyone is behind their disguises. Suddenly I spot Paul walking along on the grass, dressed as a pirate, with three small children hanging off his legs.

"Uncle Paul! Uncle Paul!" one is shrieking. "Do your scary face again!"

"I want a lolly!" yells another. "Uncle Paul, I want a lolleeee!"

"Hi, Paul," I say miserably. "Are you having a good time?"

"Whoever invented corporate family days should be shot," he says without a flicker of humor. "Get the hell off my foot!" he snaps at one of the children, and they all shriek with delighted laughter.

"Mummy, I don't *need* to go to the bathroom," mutters Artemis as she walks by dressed as a mermaid, in the company of a commanding woman in a huge hat.

"Artemis, there's no need to be so touchy!" booms the woman.

This is so weird. People with their families are completely different. Thank God mine aren't here.

I wonder where Jack is. Maybe he's in the house. Maybe I should—

"Emma!" I look up and see Katie heading toward me. She's dressed in a totally bizarre carrot costume, holding the arm of an elderly man with gray hair. Who must be her father, I suppose.

Which is a bit weird, because I thought she said she was coming with—

"Emma, this is Philip!" she says radiantly. "Philip, meet my friend Emma. She's the one who brought us together!"

I don't believe it.

This is her new man? *This* is Philip? But he has to be at least seventy!

In a total blur, I shake his hand, which is dry and papery, just like Grandpa's, and manage to make a bit of small talk about the weather. But all the time, I'm in total shock.

Don't get me wrong. I am not ageist. I am not anything-ist. I think people are all the same whether they're black or white, male or female, young or—

But he's an old man! He's *old*!

"Isn't he lovely?" says Katie fondly as he goes off to get some drinks. "He's so thoughtful! Nothing's too much trouble. I've never been out with a man like him before!"

I clear my throat. "So, er, remind me. Where exactly did you meet Philip again?"

"You know, silly!" says Katie, mock chidingly. "You suggested I should try somewhere different for lunch, remember? Well, I found this really unusual place tucked away near Covent Garden. In fact, I really recommend it."

"Is it . . . a restaurant? A cafe?"

"Not exactly," she says thoughtfully. "I've never been anywhere like it before. You go in and someone gives you a tray, and you collect your lunch and then eat it, sitting at all these tables. And it only costs two pounds! And afterward they have free entertainment! Like sometimes it's bingo or whist . . . sometimes it's a singsong around the piano . . . One time they had this brilliant tea dance! I've made loads of new friends . . ."

I stare at her for a few silent seconds.

I'm remembering that place Grandpa went to a few times, until he had a bust-up with the manager. That place full of jolly helpers, and posters advertising cheap trips to the seaside.

"Katie," I say at last. "This place. It couldn't possibly be . . . a day care center for the elderly?"

"Oh!" she says, looking taken aback. "Erm . . ."

"Try to think. Is everyone who goes there on the . . . old side?"

"Gosh," she says slowly, and screws up her brow. "Now that you mention it, I suppose everyone is kind of quite . . . mature. But honestly, Emma, you should come along! We have a real laugh!"

"You're still *going* there?"

"I go every day," she says in surprise. "I'm on the social committee!"

"Hello again!" says Philip cheerily, reappearing with three glasses. He beams at Katie and gives her a kiss on the cheek, and she beams back. And suddenly I feel quite heart-warmed. OK, it's weird. But they do seem to make a really sweet couple.

"The man behind the stall seemed rather stressed-out, poor chap," says Philip as I take my first delicious sip of Pimm's, closing my eyes to savor it.

Mmm. There is absolutely nothing nicer on a summer's day than a nice cold glass of—

Shit. I promised to do the Pimm's stall with Connor, didn't I? I glance at my watch and realize I'm already ten minutes late. Oh, bloody hell. No wonder he's stressed-out.

I hastily apologize to Philip and Katie, then hurry as fast as I can to the stall, which is in the corner of the garden. There I find Connor manfully coping with a huge queue all on his own. He's dressed as Henry VIII, with puffy sleeves and breeches, and has a huge red beard stuck to his face. He must be absolutely boiling.

"Sorry," I mutter, sliding in beside him. "I had to get into my costume. What do I have to do?"

"Pour out glasses of Pimm's," says Connor curtly. "One pound fifty each. Do you think you can manage?"

"Yes!" I say, a bit nettled. "Of course I can manage!"

For the next few minutes we're too busy serving Pimm's to talk. Then the queue melts away, and we're left on our own again.

Connor isn't even looking at me, and he's clanking glasses around so ferociously I'm afraid he might break one.

"Connor, look, I'm sorry I'm late—"

"That's all right," he says, and starts chopping a bundle of mint as though he wants to kill it. "So, did you have a nice time the other evening?"

That's what this is all about.

"Yes, I did, thanks," I say after a pause.

"With your new mystery man."

"Er, yes," I say, and scan the crowded lawn, searching for Jack.

"It's someone at work, isn't it?" Connor suddenly says, and I nearly drop a bottle of lemonade.

"Why do you say that?" I force myself to sound light.

"That's why you won't tell me who it is."

"It's not that! It's just . . . Look, Connor, can't you just respect my privacy?"

"I think I have a right to know who I've been dumped for!" He shoots me a reproachful look.

"You weren't *dumped* for him—" I stop myself. It's probably not a good idea to get into details. "I just . . . don't think it's very helpful to discuss it."

"Emma, I'm not stupid." He gives me an appraising look. "I know you a lot better than you think I do."

I feel a sudden flicker of uncertainty. What if he guesses? Maybe I've underestimated Connor all this time. Maybe he does know me. Oh, God.

I start to slice up a lemon, constantly scanning the crowd. Where is Jack, anyway?

"I've got it," says Connor triumphantly. "It's Paul, isn't it?"

"What?" I gape at him, wanting to laugh. "No, it's not Paul! Why on earth would you think it was Paul!"

"You keep looking at him." He gestures to where Paul is standing nearby, moodily swigging a bottle of beer. "Every two minutes!"

"I'm not looking at *him*! I was just looking for . . ." I take a sip of Pimm's. "I'm just taking in the atmosphere."

"So, why is he hanging around here?"

"He's not! Honestly, Connor, take it from me—I'm not going out with Paul."

"You think I'm a fool, don't you?" says Connor.

"I don't think you're a fool! I just . . . I think this is a pointless exercise! You're never going to—"

"Is it Nick?" His eyes narrow. "You and he have always had a bit of a spark going . . ."

"No! It's not Nick!"

Honestly. Clandestine affairs are hard enough as it is, without your ex-boyfriend subjecting you to the third degree. I should never have agreed to do this stupid Pimm's stall.

"Look," Connor suddenly says in a lowered voice.

I raise my head, and feel as though someone's squeezed the air out of my lungs. Jack is walking over the grass toward us, dressed in leather chaps and a checked shirt. He looks so completely and utterly sexy, I feel quite faint.

"He's coming this way!" hisses Connor. "Quick! Tidy up that lemon peel. Hello, sir," he says in a louder voice. "Would you like a glass of Pimm's?"

"Thank you very much, Connor," says Jack. Then he looks at me. "Hello, Emma. Enjoying the day?"

"Hello," I say, my voice about six notches higher than usual. "Yes, it's . . . lovely!" With trembling hands I pour out a glass of Pimm's and give it to him.

"Emma! You forgot the mint!" says Connor.

"It doesn't matter about the mint," says Jack, his eyes fixed on mine.

"You can have some mint if you want it," I say, gazing back.

"It looks fine just the way it is." He takes a deep gulp.

This is so unreal. We can't keep our eyes off each other. Surely it's completely obvious to everyone else what's going on. Surely Connor must realize. Quickly I look away and pretend to be busying myself with the ice.

"So, Emma," says Jack casually. "Just to talk work briefly. That extra typing assignment I asked you about—the Leopold file."

"Er, yes?" I'm so flustered I upend a cup of ice all over the counter.

"Perhaps we could have a quick word about it before I go? I have a suite of rooms up at the house."

"Right," I say, my heart pounding. "OK."

"Say . . . one o'clock?"

"One o'clock it is."

He saunters off, holding his glass, and I stand staring after him, dripping an ice cube onto the grass.

"I've been so stupid!" exclaims Connor, suddenly putting down his knife. "I've been so *blind*." He turns to face me, his eyes burning blue. "Emma, I know who your new man is."

My legs go wobbly.

"No, you don't," I say quickly. "Connor, you don't know who it is. Actually . . . it's not anyone from work. I just made that up. It's this guy who lives over in west London. You've never met him. His name is, um, Gary. He works as a post-man . . ."

"Don't lie to me! I know exactly who it is." He folds his arms. "It's Tristan from Design, isn't it?"

As soon as our stint on the stall is up, I escape from Connor and go sit under a tree with a glass of Pimm's, checking my watch every two minutes. A suite of rooms. That can only mean one thing. Jack and I are going to have sex.

I can't believe how nervous I am about this. Maybe Jack knows loads of tricks. Maybe he'll expect me to be really sophisticated. Maybe he'll expect all kinds of amazing maneuvers that I've never even heard of.

I mean . . . I don't think I'm *bad* at sex. You know.

But what sort of standard are we talking about? I feel like I've been competing in little local shows and suddenly I'm taking on the Olympics. Jack Harper is an international multimillionaire. He's dated heads of companies, models, and . . . and gymnasts, probably . . . women with enormous, perky breasts who do kinky stuff involving muscles I don't even think I *possess* . . .

How am I ever going to match up? This was a bad, bad idea. I'm never going to be as good as the president of Origin Software, am I? I can just imagine her, with her long legs and four-hundred-dollar underwear and honed, tanned body. . . .

OK, just . . . stop. This is getting ridiculous. I'll be fine. I'm *sure* I'll be fine. It'll be the same as doing a ballet exam—once you get into it, you forget to be nervous. Like my old ballet teacher always used to say, "As long as you keep your legs nicely turned out and a smile on your face, you'll do splendidly."

I glance at my watch and feel a fresh spasm of fright. It's one o'clock. On the dot.

Time to go and have sex. I stand up, and do a few surreptitious limbering-up exercises just in case. Then I take a deep breath and begin to walk toward the house. I've just reached the edge of the lawn when I hear a shrill voice.

"There she is! Emma! Yoo-hoo!"

That sounded just like my mum. Weird. I stop briefly and turn around, but I can't see anyone. It must be a hallucination. It must be my subconscious guilt trying to throw me, or something.

"Emma, turn around! Over here!"

Hang on. That sounded like . . . Kerry.

I peer at the crowded scene, my eyes squinting in the sunshine. I can't see anything. I'm looking all around, but I can't see—

And then, like a Magic Eye, they spring into view. Kerry, Nev, and my mum and dad. Walking toward me. All in costume. Mum is wearing a Japanese kimono and holding a picnic basket. Dad is dressed as Robin Hood and holding two fold-up chairs. Nev is in a Superman costume and holding a bottle of wine. And Kerry is wearing an entire Marilyn Monroe outfit, including platinum blond wig and high-heeled shoes, and complacently soaking up the attention.

What are they *doing* here? I didn't tell them about the corporate family day. I'm *positive* I didn't.

"Hi, Emma!" says Kerry as she gets near. "Like the outfit?" She gives a little shimmy and pats her blond wig.

"Who are you supposed to be, darling?" says Mum, looking in puzzlement at my nylon dress. "Is it Heidi?"

"I . . . Mum, what are you doing here? I never . . . I mean, I forgot to tell you . . ."

"I know you did," says Kerry. "But your friend Artemis told me all about it the other day when I phoned."

I will kill Artemis. I will murder her.

"So, what time's the fancy dress contest?" says Kerry, winking at two teenage boys who are gawking at her. "We haven't missed it, have we?"

"There . . . there isn't a contest," I say, finding my voice.

"Really?" Kerry looks put out.

I don't believe her. This is why she's come here, isn't it? To win a stupid competition. "You came all this way just for a fancy dress contest?"

"Of course not!" Kerry quickly regains her usual scornful expression. "Nev and I are taking your mum and dad to Hanwood Manor. It's near here. So we thought we'd drop in."

They're on their way somewhere! Thank God. We can have a little chat, then they can be on their way—

"We've brought a picnic," says Mum. "Now, let's find a nice spot."

"Do you think you've got time for a picnic?" I say, trying to sound casual. "You might get caught in traffic. In fact, maybe you should head off now, just to be on the safe side . . ."

"The table's not booked until seven!" says Kerry. "How about under that tree?"

I watch dumbly as Mum shakes out a plaid picnic rug and Dad sets up the two chairs. I cannot sit down and have a family picnic when Jack is waiting to have sex with me. I have to do something, quick. *Think.*

"Um, the thing is," I say in sudden inspiration, "the thing is, actually, I won't be able to stay. We've all got duties to do."

"Don't tell me they can't give you half an hour off," says Dad.

"Emma's the linchpin of the whole organization!" says Kerry with a sarcastic snigger. "Can't you tell?"

"Emma!" Cyril is approaching the picnic rug. "Your family came after all! And in costume! Jolly good!" He beams around, his joker's hat tinkling in the breeze. "Now, make sure you all buy a raffle ticket . . ."

"Oh, we will!" says Mum. "And we were wondering, could Emma possibly have some time off her duties to have a picnic with us?"

"Absolutely!" says Cyril. "You've done your stint on the Pimm's stall, haven't you, Emma? You can relax now."

"Lovely!" says Mum. "Isn't that good news, Emma?"

"That's . . . great!" I manage at last.

I have no choice. I have no way out of this. With stiff knees I lower myself onto the rug and accept a glass of wine.

"So, is Connor here?" asks Mum, unpacking chicken drumsticks onto a plate.

"Shh! Don't mention Connor!" says Dad in his Basil Fawlty voice.

"I thought you were supposed to be moving in with him," says Kerry, taking a swig of champagne. "What happened there?"

"She made him breakfast," quips Nev, and Kerry titters.

I try to smile, but my face won't quite do it. It's ten past one. Jack will be waiting. What can I do?

As Dad hands me a plate, I see Sven passing by. He's wearing dark glasses and has made no attempt at a costume. "Sven!" I call, and he stops. "Um, Mr. Harper was asking earlier on about my family. And whether they were here or not. Could you possibly tell him that they've . . . they've unexpectedly turned up?" I look up at him in desperation and he nods. He's understood.

"I'll pass on the message," he says.

And that's the end of that.

Seventeen

I ONCE READ AN ARTICLE called "Make Things Go Your Way" that said if a day doesn't turn out as you intended, you should go back and chart the differences between your goals and your results, and this will help you learn from your mistakes.

So . . . OK. Let's just chart exactly how much this day has diverged from the original plan I had this morning.

Goal: Look like sexy and sophisticated woman in beautiful, flattering dress.
Result: Look like Heidi/Munchkin extra in lurid puffy nylon sleeves.
Goal: Make secret assignation with Jack.
Result: Make secret assignation with Jack, then fail to turn up.
Goal: Have fantastic sex with Jack in romantic location.
Result: Have peanut-barbecued chicken drumstick on picnic rug.

Overall Goal: Euphoria.
Overall Result: Complete misery.

All I can do is dumbly push my food around my plate, telling myself this can't last forever. Dad and Nev have made about a million jokes about Don't Mention Connor. Kerry has shown me her new Swiss watch, which cost four thousand pounds, and boasted about how her company is expanding yet again. And now she's telling us how she played golf with the chief executive of some huge furniture conglomerate last week and he tried to head-hunt her.

"They all try it on," she says, taking a huge bite of chicken drumstick. "But I say to them, if I *needed* a job . . ." She trails off. "Did you want something?"

"Hi there," comes a dry, familiar voice.

I raise my head, blinking in the light.

It's Jack. Standing there against the blue sky in his cowboy outfit. He smiles in an almost imperceptible way, and I feel my heart lift. He's come to get me. I should have known he would. "Hi!" I say, half dazedly. "Everyone, this is—"

"My name's Jack," he cuts across me. "I'm a friend of Emma's. Emma . . ." He looks at me, his face giving nothing away. "I'm afraid you're needed."

"Oh, dear!" I say with a whoosh of relief. "Oh, well, never mind. These things happen . . ."

"That's a shame!" says Mum. "Can't you at least stay for a quick drink? Jack, you're welcome to join us, have a chicken drumstick or some quiche . . ."

"We have to go," I say hurriedly. "Don't we, Jack?"

"I'm afraid we do," he says, and holds out a hand to pull me up.

"Sorry, everyone," I say.

"We don't mind!" says Kerry with the same sarcastic laugh. "I'm sure you've some vital job to do, Emma. In fact, I expect the whole event would collapse without you!"

Jack stops. Very slowly, he turns around. "Let me guess," he says. "You must be . . . Kerry."

"Yes!" she says in surprise. "That's right!"

"And Mum . . . Dad . . ." He surveys the faces. "And you have to be . . . Nev?"

"Spot on!" says Nev with a chortle.

"Very good!" says Mum with a laugh. "Emma must have told you a bit about us!"

"Oh . . . she has," agrees Jack, looking around the picnic rug again in fascination. "You know . . . there might be time for that drink after all."

What? *What* did he say?

"Good!" says Mum. "It's always nice to meet friends of Emma's!"

I watch in total disbelief as Jack settles down on the rug. He was supposed to be *rescuing* me from all this. Not joining in. I sit down beside him, trying to think of a plan to get him away.

"So, you work for this company, Jack?" says Dad, pouring him a glass of wine.

"In a way," says Jack after a pause. "I've recently taken what you might call . . . a career break."

I can see Kerry and Nev exchanging looks.

"So you're . . . between jobs?" says Mum tactfully. "What a shame. Still, I'm sure something will come up . . ."

Oh, God. She has no idea who he is. None of my family has any idea who Jack is.

I'm not at all sure I like this. "Er, the grounds are really beautiful!" I exclaim. "Shall we have a little walk? Mum?"

We can walk around the gardens . . . and Jack and I can get "lost." Perfect.

"We're about to eat, Emma!" says Mum in surprise. "By the way, I saw Danny Nussbaum the other day in the post office," she adds, slicing some tomatoes. "He asked after you."

Out of the corner of my eye, I can see Jack's eyes brightening.

"Gosh!" I say, my cheeks growing hot. "Danny Nussbaum! I haven't thought about him for . . . ages."

"Danny and Emma used to step out together," Mum explains to Jack with a fond smile. "Such a nice boy. Very *bookish*. He and Emma used to study together in her bedroom, all afternoon!"

I cannot look at Jack. I cannot.

"You know . . . *Ben-Hur*'s a fine film," Jack suddenly says. "A very fine film." He looks at Mum. "Don't you think?"

I am going to kill him.

"Er, yes!" says Mum in puzzlement. "Yes, I've always liked *Ben-Hur* . . ." She cuts Jack a huge chunk of quiche and adds a slice of tomato. "So, Jack," she says sympathetically as she hands him a paper plate. "Are you getting by financially?"

"I'm . . . doing OK," Jack replies gravely.

Mum looks at him for a moment, then she rummages in the picnic basket and produces another Sainsbury's quiche, still in its box.

"Take this," she says, pressing it on him. "And some tomatoes. They'll tide you over."

"Oh, no," says Jack at once. "Really, I couldn't—"

"I won't take no for an answer! I insist!"

"Well, that's . . . truly kind." Jack puts the quiche down beside him, looking touched.

"You want some free career advice, Jack?" says Kerry, munching a piece of chicken.

I feel a sudden dread. If she starts demonstrating the successful woman walk, that's it. I'm leaving.

"Now, you want to listen to Kerry!" puts in Dad with pride. "She's our star! She has her own company!"

"Is that so?" says Jack politely.

"So!" I chime in, trying to steer the conversation. "Nev! How much did you say you paid for your new car again?"

But Nev isn't even listening. He's pouring himself another drink.

"Office furniture supply," says Kerry with a complacent smile. "Started from scratch. Now we have forty staff and a turnover of just over two million. And you know what my secret is?"

"I . . . have no idea," says Jack.

Kerry leans forward and fixes him with her blue eyes. "Golf."

"Golf!" says Jack after a pause.

"Business is all about networking," says Kerry. "It's all about contacts. I'm telling you, Jack, I've met most of the top businesspeople in the country on the golf course. Take any company. Take *this* company." She spreads her arm around the scene. "I know the top guy here. I could call him up tomorrow if I wanted to!"

I'm frozen in horror.

"Really?" says Jack, sounding riveted. "Is that so?"

"Oh, yes." She leans forward confidentially. "And I mean, the *top* guy."

"The top guy," echoes Jack. "I'm . . . impressed."

"Perhaps Kerry could put in a good word for you, Jack!" exclaims Mum in sudden inspiration. "You'd do that, wouldn't you, Kerry love?"

I would burst into hysterical laughter if the situation weren't so completely and utterly hideous.

"I guess I'll have to take up golf without delay," says Jack. "Meet the right people." He raises his eyebrows at me. "What do you think, Emma?"

"I . . . I . . ." I can barely talk. I am beyond embarrassment. I just want to disappear into the rug and never be seen again.

"Mr. Harper?" A voice suddenly interrupts and I breathe a sigh of relief. We all look up to see Cyril bending awkwardly down to Jack.

"I'm extremely sorry to interrupt, sir," he says, glancing around at my family as though trying to discern any reason at all why Jack Harper might be having a picnic with us. "But Malcolm St. John is here and would like a very brief word . . ."

"Of course," says Jack, and smiles politely at Mum. "If you could just excuse me a moment."

As he carefully balances his glass on his plate and gets to his feet, the whole family exchanges confused glances.

"Giving him a second chance, then!" calls out Dad jocularly to Cyril.

"I'm sorry?" says Cyril, taking a couple of steps toward us.

"That chap Jack," says Dad, gesturing to Jack, who's talking to a guy dressed in a navy blazer. "You're thinking of taking him on again, are you?"

Cyril looks stiffly from Dad to me and back again.

"It's . . . OK, Cyril!" I call lightly. "Dad, shut up, OK?" I mutter. "He owns the company."

"What?" Everyone turns to face me.

"He owns the company," I say, my face hot. "So just . . . don't make any jokes about him."

"The man in the jester's suit owns the company?" says Mum, looking in surprise at Cyril.

"No! *Jack* does! Or at least, some great big chunk of it . . ." They're all still sitting there, uncomprehending. "Jack's one of the founders of the Panther Corporation!" I hiss in frustration. "He was just trying to be modest!"

"Are you saying that guy is . . . Jack Harper?" says Nev in disbelief.

"Yes!"

There's a flabbergasted silence. As I look around, I see that a piece of chicken drumstick has fallen out of Kerry's mouth.

"Jack Harper . . . the multimillionaire," says Dad, just to make sure.

"Multimillionaire?" Mum looks totally confused. "So . . . does he still want the quiche?"

"Of course he doesn't want the quiche!" says Dad testily.

"What would he want a quiche for? He can buy a million bloody quiches!"

Mum's eyes are darting around the picnic rug in slight agitation.

"Quick!" she says suddenly. "Put the crisps into a bowl. There's one in the hamper—"

"They're fine as they are—" I begin.

"Millionaires don't eat crisps from the packet!" She plops the crisps in a plastic bowl and hastily starts straightening the rug. "Brian! Crumbs on your beard!"

"So, how the hell do *you* know Jack Harper?" says Nev.

"I . . . I just know him." I color a little. "We've worked together and stuff, and he's kind of become a . . . a friend. But listen, don't do anything differently," I say. Jack has just shaken the hand of the blazer guy and is coming back toward the picnic rug. "Just act the way you were before . . ."

Oh, God. Why am I even bothering? As Jack approaches, my entire family is sitting bolt upright, awestruck.

"Hi!" I say as naturally as possible, then glare around at them.

"So . . . Jack!" says Dad, sounding self-conscious. "Have another drink! Is this wine all right for you? Because we can easily nip to the wine shop, get something with a proper vintage—"

"It's great, thanks," says Jack, looking surprised.

"Jack, what else can I get you to eat?" says Mum, flustered. "I've got some gourmet salmon rolls somewhere. . . . Emma, give Jack your plate!" she suddenly snaps. "He can't eat off paper!"

"So . . . Jack," says Nev in a matey voice. "What does a guy like you drive, then? No, don't tell me." He lifts his hand. "A Porsche. Am I right?"

Jack looks at me with a quizzical expression, and I gaze back beseechingly, trying to convey that I'm really sorry, that basically I want to die . . .

"I take it my cover's been blown," he says with a grin.

"Jack!" exclaims Kerry, who has totally regained her composure. She gives him an ingratiating smile and thrusts out her hand. "It's good to meet you."

"Absolutely!" says Jack. "Although . . . didn't we just meet?"

"As *professionals,*" says Kerry smoothly. "One business owner to another. Here's my card, and if you ever need any help with your office furniture requirements, please give me a call. Or if you wanted to meet up socially . . . perhaps the four of us could go out sometime! Play a round? Couldn't we, Emma?"

What? Since when have Kerry and I ever socialized together?

"Emma and I are practically sisters, of course," she adds in sweet tones, putting her arm around me. "I'm sure she's told you."

"Oh, she told me a few things," says Jack, his expression now unreadable. He takes a bite of roast chicken.

"We grew up together. We shared everything . . ." Kerry gives me a squeeze. Her perfume is nearly choking me.

"Isn't that nice!" says Mum in pleasure. "I wish I had a camera!"

Jack doesn't reply. He's just regarding Kerry with raised eyebrows.

"We couldn't be closer!" Kerry's smile grows even more fawning. I try to move away, but she's squeezing me so hard, her talons are digging into my flesh. "Could we, Ems?"

Jack reaches for his glass, takes a sip, then looks up. "So . . . I guess that must have been a pretty tough decision for you when you had to turn Emma down," he says to Kerry in conversational tones. "You two being so close and all."

"Turn her down?" Kerry gives a tinkling little laugh. "I don't know what on earth you—"

"That time she applied for work experience in your firm and you turned her down," says Jack, and takes another bite of chicken.

I can't quite move.

That was a secret. That was supposed to be a secret.

"What?" says Dad, half laughing. "Emma applied to Kerry?"

"I . . . I don't know what you're talking about!" says Kerry, going a little pink.

"I *think* I have this right . . ." says Jack. "She offered to work for no money . . . but you still said no." He looks thoughtful for a moment. "Interesting decision."

No one speaks. Dad's jocular smile is slowly fading.

"But, of course, fortunate for us here at the Panther Corporation," Jack adds. "We're *very* glad Emma didn't make a career in the office furniture industry. So I guess I have to thank you, Kerry! As one business owner to another. You did us a big favor!"

Kerry is completely puce.

"Kerry, is this true?" says Mum in a sharp voice. "You wouldn't help Emma when she asked?"

"You never told us about this, Emma." Dad looks completely taken aback.

"I was embarrassed, OK?"

"Bit cheeky of Emma to ask," says Nev, taking a huge bite of pork pie. "Using family connections. That's what you said, wasn't it, Kerry?"

" 'Cheeky'?" echoes Mum in disbelief. "Kerry, if you remember, we lent you the money to start that company. You wouldn't *have* a company without this family."

"It wasn't *like that* . . ." says Kerry, darting an annoyed look at Nev. "There's been a . . . a crossed wire! Some confusion!" She pats her hair and gives me an ingratiating smile. "Obviously I'd be *delighted* to help you with your career, Ems! You should have said before! Just call me at the office. I'll do anything I can . . ."

I gaze back at her, full of sudden loathing. I cannot *believe* she is trying to wriggle out of this. She is the most two-faced cow in the entire world.

"There's no crossed wire, Kerry," I say as calmly as I can. "We both know exactly what happened. I asked you for help and you wouldn't give it to me. And fine—it's your company and it was your decision and you had every right to make it. But don't try to say it didn't happen, because it did."

"Emma!" says Kerry, trying to reach for my hand. "Silly girl! I had no idea! If I'd known it was important . . ."

If she'd known it was important? How could she not have known it was important?

I jerk my hand away. I can feel all the old hurt and humiliation building up inside me, rising like hot water inside a pipe, until suddenly the pressure is unbearable.

"Yes, you did!" I hear myself exclaiming. "You knew exactly what you were doing! You *knew* how desperate I was! Ever since you arrived in this family, you've tried to squash me down. You tease me about my crap career. You boast about yourself. I spend my entire life feeling small and stupid. Well, fine. You win, Kerry! You're the star and I'm not. You're the success and I'm the failure. But just don't pretend to be my best friend, OK? Because you're not, and you never will be!"

I finish, and look at her gobsmacked face. I have a horrible feeling I might burst into tears any moment.

I meet Jack's eye and he gives me a way-to-go smile. Then I risk a glance at Mum and Dad. They're both looking paralyzed, like they don't know what on earth to do.

The thing is, our family just doesn't *do* loud, emotional outbursts.

In fact, I'm not entirely sure what to do next myself.

"So, um, I'll be going, then," I say, my voice shaking. "I'll be . . . off! Come on, Jack. We've got work to do."

With wobbly legs, I turn on my heel and head off, stumbling slightly on the grass. Adrenaline is pumping through my body. I'm so wound up, I barely know what I'm doing.

"That was fantastic, Emma!" comes Jack's voice in my ear. "You were great! Absolutely . . . logistical assessment," he adds more loudly as we pass Cyril.

"I've never spoken like that in my life!" I say. "I've never . . . operational management," I quickly add as we pass a couple of people from Accounts.

"I guessed as much," he says, shaking his head. "Jesus, that cousin of yours . . . valid assessment of the market."

"She's a total . . . spreadsheet," I say quickly as we pass Connor. "So . . . I'll get that typed up for you, Mr. Harper."

Somehow we make it into the house and up the stairs. Jack leads me along a corridor, produces a key, and opens a door. And we're in a room. A large, light cream-colored room. With a big double bed in it. The door closes, and suddenly all my nerves return in a whoosh. This is it. Finally, this is it. Jack and me. Alone in a room. With a bed.

Suddenly I catch sight of myself in a gilded mirror, and gasp in dismay. I'd forgotten I was in the stupid Snow White costume. My face is red and blotchy, my eyes are welling up, hair is all over the place, and my bra strap is showing.

This is *so* not how I thought I was looking.

"Emma, I'm really sorry I waded in there." Jack's looking at me ruefully. "I was way out of line. I had no right to butt in like that. I just . . . That cousin of yours got under my skin—"

"No!" I interrupt, turning to face him. "It was *good*! I've never told Kerry what I thought of her before! Ever! It was . . . it was . . ." I trail off, breathing hard.

For a still moment there's silence. Jack's gazing at my flushed face. My rib cage is rising and falling; blood is beating in my ears. Then suddenly he bends forward and kisses me.

His mouth is opening mine, and he's already tugging the elastic sleeves of my Snow White costume down off my shoulders and unhooking my bra. I'm fumbling for his shirt buttons. His mouth reaches my nipple, and I'm starting to gasp with excitement when he pulls me down onto the sun-warmed carpet.

Oh, my God, this is quick. He's ripping off my knickers. His hands are . . . His fingers are . . . I'm panting helplessly . . . We're going so fast I can barely register what's happening. This is nothing like Connor. This is nothing like I've ever— A minute ago I was standing at the door, fully clothed, and now I'm already—he's already—

"Wait," I suddenly manage to say. "Wait, Jack. I just need to tell you something."

"What?" Jack looks at me with urgent, aroused eyes. "What is it?"

"I don't know any tricks," I whisper.

"You don't *what*?" He pulls away, looking baffled.

"Tricks! I don't know any tricks!" I say defensively. "You know, you've probably had sex with zillions of supermodels and gymnasts and they know all sorts of amazing . . ." I trail off at his expression. "Never mind," I say quickly. "It doesn't matter. Forget it."

"I'm . . . intrigued!" says Jack. "Which particular tricks did you have in mind?"

Why did I ever open my stupid mouth? Why? "I didn't!" I say, growing hot. "That's the whole point—I don't *know* any tricks—"

"Neither do I," says Jack, totally deadpan. "I don't know one trick."

I feel a sudden giggle rise inside me. "Yeah, right."

"It's true. Not one." He pauses thoughtfully, running one finger around my shoulder. "Oh, OK. Maybe one."

"What?" I say at once.

"Well . . ." He looks at me for a long moment, then shakes his head. "No."

"Tell me!" And now I can't help laughing out loud.

"Show, not tell," he murmurs against my ear, and pulls me toward him. "Did nobody ever teach you that?"

Eighteen

I'M IN LOVE.

I, Emma Corrigan, am in love.

For the first time ever in my entire life, I'm totally, one hundred percent in love! I spent all night with Jack at the Panther mansion. I woke up in his arms. We had sex about ninety-five times, and it was just . . . perfect. (And somehow tricks didn't even seem to come into it. Which was a bit of a relief.)

But it's not just the sex. It's everything. It's the way he had a cup of tea waiting for me when I woke up. It's the way he turned on his laptop especially for me to look up all my Internet horoscopes and helped me choose the best one. He knows all the crappy, embarrassing bits about me that I normally try to hide from any man for as long as possible . . . and he loves me anyway.

So he didn't exactly *say* he loved me. But he said something even better. I still keep rolling it blissfully around my head. We were lying there idly this morning when I suddenly said, without quite intending to, "Jack . . . how come you remembered about Kerry turning me down for work experience?"

"What?"

"How come you remembered about Kerry turning me down?" I swiveled my head toward him. "And . . . not just that. Every single thing I told you on that plane. Every little detail. About work, about my family, about Connor . . . everything. You remember it all. And I just . . . don't get it."

"What don't you get?" said Jack with a frown.

"I don't get why someone like you would be interested in my stupid, boring little life," I said, my cheeks prickling with embarrassment.

"Emma, your life is not stupid and boring."

"It is!"

"It's not."

"Of course it is! I never do anything exciting, I haven't got my own company, or invented anything—"

"You have friends who love you and whom you love," Jack said, interrupting. "You have ambitions. You have fun. You have imagination and optimism. You have . . . warmth. The only person who even *tried* to help that kid on the plane was you."

"Oh, well," I said, a little embarrassed. "Like that was a big success—"

"Don't put yourself down." He studied my face for a few moments. "Emma, you want to know why I remember all your secrets? The minute you started talking on that plane, I was gripped."

"You were . . . gripped?" I said in total disbelief. "By me?"

"I was gripped," he repeated gently, and he leaned over and kissed me.

And the point is, if I'd never spoken to him on that plane—and if I'd never blurted out my stuff—then this would never have happened. We would never have found each other. It was fate. I was *meant* to get on that plane. I was *meant* to get upgraded. I was *meant* to spill my secrets.

As I arrive home I'm glowing all over. It's like a lightbulb has switched on inside me. Jemima is wrong. Men and women aren't enemies. Men and women are *soul mates*. And if they were just honest, right from the word go, then they'd realize it! All this being mysterious and aloof is complete rubbish. Everyone should share their secrets straightaway!

I'm so inspired, I think I'm going to write a book on relationships. It will be called *Don't Be Scared to Share,* and it will show that men and women should be honest with each other and they'll communicate better and understand each other, and never have to pretend about anything, ever again. And it could apply to families, too. And politics! Maybe if world leaders all told one another a few personal secrets, then there wouldn't be any more wars! I think I'm really onto something.

I float up the stairs and unlock the door of our flat. "Lissy!" I call. "Lissy, I'm in love!"

There is no reply, and I feel a twinge of disappointment. I wanted someone to talk to. I wanted someone to impress with my brilliant new theory of life and—

Suddenly there's a thumping sound from her room. I stand completely still in the hallway, transfixed. The mysterious thumping sounds. There's another one. Then two more. What on earth—

And then I see it, through the door of the sitting room. On the floor, next to the sofa. A briefcase. A black leather briefcase. It's him. It's that Jean-Paul guy. He's in there! Right this minute! I take a few steps forward, completely intrigued.

What are they *doing*?

I just don't believe her story that they're having sex. But what else could it be? What else could it possibly—

OK . . . just stop. It's none of my business. If Lissy doesn't want to tell me what she's up to, she doesn't want to tell me.

Feeling very mature, I walk into the kitchen and pick up the kettle to make myself a cup of coffee.

Then I put it down again. *Why* doesn't she want to tell me? *Why* does she have a secret from me? We're best friends! I mean, it was *she* who said we shouldn't have any secrets.

I can't stand this. Curiosity is niggling at me like a burr. It's unbearable. And this could be my only chance to find out the truth. But how? I can't just walk in there. Can I?

All of a sudden, a little thought occurs to me. OK, suppose I *hadn't* seen the briefcase? Suppose I'd just innocently walked into the flat and happened to go straight to Lissy's door and happened to open it? Nobody could blame me then, could they? It would just be an honest mistake.

I come out of the kitchen, listen intently for a moment, then tiptoe back toward the front door.

Start again. I'm walking into the flat for the first time. "Hi, Lissy!" I call in a self-conscious voice. "Gosh! I wonder where she is. Maybe I'll, um, try her bedroom!"

I walk down the corridor, attempting a natural stride, arrive at her door, and knock softly.

There's no response from inside. The thumping noises have stopped.

As I face the painted wood I feel a sudden apprehension.

Am I really going to do this?

Yes, I am. I just *have* to know.

I grasp the handle, open the door—and give a scream of terror.

The image is so startling, I can't make sense of it. Lissy's naked on the floor. They're both naked. She and the guy are kind of tangled together in the strangest position I've ever, ever . . . her legs are up in the air, and his are twisted around her, and they're both scarlet in the face and panting.

"I'm sorry!" I stutter. "God, I'm sorry!"

"Emma, wait!" I hear Lissy shout as I scuttle away to my room, slam the door, and fall onto my bed.

My heart is pounding. I almost feel sick. I've never been so shocked in my entire life. I should *never* have opened that door.

She was telling the truth! They *were* having sex! But I mean, what kind of weird, contorted sex was that? Bloody hell. I never realized. I never—

I feel a hand on my shoulder, and scream again.

"Emma, calm down!" says Lissy. "It's me! Jean-Paul's leaving . . ."

I can't look up. I can't meet her eye. "Lissy, I'm sorry," I gabble. "I'm sorry! I didn't mean to do that. I should never have . . . Your sex life is your own affair . . ."

"Emma, we weren't having sex, you dope!"

"You were! I saw you! You didn't have any clothes on—"

"We did have clothes on! Emma, look at me!"

"No!" I say in panic. "I don't want to look at you!"

"*Look* at me!"

Apprehensively, I raise my head, and gradually my eyes focus on Lissy standing in front of me.

Oh. Oh . . . right. She's wearing a flesh-colored leotard.

"Well, what were you doing, if you weren't having sex?" I say almost accusingly. "And why are you wearing that?"

"We were dancing," says Lissy, looking embarrassed.

"What?" I am utterly bewildered.

"We were dancing, OK? That's what we were doing!"

"*Dancing?* But . . . why were you dancing?"

This makes no sense at all. Lissy and a French guy called Jean-Paul, dancing in her bedroom? I feel like I've landed in the middle of some weird dream.

"I've joined this group," says Lissy after a pause.

"Oh, my God. Not a cult—"

"No, not a cult! It's just . . ." She bites her lip. "It's some lawyers who've gotten together and formed a . . . a dance group."

A dance group?

For a few moments I can't quite speak. Now that my shock's died down, I have this horrible feeling that I might possibly be about to laugh. "You've joined a group of . . . dancing lawyers."

"Yes." Lissy nods, looking abashed. "I just . . . you know, I love the law. I love my job. But I've had this unfulfilled feeling for a while, like something was missing, like I wanted to express my creativity in some way."

An image has popped into my head of a bunch of portly barristers dancing around in their wigs and suddenly—I can't help it—I give a snort of laughter.

"You see!" cries Lissy. "That's why I didn't tell you! I *knew* you'd laugh!"

"I'm sorry!" I say. "I'm sorry! I'm not laughing. I think it's really great!" Another hysterical giggle bursts from me. "It's just . . . I don't know. Somehow the idea of dancing lawyers . . ."

"We're not all lawyers," she says defensively. "There are a couple of merchant bankers, too, and a judge . . . Emma, stop laughing!"

"I'm sorry! Lissy, I'm not laughing at you—honestly!" I take a deep breath and try to clamp my lips together. But all I can see is merchant bankers dressed in tutus, clutching their briefcases, dancing to *Swan Lake*. A judge leaping across the stage, robes flying.

"It's not funny!" Lissy's saying. "It's just a few like-minded professionals who want to express themselves through dance! What's wrong with that?"

"I'm sorry," I say, wiping my eyes and trying to regain control of myself. "Nothing's wrong with it. I think it's brilliant. So, are you having a show or anything?"

"It's a week from Friday. That's why we've been doing extra practices—"

"Really?" I stare at her, my laughter melting away. "Weren't you going to *tell* me?"

"I . . . I hadn't decided," she says, scuffing her dancing shoe on the floor. "I was embarrassed."

"Don't be embarrassed!" I say in dismay. "Lissy, I'm sorry I laughed. I think it's brilliant. And I'm going to come and watch! I'll sit right in the front row."

"Not the front row. You'll put me off."

"I'll sit in the middle, then. Or at the back. Wherever you want me." I give her a curious look. "Lissy, I never knew you could dance."

"Oh, I can't," she says at once. "I'm crap. It's just a bit of fun. D'you want a coffee?"

As I follow Lissy into the kitchen, she gives me a raised-eyebrow look. "So, you've got a bit of a nerve, accusing *me* of having sex. Where were you last night?"

"With Jack," I admit with a dreamy smile. "Having sex. All night."

"I knew it!"

"Oh, God, Lissy. I'm completely in love with him."

"In *love*?" She flicks on the kettle. "Emma, are you sure? You've only known him about five minutes."

"That doesn't matter! We're already complete soul mates! There's no need to pretend with him . . . or try to be something I'm not . . . And the sex is amazing . . . He's everything I never had with Connor. Everything. And he's *interested* in me. You know, he asks me questions all the time, and he seems really genuinely fascinated by the answers!"

I spread my arms with a blissful smile. "You know, Lissy, all my life I had this feeling that something wonderful was about to happen to me. I always just . . . *knew* it, deep down inside. And now it has."

"So, where is he now?" says Lissy, shaking coffee into the filter.

"He's going away for a bit. He's going to brainstorm some new concept with a creative team."

"What?"

"I dunno. He didn't say. It'll be really intense and he probably won't be able to phone me. But he's going to e-mail every day," I add happily.

"Biscuit?" says Lissy, opening the tin.

"Oh, er, yes. Thanks." I take a digestive and give it a thoughtful nibble. "You know, I've got this whole new theory about relationships, and it's so simple. Everyone in the world should be more honest with each other. Everyone should share! Men and women should share, families should share, world leaders should share!"

"Hmm." Lissy looks at me silently for a few moments. "Emma, did Jack ever tell you why he had to go rushing off in the middle of the night that time?"

"Er, no," I say in surprise. "But . . . it's his business."

"Did he ever tell you what all those phone calls were about on your first date?"

"Well . . . no."

"Has he told anything about himself other than the bare minimum?"

"He's told me plenty!" I say, feeling defensive. "Lissy, what's your problem?"

"I don't have a problem," she says mildly. "I'm just wondering . . . is it you who are doing all the sharing?"

"What?"

"Is he sharing himself with you?" She pours hot water onto the coffee. "Or are you just sharing yourself with him?"

"We share with each other!" I say, looking away and fiddling with a fridge magnet. "Like . . . like he told me all about his business partner, and his company."

"What about himself? As a person?"

"Yes!"

Which is true, I tell myself. Jack's shared loads about himself with me. I mean, he's told me . . .

He's told me all about . . .

Well, anyway. He probably just hasn't been in the mood for talking very much. Is that a crime?

"Have some coffee," says Lissy, handing me a mug.

"Thanks." I know I sound grudging, and Lissy sighs.

"Emma, I'm not trying to spoil things. He does seem really lovely—"

"He is! Honestly, Lissy, you don't know what he's like. He's so romantic. Do you know what he said this morning? He said the minute I started talking on that plane, he was gripped."

"Really?" Lissy gazes at me. "He said that? That is pretty romantic."

"I told you!" I can't help beaming at her. "Lissy, he's perfect!"

Nineteen

FOR THE NEXT WEEK OR SO, nothing can pierce my happiness. Nothing. I waft into work every day on a cloud, sit all day smiling at my computer terminal, then waft home again. Paul's sarcastic comments bounce off me like bubbles. I don't even notice when Artemis introduces me to a visiting advertising team as her personal assistant. They can all say what they like. Because what they don't know is that when I'm smiling at my computer, it's because Jack has just sent me another funny little e-mail. What they don't know is that the guy who employs them all is in love with me. *Me*. Emma Corrigan. The junior.

"Well, of course, I had several in-depth conversations with Jack Harper on the subject," I can hear Artemis saying on the phone as I tidy up the proofs cupboard. "Yup. And he felt—as I do—that the concept really needed to be refocused."

Bullshit! She never had any in-depth conversations with

Jack Harper. I'm almost tempted to e-mail him straightaway and tell him how she's using his name in vain.

Except that would be a bit mean.

And besides, she's not the only one. Everyone is dropping Jack Harper into their conversations, left, right, and center. It's like, now that he's gone, everyone's suddenly pretending they were his best friend and he thought their idea was perfect.

Except me. I'm just keeping my head down and not mentioning his name at all.

Partly because I know that if I do, I'll blush bright red or give some huge, goofy smile or something. Partly because I have a horrible feeling that once I start talking about Jack, I won't be able to stop. But mainly because no one ever brings the subject up with me. After all, what would I know about Jack Harper? I'm only the crappy assistant.

The only thing clouding my life at the moment is that Gloria still hasn't been replaced, and I'm still doing all her extra tasks, as well as trying to come up with copy for a new series of pamphlets for a tie-in with Endwich Bank. I made a real effort with them—but when I showed Paul my initial ideas, he was more interested in whether I'd ordered a fruit basket for his stupid mother's birthday.

Actually, his mother isn't stupid. I think she has a Ph.D. But still, it's not my job to send her a basket full of pineapples, papaya, and star fruit.

Who eats star fruit, anyway?

"Hey!" says Nick, suddenly looking up from his phone. "Jack Harper's going to be on television!"

There's an interested frisson around the office, and I attempt to look as surprised as everyone else. Jack mentioned he was going to be doing a TV interview. I didn't know it was going to be screened today, though.

"Is a TV crew coming to the office or anything?" says Artemis, smoothing down her hair.

"Dunno—"

"OK, folks," says Paul, coming out of his office. "Jack Harper has done an interview on *Business Watch,* and it's being broadcast at twelve. A television is being set up in the conference room; anyone who would like to can go along and watch there. But we need one person to stay behind and man the phones." His gaze falls on me.

"What?"

"You can stay and man the phones," says Paul. "OK?"

I knew it. I'm turning into the bloody departmental secretary.

"No! I mean . . . I want to watch!" I say in dismay. "Can't someone else stay behind? Artemis, can't you stay?"

"*I'm* not staying!" says Artemis at once. "Honestly, Emma, don't be so selfish. It won't be at all interesting for you."

"Yes, it will!"

"No, it won't." She rolls her eyes.

"It will! He's . . . he's my boss, too!"

"Yes, well," says Artemis with a sarcastic smirk, "I think there's a slight difference. You've barely even spoken to Jack Harper!"

"I have!" I say before I can stop myself. "I have! I—" I break off, my cheeks turning pink. "I . . . once went to a meeting he was at."

"And served him a cup of tea?" Artemis meets Nick's eyes with a little smirk.

I'm furious. Blood is pounding through my ears. I wish just once I could think of something really scathing and clever to put Artemis down.

"Enough, Artemis," says Paul. "Emma, you're the most junior. You're staying here, and that's settled."

By five to twelve the office is completely empty. Apart from me, a fly, and a whirring fax machine. Disconsolately I reach into my desk drawer and take out an Aero. And a Flake for good measure. I'm just unwrapping the Aero and taking a big bite when the phone rings.

"OK," comes Lissy's voice down the line. "I've set the video."

"Thanks, Liss," I say through a mouthful of chocolate. "You're a star."

"I can't believe you're not allowed to watch!"

"I know. It's completely unfair." I slump deeper in my chair and take another bite of Aero.

"Well, never mind. We'll watch it again tonight. Jemima's going to put the video on in her room, too, so we should definitely catch it."

"What's Jemima doing at home?" I say in surprise.

"She's taken a sickie so she can do a home spa day. Oh, and your dad rang," she adds cautiously.

"Really?" I feel a flicker of apprehension. "What did he say?"

"He wondered if you were ill, as you haven't called him back."

"Oh." I twist the telephone cord, feeling guilty.

I haven't talked to Mum or Dad since the debacle at the corporate family day. I just can't bring myself to. It was all too painful and embarrassing, and for all I know, they've completely taken Kerry's side.

So when Dad rang here on the following Monday, I said I was really busy and I'd call him back . . . and I never did. And the same thing at home.

I know I'll have to talk to them sometime. But not now. Not while I'm so happy.

"He'd seen the trailer for the interview," says Lissy. "He recognized Jack and just wondered if you knew about it. And he said . . ." She pauses. "He really wanted to talk to you about a few things."

"Oh." I gaze at my notepad, where I've doodled a huge spiral over a telephone number I was supposed to be keeping.

"Anyway, he and your mum are going to be watching it," says Lissy. "And your grandpa."

Great. Just great. The entire world is watching Jack on television. The entire world except me.

When I've put the phone down, I go and get myself an orange juice and a coffee from the new machine, which actually does make a very nice café au lait. I come back and look around the quiet office, then go and pour the orange juice into Artemis's spider plant. And some photocopier toner for good measure.

Then I feel a bit mean. It's not the plant's fault, after all.

"Sorry," I say out loud, and touch one of its leaves. "It's just your owner is a real cow. But then, you probably knew that."

"Talking to your mystery man?" comes a sarcastic voice from behind me, and I turn around to see Connor standing in the doorway.

"Connor!" I say. "What are you doing here?"

"I'm on my way to watch the TV interview. But I just wanted a quick word." He takes a few steps into the office and fixes me with an accusing frown. "So. You lied to me."

Oh, shit. Has Connor guessed? Did he see something at the corporate family day?

"Er, what do you mean?" I say nervously.

"I've just had a little chat with Tristan from Design!" Connor's voice swells with indignation. "He's gay! You're not going out with him at all, are you?"

He cannot be serious. Connor didn't *seriously* think I was going out with Tristan from Design, did he? I mean, Tristan could not look more gay if he wore leopard skin hot pants and walked around humming Barbra Streisand hits.

"No," I say, managing to keep a straight face. "I'm not going out with Tristan."

"Well!" says Connor, nodding as though he's scored a hundred points and doesn't quite know what to do with them.

"Well. I just don't see why you feel it necessary to lie to me. That's all. I just would have thought we could be a little honest with each other."

"Connor . . . it's just . . . It's complicated. OK? And anyway, I didn't *lie* to you—"

"Fine. Whatever." He gives me his most wounded-martyr look and starts walking away.

"Wait!" I say suddenly. "Hang on a minute! Connor, could you do me a real favor?" I wait until he turns, then pull a wheedling face. "Could you possibly man the phones here while I quickly go and watch Jack Harper's interview?"

I know Connor isn't my number one fan at the moment. But I don't exactly have a lot of choice.

"Could I do *what*?" says Connor, obviously astonished at such a request.

"Could you man the phones! Just for half an hour. I'd be so incredibly grateful."

"I can't believe you're even *asking* me that!" says Connor, incredulous. "You *know* how important Jack Harper is to me! Emma, I really don't know what you've turned into."

After he's stalked off, I take several messages for Paul, one for Nick, and one for Caroline. I file a couple of letters. I address a couple of envelopes. And then, after twenty minutes, I've had it.

This is stupid. I love Jack. He loves me. I should be there, supporting him. I pick up my coffee and hurry along the corridor. The meeting room is crowded with people, but I edge in at the back and squeeze through two guys who aren't even *watching* Jack but are discussing some football match.

"What are *you* doing here?" says Artemis as I arrive at her side. "What about the phones?"

"No taxation without representation," I hear myself responding coolly, which perhaps isn't exactly appropriate (I'm not even sure what it means) but has the desired effect of shutting her up.

I crane my neck so I can see over everyone's head, and my eyes focus on the screen . . . and suddenly there he is. Sitting on a chair in a studio, in jeans and a white T-shirt. There's a bright blue backdrop and the words "Business Inspirations" behind him, and two smart-looking interviewers sitting opposite him.

There he is. The man I love.

This is the first time I've seen him since we slept together, it occurs to me. But he looks as gorgeous as ever, his eyes all dark and glossy under the studio lights.

Oh, God, I want to kiss him.

If no one else were here, I would go up to the television set and kiss it. I honestly would.

"What have they asked him so far?" I murmur to Artemis.

"They're talking to him about how he works. His inspirations, his partnership with Pete Laidler, stuff like that."

"Shh!" says someone else.

"Of course, it was tough after Pete died," Jack's saying. "It was tough for all of us. But recently . . ." He pauses. "Recently my life has turned around and I'm finding inspiration again. I'm enjoying it again."

He has to be referring to me. He has to be. I've turned his life around! That's even more romantic than "I was gripped."

"You've already expanded into the sports drinks market," the male interviewer is saying. "Now I believe you're looking to expand into the women's market."

There's a frisson around the room, and people start turning their heads.

"We're going into the women's market?"

"Since when?"

"I knew, actually," Artemis is saying with a smug expression. "Quite a few people have known for a while."

I remember those people up in Jack's office. That's what the ovaries were for. This is quite exciting! A new venture!

"Can you give us any further details about that?" the male interviewer is saying. "Will this be a soft drink marketed at women?"

"It's very early stages," says Jack. "But we're planning an entire line. A drink, clothing, a fragrance. We have a strong creative vision. We're excited."

"So, what's your target market this time?" asks the man, consulting his notes. "Are you aiming at sportswomen?"

"Not at all," says Jack. "We're aiming at . . . the girl on the street."

"The 'girl on the street'?" The female interviewer sits up, looking slightly affronted. "What's that supposed to mean? Who is this girl on the street?"

"She's twenty-something," says Jack after a pause. "She works in an office, takes the tube to work, goes out in the evenings, and comes home on the night bus . . . Just an ordinary, nothing-special girl."

"There are thousands of them," puts in the man with a smile.

"But the Panther brand has always been associated with men," chips in the woman, looking skeptical. "With competition. With masculine values. Do you really think you can make the switch to the female market?"

"We've done research," say Jack. "We feel we know our market."

"Research!" She gives a scoffing laugh. "Isn't this just another case of men telling women what they want?"

"I don't believe so," says Jack, still pleasantly, but I can see a slight flicker of annoyance pass across his face.

"Plenty of companies have tried to switch markets without success. How do you know you won't just be another one of them?"

"I'm confident," says Jack.

God, why is she being so aggressive? I think, feeling indignant. Of course Jack knows what he's doing!

"You round up a load of women in some focus group and ask them a few questions! How does that tell you anything?"

"That's only a small part of the picture, I can assure you," says Jack in even tones.

"Oh, come on," the woman says, leaning back and folding her arms. "Can a company like Panther—can a man like you—*really* tap into the psyche of, as you put it, an ordinary, nothing-special girl?"

"Yes. I can!" Jack meets her gaze square-on. "I know this girl."

"You *know* her?" The woman raises her eyebrows.

"I know who this girl is," says Jack. "I know what her tastes are, what colors she likes. I know what she eats; I know what she drinks. I know what she wants out of life. She's size eight, but she'd like to be size six. She . . ." He spreads his arms as though searching for inspiration. "She eats Cheerios for breakfast and dips Flakes in her cappuccinos."

I look in surprise at my hand, holding a Flake. I was about to dip it into my coffee.

And . . . I had Cheerios this morning.

"We're surrounded these days by images of perfect, glossy people," Jack is saying with animation. "But this girl is real. She has bad-hair days and good-hair days. She wears G-strings even though she finds them uncomfortable. She writes out exercise routines, then ignores them. She pretends to read business journals but hides celebrity magazines inside them."

Just . . . hang on a minute. This all sounds a bit familiar.

"That's *exactly* what you do, Emma," says Artemis. "I've seen your copy of *OK!* inside *Marketing Week*." She turns to me with a mocking laugh, and her gaze suddenly lands on my Flake.

"She loves clothes, but she's not a fashion victim," Jack is saying on-screen. "She'll wear, maybe, a pair of jeans . . ."

Artemis's eyes run in disbelief over my Levi's.

". . . and a flower in her hair . . ."

Dazedly I lift a hand and touch the fabric rose in my hair. He can't—

He can't be talking about—

"Oh . . . my . . . God," says Artemis.

"What?" says Caroline, next to her. She follows Artemis's gaze, and her expression changes.

"Oh, my God! Emma! It's you!"

"It's not," I say, but my voice won't quite work properly.

"It is!"

A few people start nudging one another and turning to look at me.

". . . She reads fifteen horoscopes every day and chooses the one she likes best . . ." Jack's voice is saying.

"It is you! It's exactly you!"

". . . She scans the back of highbrow books and pretends she's read them . . ."

"I *knew* you hadn't read *Great Expectations*!" says Artemis triumphantly.

". . . She adores sweet sherry . . ."

"Sweet *sherry*?" says Nick, turning in horror. "You cannot be serious."

"It's Emma!" I can hear people saying on the other side of the room. "It's Emma Corrigan!"

"Emma?" says Katie, looking straight at me in disbelief. "But . . . but . . ."

"It's not Emma!" says Connor all of a sudden with a laugh. He's standing over on the other side of the room, leaning against the wall. "Don't be ridiculous! Emma's size four, for a start. Not size eight!"

"Size four?" says Artemis with a snort of laughter.

"Size *four*!" Caroline giggles. "That's a good one!"

"Aren't you size four?" Connor looks startled. "But you said—"

"I . . . I know I did." I swallow, my face like a furnace. "But I was . . . I was . . ."

"Do you really buy all your clothes from thrift shops and pretend they're new?" says Caroline, looking up from the screen.

"No!" I say defensively. "I mean . . . yes . . . maybe . . . sometimes . . ."

"She weighs 135 pounds, but pretends she weighs 125 . . ." Jack's voice is saying.

What? *What?*

My entire body contracts in shock.

"I do not!" I yell in outrage at the screen. "I do not weigh anything like 135 pounds! I weigh . . . about . . . 128 . . . and a half . . ." I trail off as the entire room turns to goggle at me.

". . . hates crochet . . ."

There's an almighty gasp from across the room.

"You hate crochet?" comes Katie's disbelieving voice.

"No!" I say, swiveling in horror. "That's wrong! I love crochet! You know I love crochet—"

But Katie is stalking furiously out of the room.

"She cries when she hears the Carpenters . . ." Jack's voice is saying on the screen. "She loves Abba, but she can't stand jazz . . ."

Oh, no. Oh no, oh no . . .

Connor is staring at me as though I have personally driven a stake through his heart.

"You can't stand . . . *jazz?*"

It's like a bad dream. One of those dreams where everyone can see your underwear and you want to run but you can't. I can't tear myself away. All I can do is sit in agony as Jack's inexorable voice continues.

All my secrets. All my personal, private secrets. Revealed on television. I'm in such a state of shock, I'm not even taking them all in.

"She wears lucky underwear on first dates . . . she borrows

designer shoes from her roommate and passes them off as her own . . . pretends to kickbox . . . confused about religion . . . worries that her breasts are too small . . ."

I close my eyes, unable to bear it. My breasts. He mentioned my *breasts*. On *television*.

"When she goes out, she can play sophisticated . . . but on her bed . . ."

I'm suddenly faint with fear.

No. No. Please not this. Please, *please*—

". . . she has a Barbie bedspread."

A huge roar of laughter goes around the room, and I bury my face in my hands. I am beyond mortification. *No one* was supposed to know about my Barbie bedspread. *No one.*

"Is she sexy?" the interviewer is asking, and I feel a stab of shock. I can't breathe for apprehension. What's he going to say?

"She's very sexual," says Jack at once, and all eyes swivel toward me, agog. "This is a modern girl who carries condoms in her purse."

Every time I think this can't get any worse, it does.

My *mother* is watching this. My *mother*.

"But maybe she hasn't reached her full potential. Maybe there's a side of her that has been frustrated . . ."

I can't look at Connor. I can't look anywhere.

"Maybe she's willing to experiment. Maybe she's had—I don't know—a lesbian fantasy about her best friend . . ."

No! NO! My entire body clenches in horror. I have a sudden image of Lissy watching the screen at home, wide-eyed, clasping a hand over her mouth. She'll know it was her. She'll know! I will never be able to look her in the eye again . . .

"It was a *dream*, OK?" I manage as everyone gawks at me. "Not a fantasy! They're different!"

I feel like throwing myself at the television. Draping my arms over it. Stopping him.

But it wouldn't do any good, would it? A million TVs are on, in a million homes. People everywhere are watching.

"She believes in love and romance. She believes her life is one day going to be transformed into something wonderful and exciting. She has hopes and fears and worries, just like anyone. Sometimes she feels frightened." He pauses, and adds in a softer voice, "Sometimes she feels unloved. Sometimes she feels she will never gain approval from those people who are most important to her."

As I watch Jack's warm, serious face on the screen, I suddenly feel my eyes stinging slightly.

"But she's brave and good-hearted and faces her life head-on." He shakes his head and smiles at the interviewer. "I'm . . . I'm so sorry. I don't know what happened there. I guess I got a little carried away. Could we—" His voice is abruptly cut off by the interviewer.

He got a little carried away.

This is like saying Hitler was a tad aggressive.

"Jack Harper, many thanks for talking to us . . ." the interviewer starts saying. "Next week we'll be chatting with the charismatic king of motivational videos, Ernie Powers. Meanwhile, many thanks again to . . ."

She finishes her spiel and the program's music starts. Then someone leans forward and switches the television off.

For a few seconds the entire room is silent. Everyone is gaping at me, as though they're expecting me to make a speech. Some faces are sympathetic, some are curious, some are gleeful, and some are just jeez-am-I-glad-I'm-not-you.

"But . . . but I don't understand," comes a voice from across the room, and everybody's head swivels avidly toward Connor, like at a tennis match. He's looking straight at me, his face red with confusion. "How does Jack Harper know so much about you?"

Oh, God. I know Connor got a really good degree from

Manchester University and everything. But sometimes he is so slow on the uptake.

Everyone's head has swiveled back toward me.

"I . . ." My whole body is prickling with embarrassment. "Because we . . . we . . ."

I can't say it out loud. I just can't.

But I don't have to. Connor's face is slowly turning different colors. "No," he gulps. He looks as though he's seen a ghost. And not just any old ghost. A really big ghost with clanky chains, going "Whooo!"

"No," he says again. "No. I don't believe it."

"Connor," says someone, putting a hand on his shoulder, but he shrugs it off.

"Connor, I'm really sorry—" I falter.

"You're joking!" exclaims some guy in the corner, who is obviously even slower than Connor and has just had it spelled out to him word for word. He looks up at me. "So, how long has this been going on?"

It's like someone opened the floodgates. Suddenly everyone in the entire room starts pitching questions at me. I can't hear myself think for the babble.

"Is that why he came to Britain? To see you?"

"Are you going to marry him?"

"You know, you don't *look* like you weigh 135 pounds."

"Do you really have a Barbie bedspread?"

"So, in the lesbian fantasy, was it just the two of you, or . . ."

"Have you had sex with Jack Harper at the office?"

"Is that why you dumped Connor?"

I can't cope with this. I have to get out of here. Now.

Without looking at anyone, I get to my feet and stumble out of the room. As I head down the corridor, I'm too dazed to think of anything other than I must get my bag and go. Now.

As I enter the empty marketing department, phones are

shrilly ringing all around, and the habit's too ingrained; I can't ignore them.

"Hello?" I say, picking up one at random.

"So!" comes Jemima's furious voice. " 'She borrows designer shoes from her roommate and passes them off as her own.' Whose shoes might those be, then? Lissy's?"

"Look, Jemima, can I just . . . I'm sorry. I have to go." I put the phone down.

No more phones. Get bag. Go.

As I zip up my bag with trembling hands, a couple of people have followed me into the office and are picking up some of the ringing phones.

"Emma, your granddad's on the line," says Artemis, putting her hand over the receiver. "Something about the night bus and he'll never trust you again?"

"You have a call from Harveys Bristol Cream publicity department," chimes in Caroline. "They want to know where they can send you a free case of sweet sherry."

How did they get my name? How? Has the word spread already? Are the women on reception *telling* everybody?

"Emma, I have your dad here," says Nick. "He says he needs to talk to you urgently."

"I can't," I say numbly. "I can't talk to anybody. I have to . . . I have to . . ."

I grab my jacket and practically run out of the office and down the corridor to the stairs. Everywhere, people are making their way back to their offices after watching the interview, and they all turn to gawk as I hurry by.

"Emma!" As I'm nearing the stairs, a woman named Fiona, whom I barely know, grabs me by the arm. She weighs about 300 pounds and is always campaigning for bigger chairs and wider doorways. "Never be ashamed of your body. Rejoice in it! The earth mother has given it to you! If you want to come to our workshops on Saturday . . ."

I tear my arm away and start clattering down the marble stairs. But as I reach the next floor, someone else grabs my arm.

"Hey, can you tell me which charity shops you go to?" It's a girl I don't even recognize. "Because you always look really well dressed to me."

"I adore Barbie dolls, too!" Carol Finch from Accounts is suddenly in my path. "Shall we start a little club together, Emma?"

"I . . . I really have to go."

I back away, then start running down the stairs. But people keep accosting me from all directions.

"I didn't realize I was a lesbian till I was thirty-three."

"A lot of people are confused about religion. This is a leaflet about our Bible study group—"

"Leave me alone!" I suddenly yell in anguish. "Everyone, just leave me alone!"

I sprint for the entrance, the voices following me, echoing on the marble floor. As I'm desperately pushing against the heavy glass doors, Dave the security guard saunters up and stares right at my breasts.

"They look all right to me, love," he says encouragingly.

I finally get the door open, then run outside and down the road, not looking right or left. At last I come to a halt in a small pedestrian square. I sink down on a bench and bury my head in my hands.

I have never been so completely and utterly mortified in all my life.

Twenty

"ARE YOU OK? Emma?"

I've been sitting on the bench for about five minutes, not seeing anything, my mind a whirl of confusion. Now there's a voice in my ear, above the everyday street sounds of people walking by and buses grinding and cars hooting. It's a man's voice. I open my eyes and find myself looking into a pair of green eyes that seem familiar.

Then suddenly I realize. It's Aidan from the smoothie bar.

"Is everything all right?" he's saying. "Are you OK?"

For a few moments I can't quite reply. I feel like all my emotions have been scattered on the floor like a dropped tea tray, and I'm not sure which one to pick up first.

"I think that would have to be a no," I say at last.

"Oh." He looks alarmed. "Well, is there anything I can—"

"Would you be OK if all your secrets had been revealed on television by a man you thought you could trust?" I say shakily. "Would you be OK if you'd just been mortified in front of all your friends and colleagues and family?"

There's a bewildered silence.

"*Would* you?"

"Er, probably not?" he hazards.

"Exactly! I mean, how would you feel if someone revealed in public that you . . . you wore women's underwear?"

He turns pale with shock. "I don't wear women's underwear!"

"I know you don't wear women's underwear! Or, rather . . . I don't *know* that you don't . . . But just assuming for a moment that you did . . . how would you like it if someone just *told* everyone in a so-called business interview on television?"

Aidan frowns, as though his mind is suddenly putting two and two together. "Wait a moment. That interview with Jack Harper. Is that what you're talking about? We had it on in the smoothie bar."

"Oh, great!" I throw my hands in the air. "Just great! Because you know, it would be a shame if anyone in the entire universe had missed it—"

"So . . . that's *you*? Who reads fifteen horoscopes a day and lies about her . . ." He breaks off at my expression. "Sorry. Sorry. You must be feeling very hurt."

"Yes. I am. I'm feeling hurt. And angry. And embarrassed."

And I'm confused, I add silently. I'm so confused and shocked, I feel as though I can barely keep my balance on this bench. In the space of a few minutes, my entire world has turned upside down.

I thought Jack loved me. I thought he and I—

I bury my head in my hands.

"So . . . how did he know so much about you?" Aidan's asking. "Are you and he . . . an item?"

"We met on a plane." I look up, trying to keep control of myself. "And . . . I spent the entire trip telling him everything about myself. And then we went on a few dates, and I honestly thought it might be . . . you know." I feel my cheeks flame crimson. "The real thing. But the truth is . . . he was never interested in me, was he? Not really. He just wanted to find out what an ordinary girl-on-the-street was like. For his stupid target market. For his stupid new women's line."

The realization hits me properly for the first time, and I feel a tear roll down my cheek, swiftly followed by another.

Jack used me.

That's why he asked me out to dinner. That's why he was so fascinated with me. That's why he found everything I said so interesting. That's why he was *gripped*.

It wasn't love. It was business.

"I'm sorry." I gulp. "I'm sorry. I just . . . It's just been such a shock."

"Don't worry," says Aidan sympathetically. "It's a completely natural reaction." He shakes his head. "I don't know much about big business, but it seems to me these guys don't get to the top without trampling over a few people on the way. They'd have to be pretty ruthless to be so successful." He pauses, watching as I try only half successfully to stop my tears. "Emma, can I offer a word of advice?"

"What?" I look up, wiping my eyes.

"Take it out in your kickboxing. Use the aggression. *Use* the hurt."

I blink in total disbelief. Was he not *listening*?

"Aidan . . . I don't *do* kickboxing!" I hear myself crying shrilly. "I don't kickbox, OK? I never have!"

"You don't?" He looks confused. "But you said—"

"I was lying!"

There's a short pause.

"Right," says Aidan at last. "Well . . . no worries! You could go for something with lower impact. Tai chi, maybe." He gazes at me uncertainly. "Listen, do you want a drink? Something to calm you down? I could make you a mango-banana blend with chamomile flowers, throw in some soothing nutmeg."

"No, thanks." I blow my nose, take a deep breath, then reach for my bag. "I think I'll go home, actually."

"Will you be OK?"

"I'll be fine." I force a smile. "I'm fine."

But of course that's a lie, too. I'm not fine at all. As I sit on the tube going home, tears pour down my face one by one and land in big, wet drips on my skirt. People are whispering, but I don't care. Why would I care? I've already suffered the worst embarrassment possible; a few extra people gawking is neither here nor there.

I feel so *stupid*.

Of course we weren't soul mates. Of course he wasn't genuinely interested in me. Of course he never loved me.

"Don't worry, darling!" says a large lady sitting to my left, wearing a voluminous print dress covered with pineapples. "He's not worth it! Now, you just go home, wash your face, have a nice cup of tea . . ."

"How do you know she's crying over a man?" chimes in a woman in a dark suit. "That is such a clichéd, counterfeminist perspective. She could be crying over anything! A piece of music, a line of poetry, world famine, the political situation in the Middle East. . . ." She looks at me in expectation.

"Actually, I was crying over a man," I admit.

The tube stops, and the woman in the dark suit rolls her eyes at us and gets out. The pineapple lady rolls her eyes back.

"World famine!" she says scornfully, and I can't help giggling. "Now, don't you worry, love." She gives me a comforting pat on the shoulder as I dab at my eyes. "Have a nice cup of tea, and a few nice chocolate digestives, and have a nice chat with your mum. You've still got your mum, haven't you?"

"Actually . . . we're not really speaking at the moment," I confess.

"Well, then, your dad?"

I shake my head.

"Well . . . how about your best friend? You must have a best friend!" The pineapple lady gives me a comforting smile.

"Yes, I have got a best friend." I gulp. "But she's just been informed on national television that I've been having secret lesbian fantasies about her."

The pineapple lady regards me silently for a few moments.

"Have a nice cup of tea . . ." she says at last with less conviction. "And . . . good luck, dear."

I make my way slowly back from the tube station to our street. As I reach the corner I stop, blow my nose, and take a few deep breaths, trying to calm my nerves.

How am I going to face Lissy after what Jack said on television? How?

This is worse than the time that I threw up in her parents' bathroom. This is worse than the time she saw me kissing my reflection in the mirror and saying "Ooh, baby" in a sexy voice. This is even worse than the time she caught me writing a valentine to our math teacher Mr. Blake.

I'm hoping against hope that she might have suddenly decided to go out for the day or something. But as I open the front door of the flat, there she is, coming out of the kitchen into the hall. And as she looks at me, I can already see it in her face. She's completely freaked out.

Not only has Jack betrayed me. He's ruined my best friendship, too. Things will never be the same between me and Lissy again. It's just like *When Harry Met Sally*. Sex has gotten in the way of our relationship, and now we can't be friends anymore, because we want to sleep together.

No. Scratch that. We don't want to sleep together. We want to— No, the point is we *don't* want to—

Anyway. Whatever. It's not good.

"Oh!" she says, staring at the floor. "Gosh! Um, hi, Emma!"

"Hi!" I reply in a strangled voice. "I thought I'd come home. The office was just too . . . too awful . . ."

I trail off, and there's the most excruciating, prickling silence.

"So . . . I guess you saw it," I say at last.

"Yes, I saw it. And I . . ." Lissy clears her throat. "I just wanted to say that . . . that if you want me to move out, then I will."

After twenty-one years, our friendship is over. One tiny secret comes out—and that's the end of everything.

"It's OK," I say, trying not to burst into tears. "I'll move out."

"No!" says Lissy awkwardly. "*I'll* move out. This isn't your fault, Emma. It's been me who's been . . . leading you on."

"What? Lissy, you haven't been leading me on!"

"Yes, I have." She looks stricken. "I feel terrible. I just never realized you had . . . those kind of feelings . . ."

"I don't!"

"But I can see it all now! I've been walking around half dressed. No wonder you were frustrated!"

"Lissy, I wasn't frustrated," I say quickly. "Lissy, I'm not a lesbian."

"Bisexual, then. Or 'multi-oriented.' Whatever term you want to use."

"I'm not bisexual, either! Or multi-whatever-it-was!"

"Emma, please!" Lissy grabs my hand. "Don't be ashamed of your sexuality. And I promise—I'll support you a hundred percent, whatever choice you decide to make—"

"Lissy, I'm not bisexual!" I cry. "I don't need support! I just had one dream, OK? It wasn't a fantasy. It was just a weird dream, which I didn't intend to have, and it doesn't mean I'm a lesbian, and it doesn't mean I fancy you, and it doesn't mean anything!"

"Oh." There's silence. Lissy looks taken aback. "Oh, right. I thought it was a . . . a . . . you know." She clears her throat. "That you wanted to . . ."

"No! I just had a dream. Just one, stupid dream."

"Oh. Right."

There's a long pause, during which Lissy looks intently at her fingernails, and I study the buckle of my watch.

"So . . . did we actually . . ." says Lissy at last.

Oh, God. "Kind of," I admit.

"And . . . was I any good?"

"What?" I gape at her.

"In the dream." She looks straight at me, her cheeks bright pink. "Was I any good?"

"Lissy—"

"I was crap, wasn't I? I was crap! I knew it—"

"No, of course you weren't crap!" I exclaim. "You were . . . you were really . . ."

I cannot believe I'm seriously having a conversation about my best friend's sexual prowess as a dream lesbian. "Look, can we just . . . leave the subject? My day has been embarrassing enough already."

"Oh. Oh, God, yes," says Lissy, suddenly full of remorse. "Sorry, Emma. You must be feeling really . . ."

"Totally and utterly humiliated and betrayed?" I try to smile. "Yup, that's pretty much how I feel."

"Did anyone at the office see it, then?" says Lissy sympathetically.

"Did anyone at the office *see* it? Lissy, they *all* saw it. They all knew it was me! And they were all laughing at me, and I just wanted to curl up and *die*."

"Really?" says Lissy in distress.

"It was *awful.*" I close my eyes as fresh mortification washes over me. "I have never felt more . . . exposed. The whole world knows I find G-strings uncomfortable and I don't really kickbox, and I've never read Dickens . . ." My voice is wobbling more and more, and suddenly I begin to sob. "Oh, God, Lissy. You were right. I feel such a complete . . . *fool*. He was just using me, right from the beginning. He was never really interested in me. I was just a . . . a market research project."

"You don't know that!"

"I do! Of course I do! That's why he was gripped. That's why he was so fascinated by everything I said. It wasn't because he loved me. It was because he realized he had his target customer, right next to him. The kind of normal, ordinary girl-on-the-street he wouldn't normally give the time of day to! I mean, he said it on the television, didn't he? I'm just a nothing-special girl."

"You are not," says Lissy fiercely. "You are *not* nothing special!"

"I am! That's exactly what I am! I'm just an ordinary nothing. And I was so stupid, I believed it all. I honestly thought Jack loved me. I mean, maybe not exactly loved me." I feel myself color. "But . . . you know. Felt about me like I felt about him."

"I know." Lissy looks like she wants to cry herself. "I know you did." She leans forward and gives me a huge hug.

Then she draws awkwardly away. "This isn't making you feel uncomfortable, is it? I mean, it's not . . . turning you on or anything—"

"Lissy, for the last time, I'm not a lesbian!" I cry in exasperation.

"OK!" she says hurriedly. "OK. Sorry." She gives me another tight hug, then stands up. "Come on," she says. "You need a drink."

We go onto the tiny, overgrown balcony—which was described as "spacious roof terrace" by the landlord when we first rented this flat—and sit in a patch of sun, drinking the brandy that Lissy got duty-free last year. Each sip makes my mouth burn unbearably but, five seconds later, sends a lovely, soothing warmth all over my body.

"I should have known," I say, turning my glass around and around. "I should have known a big, important millionaire like that would never really be interested in me."

"I just . . . can't believe it," says Lissy, sighing for the thousandth time. "I can't believe it was all made-up. It was all so *romantic*. Changing his mind about going to America . . . and the bus . . . and bringing you that pink cocktail."

"But that's the point." I can feel tears rising again, and fiercely blink them back. "That's what makes it so . . . humiliating. He knew exactly what I would like. I told him on the plane I was bored with Connor. He knew I wanted excitement and intrigue and a big romance. He just fed me everything he knew I'd like. And I believed it . . . because I wanted to believe it."

"You honestly think the whole thing was one big plan?"

"Of course it was a plan! He deliberately followed me around; he watched everything I did. He wanted to get into my life! Look at the way he came and poked around my bedroom! No wonder he seemed so bloody interested. I expect he was taking notes all the time. I expect he had a Dictaphone in his pocket. And I just . . . invited him in." The next gulp of brandy makes me shudder. "I am never going to trust a man again. Never."

"But he seemed so . . . nice!" says Lissy. "I just can't believe he was being so cynical."

"Lissy . . ." I look up. "The truth is, a man like that doesn't get to the top without being ruthless and trampling over people. It just doesn't happen."

"Doesn't it?" Her brow crumples. "Maybe you're right. God, how depressing."

"Is that Emma?" comes a piercing voice, and Jemima appears on the balcony in a white robe and a face mask, her eyes narrowed. "So! Miss I-never-borrow-your-clothes. What have you got to say about my Prada slingbacks?"

Oh, God. There's no point lying about it, is there?

"They're really pointy and uncomfortable?" I say with a little shrug, and Jemima inhales sharply.

"I knew it! I knew it all along. You *do* borrow my clothes. What about my Joseph jumper? What about my Gucci bag?"

"*Which* Gucci bag?" I shoot back.

For a moment Jemima flounders for words. "All of them!" she says at last. "You know, I could sue you for this. I could take you to the cleaners!" She brandishes a piece of paper at me. "I've got a list here of items of apparel that I fully suspect have been worn by someone other than me during the last three months—"

"Oh, shut up about your stupid clothes!" says Lissy. "Emma's really upset! She's been completely betrayed and humiliated by the man she thought loved her!"

"Well, surprise, surprise, let me just faint with shock," says Jemima tartly. "I could have told you that was going to happen. I *did* tell you! Never tell a man all about yourself; it's bound to lead to trouble. Did I not warn you?"

"You said she wouldn't get a rock on her finger!" exclaims Lissy. "You didn't say he would pitch up on television, telling the nation all her private secrets! You know, Jemima, you could be a bit more sympathetic—"

"No, Lissy, she's right," I say miserably. "She was completely right all along. If I'd just kept my stupid mouth shut, then none of this would have happened!" I reach for the brandy bottle and pour myself another glass. "Relationships *are* a battle. They *are* a chess game. And what did I do? I just threw all my chess pieces down on the board at once and said, 'Here! Have them all!' " I take a gulp of my drink. "The truth is, men and women should tell each other nothing. *Nothing.*"

"I couldn't agree more," says Jemima. "I'm planning to tell

my future husband as little as possible—" She breaks off as the cordless phone in her hand rings.

"Hi!" she says, switching it on. "Camilla? Oh. Er, OK. Just hang on a moment."

She puts her hand over the receiver and looks at me, wide-eyed. "It's Jack!" she mouths.

I'm frozen in shock.

Somehow I'd almost forgotten Jack existed in real life. All I can see is that face on the television screen, smiling and nodding and slowly leading me to my humiliation.

"Tell him Emma doesn't want to speak to him!" hisses Lissy.

"No! She *should* speak to him!" whispers Jemima. "Otherwise, he'll think he's won!"

"But surely—"

"Give it to me!" I say, and grab the phone out of Jemima's hand.

"Hi," I say in as curt a tone as I can muster.

"Emma, it's me," comes Jack's familiar voice, and I feel a rush of emotion that almost overwhelms me. I want to cry. I want to hit him, hurt him. . . .

But somehow I keep control of myself.

"I never want to speak to you again," I say, and switch off the phone.

"Well done!" says Lissy.

An instant later it rings again. "Please, Emma," says Jack, "just listen for a moment. I know you must be very upset. But if you just give me a second to explain—"

"Didn't you hear me?" I exclaim, my face flushing. "You used me and you humiliated me and I never want to speak to you again, or see you, or hear you, or . . . or . . ."

"Taste you," puts in Jemima, nodding urgently.

". . . or touch you again. Never ever. Ever." I switch off the phone, march inside, and yank the line out of the wall.

Then, with trembling hands, I get my mobile out of the bag and, just as it begins to ring, switch it off.

As I emerge on the balcony again, I'm still shaking with shock. I can't quite believe my perfect romance has crumbled into nothing.

"Are you OK?" says Lissy anxiously.

"I'm fine. I think. A bit shaky."

"Now, Emma," says Jemima, examining one of her cuticles. "I don't want to rush you. But you know what you have to do, don't you?"

"What?"

"You have to get your revenge." She looks up and fixes me with a determined gaze. "You have to make him pay."

"Oh, no." Lissy pulls a face. "Isn't revenge really undignified? Isn't it better just to walk away?"

"What good is walking away?" retorts Jemima. "Will walking away teach him a lesson? Will walking away make him wish he'd never crossed you?"

"Emma and I have always agreed we'd rather keep the moral high ground," says Lissy determinedly. " 'Living well is the best revenge.' George Herbert."

Jemima looks blank. "So anyway," she says at last, turning back to me. "I'd be delighted to help. Revenge is actually quite a specialty of mine, though I say it myself . . ."

I avoid Lissy's eyes. "What did you have in mind?"

"Scrape his car, shred his suits, sew fish inside his curtains and wait for them to rot . . ." she reels off instantly, as though reciting poetry.

"Did you learn that at finishing school?" says Lissy, rolling her eyes.

"I'm being a feminist, *actually*," retorts Jemima. "We women have to stand up for our rights. You know, before she married my father, Mummy went out with this scientist chap who practically jilted her. He changed his mind three weeks before the wedding—can you believe it? So one night she crept into his lab and pulled out all the plugs of his stupid machines. His whole research was ruined! She always says, That taught Emerson!"

"Emerson?" says Lissy, staring at her in disbelief. "As in . . . Emerson Davies?"

"That's right! Davies."

"Emerson Davies who nearly discovered a cure for smallpox?"

"Well, he shouldn't have messed Mummy about, should he?" says Jemima mutinously. She turns to me. "Another of Mummy's tips is chili oil. You somehow arrange to have sex with the chap again, and then you say, 'How about a little massage oil?' And you rub it into his . . . you know." Her eyes sparkle. "That'll hurt him where it counts!"

"Your *mother* told you this?" says Lissy.

"Yes!" says Jemima. "It was rather sweet, actually. On my eighteenth birthday she sat me down and said we should have a little chat about men and women—"

Lissy is staring at her incredulously. "In which she instructed you to rub chili oil into men's genitals?"

"Only if they treat you badly!" says Jemima in annoyance. "What is your *problem,* Lissy? Do you think you should just let men walk all over you and get away with it? Great blow for feminism!"

"I'm not saying that!" says Lissy. "I just wouldn't get my revenge with . . . chili oil!"

"Well, what would you do, then, clever clogs?" says Jemima, putting her hands on her hips.

"OK!" says Lissy. "*If* I were going to stoop so low as to get my revenge—which I never would, because personally I think it's a huge mistake . . ." She pauses for breath. "I'd do exactly what he did. I'd expose one of *his* secrets."

"Actually . . . that's rather good," says Jemima grudgingly.

"Humiliate *him,*" says Lissy with a tiny air of vindication. "Embarrass *him.* See how he likes it!"

They both turn and look at me expectantly. "But I don't know any of his secrets," I say.

"You must!" says Jemima.

"I don't! Lissy, you had it right all along. Our relationship was completely one-sided. I shared all my secrets with him . . . but he didn't share any of his with me. He didn't tell me anything. We weren't soul mates. I was a completely deluded moron."

"Emma, you weren't a moron," says Lissy, putting a hand on mine. "You were just trusting."

"Trusting . . . moron . . . it's the same thing . . ."

"You must know *something*!" says Jemima. "You slept with him, for goodness' sake! He must have some secret. Some . . . weak point!"

"An Achilles' heel," puts in Lissy, and Jemima gives her an odd look.

"It doesn't *have* to do with his feet," Jemima says, and turns to me, pulling a Lissy's-lost-it face. "It could be anything. Anything at all. Think back!"

I close my eyes and cast my mind back. But my mind's swirling a bit from all that brandy. Secrets . . . Jack's secrets . . . Think back . . .

Scotland.

I open my eyes, feeling a tingle of exhilaration. I do know one of his secrets.

"What?" says Jemima. "Have you remembered something?"

"He . . ." I stop, feeling torn.

I did make a promise to Jack.

But then, so what? So bloody what? My chest swells in emotion again. Why on earth am I keeping any stupid promise to him? It's not like he kept my secrets to *him*self, is it?

"He was in Scotland!" I say. "The first time we met after

the plane, he asked me to keep it a secret that he was in Scotland."

"Why did he do that?" says Lissy.

"I dunno."

"What was he doing in Scotland?" puts in Jemima.

"I . . . dunno."

There's a pause.

"Hmm," says Jemima kindly. "It's not the *most* embarrassing secret in the world, is it? I mean, plenty of smart people live in Scotland. Haven't you got anything better? Like . . . does he wear a chest wig?"

"A chest wig!" Lissy gives an explosive snort of laughter. "Or a toupee!"

"Of course he doesn't wear a chest wig! *Or* a toupee!"

Do they honestly think I'd go out with a man who wore a *toupee*?

"Well, then, you'll have to make something up," says Jemima. "You know, before the affair with the scientist, Mummy was treated very badly by some politician chap. So she made up a rumor that he was taking bribes from the Communist party, and passed it around the House of Commons. She always says, That taught Dennis a lesson!"

"Not . . . Dennis Llewellyn?" Lissy says.

"Er, yes! I think that was him."

"The disgraced Home Secretary?" Lissy looks aghast. "The one who spent his whole life fighting to clear his name and ended up in a mental institution?"

"Well, he shouldn't have messed Mummy around, should he?" says Jemima, sticking out her chin. A bleeper goes off in her pocket. "Time for my footbath!"

As she disappears back into the house, Lissy shakes her head.

"She's nuts," she says. "Totally nuts. Emma, you are *not* making anything up about Jack Harper."

"I won't make anything up!" I say. "Who do you think I

am? Anyway." I stare into my brandy, feeling my exhilaration fade away. "Who am I kidding? I could never get my revenge on Jack. I could never hurt him. He doesn't *have* any weak points. He's a huge, powerful millionaire." I take a miserable slug of my drink. "And I'm a nothing-special . . . crappy . . . ordinary . . . nothing."

Twenty-one

THE NEXT MORNING I wake up sick with dread. I feel exactly like a five-year-old who doesn't want to go to school. A five-year-old with a severe hangover, that is.

"I can't go," I say as eight-thirty arrives. "I can't face them."

"Yes, you can!" says Lissy, doing up my jacket buttons. "It'll be fine. Just keep your chin up."

"What if they're horrid to me?"

"They won't be horrid to you! They're your friends! Anyway, they'll probably all have forgotten about it by now!"

"They won't! Can't I just stay at home with you?" I grab her hand. "I'll be really good. I promise—"

"Emma, I've explained to you," says Lissy in patient mother tones. "I've got to go to court today." She pries my hand out of hers. "But I'll be here when you get home. And we'll have something really nice for supper. OK? Now, go on." She opens the door to our flat. "You'll be fine!"

Feeling like a dog being shooed out, I go down the stairs

and open the front door. I'm just stepping out of the house when a van pulls up at the side of the road. A man gets out in a blue uniform, holding the biggest bunch of flowers I've ever seen, all tied up with dark green ribbon, and squints at the number on our house.

"Hello," he says, "I'm looking for an Emma Corrigan."

"That's me!" I say in surprise.

"Aha!" He smiles, and holds out a pen and clipboard. "Well, this is your lucky day! If you could just sign here."

The bouquet is unbelievable. Roses, freesias, amazing big purple flowers, fantastic dark red pom-pom things, dark green, frondy bits, pale green ones that look just like asparagus.

OK, I may not know what they're all called. But I do know one thing. These flowers are expensive. There's only one person who could have sent them.

"Wait," I say without taking the pen. "I want to check who they're from."

I grab the card, rip it open, and scan down the long message, not reading any of it until I come to the name at the bottom.

Jack.

I feel a huge dart of stung pride. After all he did, Jack thinks he can fob me off with some manky bunch of flowers?

All right, huge, deluxe bunch of flowers, but that's not the point.

"I don't want them, thank you," I say.

"You don't *want* them?" the delivery man looks baffled.

"What's going on?" comes a breathless voice beside me, and I look up to see Lissy gawking at the bouquet. "Oh, my God. Are they from Jack?"

"Yes. Please take them away," I say to the deliveryman.

"Wait!" exclaims Lissy, grabbing the cellophane. "Let me just smell them." She buries her face in the blooms and inhales deeply. "Wow! That's absolutely incredible! I've never *seen* flowers as amazing as this." She looks at the man. "So, what will happen to them?"

"Dunno." He shrugs. "They'll get chucked away, I suppose."

"Gosh." She glances at me. "That seems like an awful waste."

"Lissy, I can't *accept* them!" I exclaim. "I can't! He'll think I'm saying everything's OK between us!"

"No, you're quite right," says Lissy, sounding reluctant. "You have to send them back." She touches a pink velvety rose petal. "It is a shame, though."

"Send what back?" comes a sharp voice behind me. "You are joking, aren't you?"

Oh, for God's sake. Now Jemima has arrived in the street, still in her white dressing gown. "You're not sending those back!" she cries. "I'm giving a dinner party on Saturday! They'll be perfect!" She grabs the label. "Smythe and Foxe! Do you know how much these must have cost?"

"I don't care how much they cost!" I exclaim. "They're from Jack! I can't possibly keep them!"

"Why not?"

She's unbelievable.

"Because . . . because it's a matter of principle! If I keep them, I'm basically saying, 'I forgive you.' "

"Not necessarily!" retorts Jemima. "You could be saying, 'I *don't* forgive you.' Or you could be saying, 'I can't be bothered to return your stupid flowers—that's how little you mean to me.' "

There's silence as we all consider this. The thing is, they *are* pretty amazing flowers.

"So, do you want them or not?" says the delivery guy.

"I . . ." Oh, God, now I'm all confused.

"Emma, if you send them back, you look weak," says Jemima firmly. "You look like you can't bear to have any reminder of him in the house. But if you keep them, then you're saying, 'I don't care about you!' You're standing firm! You're being strong! You're being—"

"Oh, God, OK!" I say, and grab the pen. "I'll sign for them. But could you please tell him that this does *not* mean I forgive him, nor that he isn't a cynical, heartless, despicable user, and furthermore, if Jemima weren't having a dinner party, these would be straight in the bin." As I finish signing, I'm red-faced, and I stamp a period so hard it tears the page. "Can you remember all that?"

"Love," says the delivery guy, "I just work at the depot."

"I know!" says Lissy. She grabs the clipboard back and prints WITHOUT PREJUDICE clearly under my name.

"What does that mean?" I say.

"It means 'I'll never forgive you, you complete bastard . . . but I'll keep the flowers anyway.' "

"And you're still going to get even," adds Jemima.

It's one of those amazingly bright, crisp mornings that make you feel like London really is the best city in the world. The sun is glinting off the river and the windows of office blocks, and the dome of St. Paul's looks like a picture postcard against the blue sky. And as I stride along from the tube station, my spirits can't help rising a little.

Maybe Lissy's right. Maybe everyone at work will already have forgotten about the whole thing. I mean, let's get a bit of proportion here. It wasn't *that* big a deal. It wasn't *that* interesting. Surely some other piece of gossip will have come along in the meantime. Surely everyone will be talking about . . . football. Or politics or something. Exactly.

I arrive at the Panther building, push open the glass door to the foyer, and walk in, my head held high.

". . . a Barbie bedspread!" I immediately hear from across

the marble. A guy from Accounts is talking to a woman with a "Visitor" badge, who is listening avidly.

". . . shagging Jack Harper all along?" comes a voice from above me, and I look up to see a group of girls walking up the stairs.

"It's Connor I feel sorry for," one replies. "That poor guy . . ."

". . . pretended she loved jazz!" someone else is saying as they get out of the lift. "I mean, why on earth would you do that?"

My optimism instantly dies away, and I consider running away and spending the rest of my life under the duvet.

But I have to face them. I have to do this.

Clenching my fists at my sides, I slowly make my way up the stairs and along the corridor to the marketing department. Everyone I pass either blatantly goggles at me or pretends they're not looking, and at least five conversations are hastily broken off as I approach.

As I reach the door to the marketing department, I take a deep breath, then walk in, trying to look as unconcerned as possible.

"Hi, everyone," I say, taking off my jacket and hanging it on my chair.

"Emma!" exclaims Artemis in tones of sarcastic delight. "Well, I never!"

"Good morning, Emma," says Paul, coming out of his office and giving me an appraising look. "You OK?"

"Fine, thanks."

"Anything you'd like to . . . talk about?" To my surprise, he looks like he genuinely means it.

But honestly. What does he think? That I'm going to go in there and sob on his shoulder, "That bastard Jack Harper used me"?

"No," I say, my face prickling. "Thanks, but . . . I'm OK."

"Good." He pauses, then adopts a more businesslike tone. "Now, I'm assuming that when you disappeared yesterday, it was because you'd decided to work from home."

"Er, yes." I clear my throat. "That's right."

"No doubt you got lots of useful tasks done?"

"Er, yes. Loads."

"Excellent. Just what I thought. All right, then, carry on. And the rest of you"—Paul looks around the office as though in warning—"remember what I said."

"Of course!" says Artemis at once. "We all remember!"

Paul disappears into his office again, and I focus rigidly on my computer as it warms up. It'll be fine, I tell myself. I'll just concentrate on my work, completely immerse myself. . . .

Suddenly I become aware that someone's humming a tune quite loudly.

It's something I recognize. It's . . .

It's the Carpenters.

And now a few others around the room are joining in on the chorus.

"Close to yooooou . . ."

"All right, Emma?" says Nick as I look up suspiciously. "D'you want a hanky?"

"Close to yooooou . . ." everybody trills in unison again, and I hear muffled laughter.

I'm not going to react. I'm not going to give them the pleasure.

As calmly as possible, I click onto my e-mails, and give a small gasp of shock. I normally get about ten e-mails every morning, if that. Today I have ninety-five.

Dad: I'd really like to talk . . .

Carol: I've already got two more people for our Barbie Club . . .

Moira: I know where you can get really comfy
   G-strings . . .
Sharon: So how long has this been going on?!!
Fiona: Re: the body awareness workshop . . .

I scroll down the endless list and suddenly feel a stabbing in my heart.

There are three from Jack.

What should I do?

Should I read them?

My hand hovers over my mouse. Does he deserve at least a chance to explain?

"Oh, Emma," says Artemis innocently, coming over to my desk with a carrier bag. "I've got this jumper I wondered if you'd like. It's a bit too small for me, but it's very nice. And it should fit you, because . . ." She pauses, and catches Caroline's eye. ". . . it's a size four."

Immediately both of them erupt into hysterical giggles.

"Thanks, Artemis," I say shortly. "That's really sweet of you."

"I'm off for a coffee," says Fergus, standing up. "Anybody want anything?"

"Make mine a Harveys Bristol Cream," says Nick brightly.

"Ha ha," I mutter under my breath.

"Oh, Emma, I meant to say," Nick adds, sauntering over to my desk, "that new secretary in Admin. Have you seen her? She's quite something, isn't she?"

He winks at me, and I stare at him blankly for a moment, not understanding.

"Nice, spiky haircut . . ." he adds. "Nice dungarees . . ."

"Shut *up*!" I cry furiously, my face flaming red. "I'm not a . . . I'm not . . . Just fuck off, all of you!"

My hand trembling with anger, I swiftly delete each and every one of Jack's e-mails. He doesn't deserve anything. No chance. Nothing.

I rise to my feet and stride out. I head for the ladies' room, slam the door behind me, and rest my hot forehead on the mirror. Hatred for Jack Harper is bubbling through me like hot lava. Does he have any idea what I'm going through? Does he have any idea what he's done to me?

"Emma!" A voice interrupts my thoughts. Immediately I feel a jolt of apprehension.

Katie has quietly come into the ladies', and now she's standing right behind me, holding her makeup bag. Her face is reflected in the mirror next to mine . . . and she isn't smiling. It's just like *Fatal Attraction*.

"So," she says in a strange voice. "You don't like crochet."

Oh, God. What have I done? Have I unleashed the bunny-boiler side of Katie that no one's ever seen before? Maybe she'll impale me with a crochet needle, I find myself thinking wildly.

"Katie," I say. "Katie, please listen. I never meant . . . I never said . . ."

"Emma, don't even try." She lifts her hand. "There's no point. We both know the truth."

"He was wrong!" I say quickly. "He got confused! I meant I don't like . . . um . . . *creches*. You know, all those babies everywhere—"

Katie cuts me off with an odd smile. "You know, I was pretty upset yesterday, but after work I went straight home and I called my mum. And do you know what she said to me?"

"What?" I say apprehensively.

"She said . . . she doesn't like crochet, either."

"*What?*"

"And neither does my granny!" Her face flushes, and suddenly she looks like the old Katie again. "Or any of my relatives! They've all been pretending for years, just like you! It all makes sense now!" Her voice rises in agitation. "You know, I made my granny a whole sofa cover last Christmas, and she told me that burglars had stolen it. But I mean, what kind of burglars steal a crochet sofa cover?"

"Katie, I don't know what to say. . . ."

"Emma, why couldn't you have told me before? All that time. Making stupid presents that people didn't want."

"Oh, God, Katie, I'm sorry!" I say, filled with remorse. "I'm so sorry. I just . . . didn't want to hurt you!"

"I know you were trying to be kind. But I feel really stupid now!"

"Yes, well. That makes two of us," I say morosely.

The door suddenly opens, and Wendy from Accounts comes in. There's a pause as she stares at us both, opens her mouth, closes it again, then disappears into one of the cubicles.

"So . . . are you OK?" says Katie in a lower voice.

"I'm fine," I mutter. "You know . . ."

Yeah. I'm so fine, I'm hiding in the loo rather than face my colleagues.

"Have you spoken to Jack?" she says tentatively.

"No. He sent me some stupid flowers. Like, 'Oh, that's OK, then.' He probably didn't even order them himself. He probably got Sven to do it."

There's the sound of flushing, and Wendy comes out of the cubicle again.

"Well . . . this is the mascara I was talking about," Katie says quickly, handing me a tube.

"Thanks," I say. "You say it, um, volumizes *and* lengthens?"

"It's OK!" exclaims Wendy. "I'm not listening!" She washes her hands, dries them, then gives me a curious look. "So, Emma, are you going out with Jack Harper?"

"No," I say curtly. "He used me and he betrayed me, and to be honest, I'd be happy if I never saw him again in my whole life."

"Oh, right!" she says brightly. "It's just, I was wondering. If you're speaking to him again, could you just mention that I'd really like to move to the PR department?"

"What?"

"If you could just casually drop it in that I have good communication skills and I think I'd be really suited to PR."

Casually drop it in? What, like, "I never want to see you again, Jack, and by the way, Wendy thinks she'd be good at PR"?

"I'm not sure," I say at last. "I just . . . don't think it's something I could do."

"Well, I think that's really selfish of you, Emma!" says Wendy, looking offended. "All I'm asking you is, if the subject comes up, to mention that I'd like to move to PR! Just mention it! I mean, how hard is that?"

"Wendy, piss off!" says Katie. "Leave Emma alone!"

"I was only *asking*!" says Wendy. "I suppose you think you're above us now, do you?"

"No!" I exclaim in shock. "It's not that—" But Wendy's already flounced out.

"Great," I say with a sudden wobble to my voice. "Just great! Now everyone's going to hate me, on top of everything else."

I still can't quite believe how everything has turned upside down, just like that. Everything I believed in has turned out to be false. My perfect man has turned out to be a cynical user. My dreamy romance was all just a fabrication. I was happier than I'd ever been in my life. And now I'm just a stupid, humiliated laughingstock.

Oh, God. My eyes are tearing up again.

"Are you OK, Emma?" says Katie, looking at me in dismay. "Here, have a tissue." She rummages in her makeup bag. "And some eye gel."

"Thanks," I say, and swallow hard. I dab the eye gel on my eyes and force myself to breathe deeply until I'm completely calm again.

"I think you're really brave," says Katie, watching me. "In

fact, I'm amazed you even came in today. I would have been *far* too embarrassed."

"Katie," I say, turning to face her, "yesterday I had all my most personal, private secrets broadcast on TV." I spread my arms. "How could anything possibly be more embarrassing than that?"

"Here she is!" comes a ringing voice behind us, and Caroline bursts into the ladies'. "Emma, your parents are here to see you!"

No. I do not believe this. I do not *believe* this.

My parents are standing by my desk. Dad's wearing a smart gray suit, and Mum's all dressed up in a white jacket and navy skirt, and they're kind of holding a bunch of flowers between them. And the entire office is gawking at them as though they're rare creatures of some sort.

"Hi, Mum," I say in a voice that has suddenly gone rather husky. "Hi, Dad."

What are they *doing* here?

"Emma!" says Dad, making an attempt at his normal, jovial voice. "We just thought we'd . . . pop in to see you."

"Right," I say, nodding. As though this were a perfectly normal course of events.

"We brought you a little present," says Mum in a bright voice. "Some flowers for your desk." She puts the bouquet down awkwardly. "Look at Emma's desk, Brian. Isn't it smart! Look at the . . . the computer!"

"Splendid!" says Dad, giving it a little pat. "Very . . . very fine desk indeed."

"And are these your friends?" says Mum, smiling around the office.

"Er, kind of," I say, scowling, as Artemis beams back at her.

"We were just saying, the other day," continues Mum,

"how *proud* you should be of yourself, Emma. Working for a big company like this! I'm sure many girls would be very envious of your career! Don't you agree, Brian?"

"Absolutely!" says Dad. "You've . . . you've done very well for yourself, Emma."

I'm so taken aback, I can't even open my mouth. I meet Dad's eye, and he gives a strange, awkward little smile. And Mum's hands are trembling slightly as she fusses with the flowers.

They're nervous, I realize with a jolt of shock. They're both *nervous*.

I'm just trying to get my head around this as Paul appears at the door of his office. "So, Emma," he says, raising his eyebrows. "You have visitors, I gather?"

"Er, yes," I say. "Paul, these are, um, my parents, Brian and Rachel."

"Enchanted," says Paul with a polite incline of his head.

"We don't want to be any bother—" says Mum.

"No bother at all," says Paul, and bestows a charming smile on her. "Unfortunately, the room we *usually* use for family bonding sessions is being redecorated. . . ."

"Oh!" says Mum, unsure as to whether he's being serious or not. "Oh, dear!"

"So perhaps, Emma, you'd like to take your parents out for . . . shall we call it an early lunch?"

I look up at the clock. It's a quarter to ten.

"Thanks, Paul," I say gratefully.

This is completely surreal.

It's the middle of the morning. I should be at work. And instead, I'm walking down the street with my parents, wondering what on earth we're going to say to one another.

I can't even *remember* the last time it was just my parents and me. Just the three of us—no Grandpa, no Kerry, no Nev. It's like we've gone back in time fifteen years.

"We could go in here . . ." I say as we reach an Italian coffee shop.

"Good idea!" says Dad in hearty tones, and pushes the door open. "We saw your friend Jack Harper on television yesterday," he adds.

"He's not my friend," I reply, and he and Mum glance at each other.

We sit down at a wooden table and a waiter brings us each a menu, and there's silence.

Oh, God. Now *I'm* feeling nervous.

"So, um . . ." I begin, then stop. What I want to say is "Why are you here?" But it might sound a bit rude. "What . . . brings you to London?" I say instead.

"We just thought we'd like to visit you!" says Mum, looking through her reading glasses at the menu. "Now, shall I have a cup of tea . . . or—what's this? A frappalatte?"

"I want a normal cup of coffee," says Dad, peering at the menu with a frown. "Do they do such a thing?"

"If they don't, you'll have to have a cappuccino and spoon off the froth," says Mum. "Or an espresso and just ask them to add hot water."

I don't believe this. They have driven two hundred miles. Are we just going to sit here and talk about hot beverages all day?

"Oh, and that reminds me," adds Mum casually. "We've bought you a little something, Emma. Didn't we, Brian?"

"Oh . . . right," I say in surprise. "What is it?"

"It's a car," says Mum, and looks up at the waiter who's appeared at our table. "Hello! I would like a cappuccino, my husband would like a filter coffee if that's possible, and Emma would like—"

"A *car*?" I echo in disbelief.

"Car," echoes the Italian waiter, and gives me a suspicious look. "You want coffee?"

"I'd . . . I'd like a cappuccino, please."

"And a selection of cakes," adds Mum. *"Grazie!"*

"Mum . . ." I put a hand to my head as the waiter disappears. "What do you mean, you've bought me a car?"

"Just a little run-around. You ought to have a car! It's not safe, your traveling on all these buses. Grandpa's quite right."

"But . . . but I can't afford a car," I say. "I can't even . . . What about the money I owe you? What about—"

"Forget the money," says Dad. "We're going to wipe the slate clean."

"What?" I'm more mystified than ever. "But we can't do that! I still owe you—"

"Forget the money," says Dad, a sudden edge to his voice. "I want you to forget all about it, Emma. You . . . you don't owe us anything. Nothing at all."

I honestly cannot take all this in. I look from Dad to Mum. Then back to Dad. Then, very slowly, back to Mum again.

And it's really strange. But it almost feels as though we're seeing one another properly for the first time in years. As though we're seeing one another and saying hello and kind of . . . starting again.

"We were wondering what you thought about taking a little holiday next year!" says Mum. "With us."

"Just . . . us?" I say, looking around the table.

"Just the three of us, we thought." She gives me a tentative smile. "It might be fun! You don't have to, of course. If you've got other plans—"

"No! I'd like to!" I say quickly. "I really would. But . . . but what about . . ."

I can't even bring myself to say Kerry's name.

There's a tiny silence, during which Mum and Dad look at each other, and then away again.

"Kerry sends her love, of course!" says Mum, as though

she's changing the subject completely. She clears her throat. "You know, she thought she might visit Hong Kong next year. Visit her father! She hasn't seen him for at least five years, and maybe it's time they . . . had some time together."

"Right!" I say, feeling totally stupefied. "Good idea."

I can't believe this. Everything's changed. It's like the entire family has been thrown up in the air and has fallen down in different positions, and nothing's like it was before.

"We feel, Emma," says Dad, and stops. "We feel . . . that perhaps we haven't been . . . that perhaps we haven't always noticed—" He breaks off and rubs his nose vigorously.

"Cappu-*cci*no," says the waiter, planting a cup in front of me. "Filter *cof*-fee, cappu-*cci*no . . . coffee *cake* . . . lemon *cake* . . . chocolate—"

"Thank you!" interrupts Mum. "Thank you so much. I think we can manage from here." The waiter disappears again, and she looks at me. "Emma, what we want to say is . . . we're very proud of you."

Oh God, I think I'm going to cry. "Right," I manage.

"And we . . ." Dad begins. "That is to say . . . we both . . . your mother and I . . ." He clears his throat. "We've always . . . and always will . . . both of us . . ."

He pauses, breathing rather hard. I don't quite dare say anything.

"What I'm trying to say, Emma . . ." he starts again. "As I'm sure you . . . as I'm sure we all . . . which is to say . . ."

He stops again and wipes his perspiring face with a napkin.

"The fact of the matter is that . . . is that . . ."

"Oh, just tell your daughter you love her, Brian, for once in your bloody life!" cries Mum.

"I . . . I . . . love you, Emma!" says Dad in a choked-up voice. "Oh, Jesus." He brushes roughly at his eye.

"I love you, too, Dad," I say, my throat tight. "And you, Mum."

"You see!" says Mum, dabbing at her eye. "I knew it wasn't

a mistake to come!" She clutches hold of my hand, and I clutch hold of Dad's hand, and for a moment we're in a kind of awkward group hug.

"You know, we're all sacred links in the eternal circle of life," I say with a sudden swell of emotion.

"What?" Both my parents look at me blankly.

"Er, never mind." I release my hand and take a sip of cappuccino, and look up.

Jack is standing at the door of the coffee shop.

Twenty-two

I ALMOST CAN'T BREATHE as I see him through the glass doors. He puts out a hand, the door pings, and suddenly he's inside the coffee shop.

As he walks toward our table, I feel my facade begin to crumble. This is the man I thought I was in love with. This is the man who completely used me. Now that the initial shock has faded, all the feelings of pain and humiliation are threatening to take over and turn me to jelly again.

But I'm not going to let them. I'm going to be strong and dignified. "Ignore him," I say to Mum and Dad.

"Who?" says Dad, turning around in his chair. "Oh!"

"Emma, I want to talk to you," says Jack.

"Well, I don't want to talk to you."

"I'm so sorry to interrupt." He glances at Mum and Dad. "If we could just have a moment . . ."

"I'm not going anywhere!" I say in outrage. "I'm having a nice cup of coffee with my parents!"

"Please." He sits down at an adjoining table. "I want to explain. I want to apologize."

"There's no explanation you could possibly give me." I look fiercely at Mum and Dad. "Pretend he isn't there. Just carry on."

There's silence. Mum and Dad are giving each other surreptitious looks, and I can see Mum mouthing something. She abruptly stops as she sees me looking at her, and takes a sip of coffee.

"Let's just . . . have a conversation!" I say desperately. "So, Mum."

"Yes?" she says hopefully.

My mind is blank. I can't think of anything. All I can think is that Jack is sitting four feet away.

"How's the golf?" I say at last.

"It's, er, fine, thanks!" Mum shoots a glance at Jack.

"Don't look at him!" I mutter. "And . . . and Dad?" I persevere loudly. "How's your golf?"

"It's . . . also fine!" says Dad.

"Where do you play?" asks Jack.

"You're not in the conversation!" I cry, turning furiously on my chair.

There's silence.

"Dear me!" says Mum suddenly in a stagy voice. "Just look at the time! We're due at the . . . the . . . sculpture exhibition."

What?

"Lovely to see you, Emma—"

"You can't go!" I say in panic. But Dad's already opening his wallet and putting a twenty-pound note on the table while Mum stands up and puts on her jacket.

"Just listen to him," she whispers, bending down to give me a kiss.

" 'Bye, Emma," says Dad, and squeezes my hand. And within the space of about thirty seconds, they're gone.

I cannot believe they have done this to me.

"So," says Jack as the door pings shut.

With a set jaw, I shift my chair around so I can't see him.

"Emma, please."

I shift my chair around again with even more determination, until I'm facing the wall.

The only thing is, now I can't reach my cappuccino.

"Here." I look around to see Jack has moved his chair right up next to mine, and he's holding out my cup to me.

"Leave me alone!" I say angrily, leaping to my feet. "We have nothing to talk about. Nothing."

I grab my bag and stalk out of the coffee shop, into the busy street. A moment later, I feel a hand on my shoulder.

"We could at least discuss what happened."

"Discuss what?" I wheel around. "How you used me? How you betrayed me?"

"OK, Emma. I appreciate I embarrassed you. But . . . is it really such a big deal?"

"Such a big *deal*?" I cry in disbelief, nearly knocking over a lady with a shopping trolley. "You came into my life. You fed me this huge, amazing romance. You made me fall in lo—" I halt myself. "You said you were gripped by me. You made me . . . care for you . . . and I believed every single word." My voice has a treacherous wobble. "I believed you, Jack. But all the way along, you had an ulterior motive. You were just using me for your stupid research. All the time, you were just . . . *using* me."

Jack looks horrified. "No," he says. "No, wait. You have this wrong." He grabs my arm. "That's not the way it was. I didn't set out to use you."

How does he have the *nerve* to say that?

"Of course you did!" I say, wrenching my arm out of his grasp, jabbing the button at a pedestrian crossing. "Of course you did! Don't deny it was me you were talking about in that interview! Don't deny you had me in mind! Every detail was me! Every bloody detail!"

"OK." Jack is clasping his head. "OK. Listen. I don't deny I had you in mind. I don't deny you filtered into . . . But that doesn't mean . . ." He looks up. "I have you on my mind most of the time. That's the truth. I have you on my mind."

The pedestrian crossing suddenly starts bleeping, telling us to cross. This is my cue to storm off and him to come running after me—but neither of us moves. I *want* to storm off, but somehow my body isn't doing it. Somehow my body wants to hear more.

"Emma, when Pete and I started the Panther Corporation, you know how we worked?" Jack's dark eyes are burning into mine. "You know how we made our decisions?"

I shrug with a tell-me-if-you-like look.

"Gut instinct. Would *we* buy this? Would *we* like this? Would *we* go for this? That's what we asked each other. Every day, over and over." He hesitates. "During the past few weeks, I've been immersed in this new women's line. And all I've found myself asking myself is . . . would Emma like it? Would Emma drink it? Would Emma buy it?" Jack closes his eyes for a moment, then opens them. "Yes, you got into my thoughts. Yes, you fed into my work. Emma, my life and my business have always gotten confused. That's the way I've always been. But that doesn't mean my life isn't real." He hesitates. "It doesn't mean that what we had . . . we have . . . is any less real."

He takes a deep breath and shoves his hands in his pockets.

"Emma, I didn't lie to you. I didn't *feed* you anything. I was gripped by you the minute I met you on that plane. The minute you looked up at me and said the thing about doing the Heimlich maneuver . . . I was hooked. Not because of business . . . because of *you*. Because of who you are. Every single detail. From the way you pick out your favorite horoscope every morning, to the way you wrote the letter from Ernest P. Leopold, to your exercise plan on the wall. All of it."

His gaze is fixed on mine, and I feel myself wavering.

Just for an instant.

"That's all very well," I say, my voice shaking. "But you embarrassed me. You *humiliated* me!" I turn on my heel and start striding across the road again.

"I didn't mean to say so much," says Jack, following me. "I didn't mean to say anything! Believe me, Emma, I regret it as much as you do. The minute we stopped, I asked them to cut out that part. They promised me they would. I was . . ." He shakes his head. "I don't know, goaded. I got carried away . . ."

"You got carried *away*?" I feel a renewed surge of outrage. "Jack, you exposed every single detail about me!"

"I know, and I'm sorry."

"You told the world about my underwear . . . and my sex life . . . and my Barbie bedcover, and you *didn't* tell them it was ironic."

"Emma, I'm so sorry—"

"You told them how much I weigh!" My voice rises to a shriek. "And you got it *wrong*!"

"Emma, really, I'm sorry—"

"Sorry isn't good enough!" I wheel around to face him. "You ruined my life!"

"I ruined your life?" He gives me a strange look. "Is your life ruined? Is it such a disaster for people to know the truth about you?"

"I . . . I . . ." For a moment I flounder. "You don't know what it was like for me!" I say, on firmer ground. "Everyone was laughing at me. Everyone was teasing me, in the whole office. Artemis was teasing me—"

"I'll fire her at once." Jack makes a sweeping gesture with his arm.

I'm so shocked, I burst into laughter, then immediately quell it. "And Nick was teasing me—"

"I'll fire him, too." Jack thinks for a moment. "How about this: anyone who teased you, I'll fire."

This time I can't help giggling out loud. "You won't have a company left."

"So be it. That'll teach me. That'll teach me to be so thoughtless."

For a moment we face each other in the sunshine.

"Would you like to buy some lucky heather?" A woman in a pink sweatshirt suddenly thrusts a foil-wrapped sprig in my face, and I shake my head irritably.

"Emma, I want to make this up to you," Jack says as the woman moves away. "Could we have lunch? A drink? A . . . a smoothie?"

I can feel part of me starting to unbend; I can feel part of me starting to believe him.

"I don't know," I say, rubbing my nose.

"Things were going so well, before I had to go and fuck it up."

"Were they?" I say.

"Weren't they?" Jack hesitates. "I kind of thought they were."

My mind is buzzing. There are things I need to say. There are things I need to get into the open. A thought suddenly crystallizes. "Jack . . . what were you doing in Scotland? When we first met."

At once, Jack's face closes up and he looks away. "Emma . . . I'm afraid I can't tell you that."

"Why not?" I say, trying to sound light.

"It's . . . complicated."

"OK, then." I think for a moment. "Where did you go rushing off to that night with Sven? When you had to cut our date short."

"Emma—"

"How about the night you had all those calls? What were those about?"

This time he doesn't even bother answering.

"I see." I push my hair back, trying to stay calm. "Jack, did it ever occur to you that in all our time together, you've hardly told me anything about yourself?"

"I . . . guess I'm a private person," says Jack. "Is it such a big deal?"

"It's . . . quite a big deal to me. I shared everything with you. Like you said. All my thoughts, all my worries—everything. And you've shared nothing with me."

"That's not true." He steps forward.

"Practically nothing, then. I mean, you didn't even tell me you were going to be on television!"

"It was just a dumb interview, for Chrissakes! Emma, you're overreacting."

"I told you all my secrets," I say stubbornly. "You didn't tell me any of yours."

Jack sighs. "With all due respect, Emma, I think it's a little different—"

"What?" I'm totally shocked. "Why . . . why would it be any different?"

"You have to understand. I have things in my life that are very sensitive . . . complicated . . . very important. . . ."

"And I *don't*? You think my secrets are less important than yours? You think I'm less hurt by your blurting them out on television?" I'm smarting with anger, with disappointment. "I suppose that's because you're so huge and important and I'm . . . What am I again, Jack?" I can feel my eyes filling with tears. "A 'nothing-special girl'? An 'ordinary, nothing-special girl'?"

Jack winces, and I can see I've hit home. He closes his eyes, and for a long time I think he isn't going to speak.

"I didn't mean to use those words," he says. "The minute I said them, I wished I could take them back. I was . . . I was trying to evoke something very different from that . . . a kind of image." He looks up. "Emma, you *have* to know I didn't mean—"

"I'm going to ask you again!" I say, resolute. "What were you doing in Scotland?"

There's silence. As I meet Jack's eyes, I know he's not going to tell me.

"Fine," I say, trying to keep control of my voice. "That's fine. I'm obviously not as important as you. I'm just some amusing girl who provides you with entertainment on flights and gives you ideas for your business."

"Emma—"

"The thing is, Jack, a real relationship is two-way. A real relationship is based on equality. And trust. So why don't you just go and be with someone on your level, who you can share your precious secrets with? Because you obviously can't share them with me."

I turn sharply before he can say anything else, and stalk away in tears.

How I get through the afternoon, I don't know. I sit at my desk, my face numb, while Artemis and Nick persist with their oh-so-funny running commentary. Artemis starts by asking me if I can recommend a good set of bathroom scales. Then Nick starts dropping Dickens references into every sentence.

". . . He's a real Scrooge. Sorry, Emma, by 'Scrooge' I mean 'miser.' "

"You're so hilarious," I say without raising my head. "Really, you should have your own show."

Caroline, meanwhile, is obviously feeling sorry for me, so she comes over to my desk and makes conversation about my parents. Which, to be honest, is even less welcome.

By the time I arrive home that evening, I have a throbbing headache and feel like crawling into a hole. I open the door of the flat to find Lissy and Jemima in a full-scale argument about animal rights.

"The mink *like* being made into coats—" Jemima is saying

as I push open the door to the living room. She breaks off and looks up. "Emma! Are you all right?"

"No." I slump down onto the sofa and wrap myself up in the green chenille throw that Lissy's mum gave her for Christmas. "I had a huge row with Jack."

"With *Jack*?"

"You saw him?"

"He came to . . . well, to apologize, I guess."

Lissy and Jemima exchange looks.

"What happened?" says Lissy, hugging her knees. "What did he say?"

"He said . . . he didn't ever mean to use me. He said I got in his thoughts. He said he'd fire everyone in the company who teased me."

"Really?" says Lissy. "Gosh. That's quite romant—" She coughs, and pulls an apologetic face. "Sorry."

"He said he was really sorry for what happened, and he didn't mean to say all that stuff on the TV, and that our romance was . . . Anyway. He said a lot of things. But *then* he said . . ." I feel fresh indignation rising. "He said his secrets were more important than mine."

Simultaneous gasps of outrage.

"No!" says Lissy.

"Bastard!" says Jemima. "What secrets?"

"I asked him about Scotland. And rushing off from the date." I meet Lissy's eyes. "And . . . all those things he would never talk to me about."

"And what did he say?" says Lissy.

"He wouldn't tell me. He said it was too 'sensitive and complicated.' "

"Sensitive and *complicated*?" Jemima looks galvanized. "Jack has a sensitive and complicated secret? You never mentioned this before! Emma, this is totally perfect! You find out what it is . . . and then you expose it!"

God, she's right. I could do it. I could get back at Jack. I could make him hurt like I've been hurt. "But I have no idea what it is," I say.

"You can find out!" says Jemima. "That's easy enough. The point is, you know he's hiding something."

"There's definitely some strange stuff going on," says Lissy thoughtfully. "He has all these phone calls he won't talk about, he rushes off mysteriously from your date—"

"He rushed off mysteriously?" says Jemima avidly. "Where? Did he say anything? Did you overhear anything?"

"No!" I say, flushing slightly. "Of course not! I don't . . . I would never *eavesdrop* on people!"

Jemima gives me a close look.

"Don't give me that! Yes, you did! You did hear something. Come on, Emma. What was it?"

My mind flashes back to that evening. Sitting on the bench, sipping the pink cocktail. The breeze is blowing on my face; Jack and Sven are talking in low voices. . . .

"It was nothing much," I say reluctantly. "I just heard him say something about . . . having to transfer something . . . and Plan B . . . and something being urgent."

"Transfer what?" says Lissy suspiciously. "Funds?"

"I dunno. And . . . they said something about flying back up to Glasgow."

Jemima is clutching her head in agitation. "Emma, I do not believe this. You've had this information all this time? This has to be something juicy. It *has* to be. If only we knew more . . ." She exhales in frustration. "You didn't have a Dictaphone or anything with you?"

"Of course I didn't!" I say with a little laugh. "It was a date! Do *you* normally take a Dictaphone on a . . ." I trail off, incredulous at her expression. "Jemima. You don't."

"Not *always*!" she says, shrugging. "Just if I think it might come in . . . Anyway. That's irrelevant. The point is, you have information, Emma. You have power. You find out what this is all about—and then you expose him! That'll show Jack Harper who's boss! That'll get your revenge!"

For a moment I feel sheer, powerful exhilaration. That would pay Jack back. That would show him. Then he'd be sorry! Then he'd see I'm not just some nothing nobody girl. *Then* he'd see.

"So . . . so how would I do it?"

"First we try to work out as much as we can ourselves," says Jemima. "Then I've got access to various . . . people who can help get more information." She gives me a wink. "Discreetly."

"Private detectives?" says Lissy in disbelief. "Are you for real?"

"And then we expose him! Mummy's got contacts at *all* the papers."

My heart is thumping. Am I really talking about doing this?

"A very good place to start is rubbish bins," adds Jemima knowledgeably. "You can find *all* sorts of things just by looking through somebody's trash."

And suddenly it's like sanity comes flying in through the window. "Rubbish bins?" I say in horror. "I'm not looking in any rubbish bins! In fact, I'm not doing this, full stop! It's a crazy idea."

"You can't get all precious now, Emma!" says Jemima tartly, flicking back her hair. "How else are you going to find out what his secret is?"

"Maybe I don't *want* to find out what his secret is," I retort, feeling a sudden sting of pride. "Maybe I'm not interested."

I hunch my shoulders and wrap the chenille throw around me even more tightly.

So Jack's got some huge secret he can't trust me with.

Well, fine. Let him keep it. I'm not going to demean myself by grubbing after it. I'm not going to start poking around rubbish bins. I don't care what it is. I don't care about him.

"I want to forget about it," I say morosely. "I want to move on."

"No, you don't!" retorts Jemima. "Don't be stupid, Emma! This is your big chance for revenge! We are *so* going to get him." I have never seen Jemima look so animated in my life. She reaches for her bag and gets out a lilac Smythson notebook, together with a Tiffany pen. "Right, so, what do we know? Glasgow . . . Plan B . . . transfer. . . ."

"The Panther Corporation doesn't have offices in Scotland, does it?" says Lissy thoughtfully.

I turn my head in disbelief. She's scribbling on a pad of legal paper, with exactly the same preoccupied look she gets when she's solving one of her geeky puzzles. I can see the words "Glasgow," "transfer," and "Plan B," and a place where she's jumbled up all the letters in "Scotland" and tried to make a new word out of them.

"Lissy, what are you doing?"

"I'm just . . . fiddling around," she says, and blushes. "I might go and look some stuff up on the Internet, just out of interest."

"Look—just stop it, both of you!" I say. "If Jack doesn't want to tell me what his secret is, then I don't want to know."

Suddenly I feel completely drained by the day. And bruised. I'm not interested in Jack's mysterious secret life. I don't want to think about it anymore. I want to have a long, hot bath and go to bed and just forget I ever met him.

Twenty-three

EXCEPT, of course, I can't.

Jack's face keeps appearing in my head when I don't want it to. The way he looked at me in the sunlight, his face all crinkled up.

I lie in bed, going over it again and again. Feeling the same smart of hurt, the same disappointment.

I told him everything about myself. *Everything*. And he won't even tell me one—

Anyway. Anyway. I don't care. He can do what he likes. He can keep his stupid secrets.

Good luck to him. That's it. Gone for good.

And what did he mean by that, anyway? *Is it such a disaster for people to know the truth about you?*

He can *so* talk. Mr. Mystery. Mr. Sensitive and Complicated.

I should have said that. I should have said—

No. Stop thinking about him. It's over.

As I pad into the kitchen the next morning to make a cup

of tea, I'm fully resolved. I'm not even going to *think* about Jack from now on. *Finito. Fin.* The End.

"OK. I have three theories." Lissy arrives at the door of the kitchen in her pajamas, holding her legal pad.

"What?" I look up, still bleary.

"Jack's big secret. I have three theories."

"Only three?" says Jemima, appearing behind her in her white robe, clutching her Smythson notebook. "I've got eight!"

"Eight?" Lissy stares at her, affronted.

"I don't want to hear any theories!" I say. "Look, both of you, this has been really painful for me. Can't you just respect my feelings and drop it?"

They both look at me in silence for a second, then turn back to each other.

"Eight?" says Lissy again. "How did you get eight?"

"Easy-peasy. But I'm sure yours are very good, too," says Jemima kindly. "Why don't you go first?"

"OK," says Lissy with a look of annoyance, and clears her throat. "Number one: He's relocating the whole of the Panther Corporation to Scotland. He was up there reconnoitering and didn't want you spreading rumors. Number two: He's involved in some kind of white-collar fraud—"

"What?" I say in shock. "Why do you say that?"

"I looked up the accountants who audited the last Panther Corporation accounts, and they've been involved in a few big scandals recently. Which doesn't *prove* anything, but if he's acting shady and talking about transfers . . ." She pulls a face.

Jack a fraudster? No. He couldn't be. He couldn't.

Not that I care one way or the other.

"Can I say that both of those sound highly unlikely to me?" chips in Jemima.

"Well, what's your theory, then?" says Lissy crossly.

"It's obvious! He's had secret work done."

"What do you mean, 'work'?" I say, baffled.

"Work. *Enhancement.*" Jemima gestures to her face meaningfully.

"Jack would never have plastic surgery!" I exclaim. "He's not that kind of guy!"

"Sharpen your wits, Emma," says Jemima. "Everyone has it done nowadays. You ask Mummy. Half the cabinet . . . the Pope . . ."

"The *Pope*?"

"Compare a recent photo of Jack with an old one, and I bet you see a difference—"

I cut her off. "It's not plastic surgery! What are your other seven theories?"

"Let me see. . . ." Jemima turns the page of her notebook. "Oh, yes. He's in the Mafia." She pauses for effect. "His father was shot, and he's planning to murder the heads of all the other families."

"Jemima, that's *The Godfather,*" says Lissy.

"Oh." She looks put out. "Damn. Well, here's another one. He has an autistic brother—"

"Rain Man."

"Bloody hell." She studies her list again. "So maybe not that after all . . . or that." She starts crossing entries out. "OK. But I do have one more." She raises her head. "He's got another woman."

I feel a jolt. Another woman. I never even thought of that.

"That was my last theory, too," says Lissy apologetically.

"You . . . *both* think it's another woman?" I look from face to face. "But . . . but why?"

Suddenly I feel really small. And stupid. Have I been even *more* naive than I originally thought?

"It just seems quite a likely explanation," says Jemima with a shrug. "He's having some clandestine affair with a woman in Scotland. He's paying her a secret visit when he met you.

She keeps phoning him. Maybe they were having a row, then she comes to London unexpectedly, so he has to dash off from your date."

Lissy glances at my stricken face. "But maybe he's relocating the company!" she says encouragingly. "Or a fraudster!"

"Well, I don't care *what* he's doing," I say, my face burning. "It's his business. And he's welcome to it."

I get out a pint of milk from the fridge and slam it shut, my hands trembling. Sensitive and complicated. Is that code for "I'm seeing someone else?"

Well, fine. Let him have another woman. I don't care.

"It's *your* business, too!" says Jemima. "If you're going to get revenge—"

Oh, for God's sake. "I don't *want* to get my revenge, OK?" I say, turning around to face her. "It's not healthy. I want to . . . heal my wounds and move on."

"Yes, and shall I tell you another word for revenge?" she retorts, as though pulling a rabbit out of a hat. "Closure!"

"Jemima, closure and revenge are not actually the same thing," says Lissy.

"In *my* book they are." She folds her arms. "Emma, you're my friend, and I'm not going to let you just sit back and allow yourself to be mistreated by some bastard man! He deserves to pay! He deserves to be punished!"

"Jemima . . . you're not actually going to *do* anything about this."

"Of course I am!" she says. "I'm not going to stand by and see you suffer! It's called the sisterhood, Emma!"

I have sudden visions of Jemima rooting through Jack's rubbish bins in her pink Gucci suit. Or scraping his car with a nail file.

"Jemima . . . don't do anything," I say in alarm. "Please. I don't want you to."

"You *think* you don't. But you'll thank me later—"

"No, I won't! Jemima, you have to promise me you're not going to do anything stupid."

She tightens her jaw rebelliously.

"Promise!"

"OK!" says Jemima at last, rolling her eyes. "I promise."

"Thank you." I reach for my mug of tea and pour in some milk.

"She's crossing her fingers behind her back," observes Lissy.

"What?" I nearly drop the milk. "Promise properly! Swear on something you really love."

"Oh, God!" says Jemima sulkily. "All right, you win! I swear on my Míu Míu pony skin bag I won't do anything. But you're making a big mistake, you know."

She saunters out of the room, and I watch her, feeling a bit uneasy.

"That girl is a total psychopath," says Lissy. "Why did we ever let her move in here?" She takes a sip of tea. "Actually, I remember why. It was because her dad gave us a whole year's rent in advance—" She catches my expression. "Are you OK?"

"You don't think she'll actually do anything to Jack, will she?"

"Of course not," says Lissy. "She's all talk."

"You're right. You're right." I pick up my mug and look at it silently for a few moments. "Lissy . . . do you really think Jack's secret is another woman?"

Lissy opens her mouth.

"Anyway, I don't care," I add defiantly before she can answer. "I don't care what it is."

As I arrive at the office, Artemis looks up from her desk, bright-eyed.

"Morning, Emma!" She smirks at Caroline. "Read any intellectual books lately?"

Oh, ha, ha-di-ha. So, so funny. Even Nick got bored of teasing me yesterday. Only Artemis still thinks it's completely hysterical.

"Actually, Artemis, I have," I say, taking off my jacket. "I just read this really good book called *What to Do If Your Colleague Is an Obnoxious Cow Who Picks Her Nose When She Thinks No One's Looking.*"

There's a guffaw around the office, and Artemis flushes a dark red. "I don't!" she snaps.

"I never said you did," I reply, and switch on my computer with a flourish.

"Ready to go to the meeting, Artemis?" says Paul, coming out of his office with his briefcase and a magazine in his hand. "And by the way, Nick," he adds ominously. "Before I go, would you mind telling me what on earth possessed you to put a coupon ad for Panther Bars in"—he consults the front cover—"*Bowling Weekly* magazine? I'm assuming it was you, as this is your product?"

Shit. Double shit. I didn't think Paul would ever find out about that.

Nick shoots me a dirty look, and I pull an agonized face back.

"Well," he begins in a truculent voice, "yes, Paul. Panther Bars are my product. But as it happens—"

Oh, God. I can't let him take the blame.

"Paul," I say, raising my hand. "Actually, it was—"

"Because I want to tell you." Paul grins at Nick. "It was bloody inspired! I've just had the feedback figures, and bearing in mind the pitiful circulation . . . they're extraordinary!"

I don't believe it. The ad *worked*?

"Really?" says Nick, obviously trying to sound not too amazed. "I mean . . . excellent!"

"What the *fuck* compelled you to advertise a teenage bar to a load of old codgers?"

"Well!" Nick adjusts his cuff links, not looking anywhere near me. "Obviously it was a *bit* of a gamble. But I simply felt that maybe it was time to . . . to fly a few kites . . . experiment with a new demographic . . ."

Hang on a minute. *What's* he saying?

"Well, your experiment paid off." Paul gives Nick an approving look. "And interestingly, it coincides with some Scandinavian market research we've just had in. If you'd like to see me later, to discuss it—"

"Sure!" says Nick with a pleased smile. "What sort of time?"

How can he? He is such a *bastard*. "Wait!" I leap to my feet in outrage. "Wait a minute! That was *my* idea!"

"What?" Paul frowns.

"The *Bowling Weekly* ad! It was my idea. *Wasn't* it, Nick?" I look directly at him.

"Maybe we discussed it," he says, not meeting my eye. "I don't really remember. But you know, something you'll have to learn, Emma, is that marketing's all about teamwork."

"Don't patronize me! This wasn't teamwork! It was totally my idea! I put it in for my grandpa!"

Damn. I didn't quite mean to let that slip out.

"First your parents. Now your grandpa," says Paul, turning to look at me. "Emma, remind me—is this Bring Your Entire Family to Work week?"

"No! It's just . . ." I begin, a little hot under his gaze. "You said you were going to axe Panther Bars, so I . . . I thought I'd give him and his friends some money off, and they could all stock up. I tried to tell you at that big meeting, my grandfather loves Panther Bars! And so do all his friends! If you ask me, you should be marketing Panther Bars at *them,* not teenagers!"

There's silence. Paul looks astounded. "So, why does this older generation like Panther Bars so much, Emma? Do you know?" He sounds genuinely fascinated.

"Yes, of course I know!"

"It's the gray pound," puts in Nick. "Demographic shifts in the pensionable population are accounting for—"

"No, it's not!" I say impatiently. "It's because . . . because . . ." Oh, God, Grandpa will absolutely kill me for saying this. "It's because . . . they don't pull out their false teeth."

Paul looks staggered for an instant. Then he throws back his head and roars with laughter. "False teeth," he says, wiping his eyes. "That is sheer, bloody genius, Emma. False teeth!"

"But the tropical flavors just don't work," I add. "If you ask me, that's why the product's in trouble."

"Is that so?"

"Would *you* put papaya on your porridge?"

"Probably not," says Paul, starting to laugh again.

As I stand there, watching him, I have the strangest feeling. Like something's building up inside me, as though I'm about to—"So, can I have a promotion?"

"What?" Paul stops laughing, and there's silence.

Did I really just say that? Out loud?

"Can I have a promotion?" My voice is trembling, but I hold firm. "You said if I created my own opportunities, I could have a promotion. That's what you said. Isn't this creating my own opportunities?"

From the corner of my eye, I see Artemis pulling an amused face at Caroline.

Paul sighs. "Emma—"

His old, patronizing tone has come back. I can't bear it.

"I am not the departmental secretary, Paul!" I exclaim. "Just because you want to cut your staff budget, I've ended up doing all the menial jobs! But I've done tasks at the same level as Artemis, and I know I could do more. I know I could be an asset. If you give me the chance, I'll show you!"

Paul looks at me for a few moments, blinking, saying nothing.

"You know, Emma Corrigan," he says at last. "You are one of the most . . . one of the most *surprising* people I've ever known." He pauses. "For your information, I've hired a new departmental secretary. Her name's Amanda, and she starts in a week."

"Oh," I say, thrown. "Oh, I see."

But even so, I'm not going to give up. I screw myself up with determination. "So . . . what about me?"

There's silence around the entire office. Everyone's waiting to see what he'll say. As I meet Paul's eyes, there's a sudden warmth in them. Friendliness, even.

"Come and see me later. And we'll have a chat." He shakes his head in mock exasperation. "Now, is that it?"

"No," I hear myself saying, my heart beating even more furiously. "There's more. Paul, I broke your World Cup mug."

"What?" He looks completely gobsmacked.

"I'm really sorry. I'll buy you another one." I look around the silent, gawking office. "And it was me who jammed the copier that time. In fact . . . all the times. And that bottom . . ." Amid agog faces, I walk to the pin board and rip down the photocopied G-stringed bottom. "That's mine, and I don't want it up there anymore." I swivel around. "And, Artemis, about your spider plant."

"What?" she says suspiciously.

I survey her, in her Burberry raincoat and her designer spectacles and her smug, I'm-better-than-you face.

OK, let's not get carried away.

"I . . . can't think what's wrong with it." I smile. "Have a good meeting."

As I emerge from Paul's office later that afternoon, I feel dizzy with exhilaration. It's finally happened. I'm going to be promoted. I'm actually going to be a marketing executive! Paul was really nice. He said maybe he had overlooked my contributions in the past, and that I deserved it.

I don't quite know what's happened to me. It's not just the job—it's like I've become a whole new person. So what if I broke Paul's mug? Who cares? So what if everyone knows how much I weigh? Who cares? Good-bye, old crap Emma, who hides her Oxfam bags under her desk. Hello, new, confident Emma, who proudly hangs them on her chair.

I reach my desk and immediately dial home.

"Mum? It's Emma. Guess what!" I can't resist glancing at Artemis. "I'm being promoted! I'm going to be a marketing executive!"

Mum's cries of delight are so piercing, they nearly deafen me. Then she relays the news to Grandpa, who sends his congratulations back, and I just hang on the end of the phone and beam happily at it.

"And what about Jack?" says Mum at last, after we've planned a celebratory dinner in London. "Did you have a talk with him?"

"Yes, I did. But . . ." The ebullience seeps out of my voice. "I guess we just weren't meant for each other."

"Maybe you're right." Mum's silent for a moment. "The truth is, some relationships are supposed to last forever, and some are only supposed to last a few days. That's the way life is."

"I know," I sigh. "It's just I was kind of hoping . . ."

"Of course you were, love." Mum sounds more sympathetic than I've ever heard her. "Oh, I feel for you. You know, I once had a relationship that lasted only forty-eight hours. In Paris."

"Paris!" I say, impressed.

"It was an affair I'll never forget."

"Really?"

I'm quite surprised by this. I always thought she and Dad were childhood sweethearts. Did she go to France on a school exchange or something?

"I'd never experienced physical pleasure like it," Mum is saying. "And I knew it could never last, but that made it all the more poignant . . ." She trails off, sounding quite over-come.

"So, was this before you met Dad?"

There's silence.

"Of course," says Mum at last, and clears her throat. "Of course it was! Incidentally, darling, I wouldn't mention any of this to Daddy, if I were you."

"Why not?" I say in suspicion.

"Well!" says Mum, sounding a bit flustered. "Er, you know how he is about the French."

As I put down the phone, I'm actually quite shocked. I always thought Mum and Dad . . . At least, I never . . .

Well. It just goes to show.

"Emma?"

I look up happily, ready to be congratulated again—and jump about three inches off my chair. Sven is standing right in front of my desk. What's he doing here?

"I need to see you," he says without smiling, and beckons with his finger. "Now."

As we walk down the corridor, everyone gives us curious glances. And I try to look all calm and relaxed, like "Oh, Sven and I often have little chats together." But inside, I'm get-ting more and more nervous. Why does Sven want to see me?

We reach an empty meeting room next to the admin. de-partment, and Sven ushers me inside. He turns, his face set like granite.

It's me and the hit man. Alone.

"Emma."

It's almost a shock hearing my name on his lips, in light of the fact that I've hardly ever heard him utter a word.

"I suppose Jack's sent you," I say, forcing myself to sound confident. "Well, if he has—"

"Jack hasn't sent me. I wanted to talk to you." He walks to the window in silence, then turns around. "I heard that you and Jack had a row."

OK, this is freaky. Since when did I start discussing my love life with Sven?

"What's this got to do with you? What's your role in this place, anyway?" I jut my chin out. "Who *are* you?"

Sven seems taken aback by the question. "I'm . . . someone who tries to be there for Jack," he says.

"You'd take a bullet for him?" I say flippantly.

"I meant . . . emotionally."

"Emotionally?" I echo, feeling a sudden urge to laugh. Does Mr. Titanium Briefcase know what emotions *are*? But to my surprise, Sven looks utterly serious.

"I've known Jack a long time. Pete Laidler, too." He stops, as though that explained everything.

"Right." I shrug.

"I've never known two people as close as those two guys. When Pete went, a lot of us were worried about Jack."

Half of me wants to say, "Is there a point to all this?" The other half is getting pretty curious.

"What you should know . . ." Sven searches for words. ". . . is that Jack's never really shared himself with any woman. With anyone. Except Pete."

"Yeah, well." I can feel an old hurt rising, and look away. This day was going so well until Sven came along. "That's not my fault."

"You may think Jack's kept himself distant. But for the rest of us who know him . . . it's been extraordinary. The way he's been since meeting you." Sven's pale blue eyes bore into mine. "He changed his plans for you. These meetings he's been having were supposed to be back in the States. People have been flying around the globe—just because of you. Are you aware of that?"

Why is he telling me all this? It's like he's digging around in my feelings, trying to find my weakness.

"Whatever. It's irrelevant now." I fold my arms defensively around my body. "Look . . . why are you here?"

"There aren't many people who know the real Jack," says Sven. "I guess I thought you should hear from someone who does."

"Well, now I have. Thanks very much."

I turn sharply and head toward the door. Sven's voice follows me. "The thing is, he's worth it."

Slowly, I turn back. "What?"

Sven takes a few paces toward me. The afternoon sun's shining through the blinds onto his hair. He's actually quite nice-looking, I realize. I'm starting to see why he and Jack might be friends.

"Emma, Jack's never going to be a heart-on-his-sleeve guy. He's never going to open up as much as you'd like. That's just the way he is." Sven pauses. "As I said, he's worth it."

His face is so fixed and serious, I feel suddenly touched.

"Thanks for trying," I say at last. "But . . . it doesn't work like that."

Twenty-four

FOR THE REST OF THE DAY, I feel all upset and agitated. Not to mention totally disconcerted that Sven has turned out to be human after all. Half of me is desperate to call him back and hear more about Jack.

But I'm not going to. I'm going to be strong. Jack made his decision—and I've made mine. It's like Mum said, we were only meant to be a short-term relationship. And actually, I'm pretty much over him. I only felt a tiny pang once today, when I thought I saw him in the corridor, and I recovered really quickly.

The important thing to remember is, I've won my promotion. My whole new life begins today. Yes. In fact, I expect I'll meet someone new tonight at Lissy's dancing show. Some really tall, dashing lawyer. Yes. And he'll come and pick me up from work in his amazingly fab sports car. And I'll trip happily down the steps, tossing my hair back, not even *looking* at Jack, who will be standing at his office window, glowering. . . .

No. I am over Jack. I have to remember this.

Maybe I'll write it on my hand.

Lissy's dancing show is being held in a theater in Bloomsbury set in a small, graveled courtyard, and as I arrive, the entire place is crammed with lawyers in expensive suits on their mobile phones.

". . . client unwilling to accept the terms of agreement . . ."

". . . attention to clause four, comma, notwithstanding . . ."

There. You see. I could go out with any one of these guys. Like . . . that one standing on his own, with the glasses and the shiny black hair. I could easily walk up to him, ask him who he knows in the show. . . . We'd start chatting. . . . He's probably got a great sense of humor.

The black-haired guy looks around, as though feeling my gaze on him, and gives me a tentative smile. Without quite meaning to, I turn on my heel, and take a few steps away.

I mean, there's no need to *rush* into a new relationship. The point is, I could. If I wanted to.

No one is making the slightest attempt to go into the auditorium yet, so I head backstage to give Lissy the bouquet I've bought for her. As I walk down the shabby corridors, music is being piped through the sound system, and people keep brushing past me in sparkly costumes. A man with blue feathers in his hair is stretching his leg against the wall and talking to someone in a dressing room at the same time. "So then I pointed out to that *idiot* of a prosecuting counsel that the precedent set in 1983 by *Miller v. Davy* means . . ." He suddenly stops. "Shit. I've forgotten my first steps." His face drains of color. "I can't remember a fucking thing. I'm not joking! I jeté on. Then what?" He looks at me as though expecting me to supply him with an answer.

"Er, a pirouette?" I hazard, and awkwardly hurry on,

nearly tripping over a girl doing the splits. Suddenly I catch sight of Lissy sitting on a stool in one of the dressing rooms. Her face is heavily made-up, and her eyes are all huge and glittery, and she's got blue feathers in her hair, too.

"Oh, my God, Lissy!" I say, halting in the doorway. "You look amazing! I completely love your—"

"I can't do it."

"What?"

"I can't do it!" she repeats desperately, and pulls her cotton robe around her. "I can't remember anything! My mind is blank!"

"Everyone thinks that!" I say in reassuring tones. "There was a guy outside saying exactly the same thing—"

"No. I *really* can't remember anything." Lissy's eyes are wild. "My legs feel like cotton wool. . . . I can't breathe." She picks up a blusher brush, looks at it bleakly, then puts it down. "Why did I ever agree to do this? Why?"

"Er, because it would be fun?"

"Fun?" Her voice rises in disbelief. "You think this is *fun*?"

I peer at her anxiously. "Liss, are you all right?"

"I can't do it," she says. "I can't." She seems to come to a sudden decision. "OK, I'm going home." She starts reaching for her clothes. "Tell them I was suddenly taken ill. It was an emergency."

"You can't go home!" I say in horror, and grab the clothes out of her hands. "You'll be fine! I mean . . . think about it. How many times have you had to stand up in a big court and make some really long speech in front of loads of people, and if you get it wrong, an innocent man might go to jail?"

Lissy looks at me as though I'm crazy. "Yes, but that's *easy*."

"Well . . ." I cast around. "Well . . . if you pull out now, you'll always regret it. You'll always look back and wish you'd gone through with it."

There's silence. I can practically see Lissy's brain working underneath all the feathers.

"You're right," she says at last. "You're right. I have to do this."

"You'll be great!" I say just as a loudspeaker in the wall blares out, "This is your fifteen-minute call!"

"So . . . I'll go, then," I say. "Let you warm up."

"Emma." Lissy grabs hold of my arm and fixes me with an intense gaze. She's holding me so tight, she's hurting my flesh. "Emma, if I ever say I want to do anything like this again, you have to stop me. Whatever I say. Promise you'll stop me."

"I promise," I say hastily. "I promise."

Bloody hell. I have never seen Lissy like that before in my life. Please don't let her mess up. Please. As I walk back out into the courtyard, which is now swarming with even more well-dressed people, I've got a terrible case of nerves myself.

A horrible image suddenly comes to me of Lissy standing like a startled rabbit, unable to remember her steps. And the audience just aghast.

I'm not going to let that happen, I resolve. If anything goes wrong, I'll pretend to faint. Yes. I'll collapse on the floor, and everyone will be distracted for a few seconds, but the performance won't stop, because we're British, and by the time everyone turns back to the stage again, Lissy will have remembered her steps.

"Emma."

"What?" I say absently. I look up, and catch my breath.

Jack is standing ten feet away. He's dressed in his usual uniform of jeans and a simple jersey, and he stands out a mile among all the corporate-suited lawyers.

Don't react, I tell myself quickly. Closure. New life.

"What are you doing here?" I say. "Did Sven send you?"

"Sven?" Jack frowns. "What do you mean?"

"I . . . nothing."

I'm taken aback that Sven didn't mention our meeting. I'd kind of assumed he and Jack were in on it together.

"I called your flat earlier," Jack says. "Lissy told me you'd be here."

Lissy told Jack I'd be here? OK, I am having a big word with her.

"Emma, I really wanted to talk."

So he thinks he can just pitch up and I'll drop everything? Well, maybe I'm busy. Maybe I've moved on. Did he think of that?

"Emma . . ." He walks forward until he's only a couple of feet away, his face frank. "What you said. It stayed with me. I should have shared more with you. I shouldn't have shut you out."

I feel a moment of surprise, followed by wounded pride. So he wants to share with me now, does he? Well, maybe it's too late. Maybe I'm not interested anymore.

"You don't need to share anything with me," I say with a distancing smile. "Your affairs are your affairs, Jack. They're nothing to do with me. And I probably wouldn't understand them anyway—bearing in mind they're so complicated and I'm such a total thickie."

I turn and start to walk away.

"I owe you an explanation, at least—" Jack's voice follows me.

"You owe me nothing!" I say proudly. "It's over, Jack. And we might as well both just—"

Jack grabs my arm and pulls me around to face him.

"I came here tonight for a reason, Emma," he says without smiling. "I came to tell you what I was doing in Scotland."

I try to hide an almighty bound of shock. "I'm . . . I'm not interested in what you were doing in Scotland anymore!" I wrench my arm away and start striding off as best I can through the thicket of mobile-phone-gabbing lawyers.

"Emma, I want to tell you." He's coming after me. "I really want to tell you."

"Well, maybe I don't want to know!" I reply, swiveling around on the gravel with a scatter of pebbles.

We're facing each other like a pair of duelers.

Of course I want to know.

He knows I want to know.

"Go on, then," I say at last. "You can tell me if you like."

In total silence, Jack leads me over to a quiet spot, away from all the crowds. And as we walk, my bravado ebbs away. I'm almost having second thoughts.

Do I really want to know his secret after all? What if he's had some really embarrassing operation and I start laughing by mistake?

What if it's fraud like Lissy said? What if he's doing something dodgy and he wants me to join in? Instantaneously I decide that if he's committed a murder, I will turn him in, promise or no promise.

What if it *is* another woman and he's come to tell me he's getting married?

Well, if it is . . . I'll just act cool, like I knew all along. In fact, I'll pretend *I've* got another lover, too. I'll give him a wry smile and say, "You know, Jack, I never assumed we were exclusive!"

"OK." Jack turns to face me. "Here it is." He takes a deep breath. "I was in Scotland to visit someone."

My heart plummets. "A woman," I say before I can stop myself.

"No, not a woman!" His expression changes, and he stares at me. "Is that what you thought? That I was two-timing you?"

"I . . . didn't know what to think."

"Emma, I do not have another woman. I was visiting . . ." He hesitates. "You could call it . . . family."

Family?

Oh, my God, Jemima was right. I've gotten involved with a mobster.

OK. Don't panic. I can escape. I can go into the witness protection scheme. My new name can be Megan.

No, Chloe. Chloe de Souza.

"To be more precise . . . a child."

A child? He has a child?

"Her name is Alice. She's eighteen months old."

He has a wife and a whole family that I don't know about, and that's his secret. I knew it. I knew it—"You . . . You have a child?"

"No, I don't have a child." Jack studies the ground for a few seconds, then looks up. "Pete had a child. He had a daughter. Alice is Pete Laidler's child."

"But . . . but . . ." I'm totally confused. "But . . . I never knew Pete Laidler had a child."

"Nobody knows." He gives me a long look. "That's the whole idea."

This is so completely and utterly not what I was expecting.

A child. Pete Laidler's secret child.

"But . . . but how can nobody know about her?" I say stupidly. We've moved even farther away from the crowds and are sitting on a bench under a tree. "I mean, surely they'd *see* her—"

"Pete was a great guy." Jack sighs. "But commitment was never his strong suit. By the time Marie—that's Alice's mom—found out she was pregnant, they weren't even together anymore. Marie's . . . she's kind of proud. She wanted to keep the baby, but she wasn't going to force Pete into anything. She was determined she could do it all on her own. And she did. Pete supported her financially—but he wasn't interested in the child. He didn't even tell anybody he'd become a father."

"Even you? You didn't know he had a child?"

"Not until after he died." His face closes up slightly. "I loved Pete. But that I find very hard to forgive. So a few months after he died, Marie turned up with this baby." Jack exhales sharply. "Well. You can imagine how we all felt. Shocked is an understatement. But Marie was positive she didn't want anyone to know. She wanted to bring Alice up just like a normal kid, not as Pete Laidler's love child. Not as the heiress to some huge fortune."

My mind is boggling. An eighteen-month-old getting Pete Laidler's share of the Panther Corporation. Bloody hell.

"So she gets . . . everything?" I say hesitantly.

"Not everything, no. But a lot. Pete's family have been . . . more than generous. And that's why Marie's keeping her away from the public eye." He spreads his hands. "I know we can't shield her forever. It'll come out sooner or later. But when they find out about her, the press will go nuts. She'll shoot to the top of the rich lists. She won't be normal anymore."

As he's speaking, my mind is filled with memories of the papers after Pete Laidler died. There were pictures of him in every single one of them.

"I'm overprotective of this child." Jack gives a rueful smile. "I know it. Even Marie tells me I am. But . . . she's precious to me." He hesitates for a moment. "She's all we've got left of Pete."

As I look at his vulnerable face, I suddenly feel moved. This is what he and Sven have been trying so hard to shield.

"So . . . is that what the phone calls were about?" I say tentatively. "Is that why you had to leave the other night?"

Jack sighs. "They were both in a car accident a few days ago. It wasn't serious. But . . . we're extra sensitive, after Pete. We just wanted to make sure they got the right treatment."

"Right." I give a little wince. "I can understand that."

There's silence for a while. My brain is trying to slot all the pieces together. Trying to work it all out. "But I don't under-stand," I say suddenly. "Why did you make me keep it a secret that you'd been in Scotland? Nobody would know, surely."

"That was my own dumb, stupid fault," says Jack ruefully. "I'd told some people I was going across to Paris that day, just as an extra precaution. I took an anonymous flight. I thought no one would ever know. Then I walk into the office . . . and there you are."

"Your heart sank."

"Not exactly." He meets my eyes. "It didn't quite know which way to go."

I feel a sudden color coming to my cheeks and awkwardly clear my throat. "So, er," I say, looking away. "So that's why . . ."

"All I wanted was to avoid your piping up, 'Hey, he wasn't in Paris—he was in Scotland!' and start some huge intrigue going." Jack shakes his head. "You'd be amazed at the ludi-crous theories people will put together when they don't have anything better to do. You know, I've heard it all. I'm plan-ning to sell the company. I'm gay. I'm in the Mafia."

"Er, really?" I say, and smooth down a strand of hair. "Gosh. How . . . stupid of people!"

A couple of girls wander nearby, and we both fall silent for a while.

"Emma . . . I'm sorry I couldn't tell you this before," Jack says in a low voice. "I know you were hurt. I know it felt like I was shutting you out. But . . . it's just not something you share lightly."

"No!" I say immediately. "Of course you couldn't have. I was . . . stupid."

I scuff my toe awkwardly on the gravel, feeling a bit shame-faced. I should have known it would be something impor-tant. When he said it was complicated and sensitive . . . he was just telling the truth.

"Only a handful of people know about this." Jack meets my eyes gravely. "A handful of special, trusted people."

My cheeks are getting warmer and warmer.

"Are you going in?" comes a bright voice. We both jump, and look up to see a woman in black jeans approaching. "The performance is about to start!" she says with a beam.

I feel like she's slapped me awake from a dream. "I . . . I have to go and watch Lissy dancing," I say dazedly.

"Right. Well . . . I'll leave you, then. That was really all I had to say." Slowly Jack gets to his feet, then turns back. "There's one more thing." He looks at me for a few silent moments. "Emma, I realize these last few days can't have been easy for you. You have been the model of discretion throughout, whereas I . . . have not. And I just wanted to . . . apologize. Again."

"That's . . . that's OK," I manage.

Jack turns again, and as I watch him walking slowly away, I feel completely torn.

He came all the way here to tell me his secret. His precious secret.

He didn't have to do that.

Oh, God. Oh, God . . .

"Wait!" I hear myself calling out. "Would you . . . would you like to come, too?"

As we walk toward the theater together, I pluck up the courage to speak. "Jack, I've got something to say, too. About . . . about what you were just saying. I know I said you ruined my life the other day."

"I remember," says Jack wryly.

"Well, I might *possibly* have been wrong about that. You . . . you didn't ruin my life."

"I didn't?" says Jack, deadpan. "Do I get another shot?"

"No!"

"No?" There's a serious edge to his voice, which throws me. To cover my confusion, I reach into my bag for a lip salve.

Suddenly Jack's gaze falls with interest on my hand. " 'I am over Jack,' " he reads aloud.

Fuck.

My entire face flames with color.

"That's just . . ." I clear my throat. "That was just a . . . doodle. It didn't mean . . ."

A shrill ring from my mobile interrupts me. Thank God. Whoever this is, I love them. I pull it out and press answer. "Hello?"

"Emma, you're going to love me forever!" come Jemima's piercing tones.

"What?"

"I've sorted everything out for you!" she says triumphantly. "I know, I'm a total star. You don't know what you'd do without me."

"What?" I feel a twinge of alarm. "Jemima, what are you talking about?"

"Getting your revenge on Jack Harper, silly! Since you were just sitting there like a total wimp, I've taken matters into my own hands!"

For moment I can't quite move. "Er, Jack . . . excuse me a minute." I keep my voice bright and casual. "I just need to . . . take this call."

I hurry to the corner of the courtyard, well out of earshot.

"Jemima, you promised you wouldn't do anything!" I hiss. "You swore on your Míu Míu pony skin bag, remember?"

"I haven't *got* a Míu Míu pony skin bag!" she crows. "I've got a *Fendi* pony skin bag!"

She's mad. She's completely mad.

"Jemima . . . what have you done?" I swallow. "Tell me what you've done."

Please don't say she's scraped his car. Please.

"An eye for an eye, Emma! That man totally betrayed you, and we're going to do the same to him! Now, I'm sitting here with a very nice chap called Mick. He's a journalist. He writes for the *Daily World*. . . ."

Everything goes fuzzy for an instant. A journalist.

"A tabloid journalist?" I manage at last. "Jemima . . . are you *insane?*"

"Don't be so narrow-minded and suburban!" retorts Jemima reprovingly. "Emma, tabloid journalists are our *friends*. They're just like private detectives . . . but for free! Mick's done loads of work for Mummy before. He's marvelous at tracking things down. And he's *very* interested in finding out Jack Harper's little secret! I've told him all we know, but he'd like to have a word with you—"

I feel quite faint. This cannot be happening.

"Jemima, listen to me," I say, as though trying to persuade a lunatic down off the roof. "I don't want to find out Jack's secret, OK? I just want to forget it. You have to stop this guy."

"I won't!" she says like a petulant six-year-old. "Emma, don't be so pathetic! You can't just let men walk all over you and do nothing in return! You have to show them! Mummy always says—" There's the sudden screeching of tires. "Oops! Teeny crash. I'll call you back."

The phone goes dead.

In dismay, I jab her number into my phone, but it clicks straight onto messages.

"Jemima," I say as soon as it beeps. "Jemima, you have to stop this! You have to—" I stop abruptly as Jack appears in front of me, holding a program.

"It's about to start," he says. "Everything all right?"

"Er, fine," I say in a strangled voice, and put my phone away. "Everything's . . . fine."

Twenty-five

As I walk into the auditorium, I'm almost light-headed with panic.

What have I done? What have I done?

I have given away Jack's most precious secret in the world to a morally warped, revenge-wreaking, Prada-wearing nutcase.

OK. Just calm down, I tell myself for the zillionth time. She doesn't actually know the story. This journalist probably won't find out anything. I mean, what facts does he actually have?

But what if he does find out? What if he somehow stumbles on the truth? And Jack discovers it was me who pointed them in the right direction? *Why* did I ever mention Scotland to Jemima? *Why?*

New resolution: I am never giving away a secret again. Never, ever, ever. Even if it doesn't seem important. Even if I am feeling angry.

In fact, I am never talking again, full stop. All talking ever seems to do is get me into trouble. If I hadn't opened my mouth on that stupid plane in the first place, I wouldn't be in this mess now.

I will become a mute. A silent enigma. When people ask me questions, I will simply nod, or scribble cryptic notes on pieces of paper. People will take them away and puzzle over them, searching them for hidden meanings—

"Is this Lissy?" says Jack, pointing to a name in the program, and I start in fright.

"Yes, it is," I say before I can stop myself. OK, forget the not-talking plan.

"Right." Jack nods and turns back to the program. His face is totally calm and unsuspecting.

Maybe I should just tell him.

No. I can't. I can't. How would I put it? "By the way, Jack. You know that really important secret you asked me to keep? Well, guess what."

Containment is what I need. Like in those military films where they bump off the person who knows too much. But how do I contain Jemima? I feel like I've launched some crazed human Exocet missile fizzing around London, bent on causing as much devastation as she can, and now I want to call her back, but the button doesn't work anymore.

OK. Just . . . think rationally. There's no need to panic. Nothing's going to happen tonight. I'll just keep trying her mobile, and as soon as I get through, I'll explain in words of one syllable that she has to call this guy off and if she doesn't I will break her legs . . .

Suddenly a low, insistent drumbeat starts playing over the loudspeakers. I'm so distracted, I actually forgot what we're here for. The auditorium is becoming completely dark, and around us the audience falls silent with anticipation. The beating increases in volume, but nothing happens onstage; it's still pitch-black.

The drumming becomes even louder, and I'm starting to

feel tense. This is all a bit spooky. When are they going to start dancing? When are they going to open the curtains? When are they going—

Pow! Suddenly there's a gasp as a dazzling light fills the auditorium, nearly blinding me. Pulsating music starts to fill the air, and a single figure appears onstage in a black, glittering costume, twirling and leaping. Gosh, whoever it is, they're amazing. I'm blinking against the bright light, trying to see. I can hardly tell if it's a man or a woman or a—

Oh, my God. It's Lissy.

I am pinioned to my seat by shock. Everything else has been swept out of my mind. I cannot keep my eyes off Lissy.

I had no idea she could do this. No idea! I mean, we did a bit of ballet together. And a bit of tap. But we never . . . I never . . . How can I have known someone for over twenty years and have no idea they could dance?

She does an amazing slow, sinewy dance with a guy in a mask—who I guess is Jean-Paul—and now she's leaping and spinning around with this ribbon thing, and the whole audience is agog, and she looks so completely radiant. I haven't seen her so happy for months. I'm *so* proud of her—

To my horror, tears start to prick my eyes. And now my nose is starting to run. I don't even have a tissue. This is so embarrassing. I'm going to have to sniff, like a mother at a nativity play. Next I'll be standing up and running to the front with my camcorder, going, "Hello, darling—wave!"

OK. I need to get ahold of myself; otherwise, it'll be like the time I took my little goddaughter Amy to see the Disney cartoon *Tarzan,* and when the lights went up, she was fast asleep and I was in floods, being gawked at by a load of stony-eyed four-year-olds.

Suddenly I feel something nudging my hand. I look up, and Jack's offering me a hanky. And as I take it from him, his fingers curl briefly around mine.

As the performance comes to an end, I'm on a total high. Lissy takes a star bow, and both Jack and I applaud madly, grinning at each other.

"Don't tell anyone I cried," I say above the sound of applause.

"I won't," says Jack, and gives me a rueful smile. "I promise."

The curtain comes down for the last time, and people start getting out of their seats, reaching for jackets and bags. And now that we're coming back down to normality again, I can feel my exhilaration seeping away and anxiety returning. I have to try Jemima again.

As we reach the exit, people are streaming across the courtyard to a lit-up room on the other side.

"Lissy said I should just meet her at the party," I say to Jack. "So, er, why don't you go on? I just need to make a quick call."

"Are you OK?" says Jack, giving me a curious look. "You seem jumpy."

"I'm fine!" I say. "Just . . . excited!" I wait until he's safely out of earshot, then immediately dial Jemima's number. Straight onto messages.

I dial it again. Straight onto messages again.

I want to scream with frustration. Where is she? What's she doing?

For a few moments I stand perfectly still, trying to ignore my rising panic, trying to work out what to do.

OK. I'll just have to go to the party and act normal, keep trying her on the phone, and, if all else fails, wait until I see her later. There's nothing else I can do. It'll be fine. It'll be fine.

The party is huge and bright and noisy. All the dancers are there, still in costume, and all the audience, and a fair number of people who seem to have come along afterward. Waiters are carrying drinks around and the noise of chatter is tremendous, and as I walk in, I can't see anyone I know. I take a glass of wine and start edging into the crowd, overhearing conversations all around.

". . . wonderful costumes . . ."

". . . find time for rehearsals?"

". . . judge was *totally* intransigent . . ."

Suddenly I spot Lissy, looking all flushed and shiny, and surrounded by a load of good-looking lawyer-type guys, all of whom seem to be hanging on her every word.

"Lissy!" She turns around and I give her a huge hug. "I had no idea you could dance like that! You were amazing!"

"Oh, no. I wasn't," she says at once, and pulls a typical Lissy face. "I completely messed up—"

"Stop!" I interrupt. "Lissy, it was utterly fantastic. *You* were fantastic."

"But I was completely crap in the—"

"*Don't* say you were crap!" I practically yell. "You were fantastic. Say it. *Say* it, Lissy."

"Well . . . OK." A reluctant smile is growing on her face. "OK. I was . . . fantastic!" She gives an elated laugh. "Emma, I've never felt so good in my life! And guess what—we're already planning next year's performance!"

I gape at her. "But you said you never wanted to do this again, ever, and if you mentioned it again, I had to stop you."

"That was just stage fright!" she says with an airy wave of her hand. Then she lowers her voice. "I saw Jack, by the way!"

"Yes," I say sternly. "I heard about your little disclosure."

"Oh," says Lissy, looking abashed. "Well, I *like* him! I think you should give him another chance. So . . . come on. What did he say?"

I lean closer to her so no one else can hear. "He told me his secret."

"You're joking!" breathes Lissy, hand to her mouth. "What is it?"

"I can't tell you."

"You can't *tell* me?" Lissy stares at me in incredulity. "After all that, you're not even going to *tell* me?"

"Lissy . . . I really can't. It's . . . complicated." God, I sound just like Jack.

"Well, all right," says Lissy a bit grumpily. "I suppose I can live without knowing. So . . . are you two together again?"

"I dunno," I say, flushing. "Maybe . . ."

Should I tell her about Jemima?

No. She'll only get all hassled. And anyway, there's nothing either of us can do right now.

"Lissy! That was fabulous!" A couple of girls in suits suddenly appear at her side, and I move away as she greets them.

Jack is nowhere to be seen. Should I try Jemima again?

I surreptitiously begin to pull my phone from my bag, then hastily put it away again as I hear a voice behind me calling, "Emma!"

I look around and give a huge start of surprise. Connor's standing there in a suit, holding a glass of wine, his hair all shiny and blond under the spotlights. He has a new tie on, I notice instantly. Big yellow polka dots on blue. Who on earth chose that?

"Connor! What are you doing here?"

"Lissy sent me a flyer," he replies, looking defensive. "I've always been fond of Lissy. I thought I'd come along. And I'm glad I've run into you," he adds. "I'd like to talk to you, if I may."

He draws me toward the door, away from the main crowd, and I follow, feeling a tad nervous. I haven't had a proper chat with Connor since Jack was on television. Which could possibly be because every time I've glimpsed him, I've quickly hurried the other way.

"Er, yes?" I say, turning to face him. "What did you want to talk about?"

"Emma." Connor clears his throat as though he's about to start a formal speech. "I get the feeling that you weren't always . . . totally honest with me in our relationship."

This could be the understatement of the year.

"You're right," I admit, shamefaced. "Oh, God, Connor, I'm really, really sorry about everything that happened—"

He lifts a hand with a look of dignity. "It doesn't matter. That's water under the bridge. But I'd be grateful if you were totally honest with me now."

"Absolutely," I say, nodding earnestly. "Of course."

"I've recently . . . started a new relationship," he says in stiff tones.

"Wow!" I say in surprise. "Good for you! Connor, I'm really pleased! What's her name?"

"Her name's Francesca."

"And where did you—"

"I wanted to ask you about sex," Connor says, cutting me off in a rush of embarrassment.

"Oh! Right." I feel a twinge of dismay, which I conceal by taking a sip of wine. "Of course!"

"Were you honest with me in that . . . area?"

"Er, what do you mean?" I say, playing for time.

"Were you honest with me in bed?" His face is growing fire-engine red. "Or were you faking it?"

Oh, no. Is that what he thinks?

"Connor, I never, ever faked an orgasm with you," I say, lowering my voice. "Hand on heart. I never did."

"Well . . . OK." He studies his glass, then looks up. "But did you fake anything else?"

I look at him uncertainly. "I . . . I'm not sure I know what you—"

"Were there any . . ." He clears his throat. ". . . any particular techniques I used that you only pretended to enjoy?"

Oh, God. *Please* don't ask me that question.

"You know . . . I really . . . can't remember!" I hedge. "Actually, I ought to be going."

"Emma, tell me!" he says with sudden passion. "I'm starting a new relationship. It's only fair that I should be able to . . . to learn from past mistakes."

I gaze back at his shiny face and suddenly feel a huge pang of guilt. He's right. I should be honest. I should finally be honest with him.

"OK," I say at last, and move closer to him. "You remember that one thing you used to do with your tongue?" I lower my voice still further. "That . . . *slidey* thing? Well, sometimes that kind of made me want to . . . laugh. So if I had one tip with your new girlfriend, it would be don't do . . ."

I trail off at his expression.

Fuck. He's already done it.

"Francesca said . . ." Connor says in a voice as stiff as a board. "Francesca told me that really turned her on."

"Well, I'm sure it did!" I backtrack. "Women are all different! Our bodies are all different . . . Everybody likes, um, different things."

Connor is a picture of consternation. "She said she loved jazz, too."

"Well, I expect she does! Loads of people *do* like jazz—"

"She said she loved the way I could quote Woody Allen line for line." He rubs his flushed face. "Was she *lying*?"

"No! I'm sure she wasn't—"

"Emma . . ." He stares at me in bewilderment. "Do *all* women have secrets?"

Oh, no. Have I ruined Connor's trust in all of womankind forever?

"No!" I exclaim. "Of course they don't! Honestly, Connor, I'm *sure* it's only me . . ."

My words wither on my lips as I glimpse a flash of familiar-looking blond hair at the entrance to the hall. My heart stops.

That can't be—

That's not—

"Connor, I have to go," I say, and start hurrying toward the entrance.

"She told me she's size six!" Connor calls after me. "What does that mean? What size should I really buy?"

"Eight!" I shoot back over my shoulder.

It is. It's Jemima. Here. Standing in the foyer. What's she doing here?

Then the door opens again—and I feel faint. She's got a guy with her. In jeans, with cropped hair and squirrelly eyes. He's got a camera slung over his shoulder and is looking around with interest.

No.

She can't have—

"Emma," comes a voice in my ear, and I give a start of panic.

"Jack!" I swivel around to see him watching me with affection. How long has he been there?

"You OK?" he says, and gently touches my nose.

"Fine!" I say a little shrilly. "I'm great!"

I have to manage this situation. I have to. "Jack, um, could you get me some water?" I hear myself saying. "I'll just . . . stay here. I'm feeling a bit dizzy."

Jack looks alarmed. "You know, I thought there was something wrong. Let me take you home. I'll call the car—"

"No. It's . . . it's fine. I want to stay! Just get me some water. Please," I add as an afterthought.

As soon as he's gone, I tear into the foyer, almost tripping up in my haste.

"Emma!" Jemima looks up brightly. "Excellent! I was just about to look for you. Now, this is Mick, and he wants to ask you some questions. We thought we'd use this little room here." She heads into a small, empty office that leads off from the foyer.

"No!" I say, grabbing her arm. "Jemima, you have to go. Now. Go!"

"I'm not going anywhere!" Jemima jerks her arm out of my grasp and rolls her eyes at Mick, who's closing the door of the office behind me. "I told you she was being all hissy about it."

"Mick Collins." Mick thrusts a business card into my hands. "Delighted to meet you, Emma. Now, there's no need to get worried, is there?" He gives me a soothing smile, as though he's completely used to dealing with hysterical women telling him to go. Which he probably is. "Let's just sit down quietly, have a nice chat. . . ."

He's chewing gum as he speaks, and as I smell the spearmint wafting toward me, I almost want to throw up.

"Look, there's been a misunderstanding," I say, forcing myself to sound polite. "I'm afraid there's no story."

"Well, let's see about that, shall we?" says Mick. "You tell me the facts."

"No! I mean . . . there's nothing. . . ." I turn to Jemima. "I told you I didn't want you to do anything! You promised me!"

"Emma, you are such a wimp. You'll just let any man walk all over you and do nothing about it!" She gives Mick an exasperated look. "Do you see why I've been forced to take action? I told you what a bastard Jack Harper was to her. He needs to learn his lesson!"

"Absolutely right," agrees Mick, and puts his head on one side as though measuring me up. "Very attractive," he says to Jemima. "You know, we could think about an accompanying interview feature. 'My Romp with Top Boss.' " He adds to me, "You could make some serious money."

"*No!*"

"Emma, stop being so coy!" snaps Jemima. "You want to do it, really. This could be a whole new career for you, you realize!"

"I don't want a new career!"

"Well, then you should! Do you *know* how much Monica Lewinsky makes a year?"

"You're sick!" I say in disbelief. "You're a totally sick, warped—"

"Emma, I'm just acting in your best interests!"

"You're not!" I cry, feeling my face flame red. "I . . . I might be getting back together with Jack!"

There's a thirty-second silence. I'm holding my breath. Then it's like the killer robot jerks into action again.

"Even *more* reason to do it!" says Jemima. "This'll keep him on his toes! This'll show him who's boss! Go on, Mick."

"Interview with Emma Corrigan. Friday, fifteenth July, nine-forty P.M." I look up, and stiffen in fresh horror. Mick has produced a small tape recorder and is holding it toward me.

"You first met Jack Harper on a plane. Can you confirm where this was flying from and to? Just speak in a natural way, like you would to a mate on the phone—"

"Stop it!" I yell. "Just leave! Leave!"

"Emma, grow up!" says Jemima. "Mick's going to find out what this secret is whether you help him or not, so you might as well be—" She stops abruptly as the door handle rattles, then turns.

The room seems to swim around me.

Please don't say— Please—

As the door slowly opens, I can't breathe. I can't move.

I have never felt so frightened in my entire life.

"Emma?" says Jack, coming in, holding two glasses of water in one hand. "Are you feeling OK? I got you both still and sparkling, because I wasn't quite . . ."

He trails off in confusion, his eyes running over Jemima and Mick. In disbelief he takes in Mick's card, still in my hand. Then his gaze falls on Mick's turning tape recorder, and all the happiness seems to slide out of his face.

"I think I'll just make myself scarce," murmurs Mick, raising his eyebrows at Jemima. He slips the tape recorder into his pocket, picks up his rucksack, and sidles out of the room. Nobody speaks for a few moments. All I can hear is the throbbing in my head.

"Who was that?" says Jack at last. "A journalist?"

He looks as though someone just stamped on his garden.

"I . . . Jack . . ." I falter. "It's not . . . it's not . . ."

"Why . . ." He hesitates as though trying to make sense of the situation. "Why were you talking to a journalist?"

"Why do you *think* she was talking to a journalist?" chimes in Jemima proudly.

"What?" Jack slowly turns to Jemima with a look of dislike.

"You think you're such a big shot millionaire! You think you can use little people! You think you can give away someone's private secrets and completely humiliate them and get away with it! Well, you can't!"

She takes a few steps toward him, folding her arms with satisfaction. "Emma's been waiting for a chance to get her revenge on you, and now she's found it! That *was* a journalist, if you want to know. And he's on your case. And when you find your little Scottish secret plastered all over the papers, then maybe *you'll* know what it feels like to be betrayed! And maybe you'll be sorry! Tell him, Emma! Tell him!"

I'm paralyzed.

The minute she says the word "Scottish," I see Jack's face change. It kind of snaps. He almost looks winded with shock. He looks straight at me, and I can see the growing incredulity in his eyes.

"You might think you know Emma, but you don't!" Jemima is continuing delightedly, like a cat tearing apart its prey. "You underestimated her, Jack Harper. You underestimated what she's capable of!"

I try to speak—but not a sound comes out. Nothing in my body will work properly. I'm pinioned, staring helplessly at him with a face I know is covered with guilt.

Jack opens his mouth, then closes it again. Then he turns on his heel, pushes the door open, and walks out.

For a moment there's silence in the tiny room.

"Well!" says Jemima, brushing her hands together with satisfaction. "That showed him!"

It's as though she breaks the spell. Suddenly I can move again. I can draw breath. "You . . ." I'm almost shaking too much to speak. "You stupid . . . stupid . . . thoughtless . . . bitch!"

The door bursts open and Lissy appears, wide-eyed. "What the hell happened here?" she demands. "I just saw Jack storming out. He looked absolutely . . . like thunder!"

"She brought a journalist here!" I say in anguish, gesturing at Jemima. "A bloody tabloid journalist! And Jack found us all closeted here, and he thinks . . . God knows what he thinks."

"You stupid cow!" Lissy slaps Jemima across the face. "What were you doing!"

"Ow! I was helping Emma get vengeance on her enemy!"

"He's not my *enemy,* you stupid . . ." I'm on the verge of tears. "Lissy . . . what am I going to do? What?"

"Go," she says, and looks at me with anxious eyes. "You can still catch him. Go."

I tear out the door and through the courtyard, my chest rising and falling rapidly, my lungs burning. As I reach the road, I look frantically left and right. Suddenly I spot him, down the road.

"Jack, wait."

He's striding along with his mobile phone to his ear, and at my voice he turns around with a taut face. "So that's why you were so interested in Scotland."

"No!" I say, aghast. "No! Listen, Jack. They don't know. They don't know anything. I promise. I didn't tell them about—" I stop myself. "All Jemima knows is that you were there. Nothing more. She was bluffing! I haven't said anything!"

Jack doesn't answer. His eyes search my face briefly, then he starts striding again.

"It was Jemima who called that guy, not me!" I cry desperately, running after him. "I was trying to stop her . . . Jack, you know me! You *know* I would never do this to you. Yes, I told Jemima about your being in Scotland. I was hurt, and I was angry, and it . . . came out. And that was a mistake. But . . . but you made a mistake, too, and I forgave you!"

He's not even looking at me. He's not even giving me a chance. His silver car pulls up at the pavement, and he opens the passenger door.

I feel a stab of panic. "Jack, this wasn't me," I say frantically. "It wasn't. You have to believe me. That's not why I asked about Scotland! I didn't want to . . . to *sell* your secret!" Tears are streaming down my face, and I roughly brush them away. "I didn't even want to *know* such a big secret. I just wanted to know your little secrets! Your little stupid secrets! I just wanted to know you . . . like you know me."

But he doesn't even look around. The door closes with a heavy clunk, and the car moves away down the road. And I'm left on the pavement, all alone.

Twenty-six

FOR A WHILE I can't even move. I stand there, dazed, with the breeze blowing on my face, and stare at the point at the end of the road where Jack's car disappeared. I can still hear his voice in my mind. I can still see his face. The way he looked at me as though he didn't know me after all.

A spasm of pain runs through my body and I close my eyes, almost unable to bear it. If I could just turn back time . . . if I'd been more forceful . . . if I'd marched Jemima and her friend off the premises . . . if I'd spoken up more quickly when Jack appeared . . .

But I didn't. And it's too late.

A group of party guests comes out of the courtyard onto the pavement, laughing and discussing taxis.

"Are you all right?" says one to me.

"Er, yes," I say. "Thanks." I look one more time at where Jack's car disappeared, then force myself to turn around and make my way back up to the party.

I find Lissy and Jemima still in the little office, Jemima cowering in terror as Lissy lays into her.

". . . selfish, immature little bitch! You make me sick, you know that?"

Lissy is in full Rottweiler barrister mode. As I watch her striding up and down, her eyes blazing in fury, I'm actually pretty scared myself.

"Emma, make her stop!" pleads Jemima. "Make her stop shouting at me!"

"So . . . what happened?" Lissy looks at me, her face alight with hope. Mutely, I shake my head.

"Is he—"

"He's gone." I swallow. "I don't really want to talk about it."

"Oh, Emma." She bites her lip.

"Don't," I say in a wobbly voice. "I'll cry." I lean against the wall and take a couple of deep breaths, trying to get back to normal. "Where's her friend?" I say at last, and jerk my thumb at Jemima.

"He got thrown out," says Lissy with satisfaction. "He was trying to take a picture of a Linklaters partner in his tights, and a bunch of lawyers surrounded him and bundled him out."

"Jemima, listen to me." I force myself to meet her unrepentant blue gaze. "You cannot let him find out any more. You *cannot.*"

"It's OK," she says, sulking. "I've already spoken to him. Lissy made me. He won't pursue it."

"How do you know?"

"He won't do anything that would piss Mummy off. He has a pretty lucrative arrangement with her."

I shoot Lissy a "can we trust her?" look, and she gives a doubtful little shrug.

"Jemima, this is a warning." I walk to the door, then turn

around, trying to summon all my strength. "If anything of this gets out. *Anything* at all . . . I will make it public that you snore."

"I don't snore!" says Jemima.

"Yes, you do," says Lissy. "When you've had too much to drink, you snore really loudly. *And* we'll tell everyone you got your Donna Karan coat from a discount warehouse shop."

Jemima gasps. "I didn't!" she says, color suffusing her cheeks.

"You did! I saw the carrier bag," I chime in. "*And* we'll make it public that your pearls are cultured, not real . . ."

Jemima claps a hand over her mouth.

". . . and you never really cook the food at your dinner parties . . ."

". . . and that photo of you meeting Prince William is faked . . ."

". . . and we'll tell every single man you ever date from now on that all you're after is a rock on your finger!" Lissy finishes. I shoot a grateful glance at her.

"OK!" says Jemima, practically in tears. "OK! I promise I'll forget all about it. I promise! Just please don't mention the discount warehouse shop. Please. Can I go now?"

"Yes, you can go," says Lissy with a contemptuous nod, and Jemima scuttles out of the room.

As the door closes, I catch Lissy's eye. "Is that photo of Jemima and Prince William really faked?"

"Yes! Didn't I tell you? I once did some stuff for her on her computer, and I opened the file by mistake . . . and there it was. She just pasted her head onto some other girl's body!"

"That girl is unbelievable!"

I sink down into a chair, feeling suddenly weak, and for a while there's silence in the room. In the distance there's a roar of laughter from the party, and somebody walks past the door of the office, talking about the trouble with the judiciary system as it stands.

"Wouldn't he even listen?" says Lissy at last.

"No. He just left."

"Isn't that a bit extreme? I mean, he gave away *all* your secrets. You only gave away one of his—"

"You don't understand." I study the drab brown office carpet. "What Jack told me . . . it's not just anything. It's something really precious to him. He came all the way here to tell me. To show me that he trusted me with it." I swallow hard. "And the next moment he thinks I'm spilling it to a journalist."

"But you weren't!" says Lissy loyally. "Emma, this wasn't your fault!"

"It was!" Tears are welling up in my eyes. "If I'd just kept my mouth closed, if I'd never told Jemima anything in the first place . . ."

"She would have got him anyway," says Lissy. "He'd be suing you for a scraped car instead. Or damaged genitals."

I can't help but laugh, albeit weakly.

The door bursts open, and the feathered guy I saw backstage looks in. "Lissy! There you are. They're serving food. It looks rather good, actually."

"OK!" she says. "Thanks, Colin. I'll be along in a minute."

He disappears again, and Lissy turns to me. "Do you want something to eat?"

"I'm not really hungry. But you go," I add quickly. "You must be starving after your performance."

"I am rather ravenous," she admits. Then she gives me an anxious look. "But what will you do?"

"I'll . . . just go home," I say, and try to smile as cheerfully as I can. "Don't worry, Lissy. I'll be fine."

And I am planning to go home. But when I get outside, I suddenly find I can't bring myself to. I'm wound up with tension like a metal coil. I can't face going into the party and having to make small talk . . . but I can't face the four silent walls of my bedroom, either. Not quite yet.

Instead, I find myself heading across the gravel, toward the empty auditorium. The door is unlocked, and I walk straight in. I make my way through the darkness to a seat in the middle row and wearily sit down on the cushiony purple plush.

Two fat tears slowly trickle down my face. I cannot believe I've fucked up so monumentally. I can't believe Jack really thinks I . . . that he thinks I would . . .

I keep seeing the shock on his face. I keep reliving that trapped powerlessness, that desperation to speak, to explain myself.

If I could just replay it . . .

Suddenly there's a creaking sound. The door is opening.

I peer through the gloom as a figure comes into the auditorium and stops.

In spite of myself, my chest constricts with unbearable hope.

It's Jack. It has to be Jack. He's come to find me.

There's a long, agonizing silence. Why won't he say anything? Why won't he speak? Is he punishing me? Is he expecting me to apologize again? Oh, God, this is torture. Just say something, I plead silently. Just say *something*. . . .

"Oh, Francesca . . ."

"Connor . . ."

What? I peer again and feel a crash of disappointment. I am such a stupid moron. It's not Jack. It's not one figure; it's two. It's Connor and what must be his new girlfriend—and they're kissing.

Miserably, I shrink down in my seat, trying to block my ears. But it's no good; I can hear everything.

"Do you like this?" I hear Connor murmuring.

"Mmm . . ."

"Do you really like it?"

"Of course I do! Stop quizzing me!"

"Sorry," says Connor, and there's silence.

"Do you like *this*?" his voice suddenly comes again.

"I already told you I did!"

"Francesca, be honest, OK?" Connor's voice rises in agitation. "Because if that means no, then—"

"It doesn't mean no! Connor, what's your problem?"

"My problem is, I don't believe you!"

"You don't *believe* me?" She sounds absolutely furious. "Why the hell don't you believe me?"

I'm filled with remorse. This is all my fault. Not only have I wrecked my own relationship; now I've wrecked theirs, too. I have to do something.

I clear my throat. "Er, excuse me?"

"Who's that?" says Francesca in a sharp voice. "Is someone there?"

"It's me. Emma. Connor's ex-girlfriend."

A row of lights goes on, and I see a girl with red hair and a belligerent face, her hand on the light switch.

"What the hell are you doing? *Spying* on us?"

"No!" I say. "Look, I'm sorry! I didn't mean to . . . I couldn't help overhearing. . . ." I swallow. "The thing is, Connor isn't being difficult. He just wants you to be honest. He wants to know what you want." I summon up my most understanding, womanly expression. "Francesca . . . tell him what you want."

Francesca gives me an incredulous look, then turns to Connor. "I want her to piss off." She points at me.

"Oh," I say, taken aback. "Er, OK. Sorry."

"And switch the lights off when you go," adds Francesca.

In haste I pick up my bag and hurry along the row of seats toward the exit of the auditorium. I push my way through the double doors into the foyer, flicking the light switch as I pass, then step out of the exit into the courtyard. I close the door behind me, and look up.

I don't believe it. It's Jack.

It's Jack, coming toward me, striding fast across the courtyard, determination on his face. I haven't got time to think, or prepare . . .

And now my heart really is racing. I want to speak or cry or . . . do *something,* but I can't.

He reaches me with a crunch of gravel and takes me by the shoulders. "I'm afraid of the dark."

"What?"

"I'm afraid of the dark. Always have been. I keep a base-ball bat under the bed, just in case."

He what? I'm totally confused. "Jack—"

"I've never liked caviar." He casts around. "I . . . I'm embarrassed by my French accent."

"Jack, what are you—"

"I got the scar on my wrist by cracking open a bottle of beer when I was fourteen. When I was a kid, I used to stick gum under my aunt Francine's dining table. I lost my virginity to a girl named Lisa Greenwood in her uncle's barn, and afterward I asked if I could keep her bra to show my friends."

I can't help a gurgle of laughter, but Jack carries on regardless.

"I've never worn any of the ties my mother has given me for Christmas. I've always wanted to be an inch or two taller than I am. I . . . I don't know what 'codependent' means. I . . . I have a recurring dream in which I'm Superman falling from the sky. I sometimes sit in board meetings and look around and think, Who the hell *are* these guys?"

He draws breath and gazes at me, his eyes so dark they're almost black. "I met a girl on a plane. And . . . my whole life changed as a result."

Something hot is welling up inside me, and my throat is tight. He came back. He came back to tell me all this.

"Jack, I didn't . . . I really didn't—"

"I know." He cuts me off with a nod. "I know you didn't."

"I would never—"

"I know you wouldn't," he says gently. "I know you wouldn't."

And now I can't help it. Tears of sheer relief start flooding out of my eyes. He knows. It's all right.

"So . . ." I wipe my face, trying to gain control of myself. "So, does this . . . does this mean . . . that we . . ." I can't quite bring myself to say the words.

There's a long, unbearable silence. If he says no . . . I don't know what I'll do.

"Well . . . you might want to hold back on your decision," says Jack at last, with a deadpan look. "Because I have a lot more to tell you. And it isn't all pretty."

"You don't have to tell me anything—"

"Oh, I do," says Jack firmly. "I think I do. Shall we walk?" He gestures to the courtyard. "Because this could take some time."

"OK," I say, my voice still wobbling a bit. Jack holds out an arm, and after a pause I take it.

"So . . . where was I?" he says as we step down into the courtyard. "Oh, OK. Now, this you really *can't* tell anybody." He leans close and lowers his voice. "I don't actually like Panther Cola. I prefer Pepsi."

"No!" I say, shocked.

"In fact, sometimes I decant Pepsi *into* a Panther can—"

"No!"

"It's true. I told you it wasn't pretty . . ."

Slowly we start to walk around the edge of the dark, empty courtyard together. The only sounds are the crunching of our feet on the gravel and the breeze in the trees and Jack's voice. Telling me everything.

Epilogue

IT'S AMAZING what a different person I am these days. It's like . . . I've been transformed. I'm a new Emma. Far more open than I used to be. Far more honest. Because what I've really learned is, if you can't be honest with your friends and colleagues and loved ones, then what is life all about?

The *only* secrets I have nowadays are little essential ones. And I hardly have any of those. I could probably count them on the fingers of one hand. I mean, just off the top of my head:

1. I'm really not sure about Mum's new highlights.
2. That Greek-style cake Lissy made for my birthday was the most disgusting thing I've ever tasted.
3. I borrowed Jemima's Ralph Lauren swimsuit to go on holiday with Mum and Dad, and I busted one of the straps.
4. The other day, when I was navigating by map in

the car, I nearly said, "What's this big river all around London?" Then I realized it was the M25.

5. I had this weird dream last week about Lissy and Sven.

6. I've secretly starting feeding Artemis's spider plant Rebuild plant food.

7. I'm *sure* Sammy the goldfish has changed again. Where did that extra fin come from?

8. I know I have to stop giving out my "Emma Corrigan, Marketing Executive" card to everyone I meet, but I just can't help it.

9. That reflexology treatment I had on Tuesday didn't *really* make me feel transformed and energized like I told the therapist.

10. Last night, when Jack said, "What are you thinking about?" and I said, "Oh, nothing," that wasn't quite true. I was actually planning the names of all our children.

But the thing is, it's completely normal to have the odd little secret from your boyfriend.

Everyone knows that.

Acknowledgments

A big thank you to Mark Hedley, Jenny Bond, Rosie Andrews, and Olivia Heywood for all their generous advice.

And hugest gratitude as always to Susan Kamil, Margo Lipschultz, Kim Witherspoon, Araminta Whitley, and Celia Hayley, my boys and the board.

THE HILARIOUS
"MUST-HAVE" BESTSELLER

Confessions
of a
Shopaholic

" Too good
to pass up. "
—USA Today

A Novel by

SOPHIE KINSELLA

**Don't miss the novel that introduced the
fabulous Becky Bloomwood!**

Becky Bloomwood has everything: A fabulous flat in London's trendiest neighborhood, a troupe of glamorous socialite friends, and a closet brimming with the season's must-haves. The only problem is that she can't actually afford it—not any of it. Her job as a financial journalist not only bores her to tears, it doesn't pay much at all. And lately, Becky's been chased by dismal letters from Visa and the Endwich Bank—letters with large red sums she can't bear to read—and they're getting ever harder to ignore. She tries cutting back; she even tries making more money. But none of her efforts succeeds. Becky's only consolation is to buy herself something . . . just a little something . . .

Finally a story arises that Becky actually *cares* about, and her front-page article catalyzes a chain of events that will transform her life—and the lives of those around her—forever.

Sophie Kinsella brilliantly taps into our collective consumer conscience to deliver a novel of our times—and a heroine who grows stronger every time she weakens. Becky Bloomwood's hysterical schemes to pay back her debts are as endearing as they are desperate. Her "confessions" are the perfect pick-me-up when life is hanging in the (bank) balance.

On sale now

THE "TREAT YOURSELF" NOVEL OF THE YEAR
FROM THE AUTHOR OF
Confessions of a Shopaholic

Shopaholic
Takes
Manhattan

*Because there just
aren't enough shops
in London…*

New York Times Bestselling Author
SOPHIE
KINSELLA

Packing light takes on a whole new meaning when Becky Bloomwood (and her credit cards) head across the Atlantic . . .

With her shopping excesses (somewhat) in check and her career as a TV financial guru thriving, Becky's biggest problem seems to be tearing her entrepreneur boyfriend, Luke, away from work for a romantic country weekend. But packing light takes on a whole new meaning when Luke announces he's moving to New York for business—and he asks Becky to go with him! Before you can say "Prada sample sale," Becky has landed in the Big Apple, home of Park Avenue penthouses and luxury boutiques.

Surely it's only a matter of time until she becomes an American TV celebrity, and she and Luke are the toast of Gotham society. Nothing can stand in their way, especially with Becky's bills miles away in London. But then an unexpected disaster threatens her career prospects, her relationship with Luke, and her available credit line! *Shopaholic Takes Manhattan*—but will she have to return it?

On sale now

**THE DON'T-MISS-IT EVENT OF THE SEASON
FROM THE AUTHOR OF
*Shopaholic Takes Manhattan***

Shopaholic
Ties the Knot

Something old, something new,
something borrowed, and something else new...

New York Times bestselling author

SOPHIE
KINSELLA

There's never been a better excuse to buy a new dress . . . or two, as Becky Bloomwood walks down a whole new aisle in . . .

Life has been good for Becky Bloomwood: She's become the best personal shopper at Barneys, she and her successful entrepreneurial boyfriend, Luke, are living happily in Manhattan's West Village, and her new next door neighbor is a fashion designer! But with her best friend, Suze, engaged, how can Becky fail to notice that her own ring finger is bare? Not that she's been thinking of marriage (or diamonds) or anything . . .

Then Luke proposes! Bridal registries dance in Becky's head. Problem is, two other people are planning her wedding: Becky's overjoyed mother has been waiting forever to host a backyard wedding, with the bride resplendent in Mum's frilly old gown, while Luke's high-society mother is insisting on a glamorous, all-expenses-paid affair at the Plaza. Both weddings for the same day. And Becky can't seem to turn down either one. Can everyone's favorite shopaholic tie the knot before everything unravels?

On sale now

SOPHIE KINSELLA

From the *New York Times* Bestselling Author of
Can You Keep a Secret?

Shopaholic

& Sister

Shopaholic
& Sister

Becky Brandon (née Bloomwood) is back in a hilarious, heartwarming tale of married life, best friends, and long-lost sisters (and the perils of simply *having* to own an Angel Handbag!) . . .

What's a round-the-world honeymoon if you can't buy the odd souvenir to ship back home? Like the twenty silk dressing gowns Becky found in Hong Kong . . . the hand-carved dining table (and ten chairs) from Sri Lanka . . . the, um, huge wooden giraffes from Malawi (which her husband Luke expressly forbade her to buy) . . .

Only now Becky and Luke have returned home to London and Luke is furious. Two truckloads of those souvenirs have cluttered up their loft, and the bills for them are outrageous. Luke insists Becky go on a budget. And worse: her beloved best friend Suze has found a new best friend while Becky was away. Becky's feeling rather blue—when her parents deliver some incredible news. She has a long-lost sister! Becky is thrilled! She's convinced her sister will be a true soulmate. They'll go shopping together, have manicures together . . . Until she meets Jessica for the first time and gets the shock of her life. Surely Becky Bloomwood's sister can't . . . hate shopping?

Shopaholic & Sister

On sale now

OK. I CAN do this. No problem.

It's simply a matter of letting my higher self take over, achieving enlightenment, and becoming a radiant being of white light.

Easy-peasy.

Surreptitiously I adjust myself on my yoga mat so I'm facing the sun directly, and push down the spaghetti straps of my top. I don't see why you can't reach ultimate-bliss consciousness and get an even tan at the same time.

I'm sitting on a hillside in the middle of Sri Lanka at the Blue Hills Resort and Spiritual Retreat, and the view is spectacular. Hills and tea plantations stretch ahead, then merge into a deep blue sky. I can see the bright colors of tea pickers in the fields, and if I swivel my head a little, I can glimpse a distant elephant padding slowly along between the bushes.

And when I turn my head still further, I can see Luke. My husband. He's the one on the blue yoga mat, in the cutoff linen trousers and tatty old top, sitting cross-legged with his eyes closed.

I know. It's just unbelievable. After ten months of honeymoon, Luke has turned into a totally different person from the man I married. The old corporate Luke has vanished. The suits have disappeared. He's tanned and lean, his hair is long and sun-bleached, and he's still got a few of the little plaits he had put in on Bondi Beach. Round his wrist is a beaded bracelet he got in Tanzania, and in his ear is a tiny silver hoop.

Luke Brandon with an earring! Luke Brandon sitting cross-legged!

As though he can feel my gaze, he opens his eyes and smiles, and I beam back happily. Ten months married. And not a single row.

Well. You know. Only the odd little one.

"*Siddhasana,*" says our yoga teacher, Chandra. He's a tall, thin man in baggy white yoga trousers, and he always speaks in a soft, patient voice. "Clear your minds of all extraneous thought."

Around me I'm aware of the eight or nine others in the group moving into position on their mats. Obediently I place my right foot on my left thigh.

OK. Clear my mind. Concentrate.

I don't want to boast, but I find clearing my mind pretty easy. I don't quite get why anyone would find it difficult! I mean, not thinking has to be a lot easier than thinking, doesn't it?

In fact, the truth is, I'm a bit of a natural at yoga. We've only been on this retreat for five days but already I can do the Lotus and everything! I was even thinking I might set up as a yoga teacher when we go back home.

Maybe I could set up a partnership with Trudie Styler, I think in sudden excitement. God, yes! And we could launch a range of yoga wear, too, all soft grays and whites, with a little logo—

"Focus on your breathing," Chandra is saying.

Oh, right. Yes. Breathing.

Breathe in...breathe out. Breathe in...breathe out. Breathe—

God, my nails look fab. I had them done at the spa—little pink butterflies on a white background. And the antennae are little diamonds. They are so sweet. Except one seems to have fallen off. I must get that fixed—

"Becky." Chandra's voice makes me jump. He's standing right there, gazing at me with this look he has. Kind of gentle and all-knowing, like he can see right inside your mind.

"You do very well, Becky," he says. "You have a beautiful spirit."

I feel a sparkle of delight all over. I, Rebecca Brandon, née Bloomwood, have a beautiful spirit! I knew it!

"You have an unworldly soul," he adds in his soft voice, and I stare back, totally mesmerized.

"Material possessions aren't important to me," I say breathlessly. "All that matters to me is yoga."

"You have found your path." Chandra smiles.

There's an odd kind of snorting sound coming from Luke's direction, and I look round to see him looking over at us in amusement.

I *knew* Luke wasn't taking this seriously.

"This is a private conversation between me and my guru, thank you very much," I say crossly.

Although, actually, I shouldn't be surprised. We were warned about this on the first day of the yoga course. Apparently, when one partner finds higher spiritual enlightenment, the other partner can react with skepticism and even jealousy.

"Soon you will be walking on the hot coals." Chandra gestures with a smile to the nearby pit of smoldering ashy coals, and a nervous laugh goes round the group. This evening Chandra and some of his top yoga students are going to demonstrate walking on the coals for the rest of us. This is what we're all supposed to be aiming for. Apparently, you attain a state of bliss so great, you can't actually feel the coals burning your feet. You're totally pain free!

What I'm secretly hoping is that it'll work when I wear six-inch stilettos, too.

Chandra adjusts my arms and moves on, and I close my eyes, letting the sun warm my face. Sitting here on this hillside in the middle of nowhere, I feel so pure and calm. It's not just Luke who's changed over the last ten months. I have too. I've grown up. My priorities have altered. In fact, I'm a different person. I mean, look at me now, doing yoga at a spiritual retreat. My old friends probably wouldn't even recognize me!

At Chandra's instruction, we all move into the *Vajrasana* pose. From where I am, I can just see an elderly Sri Lankan man carrying two old carpetbags, approaching Chandra. They have a brief conversation, during which Chandra keeps shaking his head, then the old man trudges away over the scrubby hillside. When he's out of earshot, Chandra turns to face the group, rolling his eyes.

"This man is a merchant. He asks if any of you are interested in gems. Necklaces, cheap bracelets. I tell him your minds are on higher things."

A few people near me shake their heads as though in disbelief. One woman, with long red hair, looks affronted.

"Couldn't he see we were in the middle of meditation?" she says.

"He has no understanding of your spiritual devotion." Chandra looks around the group seriously. "It will be the same with many others in the world. They will not understand that meditation is food for your soul. You have no need for . . . sapphire bracelet!"

A few people nod in appreciation.

"Aquamarine pendant with platinum chain," Chandra continues dismissively. "How does this compare to the radiance of inner enlightenment?"

Aquamarine?

Wow. I wonder how much—

I mean, not that I'm interested. Obviously not. It's just that I happened to be looking at aquamarines in a shop window the other day. Just out of an academic interest.

My eye drifts toward the retreating figure of the old man.

"Three-carat setting, five-carat setting, he keeps saying. All half price." Chandra shakes his head. "I tell him, these people are not interested."

Half price? Five-carat aquamarines at half price?

Stop it. Stop it. Chandra's right. Of course I'm not interested in stupid aquamarines. I'm absorbed in spiritual enlightenment.

Anyway, the old man's nearly gone now. He's just a tiny figure on top of the hill. In a minute he'll have disappeared.

"And now." Chandra smiles. "The *Halasana* pose. Becky, will you demonstrate?"

"Absolutely." I smile at Chandra and prepare to get into position on my mat.

But something's wrong. I don't feel contentment. I don't feel tranquillity. The oddest feeling is welling up inside me, driving everything else out. It's getting stronger and stronger . . .

And suddenly I can't contain it anymore. Before I know what's happening, I'm running in my bare feet as fast as I can up the hill toward the tiny figure. My lungs are burning, my feet are smarting, and the sun's beating down on my bare head, but I don't stop until I've reached the crest of the hill. I come to a halt and look around, panting.

I don't believe it. He's gone. Where did he vanish to?

I stand for a few moments, regaining my breath, peering in all directions. But I can't see him anywhere.

At last, feeling a little dejected, I turn and make my way back down the hillside to the group. As I get near I realize they're all shouting and waving at me. Oh God. Am I in trouble?

"You did it!" the red-haired woman's yelling. "You did it!"

"Did what?"

"You ran over the hot coals! You did it, Becky!"

What?

I look down at my feet . . . and I don't believe it. They're covered in gray ash! In a daze, I look at the pit of coals—and there's a set of clear footprints running through it.

Oh my God. Oh my *God*! I ran over the coals! I ran over the burning hot smoldering coals! I did it!

"But . . . but I didn't even notice!" I say, bewildered. "My feet aren't even burned!"

"How did you do it?" demands the red-haired woman. "What was in your mind?"

"I can answer." Chandra comes forward, smiling. "Becky has achieved the highest form of karmic bliss. She was concentrating on one goal, one pure image, and this has driven her body to achieve a supernatural state."

Everyone is goggling at me like I'm suddenly the Dalai Lama.

"It was nothing, really," I say, with a modest smile. "Just . . . you know. Spiritual enlightenment."

"Can you describe the image?" asks the red-haired woman in excitement.

"Was it white?" someone else chimes in.

"Not really white . . ." I say.

"Was it a kind of shiny blue green?" comes Luke's voice from the back. I look up sharply. He's gazing at me, totally straight-faced.

"I don't remember," I say with dignity. "The color wasn't important."

"Did it feel like . . ." Luke appears to think hard. "Like the links of a chain were pulling you along?"

"That's a very good image, Luke," chimes in Chandra, pleased.

"No," I say shortly. "It didn't. Actually, I think you probably have to have a higher appreciation of spiritual matters to understand."

"I see." Luke nods gravely.

"Luke, you must be very proud." Chandra beams at Luke. "Is this not the most extraordinary thing you have ever seen your wife do?"

There's a beat of silence. Luke looks from me to the smoldering coals to the silent group and back to Chandra's beaming face.

"Chandra," he says. "Take it from me. This is nothing."

**And coming in July 2005: a brand-new
Sophie Kinsella heroine!
Meet Samantha. She's twenty-nine years old.
She's a high-powered lawyer. She has yet to
learn how to boil an egg. In short, she's . . .**

The
Undomestic Goddess

Samantha, a lawyer, has just done the unthinkable. She's made a mistake so huge, it'll wreck any chances of a partnership. Her entire career is ruined. In a total panic, she walks out of her London office, gets on a train, and disembarks in the middle of nowhere. She rings the doorbell of a large house—where she is mistaken by Trish and Eddie Geiger as an applicant for the position of housekeeper. Somehow Samantha is offered the job . . . and, in a total daze, hears herself accepting.

Little do the Geigers suspect that their new housekeeper has no idea how to switch on the oven, iron a shirt, or sew on a button. It's total domestic catastrophe. Thank goodness for Nathaniel, the kind, handsome gardener, who turns out to be quite handy in the kitchen (among other rooms!). But just as Samantha begins to enjoy her stop-and-smell-the-furniture-polish life, her past returns to haunt her . . .